Rebecca J. Caffery is a Politics graduate and enthusiast, who can always be found curled up somewhere reading romance when she isn't working on a new novel idea.

Outside of the written world she's an avid sports fan – watching, not playing – and spends her weekends watching women's football and waking up in the middle of the night to watch Grand Prix's on the other side of the world.

She began writing when she was 14 but didn't find her voice until she spent a year living in Canada.

𝕏 x.com/beckawrites
⊙ instagram.com/RJCafferyAuthor

T0300745

For my grandma Barbara and anyone with a loved one suffering with Parkinsons.

Playlist

making the bed - Olivia Rodrigo ♡
Part of Me - Noah Kahan ♡
Rush - Troye Sivan ♡
Too Well - Reneé Rapp ♡
In The Stars - Benson Boone ♡
LIKE I WOULD - ZAYN ♡
Delicate - Taylor Swift ♡
Shut Up And Drive - Rihanna ♡
No Judgement - Niall Horan ♡
I Like Me Better - Lauv ♡
Got Me Started - Troye Sivan ♡
Midnight Rain - Taylor Swift ♡
I Know it won't work - Gracie Abrams ♡
older - Devon Gabriella ♡
this is me trying - Taylor Swift ♡
Born To Be Yours - Kygo, Imagine Dragons ♡
Wish You Were Sober - Conan Gray ♡
reckless driving - Lizzy McAlpine ♡
Boyfriend - Dove Cameron ♡
Everybody Needs Someone - Noah Cyrus ♡
Whataya Want from Me - Adam Lambert ♡
R U Mine? - Arctic Monkeys ♡
Feels Like - Gracie Abrams ♡
The Show - Niall Horan ♡
Green Light - Lorde ♡
About Love - MARINA ♡

POLE POSITION

REBECCA J. CAFFERY

One More Chapter
a division of HarperCollins*Publishers* Ltd
1 London Bridge Street
London SE1 9GF
www.harpercollins.co.uk
HarperCollins*Publishers*
Macken House, 39/40 Mayor Street Upper,
Dublin 1, D01 C9W8, Ireland

This paperback edition 2024
24 25 26 27 28 LBC 10 9 8 7 6
First published in Great Britain in ebook format
by HarperCollins*Publishers* 2024
Copyright © Rebecca J. Caffery 2024
Rebecca J. Caffery asserts the moral right to be identified
as the author of this work

A catalogue record of this book is available from the British Library

ISBN: 978-0-00-868486-0

Printed and bound in the United States

Chapter One

Kian

'What do you mean he's got a broken leg?'

I should be packing for Bahrain when my agent, Will, and the team principal, Anders, decide to drop an absolute shitstorm into my life.'

'I'm not sure what more I can say, Kian, other than that it was a freak accident and Elijah slipped on the side of a pool. His leg's broken in three places, the muppet.'

Hearing the story a second time doesn't settle the riptide of stress my brain releases into my body.

It's a no-brainer at this point. My teammate's out for at least the first six months, maybe more, of the season and everything is truly about to go to shit.

I look down at my suitcase lying open on the bed. All the packing cubes in the world aren't going to make me feel better. And that's saying something, because I bloody love sorting my life into tiny, organised squares of neatness. Elijah Gutaga and I have been teammates for the last five seasons and we've developed a bond not only on the track, but off the track, too. I'm godfather to his three-year-old. He's my best mate in a world where it's hard to find people you can trust. In one of the most dangerous sports in the world, there has to be a level of trust within your immediate circle and within the wider team too. That bond, especially for the Constructors' Championship, is vital. Without this trust, everything falls apart.

It takes me way too many seconds to realise that I'm sitting in silence whilst the two people who hold my career in their hands wait for me to respond. I don't quite know what they expect me to say. Holding my nerve is one of the most important skills in this sport and it feels slightly shaken right now. Racing isn't exactly a team sport, but Elijah and I have been training together for years and we've always worked really well together.

With Elijah out, well, I don't know what that means for me.

Jeez I can't afford to think about it like that. There are already whispers about this being my retirement season – I'm thirty-three and I've been world champion four times, most recently last year. Even so, I need this to be a spectacular year in order to shut the press up.

'Okay.' I move away from the phone mic to take a calming breath. 'That's fine. It's not the end of the world. I'll give him a call. I did wonder why he hasn't returned my texts in the last twenty-four hours.'

Anders immediately pounces on my words. 'You'll be fine, Kian, and we'll make sure Elijah gets the best care. He'll definitely need surgery so we'll get Harley Street's finest surgeons on the case. We want him back and fighting fit as soon as possible.'

'So you think he might return before the end of the season?' I ask hopefully.

That would be something, at least.

'Best not to count on it at this point. We'll have to play it by ear. It depends first on how the injury heals and then his recovery. All you can do is focus on your own game plan and let us work with Elijah to support his recovery.'

'Okay, well, I'd best finish packing, then.' I survey the mess I've created whilst trying to organise myself. It's probably going to take all night. At least I can sleep on the jet.

And I can sleep well knowing we'll have London, the team's back-up driver, taking up Elijah's spot. He's come on leaps and bounds in the last year.

'Good man. That's what we wanted to hear. We'll see you and Harper on the runway first thing tomorrow.'

'Tomorr— Hang on, what?' *Did he just say* Harper? 'Did you just say Harper? As in, Harper James?'

'The one and only. We've called him up from the lower category to take Elijah's place whilst he's out. I dropped him a line before we called you.' Anders sounds completely calm about this, like it isn't the worst possible news he could be giving me right now.

Through gritted teeth I say, 'Of course. Makes sense. See you tomorrow.' The line drops and I have to resist the urge to lob my phone at the wall.

Harper bloody James.

I could write you a list of about twenty other drivers I'd rather share a podium with than Harper James.

Face like an angel but an absolute devil on the circuit. He's better known for his partying and seduction techniques than his skill on the track. Okay, maybe I'm exaggerating, because he did win the lower category last season, but his antics captured on social-media and in the press overshadow anything else he's achieved in his career. He makes the headlines every other day even in the off season and I've seen more of that guy's body than I could ever wish to. If there's a scandal in the sports pages, chances are his name is attached to it. I'm surprised that Anders is willing to put this aside and risk pissing off the sponsors – Harper James is good but he's not *that* good!

That's the only thing we've got in common, actually. Having been raised in the public eye from the second I was born, I've made enough headlines to last me a lifetime. The stories about you as a kid – and the awkward, unflattering helmet-hair pictures that accompany the lies – follow you around forever. He could do with learning that.

I shoot Elijah a text asking him to call me as soon as he has a moment. I'm sure he's devastated, and things at his end must be utter chaos right now. I can't even imagine how hard a season-ending injury has to be just days before we jet off again. I want to make sure he's okay and let him know I'll be by to visit as soon as I can.

As I hit send, my phone pings with a news blast, containing a press release I was sadly already privy to.

'Elijah Gutaga out for Hendersohm. Harper James in, with the new season just around the corner.'

Well. It's official.

The article quotes not only a tweeted statement from the

team, but also an Instagram post from Harper himself announcing his call-up. Of course he's tasteless enough to announce it shirtless in just a pair of Hendersohm shorts and baseball cap.

It's not enough that I've had to mingle with him at the occasional Hendersohm party in the past, now I'm going to be stuck with him every day for the best part of a year. All the excitement for the new season starts to drain from me. Normally, at this point I'm buzzing with energy for pre-season testing, but not anymore.

In the most insane way, I find peace from doing this sport, despite the intense pressure, and now Harper James is about to shake that all up with his bullshit attitude and recklessness on the track. I've had first-hand experience of his type and I don't need, or want, that kind of chaos in my life. He's a reminder of all that is wrong with this sport.

A few hours later, I park my packed case by the front door and pull on a jacket. It's time for my least favourite pre-season ritual – saying goodbye.

When I let myself into my mum's house, I'm instantly hit with a whiff of freshly baked apple pie. That smell used to soothe my soul as a child. Once she'd stopped touring, there was nothing Mum loved more than baking. Now, though, it's my sister who stress-bakes and it's always a sign that it's not been a good day.

A familiar niggle of guilt creeps into my stomach and I force myself to step over the threshold for the last time for the next nine months.

Cartoons are playing on the TV in the front room, which I quickly bypass, heading for what is now Mum's bedroom, downstairs. Peering in, I find her fast asleep, a contorted, distressed look pulling on her face. There's a fragility to the way her cheekbones protrude so sharply and I have to take a couple of seconds to watch the blanket on her chest rise and fall to reassure myself that she's breathing.

Not wanting to disturb her, I gently pull her bedroom door shut and find my sister amongst a mess of pots, pans, and plates in the kitchen.

'Hey, sis.' She jumps slightly, but nothing prepares me for the bloodshot eyes that meet mine as she turns to face me.

Wordlessly, I pull her into a hug, soft sobs ricocheting off my shoulders as I hold her close.

Four years ago, Elise was in the final year of her nursing degree when she found out in the same week that she was pregnant with my niece, Cassie, and that our mum had been diagnosed with Parkinson's disease. Both discoveries changed her, one for the better, the other not so much. She gave up her nursing degree and when Mum started to lose more of her faculties, Elise became her full-time carer.

Elise and her husband, Grant, rented out their house and moved into Mum's farmhouse set in several acres of land in Norfolk. Their first child, Cassie, and their second, Jesse, have been raised here for the last three-and-a-half years. I can't imagine them ever leaving now.

I admire everything about my sister, but the way she's taken care of our mum is truly something else. Especially as I haven't been here to pull my weight anywhere near as much as I wish I could. Elise would never say a bad word about that. She'll tell you she's grateful that I get to keep my career, that she more than appreciates the trust fund I've put aside for her kids to go to university or travel the world or whatever they want in the future. I wish it was enough. I wish I could do more than just pay for the best equipment and doctors and visiting support workers to make Mum's remaining time in this world comfortable.

I'm not sure how many minutes pass with us just standing there, me holding Elise up, but we never get too many undisturbed moments like this. And then Cassie is screaming her head off, causing the baby, Jesse, to cry, and we have to break apart before either of us are ready to let go.

Elise rushes off to sort them out and I make a start on the washing-up. It's the least I can do. Everything's on the draining board and the worktops are sparkling when Elise returns, peace restored in the living room, weariness carried heavily in every ounce of her body.

'I'll bathe and put the kids to bed. You go and grab yourself a glass of wine and chill in front of the TV,' I tell her. It's an order, not a suggestion.

'Lifesaver, thank you, Ki.'

I might have come over here to moan about Harper, but I can tell that now is not the time. I don't want to add to her burden when it's so clear she's already physically and emotionally worn out from the day. Even though I know she'd protest, saying she's always here, regardless, to listen.

'Who wants a story?' I call out as I enter the living room. Cassie cheers, racing into my arms so I can spin her around and Jesse springs up and down in his bouncer. I can't believe he's already fourteen months old.

Bathtime turns into a slip and slide, but it's worth it to listen to the sounds of my niece and nephew playing happily together. When they are dried and creamed, I lay Jesse down in his cot and thankfully he settles almost immediately, but Cassie is another story. Literally.

I finish one of her favourite books and she quickly requests a second, which turns into a third and it takes all my willpower to reject her pleas for a fourth. She's only three, but she's every bit as strong-willed as her mother and has the too-pretty-to-deny eyes to match.

'I've still got to go give your mum a story, so it's time for you to settle, missy. Come on, bedtime.' I tickle her sides and she screams, legs thrashing around under her duvet. I need to leave soon, and Elise won't thank me for riling Cassie up like this, but it's worth it to see the pure joy radiating off her face.

It's not the kind of bedtime I ever remember having as a kid. When we were on tour, Mum would be warming up or already on stage by the time Elise and I were put to bed, and Dad … well, the less said about that the better. I know it really matters to Elise that her kids have what we didn't, which is why I always find it so hard to resist their pleas for just one more story.

'Okay, Uncle Ki Ki, Mommy deserves a story.' She claps and then rolls on to her side to face the mountain of teddies she keeps with her. It's precious to say the least.

Pressing a kiss to Cassie's forehead, I pull the duvet up to her chin and wish her goodnight. She mumbles back but is more interested in how many of her bears she can cuddle at once. She's peaceful when I check on her after grabbing the baby monitor from Jesse's room, so I head back downstairs. One of the best things Elise and Grant ever did was make Mum's house feel like their own home so it feels like a wonderful multi-generational household.

Elise is curled up on the sofa in her pyjamas, hair scraped back, no remains of today's make-up left on her face. Her glass is full of a straw-coloured white wine and there's some crime drama on the TV. She appears calmer, but I can see in her eyes that her mind is still going a mile a minute. She'll only have one glass so she can hear Mum or the kids in the night, and yet again, I feel guilty that I'm about to disappear for the best part of nine months.

'You okay?' She asks, like it's been me taking care of the rug rats and Mum all day.

'I'm good, kid, are you?' My sister glares at me with the same stare she's been giving me since we were little – the one that reminds me that she is exactly thirteen minutes older than me.

'I'd be lying if I said I wasn't tired. Cassie's been full of beans all day and Jesse just wants to shove anything he can reach into his mouth.' I appreciate that she doesn't mention Mum and instantly feel bad about that.

'Mum okay?' It's a stupid question, because of course she isn't. She has a godawful disease which is slowly taking her from us.

The Parkinson's diagnosis came as a complete shock at first, and then within a few months we noticed every single symptom they warned us about. Elise was incredible and took it in her stride, and I just about coped with seeing it eat away at Mum for the three months a year I was around.

'Bad day. She thought I was Aunt Judith this morning.' I try to hide my wince, but a frown pulls at my sister's lips and I know she's concealing how bad it really is from me. 'Her memory is really deteriorating and it feels like the rate of decline is increasing every day.'

This is something else the doctors warned us about. Dementia. Another disease that often comes hand in hand with Parkinson's as the condition begins to worsen.

'I'm so sorry, Elise,' I apologise like she isn't my mum, too, but I know the burden is not shared equally between us. Mum will forget me first because I'm just not around enough. It will kill Elise to be forgotten, and she's the one who will have to face it every single day. It is truly the cruellest disease. I feel a stab in my heart every time Mum looks at me blankly, unable to place me as a part of her fading life, but at least I'm not confronted with it every hour of the day.

'Anyway,' Elise says as she waves the stress away, 'what's going on with you? I love you, bro, and I know you love us, but you didn't barge your way in here just to put the kids to bed.'

I groan, the lavender candle burning on the mantelpiece not doing a thing to soothe the anxiety that's been curling in my chest since the phone rang this morning. 'Elijah's broken his leg. Three places. It's bad.'

'Oh, shit.'

'Yeah.'

'Okay, so he's out for, what, three to six months? Half a season or thereabouts. Isn't that what the back-up guy is for? That's not what's got you in this funk.'

She knows me way too well. 'I think Anders has written him off for the whole season. Oh, and Harper James is his replacement.'

The room falls silent. Elise pauses the TV show to allow us to talk properly and the house suddenly feels unnervingly still.

'Look, baby bro,' she says, which only makes me want to groan louder. 'I know what's going on in that head of yours.

He's so much like the man you've desperately tried not to become, and I know you hate everything about his attitude and how he treats people, but it's temporary. *He's* temporary. Elijah's leg will heal, the team will go back to normal, and the rookie prick'll be shunted back down into the lower category faster than he's crawled up.'

And this is why she's the best sister in the world. She's the best mum, daughter, carer and, when she can finish her degree, she will be the best nurse, too. It's everything I need to hear. I know she's right. Deep down, in the rational part of me that's buried by the anxiety, I know this. My brain loves to catastrophise while hers is made of steel – or carbon fibre. I always joke that she stole all the sensible genes in the womb.

'I just...' I'm not even sure what's left to say. I just want everything to be okay. Easy. 'I thought this was going to be *the* season.' I can't find the words to say it, to say that I'm wondering if this will be my last season. I'm not sure I'm there yet. I'm not sure I'm ready to say it out loud. 'I thought this was going to be the one where everything would be—'

'You finished top of the podium last year and got your fourth world title,' she quickly interjects. 'You're already a legend. Way better than Dad ever was.'

'I know, but I still feel like I have everything to prove this year. I'd like to go for the points record, if I can.' She's heard the whispers about me retiring – and no one knows me better than Elise – so she knows exactly what I mean.

'Harper doesn't have to get in the way of that. *Elijah* doesn't stop you winning. As your second driver, he *supports* you and the team. You just have to put Harper into a little box in your head and focus on your own drive.'

If only it were that easy. We're going to be breathing each

other's air for months, sharing pits, simulators, private jets, locker rooms. The whole atmosphere is about to change and it's going to affect my performance, no matter how hard I try to prevent it. I've been around men like him before and I know what it will do to me. I don't know what Anders is thinking.

But my sister's right. I'm an elite sportsman and if I lose the mental game then I don't deserve to win. I mentally prepare a box and shove Harper James into it, padlocking it closed.

'Okay, smarty pants. You've got me there. I have every intention of bringing home the cup this season, don't worry. It's not like I don't already have four.' I shrug like it's nothing, but it means everything to me. The first one has pride of place in my home. The second lives in Mum's room, and the third was for Elise. The fourth is displayed in the premises of a local youth charity that I'm the ambassador for. I think it's finally time to bring one home for Cassie and Jesse.

'Good. Now can you let me get back to my show?' she admonishes with the most obnoxious eyeroll I've ever seen. I can't help but silently laugh.

She unpauses the TV, chucks a blanket at me, and I sink into the cosy L corner of the sofa. I fall asleep within minutes in the worst position for my back and neck, only to be woken by Jesse's screaming at 4am. It's perfect timing because a car is coming to get me in an hour to take me to the airport … to meet Harper James.

Elise comes downstairs carrying Jesse, face puffy and hair askew, grumbling about never getting a full night's sleep. I plant a kiss on her forehead and whisper my goodbyes.

'Good luck, bro. You can do this, regardless of who's in the other car. You've got this. And don't forget: we love you, whatever happens.'

I drive back home and wait for the car to pick me up. My sister's words stay with me until the second I climb the stairs to board the jet and find Harper James kicking back in a recliner, his trademark arrogant smirk curling the corners of his lips. My hope and excitement evaporate and I'm left with nothing but frustration and irritation.

'All right, Walker? How's it going, mate?'

His face is almost split in two by how wide his grin is, and I loathe him instantly. We've only met a couple of times, and we definitely aren't *mates*. Urgh.

It's going to be a long season.

Chapter Two

Harper

This is it. The shot I've been waiting for. Championship racing, baby!

Whilst I shouldn't be this excited because it's come at the expense of a guy with a broken leg, I can't pretend I'm not itching to get started and prove I'm meant for the big leagues.

Sorry, Elijah Gutaga.

All's fair in love and war, and if the team principal likes what he sees and thinks I'd be a better fit, then the spot will rightfully be mine. I'm chomping at the bit to show them what I can do with this opportunity.

The second I come off the phone with Anders and my agent, I begin throwing everything I can think of into my kit bags. We leave for Bahrain in less than twenty-four hours and I'm not even close to prepared.

Anders mentioned keeping shtum until the news about

Elijah has been officially released, but the excitement buzzing through me has me reaching for my phone to call Johannes.

The phone rings no less than twice before his gorgeous face appears on my screen, his dark skin and velvety brown eyes twinkling as he runs on the treadmill. There's a sweat towel around his neck and beads have formed on the temple of his shaved head.

'Hope I'm not interrupting,' I say in a tone that tells him I really couldn't care less if I am.

'You know I'm always at your beck and call, James.' He dabs away the sweat before reaching down to slow the treadmill and I get a glimpse of his naked chest, all curly brown hair and dark pink nipples. Christ, it just shows how pent up I am if I'm getting a boner over my best friend. We've put all of that in the past.

'Oh, of course, but I'd hate to distract you from the sweat you've built up there,' I say. He just rolls his eyes, but the treadmill comes to a stop, and it takes him a minute to catch his breath.

'I have an interview in ten and I still need to shower. Make this quick, James.'

'God, if you're going to sound that ungrateful to see me, I guess I won't tell you the big news.'

'You know I'm already out in Bahrain getting ready for pre-season, baby. I can't have you messing with my—'

'Well, you're going to be dealing with me a lot, actually.'

He grabs his phone from where he's set it up on the treadmill and eyes my smirk. His phone pings and he begins to laugh. 'Let me guess,' he says, swiping away. 'Elijah's injured and you're filling his spot?'

'You're such a dick. You couldn't just let me enjoy this? Fucking BBC news spoiling my fun, yet again.'

'They love to do that. At least in this article it's all positive and they haven't had to blur the picture to hide your hairy ball sack.'

Okay, that's not something I want to relive ever again. I always thought that if dirty nudes of me ever leaked they'd be exposing one of the many occasions I've let a hot guy blow me in the corner of a dark club, not because a fan decided to pants me in the street. Unfortunately, someone snapped a pic that captured me full frontal before I could cover up.

'Well, that's something, I guess. Did they at least use a nice photo?'

'Podium shot from last year.' I'll take that.

I made a decision at the end of last season to delete all news apps from my phone and remove the alerts I used to have for my name on Google. The media outlets don't have many nice things to say about me and they love to dredge up my past. I was there. I don't need to be reminded of it.

'Beautiful, that's what we like to hear. Although, it would have been nice if they'd used one of my recent Instas though.'

'I don't think the BBC wants to use your thirst traps, babe.' He rolls his eyes and sets me up on the countertop in what looks like a kitchenette. I have no clue where I'll be staying this time tomorrow, but I hope it's as gorgeous as wherever Johannes is. It's his second year in the big leagues. His first was with Haas and then when Ford announced their return to motor racing with Red Bull he was selected right away for their team. It suits him; he's always been the comeback kid.

'Their loss. What're you making?'

He pulls a blender from the cupboard and goes to the

fridge before showcasing to me in the most unsexy manner what he's putting in there. 'Banana, oat and peanut butter smoothie. Need some protein after that workout. That all you wanted to say? I gotta get in the shower before this interview, James.'

'I'm beyond jealous. Send me lots of pics.'

'You don't get that privilege anymore.' He gives his ass a little shake in his booty-hugging running shorts as he stretches up to get a tall glass out of the cupboard.

I don't miss that ass in the way that he and some of our other friends probably think I do. I just miss ass in general right now.

It's not that I'm in a dry spell, so to say – I get plenty of action – but I'm just a bit bored with my usual club pickings. I'm not sure why my usual scene isn't hitting the way it used to but for some reason it's not scratching the itch, so to speak. If I'm being honest, I don't really know what I want, or how to go about finding it.

Johannes was always a bit different. He'd karted a lot as a kid and a teen and then he broke his hip at nineteen and dropped out of motor racing. His recovery was tough both physically and mentally and he'd almost not come back. I wouldn't say that I nursed him during that time, but we lived together and when he was medically signed off as fit and well, we started sleeping together. It was a good time. We were best-friends-with-occasional-benefits, but Johannes decided he wanted to find someone to have more with. He wanted exclusivity and a relationship.

The way he said it was like that person couldn't be me. It makes sense. I'm the hot guy men bang in a club, not the kind they fall in love with.

17

Which is fine by me.

It didn't break our friendship, but I did move out. When I was finally called up, I was glad it was to a different team. We still FaceTime practically every day and we hang out and party whenever we're in the same city. He may treat me like an annoying, slightly younger brother sometimes, but I know he's excited we're around each other more now we've both hit the big time.

And now we've got a whole season ahead of us. He may not want to trawl the clubs for tail the way we used to, but he'll still wingman me while I do.

'I'm good. You know I got bored of seeing that peach,' I tease. We both laugh, and thankfully that topic of conversation dies. 'Anyway, thanks for ruining my fun announcement. I'm going to get packed up and I'll see you tomorrow!'

'Bye, love. See you then.' He waves into the camera and I end the call.

It's been a strange old day. I got up this morning thinking that today would be like every other day as there are still a few more weeks until the lower-category season kicks in, and now I'm packing for a flight to Bahrain for pre-season testing.

I should probably go through my gear. Or do something. What do normal people do when they find out their career's about to hit the next level? The level they've been dreaming about since they were old enough to be sat behind a wheel.

Most people would call their family, I assume, but I don't have one of those. I've already told the only important person in my life so … packing it is.

Hendersohm sends a car to take me to Gatwick just ten hours later. It's a sleek black limo with tinted windows and soft Italian leather. This is not something I've ever experienced before. This is it. This is the big league, baby!

I don't even have to walk through the airport, which is absolutely wild to me. My passport is checked as we pull to a stop on the tarmac, and I'm escorted up the stairs to a jet that can only be described as pure luxury.

It's nothing like the inside of any plane I've ever seen. There's a bloody bar at the back of it for a start, and if the warning I got about being on my best behaviour from both my agent and Anders wasn't still fresh in my mind I'd be parking myself there for the entirety of the flight. Instead, I guess I'll have to make do with the plush armchair with a ton of buttons on it. I'm hoping one will make the chair lie flat because I've never had my own bed on a flight before, either. Business-class seats, sure, but first-class seats in private jets? I can feel my heart pounding as I imagine the rest of my life as a major player.

There are also no more than fifteen seats in this section of the jet. Half of them are taken up by the team principal and senior members who usually gather behind the pit wall during the races. I think I can put faces to names for most of them, but the only one I actually know is Anna Kash, Hendersohm's PR rep. We met many a time when I was on the Hendersohm lower-category team. I'm sure she'd say, *'One too many times'*.

She hates me.

'Anna, my saviour, how the hell are you?' I offer her a fist to bump, but she just eyes me tiredly from behind her laptop.

'It'd be great if you could keep it in your pants this year,

James. A bit less time partying please, and for God's sake stop dancing half-naked on tables with your competitors.'

She definitely means Johannes, and I already can't wait to see him when we get to Bahrain.

'Noted,' I reply, before making my way to a seat on the other side of the aisle. Probably shouldn't push my luck too much with her. I need her to make me look good so I can rack up all the sponsorship deals my agent was buzzing about.

Last year I made more money than I've ever had in my life. My bank balance was looking healthy for the first time ever, but I hadn't had many brands reaching out to do deals. Probably my own fault, but here we are. The money I'll rake in this year will make my race earnings look like a drop in the ocean. Lie-flat seats on private jets will definitely feature more often.

I hope my parents see the press release.

I hope they feel like shit when they realise I've made it, despite everything they did to me. And everything they never did.

The money, the lavish plane, and all the deals that are about to come, well, that's the beginning of a whole new life for me. These things are the biggest motivators for me to push myself the way I do, but I can't ignore the thrum of excitement pulsing through me at the thought of meeting Kian Walker properly; of being his teammate.

He's been in the sport almost fifteen years now. He's won four championships and is a complete and utter legend in my eyes. There may have been a couple of posters of him on my bedroom walls during my teen years. There were also some of his dad. Tyler Heath was a legend back in the day, just as exciting off the track as he was on it. He was known for the string of women who trailed around the world after him and the mass of kids he'd supposedly fathered. It's obvious where Kian got both his looks and his talent.

I watched so many of Tyler Heath's races when I got into karting. I found loads of old recordings of him on YouTube and studied his mad skills. He was so exciting, the way he raced, reckless and exhilarating, always pushing the boundaries. But then he was booted from the sport and never raced again. One scandal too many, and he went from hero to villain. I should probably learn something from that, but the details of why he became untouchable are a closely guarded secret.

I've met Kian a couple of times before at events, but I've never had an actual conversation with him. He's always been too busy – and too high and mighty – to talk properly. I've never taken it personally; everyone wants a piece of the golden boy of motor sport. That'll be me soon. People will be knocking on my doors, looking for a piece of me, but I'll be too busy.

I'd be lying if I said I'm not also excited about getting to know Kian, picking his brain about his years in this sport. I want to know everything he knows. I want to ask him about his dad.

I'm twenty-five and finally hitting the big time, but he was called up to top-category racing when he was eighteen. I probably shouldn't tell him I know that his first top-tier race took place on his nineteenth birthday. That would be creepy.

I sink into the plush chair, kicking off my trainers and scrunching my feet into the leather as I slide it into the recline. It's a seven-hour flight and I can't wait to get comfy. I can't believe I'm here. I can't believe I'm finally getting everything I've ever wanted. A silly smile spreads across my face.

The whole plane is abuzz, small groups of important

people talking and making calls until the sound of footsteps on the stairs echoes and everyone falls silent as Kian Walker joins us.

Christ. Up close he's even hotter than in his pictures.

My big mouth, with no bloody filter, seizes control of my brain before I can think twice, and I find myself saying, 'All right, Walker? How's it going, mate?'

The grimace on his face is enough to shut me up, but then he side-eyes all the official people watching and quickly offers me a tight smile.

'Harper. Welcome to the team.'

That's all I get, though. He nudges his backpack further up onto his shoulders and makes a beeline for the chair furthest away from mine.

Everyone goes back to their own tasks until the captain tells us to buckle up and the doors are latched closed. We're taxiing to the runway before I can really, truly grasp how much Kian Walker has just blown me off. Not in the good way, either.

Outside of his stats, I don't actually know a huge amount about him. He's a notoriously private person who doesn't put much of himself online or open up to the media about his life. I know he's got two famous parents – Tyler Heath, of course, and his mum is Chastity Walker. She was a global superstar back in the day with a string of pop hits that still get played on the radio and remixed. Tyler Heath really did have it all, but then everything came crashing down when he cheated on his pregnant wife … and got the other woman pregnant at the same time.

Chastity disappeared from the limelight, heartbroken and humiliated for a couple of years. Tyler got fired from his team – for undisclosed reasons – and never got picked up by anyone else. The dark cloud of suspicion that hung over him cast a shadow on his incredible career and he never resurfaced in the sport.

But now, here I am, on the same team and plane as their son. He's got all his dad's racing prowess and his mum's work ethic and creativity. How often do you get the chance to meet your hero? More than that – to be his teammate?

As the jet begins to level out in the sky, and before I can stop myself, I unbuckle my seatbelt and head towards Kian. He chose a spot on its own at the back and I make my way over, perching on a low table by the side of his seat.

His eyes are closed and he's lying back in his seat, but that doesn't stop me. I've never been great with self-control, and it doesn't occur to me to exercise any in this moment.

'Hey, Kian.'

No reply.

I wave my hand in front of his face, like an idiot, as though that will get his attention. Obviously, he can't see me.

'Kian?'

Nothing.

I place my hand on his knee and shake it. His eyes quickly fly open.

'What the hell?' he growls, pulling earbuds out of his ears. I hadn't spotted those under the mass of hair that could desperately do with a good cut.

'Sorry, man. Just thought I'd come over and see how you're doing … get to know my new teammate.'

He shakes his head like I'm something he can't quite believe, but I'm not quite sure what I've done to cause this reaction. There are plenty of other drivers I've pissed off over the years who would be justified in reacting this way – or worse. I've slept with the odd brother or hurled a drink at a person or two on a bad night out. But Kian Walker? What have I ever done to him? Nothing. Not even a drunken mistake. I wouldn't need any fingers to count the number of night outs I've seen him on. I don't think he even showed up to the Hendersohm Christmas party last year.

'You're all good. I think I know enough about you,' he replies.

I know enough about you. That's what he says? Like, I'm glad he at least knows who I am because it would be beyond embarrassing otherwise, but the way he says it makes me think everything he knows is bad. I know I have a reputation in the media, but I'm also a bloody good driver.

'Right. Okay. Well, this has been enlightening.' I stand up and practically jog back to my seat.

Plopping myself down in the chair, I struggle to get comfortable. Not something I thought I'd have to do on a private jet, but a weird energy is eating away at me.

I toss and turn, even reclining the chair flat and pulling a fluffy blanket over me, but it doesn't work. Eventually I get out my phone and connect to the plane's Wi-Fi, then send a text to Johannes.

> I think Kian Walker hates me.

Thankfully three dots on the other side of the screen appear quickly.

> You aren't everyone's cup of tea, James. Plus, he's quite uptight and you're probably winding him up, if I know you.

I frown at the screen.

> All I did was say hi and try to get to know him, but he just said, and I quote, 'I know enough about you'.

Kian's words are still playing on loop in my mind. What the hell did he mean by that? And how could he know enough about me? There's no such thing as enough in my book.

> Oh. Well, he's not the most sociable guy with the rest of the drivers, but he and Elijah are close. Maybe he's just tired or doesn't fly well or something.

I contemplate his words. Maybe he's right, or maybe Kian's bummed that he's lost his friend and now he's stuck with me.

> Maybe.

I peer through the gaps in the seats at the great Kian Walker. He's got his eyes closed and he's curled up on his side, but still he somehow doesn't look truly comfortable, either.

He's definitely *something*. Something I can't quite make sense of, yet.

The plane soars on over continental Europe and my last thought as I fall asleep is how can I convince Kian Walker that he doesn't know nearly enough about me?

Chapter Three

Kian

It's day three of pre-season and I finally feel like I'm getting back in my groove. It's good to be out on the circuit again and in the familiar tight space of the cockpit. For someone who doesn't like to be crowded, I should probably feel beyond claustrophobic, but it's actually the one place where I feel completely in control.

These test sessions have been incredible. I've seen the improvements they've made to the car for this season, and putting it through its paces has made me feel more than confident for what's to come in my fourteenth season. The media can suck it with their speculation about me bowing out anytime soon.

I'm pulling up into the exit lane and steadily climbing out of the cockpit when I spot Harper James. Lingering. Again.

He. Is. Everywhere.

There's no escape now. Nothing I can do to avoid him, not

even if I tried. I can't even get out of my car without him hovering around me.

I take a second to hang back, adjusting to being upright again after over an hour whizzing round the track. I stretch out my back and my legs, loosening the muscles that have begun to tense, all whilst surreptitiously studying Harper's side profile.

His eyes keep darting towards me and I can tell he's waiting for me to walk past him. I can't deny I've been watching him, too. I've watched several of his laps this weekend. On the track he's something else. He seems to have no self-control at all as a person, but he's always in control of the car, making decisions that look bold and strategic but which could also just be reckless – and the result of natural talent and instinct. Annoyingly, I watched these decisions have incredible payoffs. After day one, I went back to my hotel room and watched some of his footage. He's a circuit genius. I wish I could see what goes on in that head of his when he analyses the track, because he drives like he has every twist and turn of the course imprinted on his brain. He always seems to know exactly what's coming next, and yet he doesn't overthink things. It's a level of driving intelligence I've seen from only a handful of champion drivers. My reluctant admiration of his technique grows every time I watch him.

And then he opens his mouth and ruins it all.

'Man, you can really see that you got all the good Tyler Heath genes.'

He's rushed over to me in my moment of contemplation, my race engineer, Cole, following hot on his heels. I see Cole wince from where he's crouching to get feedback on the tire feel and I have to stop myself from snarling at Harper as he steps between us.

Harper clocks the look Cole gives me, but is either stupid or deliberately trying to wind me up, because he continues to run his mouth.

'You take corners just like your dad, man! I'm so jealous. Got that proper fearlessness he used to have.'

Eyes closed, I take a deep breath and slowly remove my helmet. I look straight at Cole, ignoring Harper completely. 'The C4s felt really good on those laps. I think they'll be good for qualifying but maybe C2s for the start of the Grand Prix.'

Cole nods. 'Good to know. We noticed some graining from the tyres in the final laps, so this is something we can take into consideration with our final choices for Bahrain.' He makes some quick notes on the iPad he's carrying. Our best technicians and engineers are gathered around the screens, already analysing data from the car and scribbling down stats.

I've pushed out close to 120 laps across two sessions today, making my total for the three days 347 – almost as many as my third season record of 368. And if I need to do more then I will, because commitment and dedication and self-discipline are just as important as whatever natural talent you might have. Harper James needs to learn that this is a completely different league to the lower categories, and he won't last long if he twats about and doesn't take it seriously.

I'm presented with so many screens showing lap times and data, including my fastest and slowest ten for the day, and all the senior technicians are gathered around. I want to get a proper look at them and take it all in, but Harper's positioned himself in front of the screens like it's *his* information they're reeling off. He's all wide-eyed and excited like a puppy, and it sucks the energy out of me. Was I like that in my first higher-category season? His enthusiasm makes him seem so young, and makes me feel like an old man. Not that there's a huge age difference – he's twenty-five and I'm about to turn thirty-four – but when it comes to racing careers and our levels of experience, it's a lifetime. And I just *love* feeling like an old man when I'm already having to dodge questions about when I'm going to retire.

'This lap –' Harper taps at the screen, motioning to my second fastest '– was insane. The car looked so aerodynamic as you took the second and third bend that I thought you were going to fly off the circuit, but you seemed so in control.'

There's awe in his voice and I probably should be flattered by how he's raving about me, but I'm used to the way Elijah and I worked as teammates. We would take some proper wind-down time and then reconvene back at the hotel to analyse the data with clear heads, calmness and objectivity.

Sometimes I just need a little bit of space when I climb out of the car. Quiet is often impossible when straight away there are cameras in your face and all the pit crew and officials are hovering. I always take myself off to an empty corner, drop into a chair and just breathe for a couple minutes. Everyone who's been part of the team for a while is used to it, and I wish someone would take the boy wonder aside and tell him to chill the hell out, because he's really beginning to piss me off. So much of this sport is a mental game and I know what conditions I need in order to perform at my best – and Harper bloody James is definitely messing with the set-up that Elijah and I have honed over the last year. But I'm not good at confrontation so I tell myself that ignoring Harper is the way to go.

He'll get the message. Or one the race engineers will tell him straight when he pushes too far.

It won't be me, though. Confrontation isn't good for the mental game, either. It doesn't come easy when anxiety plagues the soul. Ash or Cole will fill him in. I trust them, they know what's best for me.

I turn away from Harper and keep my mouth shut. He was clearly expecting a response, and the surprise is enough to keep him quiet for a couple minutes. To cover his confusion, he leans over one of the technicians, Kev, and immerses himself in the way the graphics are showing off how I've performed in the new car.

'Don't worry, man,' Cole says quietly to me. 'We're already putting together your pre-season binder for you to look at later. Just let us know all your thoughts over the next couple of days.' Cole doesn't miss a trick – he's been here almost as long as I have and I appreciate that every season he goes above and beyond to keep me happy.

'You're a star. Thanks, Cole.' I clap him on the shoulder and grab my bag, rifling through to find my earbuds. With both in my ears and the noise cancelling mode on, I can leave behind the chaos for a bit. Visualisation has become everything for me when I can't be on the track or in a simulator. I imagine every bend, I feel the sensation of the drag on the track and how my body responds when the G-force is stronger than anything I've ever experienced before.

I pick a guided meditation from my Spotify favourites and sink into a comfy chair. Controlling my breathing, feeling the tensing, and releasing of my muscles, I work from head to toe focusing and relaxing. It's the ultimate calm and it's exactly what I need after the adrenaline rush of the circuit.

Except the calm doesn't last long because no more than a couple minutes into the track, I feel a big hand shaking my shoulder and know it can only belong to one person. I don't even need to open my eyes to be sure it's him. This seems to be his favourite mode of ambush.

'Harper?' I take out one earbud and crack open one eye.

'Wow, sorry. I've been stood here for, like, three minutes and you didn't even move. I thought you were in a trance or something.' He's like a kid, vibrating with energy and eager enthusiasm. I get it – it's his first higher-category pre-season. But he also did three hundred laps this weekend and I thought he'd be a bit more burnt-out.

'Just trying to have a bit of peace.' The point does not hit home, though. Either he's doing it intentionally or he doesn't know how to read the room.

'A couple of the guys are going to go get dinner and drinks tonight. Are you gonna join us?' He's changed out of his racing suit and into a pair of gym shorts and a thin vest which is cropped at his navel. I've never seen anything like it in the Hendersohm pit in my entire career.

I'm not quite sure who he's talking about when he says 'the guys'. I've seen him over the last couple of days becoming pally with drivers on other teams and I'm fairly sure I've seen a hundred pictures of him with Johannes from the Red Bull Ford team.

'I'm good. Have a great night, though.' My tone is dry and clearly indicates that I want to be left alone.

We have two weeks' *free time* in Bahrain till the first Grand Prix weekend, which gives the technicians time to make final adjustments on the cars and tweak the set-ups. The luxury of racing is that we aren't stuck sharing a hotel suite like I know some other sports teams are when they're travelling.

'No worries. I'll see you in an hour anyway for the Sports mag interview.' He takes off after Ash, a torrent of questions about the choice to include a sidepod in our car falling from his mouth. I don't envy Ash right now.

Then his words hit me. I quickly pull up my calendar and it's right there: *Sports UK* magazine interview with Harper. I don't even know how I missed that this morning. Probably because breakfast consisted of nonstop yapping in my ear from a certain rookie rather than my normal routine of readying myself for the day.

Reluctantly, I heave myself out of the chair and track down Kelsey. She makes all the travel arrangements and I need to get back to the hotel to shower and change.

'Looking good out there, Ki.' She's always full of compliments, though it's me that should be complimenting her – all the travel and accommodation so far has been flawless.

'Thanks, Kels. Could I trouble you for a ride back to the hotel?'

'You're in luck. I just called a car round for Harper. If you're quick you'll catch him.' I wrestle with the decision for a second. Kelsey's great, and I don't want to create double the work for her, but this is the last thing I want. Yet I still just smile and say a quick thank you before I turn and head in the same direction as Harper, groaning inwardly. Annoyingly, I'm just in time, despite dragging my heels. Harper is just opening the back door, and I wish it wouldn't be rude of me to climb into the front.

'Knew you couldn't keep away,' he says with a grin.

Did he...? Was his tone flirty?

The upheaval caused by Elijah's medical emergency and Harper's sudden arrival on this team is making me overthink everything. It's one of my worst habits, and the reason I spend so much time meditating and developing my mental focus. I quickly shake it off.

'Kels said she'd just organised a car for you and I wasn't about to make her call me another one when we're going to the same place.'

'If that's what you need to tell yourself, Kian. I know you're excited to get to know me. Maybe you'll come out for dinner after all?' His teasing eyes are so bright and enthusiastic – and this close up, in the golden hour of daylight remaining, they shimmer a clear turquoise blue.

Mesmerising.

Reluctantly, I see why every man and his wife are so keen to bed him right now.

I turn away from his gaze, remembering how much he annoys me. Maybe his superpower is actually persistence. He never seems to take no for an answer.

'Not really my thing. I need to get showered, do this interview and make it back in time for my class.' He clearly isn't good with *subtle* so I try to shut him down clearly but firmly.

'A class? What're you studying?' he asks, leaning into the conversation just as I'm trying to put an end to it.

'Yoga.' Flexibility is vital for athletes, and it's not like my training activities aren't already public knowledge, so I'm not sure why I feel so uncomfortable talking about this with him.

He studies me, his languid gaze drifting up and down the length of my body. Studying me from head to toe. His eyes

33

flicker with excitement, like he's enjoying what he sees, and I don't know how to take that. That is absolutely not allowed.

'James!' I snap at him.

'Sorry. Just trying to imagine you doing yoga. You don't exactly scream elegance.'

'It's yoga, not ballet. It's about control and breathing and exploring the limits of our muscles and limbs. Sound familiar?'

I know I'm being snippy, but my headspace feels warped, and I've really had enough of him. It makes me miss Elijah even more.

For once, Harper doesn't have a reply. Maybe because he agrees with me or maybe he's finally got the message. Or maybe it's because the heat in his eyes is still blazing and he can't quite look at me. Whatever, I'm just grateful for the silence.

It's only another five minutes to the hotel, but the atmosphere feels so awkward that those five minutes feel like forever before we're pulling up at the front entrance of the hotel and the driver is opening the door to let us out.

We both stride quickly across the foyer, only to end up in the same lift going to the same floor.

As I overtake him in the corridor on the way to my room, he grabs my arm.

'You wanna meet back out here in half an hour to go to the interview?' he asks, hovering at the door to his suite, keycard braced in the swipe lock. The space between us wreaks of sweat and the rubbery Nomex that imbeds its scent into your skin regardless of how long ago you took the suit off.

I'm not sure why, but I relent. You can't kick a puppy, after all.

'Sure.' I think I catch him off-guard because he fumbles his

34

keycard at the same time he goes to walk through the door, gifting me with the sight of him smacking his head against the wood when the door doesn't click open.

Thank you, universe.

It's my reward for enduring his relentless presence, and I enjoy every single second.

His face is a picture of embarrassment and confusion. He opens his mouth to say something, but instead, wordlessly, swipes his card again and disappears into his room.

Half an hour later, we meet back in the hallway. I shut down his attempts at conversation – or fangirling over my dad to be more precise – straight away and we walk the rest of the way to the lift in silence. It's peaceful, and I hope maybe, just maybe, Harper's finally got the message. But the second we step into the lift he presses the buttons for every single floor on the way down.

'What is actually wrong with you?' My exasperated outburst shocks us both.

'Wrong with me? What the hell is wrong with *you*? Why are you being such a dick?'

'Excuse me?'

I'm being a dick?

'It's our first interview together. Could you maybe seem like you're the teensiest bit excited to have me on the team?'

'It's just going to be the usual shit. How are you feeling about the season ahead? Are you ready for next weekend? Who's your biggest competitor this year? Just trot out some stock answers and you'll be fine.'

'Well, excuse me, Mr Fifteen Years in the Business, but some of us haven't had as much experience as you.'

Okay, well that's actually fair enough.

'Right. Well, the interviewer, Ava Gonzalez is a pro. But she's also respectful. Not even you could fuck this up.'

Harper visibly recoils out of the corner of my eye.

Maybe I am being the asshole here, but everything he does seems to rub me up the wrong way.

We stand in silence again, but this time the quiet makes my skin itch in a way it never has before. I sigh as we get to the media suite, but it's time to put my game face on and I refuse to let him get to me. This is going to be *my* season.

After hair and make-up, we're led over to the set and presented with two tiny stools to balance on before exchanging pleasantries with an interviewer who I'm sure I've met but can't quite place. I go to tell Harper it's not the reporter I've prepared him for, the warning on the tip of my tongue, but it's clear they're already waiting for us to start. I've done a hundred of these things and they're always the same. It'll be fine.

Little do I know that it's the calm before an absolute shipwreck of a storm.

'So, Kian, how are you feeling about all the changes? Especially with Elijah out and Harper in just a short time before the season starts?'

It's a question I've prepped for since the news about Elijah's injury broke. The answer is straightforward: send my love and best wishes to Elijah, react positively to change, tell her you're still looking forward to the season. Easy.

'Before I let Kian answer your question, let me start by

sending my well wishes to Elijah,' Harper cuts in before I can even move my mouth, stealing my lines.

Like he even cares about Elijah.

I feel my blood start to boil.

'The whole team is wishing him a speedy recovery and sending him and his family our best,' Harper continues.

To my knowledge, they've maybe met once or twice, never hung out and barely know each other.

I can't add anything to that without sounding insincere and just uselessly repeating him so I don't say anything at all.

'You must be missing your long-time teammate and friend?' the journalist asks me.

'He won't be missing him for long with me on the team,' Harper interrupts again, this time including a cheeky grin that seems to charm the interviewer, whose name I still can't remember.

'Of course I miss Elijah,' I say before the idiot can add anything else. I clear my throat and shoot Harper a death stare. 'Elijah Gutaga is one of the world's best drivers – and the best teammate that I've ever been lucky enough to race with. They don't make many like him anymore. He's going to be deeply missed on the circuit this season – by me most of all. But he's recovering well and I'm sure he'll be back before you know it.'

There's an awkward beat of silence and I become uncomfortably aware of the multitude of video cameras set up to capture every angle, ready for clips of the interview to go up on their social-media channels right away. It's nothing outside of the norm, but I hate these stupid little stools and I suddenly feel so self-conscious next to Harper right now. Every time he tries to invade the space between us, I lean the other way. He throws me off-balance. He's too familiar. Too in my face. All the damn time.

'It sounds like you don't think Harper James is ready to step into Gutaga's place.'

I snap my attention back to the interviewer.

Oh, hell.

'That's not what—'

But Harper scoffs angrily, and before I can continue, she turns her attention to him.

'Harper, how do you feel about stepping into Elijah's place in the team? You've got a lot to live up to, according to your new teammate.' The tone of her voice is cleverly goading and I don't like it. My words in the lift come back to haunt me.

'I'm not worried at all. Elijah Gutaga has had a great career, but it's time for some new blood in the Hendersohm team and the higher-ups clearly think that's me.'

What the hell?

I swivel my head to face him. The interviewer's grinning and the guys behind the camera look ecstatic with the footage they're capturing. It'll probably send them viral.

I'm not going to stand for this.

'New blood doesn't necessarily trump skill and experience. Had Elijah not broken his leg, we'd be on track for another fantastic season, especially with all the work the team have done on the car in the last couple of months.' I'm not about to sit back and let this dipshit bad-mouth one of the greats, my closest friend, and the driver whose seat he's stolen!

'But Harper, you did have a great season with Hendersohm last year in the category below, your first podium win, and there was already a lot of speculation about you being drafted as the back-up driver this year for the Championship team,' the interviewer says. She can clearly smell drama, and she's going to do everything she can to turn this into a story.

I'd seen that speculation, too, but I'd also heard whispers that management didn't like Harper's attitude and were divided about whether to take a chance on him or not. And I couldn't agree more.

'When you say *great*, you mean *record-breaking*, right? The best second category season a driver has ever had. The points were insane,' Harper boasts, looking at me with a distinct challenge in his eyes.

I've never had much of a poker face, so I'm sure it's obvious to everyone by now what I'm thinking.

'Yes, that's right,' the interviewer coos. 'And in fact, the record before then was actually held by your dad, Kian. Tyler Heath.' She turns to me.

Until this second, I was determined to keep it professional, to keep my mouth shut, and pray that the mic wasn't picking up on the way I was grinding my molars to pieces. But with her casual mention of my father, all bets are off.

'What a legend!' Harper cuts in. 'It's an honour to be compared to Tyler Heath. I was a big fan as a little kid. He was one of the reasons I got into karting in the first place. *He* wasn't afraid to take risks and try new things.'

Harper's dig hits home, and I feel my control slipping.

'There's calculated risk *on* the track, and then there's whatever you call what you do *off* the track,' I say coldly. 'Maybe they're calling you the new Tyler Heath for all the wrong reasons.' The thought was never supposed to leave my brain, but it's too late now. There's no way in hell we'll be able to get that clip edited out.

'And what exactly do you mean by that?' Harper demands.

'I proved it last year and I'm already starting to prove it in this category, too. Stats don't lie.'

His ass is in his hands, but he has no clue what he's talking about. I had a better rookie year than the so-called great Tyler Heath, and it'll take a better man than Harper James to beat that. Harper doesn't measure up.

'I'm just saying.' I shrug in a half answer.

'Sounds like you're saying I'm not good enough to be here, Walker. I earned my spot the same way you did, and the way I drive is all that matters,' Harper protests, and the interviewer leans into the developing row, as if our microphones aren't already picking up this catastrophic mess. Harper turns to face me, but I lean back a little. It's time he learnt to have a bit of humility.

'No, you're here because Elijah Gutaga broke his leg. You'd still be languishing in the lower category otherwise.'

I let the words hang in the air.

'Okay, let's call a time-out there,' says Anna stepping in. She's using a tone that says she won't take no for answer, and I'm left wondering why she allowed the interview to go on for as long as it did. It's been a disaster from start to finish. I'm sure the magazine is thrilled as this footage will be aired over and over again, drumming up endless column inches and screen time about drama and rivalry within the Hendersohm team.

Anna steers me out of the room by my shoulders, her hands like claws.

I assume I'm being led into a side room to cool off or whatever, but instead I'm handed over to a driver who's told to take me back to the hotel.

'I'm sorry,' I say, immediately contrite. 'What about the rest of the interview?' I ask, as the driver opens the car door.

'We'll reschedule,' Anna replies. I already know we won't.

I duck into the back seat of the car and lean back against the cool leather headrest, eyes closed. I've been asked many leading questions during my career as a driver. When I was just getting started, journalists loved to make comparisons between Tyler Heath and me. They loved to go on about how lucky I was to have a dad who had inspired me and helped make my dream a reality.

I've always bitten my tongue, held on to my control, and used deep breaths to get through it without revealing what I really think of Tyler Heath and the crap he used to pull. It's been years – almost two decades since I started being interviewed – and I've never had a problem.

Yet, a couple of words from Harper James and I'm close to losing it. On camera, just to top it off.

Shit.

Chapter Four

Harper

S o, Kian Walker is nothing like his dad. He's an uptight, judgmental prick.

I once watched a video of Tyler Heath chugging a beer out of a racing helmet – a sweaty, used racing helmet. It was disgusting, but I loved it. Pure entertainment. I don't think Kian even knows how to have fun.

And yet he's got an endless list of exciting brands still dying to work with him, paying him millions of dollars. Plus, he gets invited on all the cool podcasts and sports shows. It's such an incredible waste for them to have him drone on for hours about the benefits of yoga and going to bed at granny o'clock. Boring bastard!

I haven't seen him since Anna whisked him out of the interview. Heaven forbid his precious reputation gets tarnished by facing a few home truths from the new guy on the team.

Fuming, I went back to my own room afterwards and

paced out the angry energy whilst trying to figure out what the hell his problem is.

A message came through yesterday evening, calling us both to a meeting in the hotel conference room first thing, but I can't seem to get myself moving this morning. I remember the warning Anna Kash gave me when they called me to tell me they wanted me to step into Elijah Gutaga's seat this season. Clean up your act. No bad press. Focus on the job.

I've probably screwed that up already.

When I open the door to my suite a minute before I'm due downstairs, I come face to face with Kian, who's pacing the hallway right outside. Speak of the devil.

I'm still half-dressed due to waking up a mere five minutes ago when the alarm I snoozed for the fifth time became unbearable. I'm clutching my sweatshirt and sliding on my Crocs, the keycard between my lips as I look up and see him. This door must be jinxed.

'Are you taking the piss?' he asks through gritted teeth.

The thing is, I honestly can't say if I am or not. Maybe I am walking down the corridor shirtless to piss him off, because it's the only thrill I can get from him.

However, I do slip the sweatshirt over my head, trying to keep pace with him as we stride to the lift. Because of course Kian Walker can't be late. I bet the great Tyler Heath was late for whatever he damn well pleased. *He* probably didn't care. He was such a big star that he could work off his own schedule.

'That better?' I say, now fully dressed and trapped in a lift with him going down thirty floors.

I'm met with a wordless stare; from one of the hottest grumps I've ever seen. It's seven in the morning on our day off

– no media to do today, no practice on the track. So why does he feel it necessary to look *this* good *this* early in the morning?

'Were you waiting for me?' I ask, shooting him a cheeky side eye, incapable of not needling him. Yet still trying to be somewhat friendly.

He huffs out a snort through his nose, but I can't tell if he's annoyed with himself or with me, because he was *definitely* waiting for me.

'I was … hoping to catch the sunrise yoga class in the roof garden.'

Of course. Of course it's something lame. Wanker.

'I'm sure the sun will rise again tomorrow.' The lift falls silent as he doesn't dignify that with a response. He still hasn't realised that his silence only makes me more determined to pepper him with annoying questions and chat. Silence makes me restless.

'How much trouble do you think we're in right now?'

It's probably not the best question to bug him with before we sit down with the principal, but I genuinely want to know what he thinks of our situation.

He ponders for a second and I watch in the mirror as the cogs of his brain twitch into motion.

Now that I really study Kian's face, I don't think he looks that much like Tyler, after all. Tyler's quite tall – over six foot, if I remember his driver profile correctly. Yet, Kian struggles to meet that height, sitting around maybe five-eleven. Tyler's got almost jet-black hair, whilst Kian's is a warm-brown, and in certain lights looks almost auburn. They do share the same eyes, though – piercing hazel ones at that. Okay, fine, I stared at so many pictures of Kian in my late teenage years that I could have described them perfectly. But now that I'm seeing them so often in real life, it feels like they change colour every time I see them. Sometimes moss-green, sometimes warm brown, all mixed up with mustard-yellow and golden hues surrounding the pupil.

They'd be a big hit if he ever went out on the pull. Not that I can imagine Kian in a club, prowling the dance floor for a hook-up. Maybe a sophisticated restaurant or a fancy hotel bar? I'll have to ask him how he gets laid the next time I'm pestering him with annoying questions, but perhaps not when we're in the tight confines of a lift and he could easily punch me.

The door pings open with this thought and, as though he's got the hotel mapped out already – which he probably has – Kian leads us down another corridor before veering off into the conference room.

It feels a little big for the occasion, considering there's only four other people in the room and the tables are laid out for maybe thirty people or more.

Anna's sitting beside the team principal, Anders. Their assistants both hovering around with tea and coffee, until they leave and there is a moment of heavy silence. Kian and I sit down on the opposite side of the wide table. I notice *we* weren't offered tea or coffee, but I bite the inside of my cheek to stop myself from asking. Even I'm not stupid enough to push them right now.

'So, what happened?' Anders asks.

The silence between the pair of us is deafening. Neither of us wants to own up to fucking up the interview yesterday and Anders looks increasingly furious.

'I'm sorry. We messed up,' Kian finally says, hands twitching where he's got them resting atop the table. 'I think we just need a bit more time to find a dynamic between us that works.'

We? 'I don't know who you think you're speaking for, Walker, because it's definitely not me.' I glare at him as he rolls his eyes and swings out a hand, as if to say, *you see what I'm working with?*

I'm left gritting my teeth.

'Look, it's still early days and I know the change to the line-up was sudden. We haven't even raced yet, but we can't afford to fall apart on day one, so we've booked you both some private media training to sort your shit out.' Anders doesn't even try to beat about the bush. I've always admired that about him, even now when I'm on the receiving end of it.

Kian's face is a picture. It must be incredibly embarrassing for someone who's been in the industry for over a decade and in the spotlight most of his life, thanks to his parents, to be told he needs media training. That awful interview and this excruciating meeting are almost worth it for this moment alone.

I almost burst out laughing. Until I remember I'm going to have to sit through hours and hours of tedious presentations about the right and wrong way to answer questions with Mr Uptight himself.

But let's be honest, *I* wasn't the problem in the interview. It was Kian who basically told the world that I'm not good enough to be on this team and that he can't wait for Elijah to be back.

Kian automatically agrees to the sessions. Like he's almost happy to be arranging the training with Anna.

Shocker.

Obviously I can't protest in front of Anders, but I will not be attending that shit.

'Sure. Sign me up.' I force a smile and let Anna witter on about sending us an email and putting it in our shared calendar.

Yay. Go team.

We aren't even out of the room when the notification pings on both of our phones and I groan, loudly, when I see the first session is this evening.

'Anna works fast,' Kian says dryly as he strides ahead of me, always seemingly desperate to be out of my presence.

'Damage control is literally her job.' I'm blunt, but I really can't be bothered with this shit right now. I hate that his comments have actually started to get to me. I should probably just ask him why he's being such a prick, but that would mean having to be around his shitty attitude even more.

I won't be going to this media training, even if it gets me booted off the team.

I don't mean that, but it's how I feel right now. I'm more of an act-now-think-later kind of guy.

'I'm probably going to head up to the pool,' he says. He runs his hand through his hair, hesitating, and I can practically hear his teeth grinding, like he's forcing out an attempt at an olive branch, like he might be about to invite me along.

So, this is what it takes for Kian to be nice? Being bollocked by his handler.

Except the invite doesn't follow and I'm left looking at him a little expectantly as we climb into the lift. Probably like a child desperate for a party invite. Not my style, at all. Yet I still want him to ask.

I huff and he has the audacity to raise an eyebrow at me in the mirror.

'Guess I'm gonna head back to bed for a bit,' I add, not that he was courteous enough to ask if I had any plans.

And then, out of nowhere, a thought occurs to me and I cannot dislodge it. Kian Walker in tiny little Speedos. Why does it still have such appeal when he's shown himself to be nothing but a dick in real life?

'What do you swim in?' Curiosity gets the better of me and I almost need to know the answer for my own piece of mind.

'Um … the hotel pool?' He says it like *I'm* the idiot here. 'It's got two. An indoor and an outdoor one.' He has such a stick up his ass. I'm smiling and shaking my head, but he's just glaring at me like he can't quite figure out what he's said that's so funny.

'I meant clothing-wise,' I add, looking him straight in the eye and returning his challenging eyebrow raise for good measure.

'Oh.' That stops him in his tracks. He has to be well aware at this point that I'm gay. If not, he truly must live under the world's biggest rock. Maybe I've succeeded in making *him* uncomfortable.

His cheeks tinge the slightest shade of pink and his hands grip the rail at the back of the lift. I should just laugh it off at this point, because I actually don't want him to think I'm some perve who's going to be watching him change in the locker room or whatever, but his reaction is interesting.

It doesn't look like he's actually angry that I'm sticking my nose where it doesn't need to be. *Very interesting indeed.*

It takes twelve floors before he finally collects himself and says, 'Normal swimming trunks,' like it's no big deal. But I watched him before he said anything and it looked like he really turned that answer over in his head.

I don't say anything more. Of course, he gave the most boring answer in the world, but it's his reaction that's provided me with something to think about.

Like, maybe he's not as straight as I thought he was.

'Disappointing,' I mutter, but my heart's not in the teasing anymore. Kian really does suck all the joy out of everything.

When the lift gets to our floor, he's out of there so fast that I'm left blinking in the glare of the lights, while he's disappearing down the corridor and into his suite.

I do love that we're getting along so well.

I make good on my words and climb back into bed, as it's still not even 9am. Except going to sleep with the image of Kian in just Speedos is not a good idea.

Because I end up dreaming of him in a deserted pool, the teeny-tiny Speedos abandoned on the side, the two of us getting hot and heavy in the glow of a thousand stars.

Until Anders walks into the dream and ruins everything.

It's almost eleven when I shoot awake, sweat beading on my forehead and a raging hard-on in my boxers. I groan, brilliant, another issue caused by Kian.

Can I really blame this one on him? Or is this my punishment for messing with him? I think about him blushing in the lift, which does nothing to help my current situation. I think about him gripping the rail and I'm wishing to be lost in my dream again.

I grab my phone to check for notifications. I need a distraction. Nothing interesting comes up except a text from Johannes saying we're staying at the same hotel and do I want to get dinner this evening. Of course I do.

In the bathroom, I fire back a text agreeing to meet him in the hotel restaurant, before hopping in the shower to deal with my next Kian problem.

It's not even a satisfying release when, with only a couple of tugs and a vision of Kian gripping that bar in the lift, I cover the tiles and shower floor with cum. Hey, a guy can dream.

My agent rings as I'm stepping out of the shower and I fill the rest of the afternoon looking through the brand portfolios who are interested in working with me, the pile so much bigger after seeing my performance during pre-season. There's so many I'm almost late for dinner with Johannes.

'I'm sorry, I'm sorry,' I say as I finally arrive at the table where Johannes has been waiting. 'It's been an unexpectedly busy day. But I'm here now; you have my full attention.'

Except he doesn't, because my phone starts to ring. I don't even need to look at the screen to know it's Kian calling me because I haven't shown up for our media training. Surely, if he knows me as well as he says he does, he can't actually have expected me to show up.

'You sure you don't need to get that?' Johannes asks, but I just shake my head. 'Nils had dinner here last night and apparently the steak and blue-cheese salad is really good.'

'Well, if your new bestie thinks it's good I suppose I'll give it a try,' I tease, though I am envious that Johannes has been lucky enough to get a great teammate, someone who actually seems pleased to spend time with him.

'He's nice. Leave him alone. Just because your idol doesn't like you, no need to be bitter.'

We both order the recommended salad and slump into the booths with glasses of iced lemon water. 'I can't believe we're being sensible,' I groan.

'I'm doing a shoot tomorrow where I need to be behind the wheel of a car, can't be hungover, man. Plus, aren't you on the Sky Sports breakfast thing tomorrow? You realise they'll want you in the green room first thing right?'

I do. Thankfully, my agents got me an assistant who keeps my diary nice and tidy and easy for me to decipher where I need to be and when. I could still do with a drink or two after this morning.

The ringing in my pocket begins again and I flash Johannes the screen. 'My handler. Apparently, he can't get enough of me.' Johannes just chuckles and I reject the call again, only for it to start going off straight away.

Jesus, Kian. Get the message.

My phone bleeps for the fourth time and Kian's name fills my screen yet again.

'Blimey, he's obsessed with you,' Johannes says.

'Tell me about it. All because I didn't meet him for that media training.' I lock my phone and place it face down on the table. He's not about to ruin my evening with his sour mood.

'Wait, are you supposed to be there right now?'

I nod.

'Jesus, Harper. I know dinner with me is the most important thing in your life, babe, but you're in the big league now. You need to make more effort for the team, especially if this was training ordered by your principal. You're gonna be in so much trouble tomorrow.'

He's probably right, but I'm not ready to deal with the fallout just yet. That's tomorrow's problem.

Rolling my eyes, I shake off his comments. 'Christ, when did you get so sensible?'

'When I realised I'm replaceable. There are so many junior drivers coming up the ranks with insane skills and if I step out of line they won't hesitate to cut me. It's all money for them, Harps. If we aren't making it, or we're losing them sponsors and bringing them bad press, it's over.'

His words hit me like the iced water I've been drinking so far this evening, cold and choking. Johannes used to be the life of the party; he used to be me. Just a year older than me, he was in his rookie Championship season this time last year. He's learnt all the lessons and I should probably be listening to him. Yet I miss the guy who was nothing but fun when we were in lower categories, who'd sneak out when we were just eighteen or nineteen to a bar in every city to get trollied and pick up hot guys.

'I get what you're saying, but I don't need media training,' I protest. 'It was Kian who sat there basically saying I don't compare to his friend, like boo-fucking-hoo. Cry me a river. And then he got all huffy because the interviewer mentioned that I beat his dad's record and compared *my* talent to Tyler Heath's instead of Kian's.'

'I saw the clip. It went pretty viral, Harps. I'm just saying, you need to play the game a bit. Once I did, I feel like they backed off. I win points and they don't say shit when I go out too much as long as I don't get papped doing something stupid. Nobody cares what you do in your spare time when you're in the lower categories. It's different now.'

Deep down, I know he's right, but it's too late regardless. I've missed the session and I'm sure Kian's already blabbed to management that I didn't show. He probably sat there like a good little boy and took his punishment.

'I'll reschedule. Don't stress about it. Kian would still be annoyed at me even if I'd have shown up.' There'd been little puffs of smoke leaving his ears as we sat in Anders's makeshift office like naughty schoolboys. I know he blames me and resents me for putting him there, even if it was actually his fault.

'Are you even trying with him?'

'He's not trying with me.'

'Can you hear yourself right now, Harp? You sound like a child.'

I stick my tongue out at him just to prove his point, before slumping back into the small booth.

'Can we talk about something else? I'm bored of talking about Kian bloody Walker. Let's just enjoy the evening and toast these boring old glasses of water to our first Championship race together?'

He clinks his glass against mine and the world settles back into place. This is what I thought it would be like when Jo and I were karting babies and top-class racing was just one big dream. Now look at us. We've made it.

Johannes walks me back to my room and just like that our blissful bubble pops at the sight of a very furious Kian skulking outside my room.

He eyes Johannes wearily. 'Johannes.' He nods.

'Kian,' Johannes claps me on the shoulder, pushing me towards my new teammate. 'He's all yours.'

'Traitor,' I mutter under my breath as Johannes returns to the lift, heading to his own floor.

'What the fuck, Harper?'

'What the fuck Harper what?'

I know why he's here, but I'm relaxed now and I can't resist.

'Do you not take anything seriously?' It's a wonder he has any teeth left at the rate he grinds them to try and keep his temper in check. Kian spots the smirk on my face and I know that's what sets him off.

'I can't tell whether you think you're too good for them to fire you, or if you're actually just completely stupid.'

'It's media training, Kian. Chill out.'

He snorts and shakes his head.

'I don't know why I'm bothering. I hope you *do* keep fucking up, James, because then Anders'll drop you and I'll get a decent teammate who's actually in with a chance of winning.'

And with that he walks off, head held high. What a prick. Where does he get off underestimating me?'

I almost wish Johannes had stayed so he could have seen what I was working with.

My first qualifier comes around quicker than I could ever expect and even though I'm the new kid on the track, the crowds are howling for me as we make our way into the Hendersohm garage. Fans throw T-shirts at us and I'm surprised when Kian stops to sign every single one of them and shake hands with each kid looking for anything they can get from their idol. He's always so focused on the work. No time for anyone or anything. Or maybe it's just no time for me.

The atmosphere inside the garage is something else,

though, abuzz with technicians, analysts, designers, agents, and the big boss himself, Anders. Everyone's gearing up for the start of the season. I'm just glad to be coming in on a season where the cars only had to have tweaks from last year because it was so bloody good, so I don't have to work out the kinks in a completely new, rebuilt car that's still being reworked by the technicians.

Anders talked a big game during pre-season about there being no number one at Hendersohm because it's not how his team rolls, but everyone knows the top seat belongs to Kian. Does he even realise that the whole team revolves around him and what he wants? He's the bright flame to their busy, fluttering moths. I guess we'll see what happens this weekend.

Will they hold me back if I'm closing in on Kian? How many technicians will be on *my* car making sure *my* tyre changes are just as quick as Kian's?

It's going to be interesting, to say the least.

And it turns out to be even more interesting than I could ever have anticipated.

The guy I've watched and worshipped for years crumbles.

He struggles to get going, and can't keep up the pace on some of the more brutal corners of the Bahrain track, and overall, it's a less-than-stellar performance.

I actually finish ahead of him, setting a lap time that delights both me and the wider Hendersohm team. Ash, my race engineer and the guy who will live in my ear for the season, is screaming about how good it is for a rookie.

Kian's still out there trying until the last minute, but it's not enough. I hear Cole tell Ash that Kian's only made P8, whilst I'm in P4. It's a switch-up in positions that I don't think anyone was expecting, least of all Kian. I can only imagine what's going through Kian's mind when he hears that he's eighth to my fourth.

Who's the number one driver now, Kian? Who's the one at risk of getting dropped? Media training, my ass. There's been no fallout from me missing the session yet, and if they had any concerns about me being worth it, well, looks like I am…

All the air leaves the garage when Kian enters. He's silent at first, and then I've never seen anger like it. He slams his helmet down so hard it practically bounces off the table and onto the floor, and I'm surprised the visor doesn't shatter with the sound it makes. He has every right to be frustrated. Finishing eighth when he should have been top three is not good during the qualifiers. Even I'm not quite sure what happened out there today.

No one says a word, and you could cut the tension with a knife, Kian's fury drowning out the crowds in the stadium behind us. I find myself fascinated by the interplay of emotions on Kian's face, and I'm unable to look away.

Then he releases a breath and it's like watching a balloon deflate. The experience for me is cinematic, and seems to happen in a kind of terrible, slow motion. The fight and anguish drains from his face and body until he becomes the serene and unflappable Kian Walker again, and he quickly begins apologising to everyone.

I can't put my finger on the word I'm searching for to describe him right now. He's like four seasons in one day, a force of nature that contains both chaos and calm in one bright, beautiful shell. Anna pulls him to the side, and before I know it, he's out of there. No media for him right now and it's probably for the best if he's already dented a helmet. They cost thousands to construct and then meld perfectly to the skull so that they can protect us from whatever the track throws at us.

I'm left to face the team on my own. Everything feels weird, and I'm strangely disappointed. I should be excited – P4 in my first qualifier – but the press only wants to talk about Kian's disappointing performance, so my achievement is entirely overshadowed.

Because of course everything has to be about Kian Walker.

Kian bloody Walker.

Chapter Five

Kian

I really shouldn't have been shocked that Harper qualified in fourth place after seeing his performance in pre-season and his record-breaking win last year in the lower category, but I am. I have no clue how he does it when he seems to do zero preparation and treats the whole thing like a joke. How does he collect himself when shit happens? How does he focus? What are his coping strategies? I don't understand how going out and partying with his competitors *helps* his race.

And yet both of them qualified ahead of me. Both of them.

What the hell is going on?

With the Prix tomorrow, they won't be able to go out and get smashed tonight. Not the night before a race. Harper's not that stupid. Or at least I don't think he is. He might idolise Tyler Heath, but he wouldn't make the same mistake that cost my father his place on the team.

Would he?

Tyler always claimed he was fired unfairly because the team bosses didn't like some of the choices he'd made in his personal life, but Mum told me he'd had to be breathalysed the morning of a race and was found to be over the limit to drive. It wasn't the first time he'd had a problem with his drinking, and I guess they finally had enough. He was a danger to himself and to others. And he always did whatever he wanted without a thought for who he hurt or how anyone else would suffer. Always.

Being fired for drinking was a humiliation he'd paid a lot of money to keep quiet, and I'm surprised to this day that the story has never leaked. He made Mum sign an NDA as part of the divorce agreement. I'm sure if my sister and I had been old enough he'd have forced us to sign one, too.

Luckily, he doesn't hold any power over me, and he never will.

In my rookie years, I carefully spun the narrative to be all about how my mum had taught me and my twin to dream big and follow through. How it had been hard work and dedication that got me here. Nothing genetic about it. I owe my success to Mum and to Elise – my dad has nothing to do with it. Gradually, people stopped asking.

And now here I am, throwing it all away and qualifying eighth. *Eighth!* This isn't like me. It isn't like me, at all, but I just can't seem to get it together. Ever since I heard Harper was joining the team, my head has been a mess.

I'm back at the hotel in a blur of anxiety, showering off the day and desperately trying to get my shit together when my phone starts to ring with a FaceTime from Elise.

These were my favourite parts of the day when I was younger. She'd call me and tell me about her nursing course, when she first started dating her boyfriend, now husband, and about all her exciting friends who loved to do wild things at uni. Now, whenever the phone rings, I dread that she's calling with bad news about Mum.

It doesn't stop me answering quickly, though. It's not too late in the UK and the biggest smile cracks across my face as I open the video call to find my niece taking up most of the screen.

'Uncle KiKi,' she cries happily, clapping as my face fills her screen. 'Uncle KiKi, I did finger painting today.' Elise flips to the back camera and I'm met with at least ten sheets of paper covered in swirls of different coloured paint. And this is all it takes to restore my happiness.

I breathe out and let Cassie explain her wandering thoughts about a couple of paintings before she gets completely distracted telling me about a bedtime story TV show she's been allowed to watch.

'Miss you, Uncle KiKi. Mummy says you're going to win me something, like Daddy does when we go to the fair.' My heart beats faster at that. I can't let her down. Her excited little face... It would break my heart.

'I'm definitely going to try, sweetheart. A big gold cup. How does that sound?'

She cheers with utter glee and then drops the phone, her voice fading out into the background as she runs off to find her dad to tell him.

Elise picks it up from the floor and for once I'm caught off guard by the paint streaks on her face instead of the tiredness in her eyes.

'Sorry about that. She's had too much sugar. Grant took her to the fair today at the park. She's had a concoction of doughnuts and candy floss for dinner.'

I shake my head because I love that kid too much to care about her throwing me on the floor.

'It's fine. You look really well, El.'

'It's been a good day. The kids are happy. It's nice to have Grant at home. Mum held Jesse today and knew who he was. So, my heart is very full.'

I remember what she said to me when she sat me down and told me that the Parkinson's was now considered advanced; that we should be making every memory possible with Mum, treasuring the good days and just being glad she's still here on the bad ones. I'm not surprised she looks content.

'God, El. I'm sorry I wasn't there for that.' There's a heaviness in my heart that I'm missing all these good moments. I should be making the most of them, too.

'I'll send you all the photos, don't worry. She asked about you this evening. Even when you're not around you're still in her mind.'

I choke down a big old sob at her words. I'm really missing them all so much today.

'We didn't see the qualifiers, but I saw you finished eighth when I checked the news. Just remember, tomorrow's another day and your race days are always better than your qualifiers.'

She isn't wrong. For someone who actively refuses to watch most of my races out of fear of seeing me crash, she knows a lot about my stats.

'We love you so much, Ki. Just wanted to drop in on you before we get the kids to bed. It's already way past their bedtime.' I'm grateful she's made the time; she probably saw today's result and knew that I needed them right now.

I love my sister so much.

'Love you all, too. Kiss both of them goodnight for me.'

'Hope you aren't forgetting me,' her husband, Grant, says with a grin, appearing behind her, Jesse fast asleep on his hip as he heads for the stairs.

'Kiss the big baby for me too.' I make kissing noises into the camera and then the line cuts off and I'm back to being alone in my hotel.

Again.

The next morning I'm whispering a mantra under my breath as I head into the garage and suit up.

'Yesterday is forgotten, today is a new day, I've got this.'

I repeat it over and over in my head, trying to get that laser-focus to kick in.

The muscles in the back of my neck don't feel quite so coiled with anxiety anymore, and my mind's on the prize. I fell asleep visualizing giving that cup to Cassie. This is my motivation now. The wins aren't for me; they're for her and Jesse. Everything I do is for them – not just to give them trophies but to give them a better life. A life I didn't get.

Don't get me wrong. Mum always made sure we wanted for nothing, but the gifts she gave us were to plug the parental-sized hole in our life. Dad was physically gone and a lot of the time it seemed like Mum was mentally checked out. That wouldn't be Cassie and Jesse, they'd constantly know they were loved and treasured.

'Yesterday is forgotten, today is a new day, I've got this.'

I roll my shoulders back as I walk out into the Hendersohm pit, the rush of noise around me so familiar that it's not even distracting. There's people in the stands holding up posters with my name on. I've got this.

I don't know where Harper James is and I don't care. He's not my problem.

'Yesterday is forgotten, today is a new day, I've got this,' I whisper to myself.

The crowd cheers when I wave, and I feel the roar well up inside me.

'Yesterday is forgotten, today is a new day, I've got this,' I say again.

It's one bad qualifier. It's not over until the chequered flag. No more catastrophising.

I'm calm and in control as I climb into the cockpit. Cole checks that I'm comfortable and that everything feels good.

'Yesterday is forgotten, today is a new day, I've got this.'

I nod as he steps back, the halo settling around me.

'All right, Kian. Keep your focus. You've got this.' Cole's voice has been in my ear for years, and it's reassuring that he hasn't lost faith in me either.

'Thanks, Cole. Let's do this!'

Yesterday was admittedly a little shaky, but I always seem to perform better when I'm wheel to wheel with every other driver on the track. Even if that includes Harper, who I can't help but see is waiting to go in fourth.

Starting in eighth isn't ideal, but the second the race starts I feel myself slipping back into the focus that's got me where I am today.

Everything feels good around me – the halo is secure, the steering feels smoother, the skid on the track so much better than yesterday. It doesn't take me long to feel the thrill of driving again.

I start moving up, first P7 and then P6. I feel good, I feel settled, and I'm starting to enjoy myself. That trophy will be Cassie's, just like I promised.

It takes a couple of laps, but I'm powering in to P5, Harper just ahead of me. He hasn't managed to move up at all, but he's maintained his position, so I've got to give him that at least. I'm determined to take him. I cannot finish behind this little twat who seems to know how to push every single one of my buttons.

But he's got some impressive little techniques to force me into bad positions behind him so I can't sneak past. We don't run a policy at Hendersohm where driver one has priority. I know some teams have a strategy and they work together as a pair, but that's not how we do things. Elijah and I were always equals on the track, and that worked for us.

But there's something about the way Harper's driving that really pisses me off. It's like he's teasing me with opportunities and then swinging in to close them off the second I take the bait and go for it. He's playing with me.

But I've got years of experience under my belt. I know this track, I know the car, I know what I'm doing.

'Cole, what's the difference?' I ask.

'Point six,' he replies.

So, when I see the opportunity, I open the DRS and gain an advantage, sliding past him with the grace and poise of a ballet dancer.

It's unbelievably satisfying.

Take that, you arrogant twat. Watch and learn how the big boys do it.

But when I move up into P3, Harper's right behind me.

I just need to tune him out and focus on my own race, my

own schedule, my own routine. He's a rookie. He's good, but he's a rookie. I'm the reigning champion and I'm defending my title. One bad press interview doesn't change that.

I'm pulling overtaking manoeuvres that feel as natural to me as breathing, until I'm nearly up front where I belong. It's easy to feel content here, especially when I've only been able to see one person up ahead of me for the last half a lap. Whoever it is, I'm close enough to see that their car is bouncing almost out of control. If we weren't racing, I would think they were listening to ACDC up ahead.

'Can you confirm I'm in P2, Cole?' I ask over the headset, just in case I've been so in the zone that I've missed something.

'P2 confirmed. Just Yorris out ahead of you.'

So, only one rogue Ferrari guy to fly past and with how bad he looks and how good I feel, I'm confident it won't be difficult.

The last third of the race sitting up front, almost leading the pack, feels like the heaven I've spent the last decade and a half building. My eyes are on the road and with Cole in my ears there's nothing we can't do. We're unstoppable. Not even Yorris will stop me.

'Three laps to go, Ki. Straight coming up.' I take the bends, watching mostly for the narrow one, and the second I hit the straight I'm on max power, looking for the sweet spot and then flying past Yorris and whatever issues he's facing.

'P1!' Cole tries not to shout, but there's an eruption going on behind him in the garage.

I'm three laps from smashing out of the first race of the season, my mind sharp and the car performing, as I pass the line for one of the last times. Two laps, just two laps from victory. So close and yet so far because before I know it there's a car up my ass locking on to me, and I can feel them being pushed by a car right behind them, too.

'Give me P2 and P3, Cole.'

I need to know what I'm up against right now so I can plan how to handle these final laps and still keep pole position.

'Yorris in P2 and James in P3,' Cole confirms, and for a second I almost lose focus. He can't be right.

'Can you confirm P3 again, please?' There's no way. It's one thing for a rookie to shit out a good lap in qualifying, but another for them to be battling for podium in their first race.

'It's Harper, mate. Really battling with Yorris. Might be one of those moments for the history books.'

Fuck this. I banish any thought of who's behind me. I have to focus on *my* drive right now. My back's killing me as I push right up against the seat, like that's going to maximise my speed. I know I can ignore it for two more laps and keep up the pace without flying off the track in a heap of metal.

'Yesterday is forgotten, today is a new day, I've got this.'

The final lap is called into my headset and I'm really bloody pushing now. It's not like other seasons where it's felt like I'm fighting with the car by the last couple of laps, but I can still feel every bit of G as I tap the brake ahead of the corner to keep me from ending up too close to the wall. It's painful in my neck and spine, but exhilarating at the same time.

This is what I live for.

'How far behind?' I'm asking as the last turn of the lap approaches.

'P2 point eight. P3 one point four.' It's reassuring enough. I can work with that.

And I absolutely do. I floor it on the last straight and then I'm flying over that line like my life depends on it. Inside my ears, the garage erupts into a chaos of noisy celebration. I can't wait to be out of this car and celebrating with my team.

'Thank you, Cole,' I murmur into the headset, beyond glad that one of my favourite team members is with me for the fifth year in a row.

'You're always welcome, superstar. Anders is crying. First race and he's got both Hendersohm drivers on the podium.' There's still so much shouting going on in the background at his end that I have to check I heard him correctly.

'Harper stayed in P3?'

'Indeed he did. Everyone's the best kind of shocked right now.'

It's carnage in the garage. My back aches as much from the backslaps and hugs I've been pulled into than it does from the two hours I've spent enduring G-force speeds in my car. Champagne corks fly around the room, the popping sound only causing people to scream our team name more and more. I get handed a magnum with Hendersohm branding on it and I take a swig before handing it on to Ash. Seconds later he has Harper on his knees in front of him and he's pouring the frothy bubbles down the rookie's throat.

The Netflix videographer is floating around, so that's going to make for some interesting footage.

Not my problem, I quickly remind myself.

I need to focus on what I'm doing and Harper James can take care of himself. If Anders is happy to take a chance on him, then that's his decision.

Yet the frustration still threatens to ruin my joy. That Harper James can just waltz in here, treat all the careful training, scheduling, and clear instructions from the team principal like a joke, and still get on the podium.

Speaking of podiums, as Harper nudges past me to step onto the third-place box, he shoulder bumps me hard enough that I stumble slightly. In full view of all the fans, the press, everyone.

That's rookie sportsmanship for you. He's such a sore loser.

It takes grace, dedication and commitment to be a winner. He's not mastered that yet as he proves what an arrogant little twat he truly is.

When I step up onto the podium and take the medal for first, I can feel the waves of annoyance coming off him. Yorris, on the other side of me, seems oblivious to the tension.

And then, when it's time to shake hands with each other for the inevitable press photos, I turn to Yorris first and we congratulate each other. I don't know him very well, but we've shared a podium many times before and we know the drill. Shake, eye contact, then look out at the press for the photo op. When I turn to Harper, though, and go to shake hands with him and do the same, he pretends not to see me – or to understand the established order of how this is done – and he reaches around me to shake hands with Yorris and congratulate him.

I'm left holding out my hand and looking like a total turkey in front of the thousands of fans and the global media. Cameras click and flash and I know this will be front-page news in the sports press.

Even when he finishes with Yorris, Harper acts like I don't exist and turns to step off the podium.

'You're such a sore loser,' I say under my breath and he turns to give me a look that would put me six feet under if such a thing were possible.

I can't help laughing at his petulance, but I admit that it's easy to be the bigger person here since I'm the one that got the win. But when I turn my head, I see Anders watching and I feel chagrined.

Anders is like a father to me. He's certainly been more of a father to me than mine ever was. He has nurtured my career, and the way he supported me when Mum was diagnosed with Parkinson's – and the way he continues to support me – will put me forever in his debt.

Now I feel bad for embarrassing him in this way. It matters how the team appears in public. It matters what our reputation is. It matters to the sponsors, to the team owners, and to the team's bottom line. It's not too much to ask that we keep private hostilities from spilling over. We're afforded approximately thirty minutes of uproar to enjoy the celebrations, shake hands with VIPs, sponsors, and autograph-hunters before Anders waves me over to him. He's already got Harper welded to his side with an arm around his shoulders that appears jovial but is probably like an iron band.

I already know this is not going to be good.

When Anders has us both in his grasp, amidst the deafening noise of the team's celebrations, he says in a low voice so that only Harper and I can hear, 'Great performance on the track, boys. An excellent start to the season. But listen carefully to what I'm about to say. No more dick swinging, no more petty infighting, no more bullshit. From now on, you put on a united front. This is your final warning. Fix it or fake it, I don't care which, but if the press, sponsors and VIPs don't come away with the impression that you boys are best buds, then you'll both be looking for a new team. Are we clear?'

I feel a weight drop into the pit of my stomach. My throat

feels tacky and I can't swallow. I cannot lose my place on this team. Not that way. It would crush me.

To be fired, like my father was, for something so stupid … I don't think I'd ever get over that.

'Of course. I apologise for the unprofessionalism. I know I'm not great with change, and I don't think I've handled the upheaval very well. But that doesn't justify how I've been acting…'

Even to my ears, the words seem desperate, and maybe they are. Maybe I'm a thirty-three-year-old facing the end of his career who's desperate not to become the person he despises most in the world, but I will only be going out on my own terms. I've worked my entire life to shrug off the comparisons between us, and I will not fall at the final hurdle.

Harper's head spins round so quickly to face me, it almost gives *me* whiplash. He's eyeing me like he's not quite sure what to make of this version of Kian Walker. I'm just hoping he's not about to argue with me about this. After all, it's mostly his fault.

'I think maybe you two just need to get to know each other a bit more. You don't have to love each other – hell, you're still each other's competition – but you need to get yourselves under control. This is a spectator sport, and everyone's watching. How you talk about each other and to each other in public matters. It's also a team sport, so act like a bloody team. Is that understood?'

I nod, rapidly, but Harper is still dead quiet.

'Sure,' he finally agrees, and again I'm reminded of a petulant child. In that, I'll need to be the grown-up here.

I'm trying to think of an activity that we can do together,

something we have in common that we can use to settle this situation between us.

'The gym maybe?' I suggest.

'Huh?' Harper replies, clearly not following my chain of thought.

'We could start working out together and post some clips on social media. It'll be good for our driving and we can try to get to know each other a little bit more.' Harper's still acting like a sulky teenager being reprimanded by a teacher he clearly doesn't respect. All I can do is take the high ground. He might not grasp what's at stake, but I do. Maybe I just have more to lose. 'That's my bad, man. I should have welcomed you properly to this team.'

Maybe I have been unwelcoming, bordering on unfriendly. He's not to know that comparing me to father dearest would put my back up, but I'm also not above being the bigger man. He just always seems to know exactly what to say and do to push my buttons. Just when I think I've got my shit together, he makes a comment that leaves me floundering in the deep end.

Anders smiles at both of us, and my suggestion is clearly a hit, yet Harper is still taking his sweet time agreeing. For a second, I almost think he won't, that he'd rather throw away the biggest opportunity he's ever had for the sake of his own pride.

'Sure,' is all he offers to this conversation again. It'll have to do.

'Brilliant. I knew you two wouldn't let me down. The sponsors are incredibly excited for this pairing and what you'll accomplish this season. Let's not waste this momentum.'

Anders has always cared so deeply about the team, and I

know better than anyone that the team is bigger than any individual driver. Motor racing is a multi-billion-dollar industry, and managing a team means being ruthless when it comes to making money. Anders may love Hendersohm, but he's not in this for shits and giggles. If he can't get his drivers under control, the owners might just decide to fire *him*. If sponsors are turned off by our bickering and start looking elsewhere … well, suffice it to say that this cannot be a loss-making venture. So, I understand his need to keep everyone happy.

Harper disappears back into the celebration, whilst I slink off back to the hotel. I don't have the heart to join in with everyone else. All I need right now is to catch up with the family and sleep. When did winning start to feel so exhausting?

I turn my phone back on and I'm barraged with texts, mainly from friends and family back home. But there are also several from Elijah congratulating me on my first win of the season.

Sadly, Harper's antics on the podium have gone viral. No wonder Anders was so pissed off. Some of the reporters are even claiming that the supposed rift between Harper and me is my fault. Apparently, despite today's performance, my best days are behind me and I'm standing in the way of a new generation of superstar drivers. The same people who called me the golden boy of Championship racing for more years than I can remember are as good as calling me grandad. Where do they get this bullshit from? I mean, did they not watch me today?

It's almost enough to make me truly consider retiring this season. Giving the press what they want.

But I'm not a quitter. And I won't let one arrogant rookie throw me off my game.

Chapter Six

Harper

I'm standing outside the gym, the door cracked open enough that I can see Kian in the mirror. His shoulders are hunched as he waits at the bicep curl machine. There's a sheen of sweat on his forehead that says he's started without me, but the way he keeps glancing at the clock tells me he thinks I still might turn up.

I know this makes me sound like a whiny kid, but it's not my fault he decided to be an asshole first. I can't believe I ever looked up to this guy, when all he seems to do is look down his nose at me. What's wrong with wanting to have a good time? To work hard but play equally as hard? Not my fault he's boring as fuck and acts like a middle-aged woman. Who wants to do yoga and be in bed by nine when we are literally in our prime?

Still. I should go in. I almost want to, even if it's just to ogle Kian in the little shorts he's wearing.

Yet something stops me.

If I'd continued with the therapy I'd been forced to attend when I came out of the foster system at eighteen, I'd probably have been told it was because I don't deal well with anxiety and handing over control to other people. It would make a lot of sense if you'd ever met my parents. Not that I need to contemplate my emotional trauma right now in the hotel hallway.

I'm frozen in place, lingering as Kian paces over to the wall, setting up a skipping rope and a bunch of weighted balls at his feet. He then whips a tennis ball out of his shorts pocket and bounces it quickly off the wall, getting in some reaction rate reps before his strength training.

I wish I didn't admire his utter commitment to the sport. It would be easier to hate him that way. He does this every single day except race days. It's everything to him. He's clearly given motor sport his whole life, which also means it has the power to tear him apart.

I love the sport, too, and hope I have a long career in it, but I won't give anything or anyone that power. I want to enjoy *right now*. And right now, I really don't want to give Kian Walker the satisfaction of going in there to train with him.

Decision made; I leg it. Running away from something else I don't want to do. Yet again.

Instead, I persuade Johannes to go for dinner with me in the hotel restaurant again. We snap a ton of selfies and I post them to my story. These are immediately picked up and shared by press and fan accounts until I swear the entire world is watching our every move. It's exhilarating to feel like so many people care what I do.

We're just paying the bill when I catch a glimpse of Kian

going from the gym to the lift in the hotel lobby. For a second, he looks so dejected as his eyes glance between the empty plates and glasses on our table and how Johannes is laughing about something his teammate, Nils, did on the flight over here.

Then he catches me watching him and he instantly schools his face into the pissed-off look he wears just for me.

I'm an asshole and I know it.

He's trying. Like, really trying, and I'm being a dick. It's worse that I know this and yet I'm still struggling to just take the bloody olive branch he's offering.

'Hello? Earth to Harper.' Johannes snaps his fingers in front of my face and I watch as Kian walks with a defeated air towards the lifts.

'Sorry, sorry. I think I'm just tired. Hang on a second, I just need to go do something.'

I slide out of the booth and stride across the hotel lobby towards the lift Kian's waiting for. The doors start to open as I'm just five seconds away, and my strides turn into a sprint so that I make it just in time to keep the doors open.

'Are you kidding?' he grumbles.

He smells like a gym locker right now, and I hate that it's so appealing. I want to lean in to him, get up close and take a deep breath, inhale his woodsy, masculine scent. I remember how he looked in his vest and shorts in the gym and have to physically shake my head to get rid of the image.

A queue starts to form behind us and we both step out of the way to let people into the lift.

'You're such an asshole,' he says through gritted teeth as the lobby empties around us and the lift departs. 'Why did you stand me up?'

He doesn't call another lift, so we're clearly having this out here and now.

I sigh.

'I mean, technically I didn't. You sent me a time and a place. I never said I'd be there.' It's petty, because I replied to his message with a thumbs-up. I had every intention of going, and I did … sort of. I mean, I went there. I just didn't go in.

'Please, educate me on the meaning of the thumbs-up emoji!'

'That was to let you know I'd seen the message, not to tell you I'd be there. I wasn't feeling it, so I decided to get dinner instead.'

He finally peers over my shoulder in the direction I came in, quickly spotting Johannes at the table I abandoned.

'I can see that. God forbid you miss an opportunity to update your socials and hang out with the competition. Clearly, getting shitfaced and posing for pictures is more important than the team you're actually on. Did nothing Anders said earlier get through your thick head?'

'Best friend.' When Kian raises an eyebrow at me, tilting his head slightly, I clarify for him. 'He's my best friend. And we weren't getting shitfaced. We were having dinner. Go and sniff my glass if you don't believe me. Just sparkling lemon water all evening.' I don't mention that this was Johannes's doing not mine and I'd have happily taken a vodka soda if he hadn't overridden any alcohol consumption this evening.

'He's our competitor. One of the biggest, if the predictions are anything to go on. I don't get it. Do you just not give a shit about your career? Is this all a bloody joke to you? Elijah's sitting at home dreaming of being here and his spot is being wasted on you.'

77

I'm so sick of his constant judgement and criticism. He's talking about my best friend in the whole world. The only person whose been by my side through thick and thin, there's nothing that can replace Johannes. Not a team or this sport.

'You're also one of my biggest competitors,' I tell him. 'Yet you've been trying to get me to hang out with you in the gym or in the pool or in those boring media sessions. So which is it? Should we be socialising together or not?'

He turns to me and takes a step closer.

'It's not the same and you know it. We're on the same fucking team! Or do you just not understand the concept of a team? Have you got any fucking brains at all? We're supposed to make each other better for the sake of the Constructor's Championship and Hendersohm as a team.'

I know he's right, but he's being such a wanker about it. I don't think he knows any other way to be than patronising. Back in the lower categories, I always made the effort to be at least friendly with my teammate. Maybe too friendly, considering I used to stick my dick in Johannes when we were both driving for the same team.

So, I find myself back on the defensive. 'Me and Johannes have been in each other's lives since our early karting days. I refuse to give that up because we're racing against each other. Would you stop socialising with Elijah if you're on different teams next year?'

I'm met with silence before he sighs. Score one to me.

'Fine, do whatever you like. I've tried. Don't be surprised when Anders drops your ass back down because you don't show any commitment.'

'Maybe it's your ass they'll be dropping, old man, now they've got new blood on the team.' Kian's eyes darken momentarily and I can't help but be amused. If looks could kill, I'd be buried under the Albert Park Circuit.

'Don't get too cocky, rookie. A couple of good performances are nothing when there's still twenty to go. You might have pulled off the odd risky move, but it wasn't exactly difficult to overtake you. And when everyone else sees that you're a joke, too, you won't be seeing much more of the podium.'

He's so bloody sure he knows what I'm like, it could almost knock my confidence. But this is just words, and I've got a P3 under my belt already.

I'm not delusional enough to think I'm the best in the world – yet. But I earned this opportunity, even if it did come at the expense of Elijah's broken leg. Maybe finishing on the podium in my first attempt has gone to my head, but it's not like I could ever forget that I'm the number two driver around here with Kian throwing his every bit of wisdom and experience at me.

There was still a long way to go, he wasn't wrong. I wasn't about to get ahead of myself thinking I could take it home after coming third a couple of times.

Kian looks satisfied as he presses the call button and leans against the wall next to the lift, as if he's shut me up. He hasn't. He could never. I'm going to be here for as long as they'll have me, battling Kian bloody Walker until I've proven myself.

Maybe Elijah will come back in three months' time, leg all healed, and take my seat. Or maybe Hendersohm will realise that Kian's been around enough and they do need new blood. It's all to play for, as far as I'm concerned.

'Well, enjoy your night. I'll be in the gym at 7am. You'll join me if you know what's good for you, but I can almost guarantee you probably won't.' The lift pings behind him with perfect timing and he saunters in. He pushes the button and the doors close, giving him the last word.

Fuck. I stand there like an idiot as I watch the number go up and up and up, not sure that could have gone any worse. Johannes appears behind me.

'I won't lie, I really enjoyed watching Kian handing your ass to you. I like the guy even more now.'

'Get lost,' I grumble. 'Can we go get dessert? I know we shouldn't but I need something sweet right now.' I saw a picture of the biggest slice of chocolate cake on the menu and there's nothing I want more right now – except maybe to get drunk. Thank God for this hotel having a luxury restaurant right here in the lobby.

'You wanna eat your feelings, Harp? You must really be gutted that your idol won't take any shit from you.'

'Don't make me tell you to get lost again.'

'Don't tell me you've fallen out of love with him? Back in the day, you used to—'

I scramble to cover his mouth with both of my hands until he surrenders, licking my palm so I let him go.

'*Used to*, past tense.' Ending the conversation, we go back into the restaurant. I flag down a waitress and order us a big piece of chocolate fudge cake to share. I'll be paying for it in the morning. Not in the gym at 7am with Kian, though.

'I hate you,' Johannes says when the cake is quickly brought out to us alongside two forks. 'Not as much as Kian hates you, but still.'

'Is it too late to see if another team wants me? Reckon Nils would like to swap?'

'I do love you, but us being on the same team again would be a nightmare.'

I'd probably kill to be on the same team with him again, like we were once upon a time. But he's probably right. We'd get each other in way too much trouble; the team wouldn't be able to handle us.

'Yeah, I'm too good for you now. I'd make you look bad.'

'Whatever you say, James, whatever you say. How about tomorrow you go lick ass with your *loverrrr* and make things right?'

Whilst I can't deny that rimming Kian Walker sounds hot as hell, I don't think I could get him to remove the stick up his ass long enough to get my tongue up there.

'I'll pass. Now hand me the fork. I need this.'

He complies, but the cake does nothing to fix the fact that I know tomorrow I might actually have to submit to Kian and meet him at the gym.

Chapter Seven

Kian

Since Bahrain, Harper and I have done a pretty decent job at playing nice. If you can call working out together and sitting opposite each other on the jet without bickering, playing nice. Not even the bitch that is jet lag has caused us to squabble. Yet. Especially as jet lag in Australia seems to be worse than jet lag in any other country. It hits me like a ton of bricks every year. Not that it seems to cause any disruption to Harper's sparkling personality, he still seems to operate at high speed. Except he's also been behaving, I even heard him turn down going out this evening when Johannes asked him right in front of me.

The clock on the bedside table blinks at me as the time ticks over to 5am. I'm not sure how long I've been asleep or if I even slept at all.

Sadly, the curtains are doing a poor job of shielding my

gritty eyes from the blisteringly bright sunlight, so there's no way of me going back to sleep even if I tried.

It's evening in the UK. I could call Elise and check in, but I only spoke to them eight hours ago when I couldn't sleep the first time round. Instead, I settle on firing up my laptop to assess what Netflix in Australia has to offer. A cooking show catches my attention and I curl around the laptop in the hope of having a restful morning.

Harper and I don't have plans to work out until 9am, at his insistence that my 7am starts were much too early for him. It's a tiny compromise to keep Anders off both of our backs. I might as well make the most of being awake already, but not having anything to do.

I'm halfway through the first episode when my phone starts ringing. To my surprise, it's Harper. Before 7am, nonetheless.

'Hello?' I answer cautiously. What could he want at this time of the morning? Or, come to think of it, at any time?

'Can you come to my room?' His voice is quiet and croaky and I'm almost afraid to ask why.

It was one thing being civil and trying to learn to be teammates. And another to be asking favours before the crack of dawn.

Has he got someone in there who shouldn't be hearing this call? What kind of mess has he got himself into now? Yet another shitshow he wants to drag me into and then expect me to clean up. Whatever it is, I want no part in it.

'Hi Kian, how are you? Thanks for asking, Harper, I was great until this call. Do you have no manners at all?' I let out an exasperated sigh. 'No, I can't come to your room. It's five in the morning.'

'Kian.' Oh no. This pleading tone is new, and I'm a sucker for a lost cause. 'I, uh...' The line goes quiet for a couple of seconds and then I hear the awful sound of someone retching and, worse, vomit hitting the surface of water.

'Are you okay?' What a stupid question when he's clearly got his head in the toilet. My flash of compassion is gone in an instant. 'Did you seriously just call me because you're hungover? What is it you imagine I can do to help?'

'Mmmm... Don't have a hangover.' He starts to cough and I have to pull the phone away from my ear as he heaves into the toilet again.

'Sure, sure. The sick doesn't lie.'

'Not a fucking hangover, *mate*.' He sounds pissed off. 'I've been up all night. My stomach hasn't been right since I got into bed.' There's a pitiful shake in his voice. I consider that if he were hungover, I don't know why he would advertise it to me. The way he parties, he must be permanently wrecked, so if anyone knows how to deal with hangovers it's him. If he's as much like my father as I think, they're probably his speciality.

Then again. I did see him right in front of my eyes last night decline a night out on the town with some of the other drivers, instead settling on just going for a quick meal with Johannes.

'Still doesn't answer the question of why you're calling me,' I say.

'Please, just help me.'

Why am I such a pushover? I hate that I'm so close to caving.

'Isn't there someone else you could have called? Like Johannes, or if you're unwell the team doctor?'

'I can't. It's so early and you're always awake.' Oh, so I'm just the convenient call brilliant.

84

'What do you expect me to do?'

'I've drunk all the bottles of water and the ginger ale in the mini-fridge. Have you got any left in yours? Could you bring me something to sip on whilst I lie on the bathroom floor? And maybe some ice? Please.' He sounds pathetic and desperate, and I fight the instinct to immediately cave to his demands. But then I realise this is the first time he's actually used a pleasantry with me.

'Okay.' Ending the call, I roll out of bed and pull on a pair of sweats and a clean T-shirt. There's a stock of bottled water and sports drinks in our mini fridges so I grab a couple of each and make my way down the corridor to his room. I knock on the door and he calls out that he's put it on the latch. I try the handle and slip into the room.

Christ! It reeks in here.

The thick smell of sick hangs in the air and I quickly dump the bottles on his bed, cover my mouth and nose with the hem of my T-shirt and try not to gag as I race to open the windows. Opening both, grateful for the fresh air that rushes into the room. Luckily, the retching in the bathroom has stopped, but when I open the door I'm met with a very sorry state.

He's as pale as a ghost, eyes bloodshot and face flushed. He's curled around the base of the toilet, his cheek pressed to the cold tiles of the floor.

'You look bloody awful.'

He eyes me with a frown, noting I'm empty-handed, and I realise I've left what I came with on his bed.

'Thanks for stating the obvious,' he croaks out, his throat sounding as rough as gravel on a cheese grater.

I hold up a finger to him, indicating that he should wait

there, though he's clearly going absolutely nowhere. I get the drinks and return.

'Sip this,' I say, kneeling next to him and handing him the bottle of water, 'and then drink some of this.' I pop the sports drink next to him. 'You'll be dehydrated after being so sick so you need to get some electrolytes into your system, too.'

He unscrews the cap quickly and begins to glug it down. I almost want to swat the bottle out of his hand because he's only going to make himself throw up again doing that. Instead, I just steady his hand and hold the bottle for him. 'Sip,' I command, 'otherwise you're going to end up being sick again.'

He glares at me in response, almost as if he's questioning why on earth he should listen to me. His stomach begins to grumble again, and he finally listens, restricting himself to small sips. Hey, he's the one who called me instead of literally everyone else on the planet and I still don't have a clue why.

Having done my job, I think about leaving. I really should … except his skin looks like death and his eyes are closed in pain. For the first time since we started working together, he looks vulnerable and alone. My sister might be the nurse in the family, but she's not here and I can't leave him on his own in this state. I need to look after him. No matter how annoying and infuriating he is. There's a sheen of sweat across the top of his forehead and when I lean in to get an idea of his temperature, I can instantly feel he's hot.

'I think you're running a fever. How about I go sort you out some fresh clothes and then you can get changed and get back into bed.'

He groans, but eventually nods.

It's weird to be rifling through Harper's messily packed kit bags, but I find what I'm looking for in the shape of a baggy T-shirt and some boxers, which look a size too big. Not that I know what he's packing down there. I quickly shove that thought out of my brain.

I slip back into the bathroom, finding him exactly where I left him, pitifully clutching his stomach on the floor. 'Do you think you can stand?' I ask from the doorway and he shakes his head, before taking a couple more sips of water.

Christ, he's really going to make me do this.

Crouching on the floor next to him, I gesture to the sweat-soaked T-shirt, which is clinging to his torso. 'Am I okay to take this off?'

He nods, but the second my fingers skim the hem of his shirt he inhales a shaky breath. He doesn't have to tell me this is awkward. I'm quick but careful as I strip him out of it; a sheen of sweat coats his chest and stomach.

'One second.' I pause, grabbing a washcloth from the hotel-provided pile and drench it in cold water before wiping him down.

His sweatpants are next, luckily with him being stretched out on the tiled floor I whip them off in one swift movement. I shouldn't be surprised he's naked beneath them, he seems like the type to enjoy going commando. Getting a clean pair of boxers on him proves to be much more difficult than taking off his sweats, but we make it work without the world ending over how weird this is.

I give him another second to enjoy the coolness of the cloth on his chest before drying him off with the hand towel and pulling the new, oversized T-shirt over his head.

The whole time, he's been watching me, eyes half-lidded. I'd describe it as awe if he didn't look moments from passing out.

'Come on, let's get you to bed.' I tuck my arms under his shoulder to lift him off the floor and move one around his waist for support as we trudge back into the bedroom, before lowering him down on the bed.

He's lethargic and looks damn exhausted as he shuffles across the bed. Why does this make me want to do nice things for him?

I find myself pulling back the duvet currently on his bed and grabbing a spare sheet from the wardrobe to drape over him. 'You don't want to overheat, so get comfy under this and then when your temperature comes down grab the duvet again. I should probably call the team doctor and ask for his opinion in case it isn't just food poisoning and you have a stomach bug or something.'

'No!' he calls out, quickly interjecting. 'Don't notify them. They'll just think I'm hungover and I don't need a bollocking right now.'

'Okay, okay.' I'm holding my hands up defensively, but I can kind of see his point. We've both been chewed out enough recently by management. 'I just don't want you to get worse and not know what to do.'

A moment of realisation zings through me. 'My sister is a nurse. How about I call her if you don't perk up within the next twelve hours? Food poisoning – if that's what this is – can get really bad, or it might be something else and you actually need medical attention.'

'Sure. Not like she reports to the team or whatever, right?' Harper's struggling to keep his eyes open at this point, but every time he seemingly gets comfortable, he has to reach up and swipe his matted, sweaty curls off his head.

Something weird has come over me, because seconds later

I'm in his bathroom, dampening yet another flannel with cold water, wringing it out and folding it into the perfect forehead size for Harper. Just call me Florence fucking Nightingale.

'Am I okay to put this on your head?' I dangle the cloth in front of him and he nods, so I sweep the curls off his forehead and replace them with the soothing flannel.

The noise that escapes his lips at the contact of the icy coolness on his forehead should be illegal, and my groin definitely shouldn't be twitching.

The man is sick, Kian. Come on.

'Thank you,' he mumbles as he finally relaxes into his pillow.

I'm not sure how long I've been perched on the side of his bed for, but it's definitely a couple of hours. Between scrolling social media and sending some emails, I've been checking on his fever every half hour or so, and I've done that at least three times. He's still running warm, but nowhere near the scorching temperature his forehead was the first time I checked.

He's not stirred for a while, either. For the first hour or so he thrashed under the sheet, arms wrapped around his stomach, and I was convinced he was going to wake up and be sick again. Eventually, however, he settled.

I check the world clock on my phone and it's probably an okay time for me to call Elise, just to check I'm doing everything I should, so I slip into his bathroom and click her name on my phone.

'Morning,' she says cheerfully and I'm glad to hear it, if I'm honest. She's sounded down the last couple of times we've spoken, even if she won't openly admit things are hard right now.

'Morning,' I whisper back and she immediately laughs.
'What?'

'I thought the day would never come. Whose place are you
calling from this early in the morning that has you whispering
to your big sis?'

Oh, brilliant. I don't know who she thinks I am, but she
can't for a second imagine I'm hiding in the bathroom of a
hook-up, can she?

'Christ, El. Get your head out of the gutter. I just need some
medical advice. About food poisoning.'

'Are you not well?'

'No, it's not me.'

'So, who? Gotta know the patient before I can tell you the
fix.' I roll my eyes because it's not like I'm asking her to
diagnose a dramatic condition. I just want to check I've done
everything I need to.

'Elise…'

'Kian, humour your big sister, please. You never have fun
stories to tell me.'

Yeah, because looking after a vomiting rookie has been so
much fun.

'Sounds like Harper ate a bad burrito and spent half the
night chucking up his guts. He was running a fever but is
starting to cool down now. I hydrated him before he slept and
tried to keep him cool. Just need to know anything else I
can do.'

'Oooooh, I can't believe you're looking after Harper James
right now. Like, I swear, all I've heard from you nonstop is
what a pain in the ass he is.'

'He was sick, El. What should I have done? Just abandoned
him?' That shuts her up because there isn't a world in which

she would tell me to leave someone to look after themselves when they weren't doing great. 'Is there anything more I can do for him?'

'Make sure when he wakes up that he takes a painkiller of his choice. He'll probably have a sore throat from being sick and a raging headache from being dehydrated, even if you've given him water. Also, he needs to eat something today – small and often is key – as his stomach will be empty.'

I wasn't planning on leaving straight away, but I also didn't plan to be here when he woke up. Yet now I have no choice. Elise would be disappointed if I left him in his hour of need.

'Sure. I can do all of that. I'll get him some room service or something when he wakes up.' If I get them to leave it at the door, they won't even need to know I'm in here. I could just pretend to be Harper on the phone.

'You're a good guy, Kian, taking care of him when he's been nothing but a dick to you.'

Talking about taking care of people… 'How is everything at home?' I say, I ask every day, but it still doesn't feel like enough.

'We're good. Kids are tucked up in bed and Grant's here for another day as a conference he was meant to be speaking at was cancelled. Mum's been in her chair today – I gave her breakfast in it and everything. She remembered how much she loves cornflakes, so Grant's been out and bought several boxes.' Elise sounds pleased – vibrant, even – that Mum's had a good day. It's so good to hear right now.

Yet pinpricks sting my eyes and I have to control my breath out, completely hollowing my cheeks, to stop myself from crying about these moments I may never get to see first-hand again. And the guilt. The guilt that El's doing it all…

'I'm glad, Els,' I croak out, my throat feeling dry as I swallow down another round of fresh tears. 'Give everyone a big kiss from me, especially Mum. Tell her I love her so much.'

'I will, every day, Ki. She knows you do.'

I'm not sure Mum does know. Neither me nor Elise can be sure. She may never know again how much her son loves her – or even that she has a son. God! I can't cry in the same room as Harper. If he wakes up right now, he'll never let me forget it, and who knows who else he'll tell. Johannes, probably.

So, after we say our goodbyes, I busy myself with the mess that is Harper's room. There's nothing like tidying and organising to help me feel in control.

The hotel provides a laundry bag in every room and whilst I make the most of it when I'm on the road, it doesn't look like Harper does. There are little mounds of worn clothes all over his floor, plus the clothes he vomited in which I left in the bathroom. I gather them all up in the bag, fill out the form for the express twenty-four-hour turn-around and pop them outside his door for collection.

It's yet another thing Harper won't appreciate, but there's nothing worse than being unwell and being in a messy room. Or having to put dirty clothes on.

A little nap won't hurt either of us. We're heading towards mid-morning now and the curtains aren't doing enough to stop the light streaming in. I close the windows and put the AC on – the smell has finally gone and the heat will soon become unbearable. I wedge the curtains tightly closed around the edges using Harper's discarded shoes to hold them in place. The darkness is a relief, and the AC starts to take the edge off the warmth that's been building.

I'm not prepared to do my back in my trying to sleep in one

of the armchairs – I'm too old and my body is too important to my career. I tell myself that if I stick to the very right-hand side of the bed, this won't be weird. I peel off my T-shirt and slide into the bed – on top of the sheet I gave him, obviously – and let my head hit the pillow.

It's a relief when I finally close my eyes, the jetlag making my brain feel groggy. A couple more hours' sleep will make me feel more like myself – this day has already been like an out-of-body experience. I set an alarm, because I'm due to meet the media team to film some bits for the Hendersohm TikTok later this afternoon.

And then I let myself drift off.

In Harper's bed.

It may be a stupid thing to do, I think, but it's too late because the world goes dark.

Chapter Eight

Harper

I'm not sure what time it is, what day it is, or even where I am.

There's a growling in my stomach and a pounding in my head. The room is pitch black, but I feel like it was just as dark the last time I woke up, so I can't decipher how much time has passed.

Damn, I don't remember ever feeling this rough. I crack open one eye, and the room spins a little. It's only then that I realise the curtain has been wedged against the window, creating a complete blackout effect. Are those … my shoes?

When did I do that? How? Am I experiencing memory loss? Is this normal after food poisoning?

I try to roll over, but end up smacking straight into another warm body.

Bloody hell!

What's going on? Am I dreaming? I'd never let a hook-up

stay over. I hate this. I hate that I can't gather my thoughts, and when I move again my back aches like hell.

There are soft snores coming from my bed partner and when I try to get up out of bed my foot hits a cold, wet cloth. What happened in here?

Pausing for a moment, while the room stops spinning, I try to think.

I went for dinner. Johannes and I and a couple of the guys from the pit. Cole and Ash maybe? One of the younger assistants. We'd left after dinner, keeping my promise to Kian that we wouldn't go out drinking so I'd be up in time for the 9am workout. We had Mexican, I think. The vivid colours of a place that looks like a dive bar come to mind.

Whilst I hadn't drank, Johannes had. He'd carried on to a bar alone, having already had several margaritas at the Mexican place and downing a couple shots at the bar when I was trying to get us out of there. I remember being worried. He seemed out of sorts; I'm not sure if I asked him about it, though, so I file that mental note away until I can make sense of my current peculiar situation.

My stomach gurgles and the rawness of my throat plus the bad taste in my mouth begin to make sense. I was sick.

Here.

I remember the coolness of the marble bathroom tiles beneath me as I vomited. Still, that doesn't explain my snoring bed friend.

The half-naked guy chooses this moment to roll over, still fast asleep and … well, well, well. I definitely don't feel great, but it's hard to feel like shit when you've got Kian Walker in your bed.

It all starts to become clear. I came back here and felt so

unwell that I couldn't move off the bathroom floor. My body felt heavy and every time I tried to get up my stomach began to cramp, and I was sick again.

Oh, God … and then I'd called Kian. Of all people! Why him? I grab my phone and shockingly it looks like I texted Johannes, too. Apparently I called him a couple of times but got no answer. That's strange, especially as we're staying in the same hotel, but he was well on the way to being drunk when we left the restaurant. He probably just passed out and missed the calls.

So, Kian had come to take care of me, huh? Closing my eyes, I can almost feel his big hand on my back as he guided from the bathroom to the bed. I definitely remember the cool washcloth on my forehead and the feeling of being looked after.

I should be embarrassed that he saw me in such an awful state and later I probably will be, but right now I feel … grateful. There haven't been many moments in life that I've felt that way. Johannes got me through the hangovers and the odd case of flu when I was starting out and travelling internationally for the first time, but he has an easy, casual nonchalance about him whereas this…? This felt nice. But also weird that it was Kian. I try and fail to reconcile the uptight prick I've come to know with the kind, caring man who put me to bed with unexpected gentleness. Needless to say, I'm finding this scenario very confusing right now.

I imagine telling fourteen-year-old Harper that one day he'll be half-naked and sharing a bed with his crush. I watched Kian's first season, glued to the TV, as this guy started to take the world by storm, brushing off every comment about his father in all the interviews I watched. I couldn't ever understand why because Tyler Heath was a legend, but it gave me goosebumps.

I was just this angry teen in his millionth foster placement, trying to convince his new parents to spend some of the money they got paid each week to look after him on karting lessons. Then there was this new driver, refusing to be defined by who his parents were. He didn't want to be a global sensation just because his mum was once a massive pop star and his dad a champion driver. He wanted to succeed on his own merit, or not at all – and it was so exciting to watch him race.

I could appreciate that, even as a teen.

I turn to look at him and the room starts to spin again. It's hard to make out much in the blackout conditions he's created in the room, but I'm not going to miss this opportunity to really look at him. The headache doesn't improve, so I slide back under the cool sheets and allow myself to have this.

The Melbourne sun may have bronzed his face and shoulders, but his chest and stomach are pale, coated in thick wafts of brown hair. I manscape because I know I get papped shirtless – okay, let's face it, I like to show off – but Kian clearly doesn't bother. I want to reach out and stroke it. I want to thread my fingers through and see if it's as soft as it looks.

Men like this have never been my type. I usually go for the prototypical twink – lanky and scrawny, someone who wants to be dominated; guys with soft features and a praise kink. Kian doesn't fit into any of those categories. He has sharp features and he only has to go a couple of days without shaving to pull off some impressive facial hair. And I can't for one second imagine him enjoying me telling him what to do. If anything, it would probably be the other way around.

That stirs something in my stomach that feels thrilling.

I'm surprised to find I'm enjoying seeing Kian like this. I've got so used to him being an insufferable asshole that the change is freaking me out. Except, it's not. Instead, I feel settled. Comfortable.

Peaceful. It's the only word I can think of to describe Kian's state right now. There's a thick fan of brown lashes brushing the tops of his cheeks and a smattering of sun-induced freckles across his fair skin. He's not wearing the forced, tight smile he often puts on around me, when it's like he's constantly biting his tongue and trying not to let on to the rest of the world how much he despises me.

I smile to myself as I admire him now. And then those same lashes start to flutter, and I am plunged into the most awkward moment of my life as we lock eyes.

Busted!

We're sharing a bed and I'm lying here, awake and staring at him while he's shirtless and drooling into my pillow. A line of sweat rolls down my spine and I don't think I can pretend the cause is anything other than the man in my bed.

It takes one too many seconds for me to look away from him, and when I look back, he's jumped out of bed.

There's a panicky look on his face as he paces for a second, like he's trying to recall why he's here. I'm still watching him – I can't seem to stop – and when he notices, he disappears into the bathroom.

He's probably trying to think of a way to leave without this being awkward – although that ship might have sailed. He's been here for hours and hours, looking after me, and he fell asleep beside me. It's more than someone who acts like he hates me should ever do.

I hear the water start to run in the basin and I prepare

myself for the inevitable uptight excuse he's about to deliver and the sharp exit he will make back to his own room. I hate that I'm almost disappointed that he's leaving, because why should I care what Kian Walker does with his day off?

Yet when he returns from the bathroom, he just hands me another wet washcloth and I can't deny that the cold material against my forehead makes me feel a hundred times better. I also can't deny, even though it causes something to twist up in knots inside of me, that I like the way he takes care of me.

'You know,' I say, 'if we can do this, surely we can find a way to get along. Truce?' I'm not sure if it's the fact that I feel completely wrung-out that's making me consider trying or if it's the fact he's looking at me with something other than pure disgust in his eyes, but I'm running with it.

'A truce? A compromise?' he asks wearily from where he's now perched on the edge of the desk. Sadly he's put his shirt back on.

'Trying each other's worlds. You want me to give your yoga, media training, early-bedtime life a go, but you should try my way, too. Isn't that the definition of compromise?'

I think for a second that he's not going to go for it. He's made it crystal clear that he doesn't approve of my lifestyle. I don't even know if he'd have a good time if he did come out for a drink after a win or whatever, but it's worth a try.

'Define your way?'

I roll my eyes. He makes it sound like a boring business deal.

'Relax a bit, come out for drinks to celebrate, maybe even go to a club.'

There's a look of utter terror in his eyes and I almost laugh, but it gets trapped in my completely wrecked throat and turns into a cough.

Kian quickly hands me a bottle of cold water and a small voice in the back of my head reminds me to sip, not gulp, it.

'Look, you do you, okay? But it's not my scene. Can you imagine me getting drunk in a club? Because *I* can't. And dancing? Dancing is a big no.'

Sure, I can imagine he might be a little awkward at first, but I'd get him to loosen up. I'd have him grinding up a storm in no time if he'd just let me get my hands on him. A little guidance never hurt anyone.

'You don't need to drink or dance to have a good time. Just … loosen the strings a little. Try and relax a bit. I don't get it – you're nice to all of the guys in the garage and to the broader team, but it's like you don't want friends.'

A look of contemplation passes over his face, brows tugged tight like he's thinking about how to respond. I know he's wondering whether to open up to me or not. He's trying to decide if he can trust me.

'It's not… It's just…'

Well, I guess I got the answer to that one. No opening up, no trust.

'If you come out with me after our next win, I'll join your workouts and I'll do the stupid media training—'

It's his turn to interrupt me this time. 'You'll find it helpful. They'll help you tone down the sarcastic comebacks and think before you speak.'

I don't care what he did for me – I'm not taking that!

'Says you, who can't keep his temper in check anytime Daddy's mentioned. I don't get that, either – you've already had a better career than him, like, twice over and you could probably make that *three* times over if you don't retire this year.'

He visibly riles. Well, that clearly touched a nerve.

'I fucking hate that word! Retire, retire, retire! Why is that all the press wanna talk about? How about the amazing start to the season? Or the work I do as an ambassador for the youth charity—?'

'Come on, old man—' I joke, but stop when I see his face.

Not the time, Harper. Not the time.

I start over. 'I thought this was one of those things the team had fed to the press. Like, you'd already spoken about it, and they were giving the papers lines and hints about it, making a buzz about your last year to hype up the media. I'm guessing not?'

'No! For fuck's sake. No. I've spoken to Anna about trying to put a stop to it, but everyone loves to speculate and it's all I ever get asked anymore. I don't know if … I haven't thought… I'm not even thirty-four yet.'

The contortion of his face is torturous. I can see every single struggle he's having with this decision.

Even though I'm only twenty-five, I understand that making this decision comes around so quickly, regardless of what sport you're in, and deciding whether to go out on a high or slowly fade away is a tough one.

'So, there's still a chance it might be?'

'Isn't there a chance it might be anyone's last season? I could crash this weekend and never be able to drive again, or Hendersohm could choose not to renew my contract with them and no other team picks me up. And the same is true for any of us. It is what it is, and I'll cross that bridge at the end of the season. But if I go it'll be *my* choice.' His words and tone are firm – not that that would matter with any journalist. They'll still print the reasons they think he might retire, anyway.

Uncomfortable with the intimacy of the conversation, I decide it's time to get up. I go to climb out of bed and notice something's different about the room. The carpets are clear, my kit bags are tucked into the provided storage, and the fan mail I was given when we arrived is stacked neatly on the desk. There's no way I did this last night.

'Did you, um, tidy?' I ask as I scan the room for all of the clothes that once resided on my floordrobe. I had one in every country.

Maybe this was all a carefully orchestrated prank and he's hidden all my clothes or burnt them as revenge. That would actually make more sense than him *tidying my room*.

'Yeah. It was an absolute pigsty in here. When did you last do laundry?'

Wracking my brains, I couldn't think. I definitely hadn't since I'd got here. Maybe I had in Saudi? I can't remember. 'I bring a lot of clothes with me, so it's fine. Where's … the stuff I was wearing last night?'

'In the laundry bag, where it belongs. While you were sleeping I took a bunch of your dirty clothes and put them in for an express service.'

He makes it sound like nothing, but I am shocked into silence.

It was almost too much – the cold washcloths, the tidying, the *looking after*.

It makes my skin feel tight. I can't imagine why he'd do this for me.

'Uh … thank you? You really didn't need to do that.'

'No, I definitely did. The clothes would probably have

started putting themselves in the bag otherwise. Did your parents never teach you to clean up after yourself?'

I never, *never*, speak about my upbringing in public or to the press. There's no way he could know I don't have parents, or any kind of people who've earned that title. There's no way he could know how that comment is like a dagger through my heart, yet it breaks the spell I've apparently been under completely.

'I think I'll probably be okay now. You can go.' I don't mean for it to sound so dismissive when he's clearly, by any objective standards, been really good to me in the last few hours, but I'm done. I don't want to continue this conversation.

'My sister said you need to eat little and often to settle your stomach. I was going to order some toast or something for you on the room service menu.' His tone is defensive, as if he doesn't understand why the mood has suddenly soured. I can't blame him, but I'm over this domestic little fairy tale and need my own space again.

'I'm sure I can manage that by myself.' I actually cross my arms over my chest for good measure and he finally gets the message. He backs towards the door.

'Suit yourself, but I expect you in the gym with me tomorrow morning. Then, maybe, if we win, I'll come out with you, okay?'

I'd almost forgotten with the way all the air has left the room, that we agreed to that. I nod quickly.

'Yeah, yeah, tomorrow,' I say. My jaw is so tightly clenched at this point that I'll probably need his stupid yoga routine anyway to loosen my neck and traps.

He cracks the door and comically peers left and right to make sure no one sees him leave, even though we've done nothing wrong, and without another word slips into the corridor. The door closes behind him with a finality that feels like a relief and also like a bereavement.

The air whooshes back into the room and I can finally breathe again. It's not really breathing, more like panting, as though my lungs are desperately trying and failing to make use of all the air I'm taking in – but I'll take it over not being able to breathe at all.

Combined with the sore throat from throwing up and my incredibly empty stomach, the panting isn't doing me any favours. I desperately need to collect myself and wipe all memory of this morning from my brain. Spend what's left of this day off resting and rehydrating. Kian said his sister basically advised that, and she's a nurse so I should probably listen. I'm definitely not ordering a couple of rounds of toast from the room service menu because Kian told me to.

I don't care what Kian thinks *at all.*

Chapter Nine

Kian

We smash the Australian Grand Prix out of the park. It's the second time Hendersohm have had two podium places so far this season and I could not be happier to be back on top of the world in first place.

It's a strong start to the season, and as I reflect back on some of the reasons for this, I grudgingly acknowledge that Harper has brought out the competitive side in me – and maybe this is giving me an edge on the track. Having to look after his sorry ass the other day had an upside: it finally got him to commit to joining me in the gym. He's actually making the effort, rather than acting like he's just here to prove a point to our principal, which is nice.

It starts on the treadmill. He picks the one right next to me and at first we warm up gently. I up my speed to a jog and he's quick to follow. I increase my speed again, and he matches it; I notch it up again, and he's there alongside me, upping his speed to catch me and then I'm upping mine. It goes on like that until we're both working hard, practically sprinting, but I can't stop myself. I can't bear to let him win. To win what, I have no idea, but it's exhilarating. My whole body's on fire, both with excitement and how hard I'm pushing it. I can't remember the last time, outside of being in the cockpit, when I felt this *alive*.

Eventually, he hits the stop button and I experience a moment of intense triumph, before quickly following suit. We pant like dogs as the machines slow us both to recovery walking pace, our gym towels unable to mop up the sweat pouring down our faces quick enough.

It's the most fun I've had in ages. With Harper James, of all people!

'What do you squat?' he asks between glugs of a purple-coloured sports drink.

'One forty. Depends on reps. What about you?'

'One forty.' He doesn't sound sure, though, and I feel like he's probably going to recklessly try to prove it to me and we'll have another driver out on injury.

'Well, I'm doing upper body today now that my cardio's done,' I say, 'so you can save your squatting skills for another time … if we're doing this together?' He doesn't attempt to fight me on this, which is nice for once, and instead follows me to a bicep machine.

Yet we continue to compete, trying to outperform each other on every setup. But the strange thing is that it's actually a laugh, and I enjoy my routine more than normal. I definitely push myself harder than usual and I have to admit that maybe this new injection of fresh motivation is long overdue in my gym workout.

Now, unfortunately, it's time to keep up my end of the bargain. I'm dressed in what Harper has deemed my going-out clothes – a short-sleeved navy blue shirt and denim shorts that feel a little snug. We're at a bar that he considers appropriate for the celebration and which I would never have come to in a million years if I hadn't agreed to this deal.

Harper and Johannes charge towards the bar and I find myself wandering in search of a booth that's a little more out of the way from everyone else. I hate feeling like I'm on show all the time.

They return quickly, two glasses of something dark and stormy in Johannes's hands and a bottle of beer clutched in Harper's. Fuck's sake! I was crystal clear that I just wanted water. Neither says anything as they sidle into the booth around me, matching grins on their faces because they've clearly intentionally ignored everything I said.

I don't think I've ever been more uncomfortable in my life. I sneak a peek at my watch. It's early morning at home. I could be chatting to Elise, giving her some adult conversation before the kids get up and she has to start Mum's morning routine. The need to be there, even if only virtually, is greater when Grant's away at a conference.

'So, Kian, this guy finally dragged you out, huh? How're you enjoying Oz? S'pose you've been coming here for the last decade. Does it ever get boring?' I know Johannes is just trying to be nice, but I only ever see the inside of the hotel, the track, and whatever venues I get dragged to for interviews.

I wrack my brains for what it was like ten years ago when I was more their age, when life was easier and the pressure wasn't so great. I was never a big partier, but I did a bit of sightseeing here and there.

'It's nice to be in the warm, but I can't say I've seen a lot of it this time round.'

'I'm telling you,' Harper starts, the rim of his glass of whatever perched against the bottom of his lip, 'he doesn't leave the hotel until qualifiers. He does yoga in his room!'

Rolling my eyes, I almost groan. Not the yoga thing again. I will probably never live this down.

'Nothing wrong with yoga,' Johannes says, and my jaw almost drops. I was prepared for the pair to gang up on me. I imagined I'd spend the next hour – the amount of time I agreed I'd stay out for – being teased. 'The team trainer is quite big on it. He got me into it last year and it helps me loosen up after being cramped into a cockpit for hours at a time. I got that neck strain last season, d'you remember? Yoga's what fixed it. Well, it's what's prevented me getting it again, anyway. I swear by it now.'

'Oh, God. You'll be doing downward dog together before you know it and then *I'll* be forced to join in.'

I snort. I very much doubt that. But it does bring home to me that Harper's in his first top-category season. He's never had all these trainers and specialists and professionals trying to micromanage every aspect of his fitness before. He's also still got the invincibility of youth that makes you sneer at the advice of older people. He hasn't had any major injuries yet and he hasn't felt his body let him down. His energy is infectious, though, and I find myself hoping, that for his sake, his arrogant confidence doesn't lead him to make a reckless decision now that he comes to regret in the future.

God, when did I start caring about Harper James's future?

Luckily, Johannes just laughs off Harper's suggestion and I sink into the booth a little. The time blinks in the corner of the TV screen that's showing a rugby game. Just fifty more minutes and I'm out of here.

We talk some more about today's results and about flying to Azerbaijan for the next race. Apparently, it's one of Johannes's favourite circuits. Never heard that one before. I didn't think anyone was a big fan of it. I don't mind it myself, but it's too split in half for me to really enjoy it. One side is wide and open, full of beautiful straights where you can push your speed to the max. The other is tight and twisty, full of punishing turns that make you pay for every fractional mistake tenfold. It takes a lot of concentration to flip between these two states. I guess that's part of the challenge, but it's not where I feel at my best.

'Let's dance,' Harper quickly suggests, as the motor racing conversation dies down.

I'm quick to shake my head, and before I know it Johannes is hopping out of the booth and pulling Harper onto the dance floor, screaming something about it being their song.

As Harper grinds – yes, full-on grinds – against Johannes, I wish I'd never agreed to come. The hour isn't up yet, but I promised Anders I'd do my part – make an effort, compromise, be a good teammate. Well I'm here, aren't I? Though I can't currently see how this is making me a better teammate because there's a fiery pit of something I don't want to name brewing in my gut. It's vicious and attacks my stress levels more than the guilt does.

Johannes's hands are roving up and down Harper's body. When they land on his hips, the T-shirt he's wearing rides up, leaving a delicious smattering of blonde hair on display leading down into his stupidly tight denim shorts.

It's not like I am or ever have been blind to Harper James. I refuse to accept that he's quite the sensation the fans claim he is. I mean, he *is* hot – that's undeniable – but it's more than that. He's beautiful in the most classic sense of the word. His features are like something one of the great sculptors of the past would carve – godlike, perfect, clean. And then there's his ass. It's lean, firm, shapely and would tempt anyone to sin. Of course I've noticed. But then there's also his sharp, sarcastic tongue…

He throws his head back onto Johannes's shoulder. His eyes closed, a couple of slick curls cling to his damp forehead as he writhes and twists on the dance floor. Fuck. I absolutely do not want this image of Harper James to become engraved inside my brain.

And yet, I can't look away. There's an uncomfortable stirring in my shorts that makes sitting in this sticky booth that little more uncomfortable. I didn't want to come here and now I can't leave – trapped between the terms of our deal and the compulsion to keep on watching him.

This is so wrong. So, so wrong. I desperately want to leave, but I also really, really want to go up there and slide in between the pair. I want to be the one Harper is writhing against. I want to forget about all the crap in the world, all the pressure, all my responsibilities, and all the ways I am failing my sister, and just lose myself in Harper. That's what I want.

I'm supposed to be here to build a relationship with my teammate. To become friends with him so we can work together.

But the burning desire inside of me is not for friendship. It's just for him. His body held against mine. His ass in my hands. My lips on his—

I should leave, but if I walk outside now everyone's going to get a good look at the tent I'm pitching and it'll probably end up on the front page of some Australian tabloid. Or someone's Instagram.

And then everyone would know. And even worse than *everyone* knowing is if *he* knows, if Harper sees the way I'm looking at him.

I feel a sudden panic rising inside me and my breath hitches. And then it happens.

Fuck.

It happens in a kind of feverish slow motion and I cannot look away. His eyes open and our gazes meet. It's electric, instant fireworks. It's almost like he can hear every single one of my dirty thoughts because he looks me up and down in an assessing way, and then grins like a Cheshire cat.

Too late. It's too late. He *knows*.

He beckons me with a single finger. He's also bloody delusional. The only place I'm going is back to the hotel. Not a chance in hell he'll get me out on that dance floor.

I shake my head and he pouts, full on model pout, but before I know it he's focused back on dancing with Johannes.

The spell is broken.

The moment is over.

He doesn't know anything, and, quite frankly, he doesn't care.

That's the thing with Harper, I'm learning. I'm pretty sure everyone is disposable in his life. No one ever spends more than one night in his bed. He's all hook-ups and fuck-buddies. No one means anything to him, and no one gets close. He and

Johannes are obviously friends, but I don't know whether they were ever together or not. Either way, I don't think they're sleeping together now. I don't get that vibe.

It's kind of sweet in the most messed-up sense of the word sweet. Harper seems to either dislike or distrust most other people in his life, but Johannes just seems to be his person. The only one he'll let close.

If I ignore the green pit of something I refuse to call jealousy, I can see how they'd be cute together. I'm not super familiar with Johannes's stats as he didn't make much of an impact on the track last year, but this season is different. His antics outside of the track seemed to have calmed down and he's coming on leaps and bounds to be a true competitor this year. Especially since he's part of the new Ford-Red Bull team. I only hope Harper will learn from his friend and find a way to focus on his driving. This moment in time is perhaps not the best example of that, but amidst the pressure of competition it's important to blow off steam. Looking at them now, it's clear that what they have in common is how they choose to do that. It's only 9pm and neither of them is smashed, so it's pretty tame in comparison with what it could be.

I try to take that onboard and feel as relaxed as they look, but I'm wound up like a tightly coiled spring. This is not my idea of blowing off steam. If anything, I'm reaching boiling point.

Shit.

Why did I agree to this?

I look at the snacks that have been delivered to the table and consider scoffing the lot, just to give myself something to do. I have a strict diet, though, since every gram of weight is carefully controlled so that the car and I together hit the exact perfect mass for peak performance. I push the bowl away and instead focus on rolling the bottle of beer, which is getting slightly warm now, between my palms and picking at the label. Anything to avoid looking at the pair of them on the dance floor.

I must look bored, because when the upbeat song drifts into something slower, Harper appears suddenly back at the booth.

'What do I have to do to get you up on the dance floor?'

He leans across the table, on his elbows, invading my space. His face is too close to me for comfort and I can smell him – which is definitely not helping.

It's almost like he's taunting me. Perhaps he thinks that if he gets close enough, he'll get his way.

Maybe that's how it is with him. That's probably how he bags all the bloody men. But why is he using this technique on me? There's no way he has any clue that I'm bisexual; no clue that I could be interested. Not that I am. I'm not interested in him.

'I'm all good here, *mate*. Go back and enjoy… Johannes. You'll have a better time without me.' I absolutely hate the way that comes out. I should have just left it after saying I'm all good. Now he's eyeing me like the cat that's got the cream. He doesn't know, I tell myself. He doesn't know. This is just feeding his already massive bloody ego.

'Oh. *Ohhhh.*' He's grinning now, his massive bloody ego inflated even further. 'Green isn't your colour, handsome.'

I make a show of looking down at my navy shirt and frowning in confusion. 'Are you colour blind?'

'Arise, oh green-eyed monster, and join—'

'Screw you.'

'Ha! I knew it!'

God, I hate how smug he looks.

'I knew you were enjoying the show. Thanks for confirming that one at least.'

'Congratulations, Sherlock. I'm bisexual. Alert the media. What do you want, a medal?'

Why am I so bothered that he knows? It's not a secret. I've just never officially announced it to the public. But if anyone asks, I don't try to hide it.

It's the way it makes him smirk that pisses me off, like he thinks I've been checking him out. Which I haven't – apart from just now, of course.

'Wow, racing is really queer this year.'

I don't ask what that means. I'm obviously aware of me, him and Johannes, but I wasn't in the know about anyone else. Didn't even have an inkling. There was one good way that he'd probably know who else wasn't on the straight side, but I couldn't bring myself to think about it. Not too hard anyway. I'm sure tonight, when I can't sleep, I'll probably be turning the idea, over and over, of Harper sleeping with other drivers.

'Does anyone really care anymore?'

None of the teams come across as particularly homophobic. If they are they've kept it in their garage.

'I have one of the best gaydars going, and even I didn't realise you were bi. Don't you realise that you present straight, or do you do it intentionally? Every third comment on the Instagram page when they post anything about me or Johannes is regarding our sexuality.'

Now *that* I didn't know. I didn't want to seek it out either, there was no desire for me to read the gross words I'm sure some shitty fans might be throwing around.

'Well, maybe it's just because I don't get papped falling out of clubs with obvious hook-ups, or with my dick out in the street,' I say.

I know this is only half the story, but Harper really doesn't help himself.

'So, it's my fault? I deserve to be trolled by ignorant fuckwits? I deserve to get death threats because I'm not doing yoga alone in my room at 3am?'

'That's not what I'm saying. I—'

'What *are* you saying? Because right now, all you're doing is ruining the vibe. I invited you to relax and enjoy yourself, not to sit here in judgement like some dried-up old prune.'

'Yeah, that's right, blame me. It's always *my* fault, isn't it. When will you learn to take responsibility for your own actions? Some of us take our careers seriously.' I'm so worked up now that I can't stop myself. 'I knew coming here was a mistake. I don't know what they were thinking when they put you on the team. You're nothing compared to Elijah. You're a bloody child.'

I see the impact of my words on his face and I instantly regret what I've said, but it's too late now. It's far, far too late.

'Whatever you say, *Grandpa*. No wonder all anyone can talk about is when you're going to retire. At least your dad went out with a bang. I've stepped in puddles with more personality than you.'

I know I probably deserve that, but he has a way of cutting to the bone that plays on all my insecurities. For a second, I'm speechless.

All I want now is to be out of here.

'Well, this has been fun,' I say sarcastically as I stand up. 'Enjoy the rest of your evening.'

Our temporary truce is over, and I turn and walk away.

I definitely hear him mutter something that sounds like *boring bastard* under his breath, but I don't stop. I am so done with this shit. And I'm so, so done with Harper fucking James.

I contemplate calling an Uber to take me back to the hotel, but decide to walk instead. It's still a balmy night in Melbourne, and I need to walk off the mood I'm in.

Harper's been nothing but trouble since the moment he took Elijah's place. I've tried, I really have, but there's something about him that just riles me up. All thoughts of the benefit of fresh blood and competitive spirit have drained away and I'm left feeling … empty. Alone. And just really, really tired.

I dread being at odds with him again, and I know he will make no attempt to hide his contempt in front of Anders, the media, or anyone who'll listen. This was supposed to be a brilliant season – my best to date, even – and now it's turning into a constant battleground with no winners.

I tell myself I don't care what Harper thinks. I can't care, because I can't afford to. I'm not the life of the party. I never was. It's got nothing to do with being old in the sport, despite what Harper might have to say on the matter. If you look at the average age of drivers now, I'm only slightly above the line. There are guys five, six, and seven years older than me who're still competitive in top tier racing. I started young, that's all. Alonso's over forty. I could have another decade ahead of me, if I wanted. If there weren't so many youngsters coming up from the lower ranks -right now, I'd be right around average. It's just the current cohort that's pushing me into the upper age bracket.

But that's got nothing to do with why I don't fit in with Harper and Johannes. I've never been into that scene, even when I was a teenager or in my early twenties. I never understood the fascination. I wanted to race and win. That's all I ever wanted. To race, to win, and then to go to sleep. Is that too much to ask?

Probably.

Definitely, according to Harper. Maybe this is what he needs in order to be at his best, but it certainly isn't what *I* need. Maybe...

No. Surely not.

A thought occurs to me. Have I underestimated Harper? Is this all part of an elaborate plan to throw me off my game? Is he actually ... strategic? Is he actually some zen, chess grandmaster who's actually ten steps ahead of me?

Now you're really losing it, Walker.

He's just an overexcited rookie who doesn't know his ass from his elbow.

Don't think about his ass.

I can feel myself spiralling into a vortex of overthinking. None of this is helping me.

I take some deep breaths and try to control my thoughts. I look at my watch. There's still time to call Elise, and nothing works better to ground me and remind me of my goals and priorities than my sister and her kids. A trophy for Cassie. Defending my title on the track. Making my family proud.

Fuck Harper James.

Chapter Ten

Kian

There are at least six pairs of eyes on us as we sit next to each other on the jet.

Anna's jaw is practically on the floor as she looks up from where she's frantically typing on her laptop. Her surprise quickly morphs into joy with a beaming smile that tugs her whole face upwards. I've never seen her look so happy in all the years I've known her. She gives me a little wink and a subtle thumbs-up.

Urgh.

No one needs to know about the argument Harper and I had in the bar after the podium finishes in Melbourne. We've smashed out a whole other Grand Prix in Azerbaijan since then. The highlight reel consisted of me not only qualifying first, but also finishing top of the podium, again. That's three out of four so far this season. More evidence, if I needed it, that my approach works.

Harper finished fourth in both the qualifier and the race, which is actually incredibly impressive for a rookie in his first season. Maybe, I grudgingly acknowledge, his approach works for him.

Since the night out with Harper and Johannes, I've calmed down. A little. I'm not so angry anymore, at least. The truth is, I can't deny that something has changed the way I look at Harper. It's not something I would ever openly admit or, heaven forbid, act upon, but there are flickering thoughts of him on repeat in my mind. Maybe I'm sexually frustrated – I can't remember the last time I had sex. But no matter how much meditation I do, or how many cold showers I take, I cannot rid my mind of the image of his shirt riding up, of the sandy skin of his belly with its blond fuzz. Or his curly hair against his damp forehead as he writhed against Johannes on the dance floor. It has fuelled many hot jerk-off sessions. The cold spray, like a thousand tiny needles piercing my skin, only made me hotter as I took myself in hand and fantasised about teaching the rookie a proper lesson, with my dick in his mouth. Even now, sitting beside him, the scent of him in my nostrils, I have to call upon every single meditation mantra in my arsenal to maintain my neutral expression and composure.

He went out with a few of the other drivers, including Johannes, after we all finished top five in Azerbaijan, and I even dragged my sorry ass out to the dinner portion of the celebration. I saw it as a compromise, but on my terms this time. I made conversation with the other drivers and techs, and I didn't even clock-watch. I enjoyed an ice-cold glass of sparkling water and no one expected me to get up and shake my ass. Better yet, I didn't have to watch Harper shake his.

'Why are they looking at us like we've both got two heads?'

he stage-whispers to me as the jet door is closed and the steps are dragged away on the tarmac. The rest of Hendersohm are indeed still watching us like we're animals at the zoo. They're clearly expecting a show of some kind, but I'm not about to risk everything I've worked for my entire life. In public, Harper and I are exactly what Anders demanded of us: a team.

In private … well, that's another matter.

'Might be something to do with us breathing the same air and not fighting about who gets the bigger portion.'

He responds with an easy laugh and slowly everyone goes back to what they were doing before.

We've clearly got the same idea about keeping Anders happy. We didn't plan this. I took my usual, preferred window seat looking over the wing – and he casually plopped himself down next to me like it was the most natural thing in the world.

So he *is* capable of behaving like a grown-up when he wants to.

Don't be a dick, Walker, I think to myself as I put my noise-cancelling earbuds in and tune out the world for the flight to Miami. I offer him a piece of gum to make up for it, which he takes.

It'll be all right, I tell myself. *We're going to be all right.*

Which is exactly when it all goes to shit.

My phone startles me awake in the middle of the night.

I blink as the world comes into focus. It's 4.18am and Harper's name is flashing across the screen.

There's a new level of frustration unlocked inside of me,

because this call undoes all of the good work we've been putting in. I almost don't answer, but on the sixth ring I hit the green button and scratchy, tinny music blasts down my ear.

I don't wait for him to speak.

'This is really bloody selfish, James! I don't know why you think this is okay. You know how important sleep is in the days leading up to a race. I have a routine. I have a system. I need to get in the zone. You know all this and yet you still wake me up in the middle of the night just two days before the race!'

'Kian?'

He sounds plaintive. Lost.

'Harper? What's wrong? What's happened?'

My mind races as I imagine all sorts of horrendous scenarios. A terrible accident, a career-ending injury, gun violence.

'Harper? What the hell's going on?'

'Kian … come you … can you … come you and get me?' His words are slurred and he can barely get them out in the right order. 'Can't rememem-r-r-ememember the name of … th'otel.'

And then it hits me. He's drunk. Harper James is blind drunk.

Here we go again.

The moment I start to let my guard down with him! The exact fucking moment!

And yet, I swing my legs out of bed and pull on a pair of loose sweats. I call an Uber and in the six minutes it says it will take for it to get here, I grab a T-shirt, a hoodie, my phone and my keycard. I shove my feet into my shoes and blink at the bright lights as I stagger towards the lift and press the button.

Yes, I'm going to get him, but make no mistake: I'm absolutely fucking livid.

'Get in,' I say roughly, as I manhandle my teammate into the back of the Uber.

I found him half collapsed on the pavement outside a club where a bouncer had deposited him and was vaguely keeping an eye on him. I nod to the man and desperately hope he either doesn't recognise us or doesn't care.

Fuck.

I slide in beside Harper and ask the driver to return us to the hotel. Harper's lucky we're not alone here, otherwise I'd be going absolutely berserk. We can't afford to have any of this leaking to the press.

'Hhhhh … he left me,' Harper murmurs as his head hits my shoulder. 'Everybody leaves me. But never him. Tonight … he … he left me.'

The words are sad, and for a moment I'm worried he's about to start crying, but he's just drunk. This is what happens when you drink like a fish. When you rely on alcohol to lift you up or bring you down or make you forget. *It* starts to consume *you*. It scrambles your brain. It turns you into someone else.

I should know.

I don't know what to say to him, but it doesn't matter anyway, because his breathing levels out and soft snores fill the back of the taxi as we slip through the Miami streets. It's 5am, but there's a surprising amount of traffic.

It's forty minutes back to the hotel and he sleeps through

almost every second of it. While I'm grateful for the silence, inside I am absolutely fuming.

It makes total sense now, the way he idolises Tyler Heath. My dad. The great Tyler Heath. Oh yes, he was truly great.

A great drunk.

A fantastic cheat.

And even better liar.

He used to hit the motor racing party circuit harder even than he hit the track. Until it all caught up with him and then it didn't matter how great he was behind the wheel. None of it mattered.

Fuck him. And fuck Harper James.

And yet, I find myself wondering, *who* left him? I don't even know who he went out with tonight. I don't spend a lot of time scrolling social media, especially during the season. I find it ruins my concentration and eats away at my ability to focus. One split-second decision on the track could cost me the title. Or my life.

Sliding out my phone from my sweats' pocket, I pull up Johannes's Insta stories – it seems like a pretty good place to start. And there he is. The man whose body has been haunting my shower time is sandwiched between Johannes and a half profile of a guy who looks familiar. Long wavy brown hair that, if I wasn't so tired, I'd probably remember who it belongs to. There's a series of photos that Harper's been tagged in. The three of them are chilling at the bar, captured in various poses throughout the evening, gradually getting drunker and wilder.

The final photo shows Johannes with his arms around the man with the chocolate curls. The way they're looking at each other it's clear they're about to kiss, and a few feet off to the side, his face half in shadow, is Harper. The expression in his eyes is hard to read at first, but not if you know him like I now do. I doubt Johannes even knew Harper was in the photo when he uploaded it, but I zoom in so I can get a closer look. There's pain there for sure, but what hits me deep in the pit of my stomach is the despair.

I scroll forwards and there's a four-hour gap of nothing, before a blurry image appears. It seems to show a set of abs against a crumpled white sheet, lit artistically from the side, and splayed over the chest is a head of curls that are easily identifiable as belonging to the gorgeous man from the bar. There's no text to accompany it, just a small red heart in the bottom corner.

It doesn't take a genius to read between lines: Johannes hooked up with the hot guy from the bar, and Harper drowned his sorrows. Quite why Johannes posted this to his stories I'll never understand, and I suspect he'll get an early morning wake-up call from his PR team telling him to take it down, but the damage to Harper has been done.

Is this what Harper meant? Did he feel like Johannes abandoned him tonight for whoever this man is? Surveying Harper's face I'm trying to figure out if it's heartbreak etched in his face?

Is that what this has been about all along? Is Harper in love with Johannes? I almost feel pity for him because that kind of unreciprocated love – must be awful. Having to see the person you love go home with someone else – must be gutting.

It makes sense when I look back at the last few weeks. Harper moved so freely when he was dancing with Johannes. His eyes lit up with every touch, and they looked like they fitted so well together.

I sigh and lean back against the headrest. Beside me,

Harper shifts and then is peaceful again, his cheek firmly pressed into my neck.

I wish I didn't feel so much sympathy for him. It would be easier to hate him, but I don't.

The sun's starting to rise as I guide him down the corridor to his room, his arm around my neck and mine virtually holding him up around his back. This is going to look so bad if someone sees us right now.

He's starting to come round, the bright lights of the hotel clearly having an effect, but it's making it harder for him to coordinate as he rebuffs my every touch.

'Where's your keycard?' I ask, not wanting to risk patting down his pockets. Not when he's wearing the skinniest jeans I've ever seen on such ripped thighs.

He shrugs in a way that would be comical if I weren't annoyed with him, and I lean him up against the wall while I decide what to do.

There's nothing for it. I have to pat him down, but my search comes up frustratingly empty. He's managed to hold on to his wallet and phone – full credit to the bouncer, I suspect – but there's no sign of his keycard.

Brilliant. Just brilliant.

'You're a twat,' I say. 'I can't ask reception for another keycard without alerting them to your current state. In any case, I can't leave you here on your own and I'm not dragging you back down there. Argh! Why are you such an idiot?'

Two days before qualifiers. Two days, and he decides to be this irresponsible. Never mind the impact his own performance will have on the team – now it's affecting me, too.

'Your bed it is, then,' he suggests cheekily, and for a second the wickedest smile I've ever seen flashes across his face. It's so fast that if I hadn't been looking right at him, I'd have missed it. I almost want to leave him in the corridor to figure it out for himself.

Yet here I am, reliable as ever, leading him like a dog on a leash to my room. This should not be happening. I don't fancy sleeping on the floor, but we can't share a bed again. We just can't. Although it's nearly 6am, with jetlag and everything, I'm still in desperate need of a few more hours of sleep, but it looks like I don't have a choice.

A heavy groan escapes Harper's lips as I plop him onto my bed. His lids flick open and I'm surprised by the bright eyes that meet mine, like his sober, rational mind has finally woken up. If he even bloody has one.

'Mmmm. Why is your bed comfier than mine?' He grabs one of the pillows and punches it to create a little nest for his head. 'Like a cloud. So soft. Mine's too … springy.'

I don't want to know how he's tested that, my brain doesn't need to produce any images right now of Harper bouncing around. Naked. With some other guy.

'You want anything?' I ask. 'Glass of water, maybe?' Of course he shakes his head.

I pull a spare blanket and pillow from the wardrobe and begin to make myself a makeshift bed on the floor. Both my back and my hips are going to hate Harper for this, but it feels like the smarter choice compared to the impact that sleeping next to him will have on my psyche.

I turn around and he's undone his jeans and he's desperately trying to kick them off. Of course they get stuck halfway down his thighs, leaving him trapped in just his boxers and an unbuttoned shirt. The trouble he's having with his coordination right now would be comical if the sight of him undressing weren't being burned into my retinas.

'Whaddaya doing?' he slurs. 'I won't bite…' He gives me the cheekiest little side-eye. 'Unless you ask me to.'

Shaking my head at him, I try to hide my actual reaction with a disapproving look. He, on the other hand, seems unaffected and continues to kick at the stiff denim without success. I could leave him like this, hogtied by his own incompetence, but I'm not sure the thought of him rendered physically submissive in this way will help my peace of mind.

'You need some help there, buddy?' I ask.

He hums his approval and in the blink of an eye, my hands are on him again. How is this the second time I am undressing Harper James?

'Stop kicking – you're making it worse!' I say, exasperated by his futile attempts to help.

'Johannes says they make my *aaaaassssss* look great.'

Even I can't deny that.

'How's that working out for you?'

'Not. Great. K-Kian.' He annunciates his response with intense effort and then looks up at me. He stops squirming and then says, 'Tobefair –' it comes out as all one word '– I'm not alone, am I? *You're* here.'

His hand clasps my wrist, stopping me from walking away.

'It's not like you gave me a choice, did you? When you call me drunk and alone, thrown out of a club for God knows what. I couldn't just leave you, could I?'

'Ev'ryone else did,' he says with a bitter, self-deprecating laugh.

It's getting harder to ignore his throwaway comments. It reminds me that I actually don't really know him at all. I know he's a party boy who doesn't take anything seriously, and who knows how to push all my buttons, but that's it. I don't know anything about his family, his goals, or his life outside the circuit. We're teammates, and somehow also strangers.

I sigh. When did I start feeling sorry for the asshole who's been making the last couple of months an absolute misery? Okay, not an *absolute* misery, but harder than they needed to be.

He's still clinging to my wrist like it's a lifeline. He pulls himself up into a sitting position until we're so close I can feel his breath on my face. I expect him to stink of beer and disappointment but instead I get a sweet, fruity aroma, as though he's spent all night drinking cocktails.

'Sometimes, I think you're one of the most boring people I know.' He's smiling as he speaks, suddenly able to articulate his words as though the drunken fog has momentarily cleared so he can impart these words of infinite wisdom. 'But then other times you look at me so ... primal, you know? And it makes me wonder...'

'No, I do not know. What are you going on about?' My tone is defensive, and I hope he's too pissed to notice. Instead, he suddenly tightens his grasp on my wrist.

No wonder his steering control is so good with this grip.

'Aha! See...! Your eyes lit up. Bet you love a pair of cuffs, tough guy.'

'Shut up, James.' I try to pull away, but even when he loosens his hold there's something still rooting me in place.

He doesn't know. He can't. Nobody does.

I've dated both men and women, but I've only ever been romantically linked to one person – who happened to be a woman – and I haven't left a trail of beefcakes, starlets or wannabes to sell stories to the tabloids about what I'm like in bed. So nobody knows. Except…

Clearly, Harper's a little bit more observant.

'Tell that to your little friend, Mr Half Chub.' He stares down at my crotch.

He's right. There's no hiding a semi in the grey joggers I'm wearing, especially when I didn't put underwear on in the 4am haze of the dash to get my Uber.

'Would you just roll over and start sleeping off the inevitable hangover? You've got bigger things to worry about than whether I'm hard or not.'

'I'm barely touching you.'

This time, I properly shake him off and he releases me without a fight. Except, his hand moves to my thigh, his fingers creeping up the soft cotton of my joggers and I don't want him to stop.

'You're so … responsive.'

His fingers dance higher and higher up my thigh until the pads graze over my erection. I'm fully hard now. There's no denying it. But I'm not alone. His dick is tenting in his boxers and I can't help but lick my lips.

I've seen clickbait headlines in the past about guys coming forward with stories about the *'best night of their life with Harper James'*. Most of the time I just thought it was glory hunters hoping for their five minutes of fame, or trying to get Harper to come back a second time. Even I know that's not how he worked. You get one chance with Harper James and that's it.

Is this mine?

I've thought the question before I have a chance to work out whether I want it to be.

I almost shake my head at my own thoughts.

Absolutely not. There's no way I want to be a notch on his very big bedpost. He's also way too drunk to be able to consent to anything.

But now he's stroking me through my sweats and I don't want him to stop.

'What are you doing?' I ask, the words coming out breathless.

'Anything you want, sweetheart.' The term of endearment sounds dirty on his lips.

What does *anything* even mean? A blow job? A hand job? Does he want me to fuck him? Is he a bottom or a top? Or both, like me?

I've been with men before, but not for a while. I know what I'm doing, I just never expected to be contemplating doing it with Harper James.

Except I want to. Every feather-light touch is driving me crazy. The pounding of my own heart rings in my ears and I know I'm starting to pant. It's almost sensation overload. Too much. Too much him.

'What do you want, Kian Walker?' He says my full name like I hold some kind of power here. I don't. I am flooded with the instinct to submit to him and just let him do whatever he wants. I'm sure anything would feel good at this point.

His other hand comes up to cup the side of my face, angling my head so I'm forced to look him in the eye. They were glassy maybe half an hour ago, and he was almost out of it, like the alcohol had dulled his shine. Now they're the clearest blue I've ever seen. Crystal, like the colour of the sea. He seems to be completely back in control. That drunk guy who was upset about being abandoned by his friend is gone, and cocky, swaggering Harper James, rookie and social-media fuck-boy, is back.

I can't speak. What would I even say? Instead, I lean into his touch so that we're knee to knee on the bed. If he didn't want this – hell, if I didn't – then now would be the time to back off. No impossible lines would have been crossed. We could put this down to a drunken mistake on his part and a sleep-deprived one on mine.

But, nope. We're both leaning closer and in an electric moment our lips touch. Lightly at first, apprehensive, almost like there's been more than a flirty five-minute build up to it. Maybe there has. Maybe it's been a few weeks. Maybe it's been more.

It's been there in the back of my mind every time I catch a glimpse of his bare skin, his playful smile, his beautiful blue eyes. The vulnerability beneath the mask.

The snark from him that never failed to rile me up. Yeah, he's been on my radar for more than five minutes.

Not that I ever expected this.

In a swift move, I'm pinning him to the bed and we're both thrusting against each other, clothed erections brushing as we tussle for dominance in the kiss. It's wild. Thrilling. Like nothing else I've ever experienced before.

I'm more turned on than I have been in years, like I could cum from just this level of contact alone. Harper's hand snakes around my waist and he yanks my sweats down, exposing my buttocks. I twist my hips so the joggers come off completely so my dick has room to breathe.

He breaks the kiss only to pull off his shirt and throw it to the floor. I manage to kick off my sweats from around my ankles whilst trying to keep my lips in contact with any part of his skin I can get access to.

It's rabid. I'm like a wild animal searching for my next meal. My teeth nip at the skin of his jaw, neck, collarbone, and down to his nipple. Lost in the taste of his salty skin, I feel like I'm losing my mind. It's sheer perfection as I swirl my tongue around the little pink nubs, and Harper's hand finally makes contact with my erection. It's both a relief and a torment.

He fists my dick with his grip and I'm groaning against his mouth. Oh, God, it's incredible. It's too much and not enough at the same time and I feel a great wave starting to build inside me.

'Kian...' he moans, and his raspy voice saying my name catches me completely off guard.

It's like a bucket of freezing cold water being thrown over me, stilling all my movements as I meet his eye. The questioning look I see there is concern but also confusion.

'Fuck.'

I breathe out harshly, my forehead resting against his. The wave recedes like an enormous falling tide as I finally come to my senses.

And then I'm pushing off Harper and he lets go of my dick to raise both hands in a kind of awful parody of a man being arrested by the police. The look in his eyes is hurt, but it's also, I realise painfully, resignation. Somehow I know this isn't the first time he's been rejected like this, and I want to comfort him, to reassure him, to say *it's not you, it's me*, but I don't.

'We can't do this. Fuck! This was so stupid.'

I'm pulling on my sweats so fast the fabric burns my heated skin. I stumble as I try to get my feet into my slides, the momentum of my exit overbalancing me in my desire to get out of the room.

It's only when I'm in the corridor that I remember this is *my* room and Harper doesn't have the key card for his, and this situation is only going to be more awkward to sort now.

Fuck. Fuck. Fuck.

So, bare-chested and embarrassed, I humiliate myself at the reception desk by pretending to be Harper and saying I've lost my key, then take the lift back up to our floor where I slip into his room and lie down on the bed, desperate to pretend that none of this is happening.

Because apparently, the only thing I'm good at tonight is avoidance.

Chapter Eleven

Kian

A day and a half later, I'm still falling apart. I can't think, I can't sleep, I can't focus.

Yet Harper bloody James is rocking some kind of weird glow. I'd call it post-orgasm, but neither of us came.

I'm undeniably envious at how he's bounced back so quickly from our aborted fuckfest. I'm also … hurt? Offended? I can't quite articulate how I feel about the fact that he seems completely unaffected by what happened between us. Especially since it feels like my whole world has been plunged into the kind of chaos that does not bode well for my upcoming performance. Every time he looks at me my skin prickles and I have to look away – my nerves are completely shot. I can't sleep because whenever I close my eyes, I see his hand on my cock, I feel the pressure of his tight grip, the sensitive pull as he tugs, the tightening of my balls … I'm struggling to remember to do even the most basic things as I prep to get in the cockpit.

Stupidly, I haven't brought my earbuds with me to the track, because when I woke up this morning, gritty-eyed from restless tossing and turning, I should have been visualising the course here in Miami and thinking about what I needed today. But all I could think about was Harper.

Is he thinking about me?

Probably not, I tell myself harshly. He does this all the time. He's used to it, used to that rush of adrenaline, the feeling of weightless falling and delicious anticipation.

I sound like a bloody teenager with a crush, for fuck's sake!

I tell myself that it only seems meaningful because the last time I had sex was, like, eight months ago. It had been quick, like scratching an itch, and exactly what we'd both been looking for – something to take the edge off.

I haven't had a serious relationship in almost four years. Christine and I were together for eighteen months. She broke things off shortly before I was heading off for pre-season training because I wasn't home enough and she couldn't face another season before the little I had to give was hers again. I wasn't 'present' she claimed, even when I was around. And I don't blame her – the way I have trained myself to be able to focus has always been my superpower. It's one of the reasons I have such a strict and disciplined routine. It's why I don't drink or go out partying. When I get behind the wheel, I need to know that I'm one hundred percent committed to winning. No distractions.

What made it worse, at that time, was that during the break between seasons, Mum got her Parkinson's diagnosis and my sister was really unwell with chronic morning sickness. I felt overwhelmed and anxious, and there was nothing left in the tank for Christine after caring for my mum and my sister.

We parted amicably, and I went on to start pre-season training without looking back. Any spare mental or emotional capacity was taken up with family stuff, and I was able to compartmentalise on the track with no problem.

Unlike now.

The feel of Harper's lips on mine is seared into my brain. I can feel the imprint of them still on every inch of my skin — even places they hadn't touched.

There was no amicable parting of ways with Harper. He swaggers about with his usual arrogant nonchalance and I am a pathetic ball of anxiety and awkwardness. In public – in front of Anders and the team, the media, and basically anyone else – we continue to maintain what passes for a friendly truce.

In private … well, there is no private. I make sure that we're never alone together. I do everything I can to forget about it. Yes, I know, very mature.

'You okay?' Cole asks. 'Your heart's racing.'

Of course, he's got all the data from the various monitors for both the car's health and mine on a screen in front of him.

Great. Just Great.

While I've been off in my own world, on a trip down memory lane, Cole's been watching me have a minor heart attack. The world of knowing what Harper James feels like underneath me is really messing with my concentration. It's not a fun place to be. Zero out of ten, would not recommend.

Enough, Walker! For fuck's sake.

I don't know what to tell Cole. He's my eyes and ears when I climb in the cockpit so I should probably be honest about where my head's at, but there's no way I'm admitting any of this. Denial it is!

'Just trying to get myself in the zone. Forgot my earbuds and I've got a bit of a headache coming on.' I rub my temples for good measure. I can feel the stress tugging at the back of my head, making my forehead feel tight. Good thing it's only practice – the final one before qualifiers – but not race day.

'Let me get one of the runners to grab you something with electrolytes in it, so you don't start to flag; down it and then get going,' he says, signalling to one of the team to grab a drink from the fridge in the garage.

If only electrolytes could flush Harper out of my system.

One of the elite performance coaches that Hendersohm brings in says that sometimes the only way out is through. You can't avoid a problem forever, nor can you find a way around it; you have to accept the truth and face the problem with courage. *Let yourself feel it, but keep pushing through*, he used to say. If Harper is my problem, then...

Shit. Maybe the only solution is a naked rematch. Maybe that's the only way to get him out of my system.

One of the guys comes running over with my favourite brand of sports drink – the blue flavour. I offer him my thanks but he's already being called off to do something else.

'It's only practice,' Cole reassures me. 'See what happens out there and then bring your absolute A game tomorrow. Get some laps in to shake off whatever's eating away at you.'

And now I have images of Harper eating me out. Thanks Cole, super helpful.

I feel immediately guilty, because how could he possibly know?

'Yeah, thanks, mate. I think I must just be a bit dehydrated.'

For the walking thirst-trap that is Harper James.

Cole gives me an odd look as I continue to chug the sports drink. He points out something on the monitor playing footage from this morning. I'm waiting for my allocated turn on the track but Yorris, Johannes and the two McLaren Swedes have already done their laps. They're my biggest competitors this season, I reckon.

I should probably be including Harper in that running order, too, since he's in the top five positions more than he's not. I hate to admit it, but he's doing better than Elijah did at this point last season.

Cole and I look for ways that our competitors' cars betray them and point out micro-errors that indicate where their weaknesses are when driving. Especially with the Swedes, who are brothers. They work so well together as they try and box off P1 and P2 – precisely what Harper and I don't do. I'm constantly on the lookout for opportunities to slip past them or to maintain the lead. The older brother, he's fearless, with a killer instinct on the track. It's like a natural gift. The younger brother can sometimes be induced to panic if you put enough pressure on him. He's the weaker of the two, and I'm always confident I can take him.

It's an interesting dynamic, siblings racing together. I'm glad I don't have to do it, that's for sure. Elise is as tough as they come and I've always looked up to her, but she's got the killer instinct of a buttercup.

'Feeling ready to get out there?' Cole asks after I drain half the bottle of blue liquid.

I nod. I need a great practice session to put me in a good headspace for the qualifiers tomorrow. To make sure my head's in the game.

Balaclava secure and helmet donned, I climb into the cockpit. My second home. Cole's voice snugly back in my ear; the familiar cadence of his breathing is calming as I wait to be told I can go.

Miami's track might be newer, but it was my favourite to race last year. It's just three long straight runs that I know how to exploit to my advantage, and then some elevations on certain bends that feel thrilling to fly over.

The flag drops for me to go and the main man is already chattering encouragement in my ear.

'Push mode, push mode,' Cole's saying and I ramp up the throttle and tear down the first straight. 'Oh, and Kian? Try to have fun, won't you?' That has me smiling and laughing to myself as I brace my body against the G-force of the first bend.

Free practices are so much fun in Miami. The sun might be blaring down on us, but there's an atmosphere in the arena that lifts me out of my funk of the last thirty-six hours as I zoom past the stadium that houses the Miami Dolphins. I notch up the speed and feel the car respond, and that's when the fun finally kicks in.

I'm trying not to think too hard about anything other than my foot on the gas, my hands on the steering wheel, and the way the moulded seat hugs my body. I mentally catalogue anything that doesn't feel right on the tracks, passing on the info to Cole who will work with the technicians ahead of tomorrow's qualifiers. Finally, I start to feel like myself again.

I pull into the garage after fifteen laps and climb out, discussing with Cole and the team what tweaks we can make for tomorrow that will address the sluggish third quarter. Cole and I then look at the specific data and I give him my overall report on today's session.

Those fifteen laps are all I needed today. Sometimes I need more, but I'm good for today. I'm glad my schedule is packed. I need to keep this positive mindset and the flow that I found on the circuit. I have a big *'from the track'* interview to do for ESPN and then I've got a gym session with my personal trainer followed by an evening of sports massage and stretches. Perfect.

I love my routine. It keeps me sane – and winning.

And then I walk into the interview and am completely blindsided by the host introducing a set of questions on my father. I look around for Anna. This is definitely not on my list of approved topics. It's actually on the blacklist, the only thing on there that Anna knows to emphasise with anyone wanting to interview me.

'We had Tyler Heath on earlier this morning, talking about how the first part of the new season is going for you and the line-up at Hendersohm. What do you think he had to say about your performance?' Kelly Sikes asks. She was one of my favourite sports presenters to watch, until now.

I don't care what he's said about me. I'm sure it's been nothing but good things because he loves to talk about me when I'm doing well and whenever it'll bring him in a couple of quid. But quite frankly, his opinion is irrelevant.

'I've got my eyes on another top-of-the-podium finish this season,' I say. Despite being forced into media training at the very beginning of the season – which I still blame on Harper – I'm actually good at this. It's hardly the first time I've neatly sidestepped any mention of the connection between me and my infamous father.

I laugh along as she plays me soundbites of the earlier clips. He says things like, 'he's just like his old man on the track,' and that 'I couldn't be prouder of the driver Kian's become over the last decade.'

It's enough to make me want to vomit, but I fake pleasant acquiescence and quickly find a way to move on from the topic.

Thankfully, the rest of the interview is painless. We talk about how the Miami Grand Prix is becoming as big as the Super Bowl each year, and what I'm excited to see and do while I'm in America.

I'm sure she's not expecting me to gush about the beach yoga, but Anna's always saying I need to come across with a bit more warmth and 'emotional authenticity'. I know this is to counteract my refusal to discuss Tyler Heath, and to court sponsors, so I go on about mindfulness for a bit and show my enthusiasm for the sunrise beach crowd. If Kelly is surprised, she hides it well.

Then she blindsides me again.

'I hear there's going to be a Kian Walker night at one of the bars in the gay village. Will you be attending that?' Not even I've heard about this night that's apparently being thrown in my name, but I definitely won't be putting in an appearance.

'While that sounds very cool and I'm honoured, it's not really my scene. However, if you let me or the team know which bar it is, I'll get some signed merch down to them.' It's the least I can do if I'm not going to go, and I don't think Anna will object.

We end the interview on that and Kelly's assistant hands me a business card with the name of the bar so I can get in touch. I'll put the Hendersohm PR team on that straight away so I can focus on tomorrow's race.

I'm lucky enough not to cross paths with Harper for the

rest of the day. Physically, I'm doing a great job of avoiding him. Mentally, I'm actually feeling pretty robust after this afternoon's session on the track. I'm so focused on *not* thinking about him, however, that I miss the window of time to call Elise to say goodnight to the kids.

I eat what the hotel calls a 'soul bowl' alone in bed. I stay off social media and go through my night-before-a-race meditation routine. When I finally close my eyes to fall asleep, Harper James swaggers into my thoughts as though he'd never left.

I haven't had sex dreams like that for a long time.

Needless to say, I go into the qualifiers half-asleep. Maybe even dangerously tired, to the point that I down two espressos in the garage and have to splash my face with ice-cold water.

It's not my best pre-race warm-up, but it has to be done. The first two knockouts go fine – nothing special, but nothing truly awful. I'm in P6 going into the final qualifying round which is not where I want to be, but it definitely could be worse.

Yet, the second they let us go for the third time that day, I know something's really, really wrong. I'm pushing the pedal and I'm still going forwards, but the car feels like it's shaking. The engine is shuddering and spluttering as if it can't find the energy to go any faster.

Maybe the engine and I are one, because I am eerily familiar with the feeling. It's unsettling to have my inner turmoil reflected in the inanimate beast that's normally growling and rumbling with barely leashed power. Today, neither of us has the edge.

'What's going on, Ki?' Cole asks.

'You tell me, mate!'

I'm not quite limping yet, but after one semi-decent lap everyone overtakes me and I just want to crawl back to the garage. For the first time in my career, I feel like giving in and going home.

Cole is buzzing in my ear with suggestions and feedback, but nothing's working.

'Just can't get going. Doesn't feel like the car's even reaching half-throttle let alone full.'

'Engine seems shot mate, sorry. It's not putting out what we'd like. Everyone's pissed off in here right now,' Cole quickly replies.

Slamming my fists against the steering controls, I let out a deep, earth-shattering roar of frustration.

'I thought we sorted this yesterday!'

I feel my temper flare. I'm really angry now – and only some of it is due to the technical failure of the car. I know I'm annoyed with myself – for losing focus, for getting side-tracked by Harper, for a missed opportunity that could cost me the trophy.

It feels like the engine's about to fail completely, so I have no choice but to slow even more. I'm limping along now, and trying not to deafen Cole as I take out my frustration on his eardrums. I never really got going in these qualifiers, and the stats Cole's giving me show I've hit nowhere near the numbers I expected. Come race day, I'm going to be staring at the exhausts of people I should have in my pocket. I don't need to see anyone else's lap times to know that.

At least I'll still be top ten. I hate relying on other people having a worse day in order to do well. That's not what elite performance should be about.

'Where am I sitting?' I ask Cole as the engine shudders.

'P9. Everyone else is almost finished so that's where you'll end up.' What he's saying is I shouldn't even try and finish. I should just get out now and let them pick the car up and return it to the garage. The team's going to have an all-nighter to get it fixed and ready for tomorrow. I don't envy them, but they're not the ones out here doing the driving. The most useful thing I can do is rest up and come back with a good strategy for the race.

Thankfully, it's not a sprint weekend so I'm not losing out on possible extra points. Silver linings and all that.

'Harper's position?' I ask once I'm stationary on the side of the track. I wait for the go-ahead that says it's safe to climb out, and I want to have time to compose myself before I face anyone.

'P4.'

Damn it! That motherfucker!

His first time on this Miami track and he's gone and crushed it.

It's like he's coated in Teflon. Nothing sticks!

If I wasn't so annoyed at myself and at the situation I'd probably find his skill a turn-on.

'Track's clear. You can step out now.' Following Cole's instructions, I walk the final few metres to the finish line. Walking over it on foot instead of speeding past is a weird feeling.

Of course, the first bloody thing I see is Harper hugging Johannes. The pair jumping up and down like little children at Christmas.

Does he not understand the concept of a team?

Was he not crying over Johannes just the other day?

For fuck's sake!

'Who finished P1?'

I'm glad to still have my helmet on so no one can see my face.

'Johannes,' Cole says simply.

Fantastic. Fan-fucking-tastic.

They are going to be truly insufferable.

From where I'm standing, I contemplate whether I can get past them without having to acknowledge them, but I'm sure all eyes are on me because of my poor performance today, and if I dodge two of the better top finishers – one of whom is my teammate – it'll reflect poorly on all of us.

Time to put on your big-boy pants, Walker.

So I get it over with, striding up to them, offering my congratulations, fist-bumping and clapping backs and shoulders, before retreating to the Hendersohm pit to lick my wounds. I prepare myself for a barrage of questions from the technicians about how the car actually felt at different points, and I'm quick to engage in the discussion, because I need the car to be perfect tomorrow if I have any hope of getting out of P9.

I'm afforded only five minutes of downtime before Harper swings by to collect me for the post-qualifying meeting in the Hendersohm garage.

'You okay?' Harper asks.

This is the first time I've been alone with him since the other night.

I grunt in response, not quite sure how to dredge up eloquence appropriate to this situation. I definitely don't want to talk about what happened. The only thing I want to know is how he does it. How does he manage to go through life without anything touching him?

'I don't know how you just did that.' The honest truth rolls bitterly off my tongue.

'Did what? Qualify fourth? Mate, you're normally above me. You know how better than I do.'

I don't know if he's deliberately misunderstanding the question or if *this* is exactly how he does it – by not overthinking.

Or by not thinking at all.

'You're like a worm in my brain, James.'

I try to shrug it off, but this moment's too important, I need Montreal under my belt to keep me in good standings to take home the Drivers' Championship this year.

'Was it my magic kisses?' he teases.

I'm horrified by the heat that rises in my cheeks and the way my body betrays me. He always seems to know exactly what buttons to push to get me off-balance.

'Fucking hell! Maybe I should go round kissing all the competition if it's gonna have this kind of effect.'

'Fuck off,' is all I manage to say before our conversation is no longer private.

As we arrive at the team meeting, I am wound up so tightly that I can barely speak. Harper James is living rent-free in my head right now, and he knows it.

The little fucker knows it.

He goes around doing whatever the hell he wants, kissing whoever he wants, shagging whoever he wants, and he's still killing it on the track!

He only has to look at me the wrong way and I fall apart.

I can't believe I convinced myself yesterday that the answer was to sleep with him, to scratch the itch so I could stop letting the intrusive thoughts win.

Maybe I really am getting old.

He doesn't have magic kisses, but he is a distraction and I can't take that right now.

I just need to stay away from Harper. That's what this comes down to.

Chapter Twelve

Harper

Never did I think one kiss could have the power to reduce a grown man to a jittery mess. Miami was a technical issue, but there's no doubt it affected Kian's performance in Monaco and Spain, placing him P2 in both. There was some chat in the garage about *ongoing* problems with his car, but we both know that's not what his problem is.

At first, I thought we'd get past it quickly, but he takes everything so damn seriously. You'd think he'd never had a one-night stand before. Not that we even got that far before he freaked out. He really could do with loosening up a little.

He's gone from scowling at me constantly to now going out of his way to avoid me entirely. Unless we're surrounded by the Hendersohm team or out in public, he's a ghost. He's obviously tweaked his routine to be wherever I am not at any given moment. And *he* calls *me* immature!

I thought maybe he'd cut himself off from everything

except driving, press and working out. But then I stumble across a realisation that while he's been dodging my company as though I'm carrying some kind of infectious plague that might tempt him away from being a boring bastard, he seems to have become pally with Anders's son, Jackson.

Jackson was raised on motor racing. He eats, sleeps and breathes it. He started out with a blog that turned into a popular podcast with expert guests, and he's regularly called upon as an industry expert to comment on everything from chassis design to track safety to driver stats. He's a nepo baby, for sure, but he knows his stuff.

He hasn't been working the media circuit quite so heavily this season, which seemed strange to me at first. Instead, he's been travelling with us a lot, working closely with his father and being invited to senior leadership meetings about strategy and finance. If I didn't know better, I'd think Anders was grooming him to take over.

I don't know how long Jackson is going to be hanging around, but he's certainly making the most of the opportunity to work out with golden-boy Kian while he's with us. I'm not sure who's sucking up to who, but they can have their little bromance. It makes no difference to me.

Working yourself up about shit like that – getting ahead of yourself and worrying about the future – is for people like Kian. I deal with what's right in front of me – in life and on the track – and so far it's served me well. Overthinking is the best way to get left behind by younger, hungrier, faster people who'll take risks that you're not brave enough to. If Elijah comes back next year, someone else will want me and I'll win for them instead. In any case, the best thing for me to do is win and hope Anders isn't stupid enough to let me go.

Having said that, it does seem like lately, whenever I enter a room, Kian's always mid-conversation with Jackson. They've always got their heads bent towards each other or they're on the way to the gym together. I'm not jealous – it just seems like mighty convenient timing. A paranoid person might worry that Kian's persuading Jackson to drop a word in his dad's ear about kicking me off the team, but that's not me. And why would Anders do that when my results speak for themselves?

If Kian asks I'll tell him to his face that he's being childish. So what if we kissed? That was weeks ago, he needs to move on. And yes, maybe it enthralled me to the point I haven't looked at another man for the last four weeks.

Never in my life would I have thought I'd finish in P3 at the Monaco Grand Prix and not hit the town hard afterwards with at least one hot gazillionaire. I made it to the casino and didn't even scout the talent that was there. I know there was more than one blue blood gambling away the family jewels who couldn't keep his eyes off mine, but I wasn't interested.

I shiver at the thought.

It was definitely just exhaustion though. The step up from lower-category racing was obvious as we navigated deeper into the season. Plus, Johannes hadn't been going out at all really, so I've lost my usual wingman. That's the explanation I'll be using if anyone asks.

Now we're in Montreal, one of my favourite places in the world, and I feel more like myself again. Settled. Ready to put any thoughts of that night in Miami to the back of my mind permanently.

Until Johannes asks me if I hooked up with anyone in Monaco.

We're in a café in Montreal, doing some people-watching

and catching up – I haven't seen him much recently, his time has been occupied with someone or something he's not telling me about – when Jackson and Kian step inside.

They're laughing and joking, Jackson's clapping his hands on Kian's shoulders as he tells him the coffee's his shout.

Jackson's dark brown curls are so slick with sweat that they almost look black and Kian's flushed in the face. They're in full workout gear, so they've clearly been for a run, but for a second my mind drifts to another activity that would leave the pair sweaty and panting. All of a sudden, I'm feeling growly. I put it down to lingering tension with Johannes after he abandoned me for some no-name guy that he refuses to talk about. Even though I'm usually able to shrug these things off. Did I want to shag Kian that night? Yeah, I did. But it's not like I've been obsessing over why he freaked out so much just when we were getting to the good stuff. He's got a stick up his ass, and though I know he'd have more fun with my dick up there instead, that's his issue, not mine. I've barely given it any thought. I really haven't.

But as I look at him with Jackson and see how easy and relaxed he seems, I'm actually kind of pissed off. Why does he save the worst of his personality for me? I thought Kian didn't do this. I thought he didn't do hook-ups. To my knowledge, he hasn't shagged anyone all season – male or female. So why's he suddenly all over Jackson like a rash? He doesn't even seem to be friends with many people on the circuit, outside of Cole. Yes, he's *friendly* with everyone, but there's a difference between that and friendship.

'Hello? Earth to Harper.' Johannes waves his hand in front of my face, wrenching my attention from Jackson's arm which is casually slung around Kian's shoulder as they order their drinks.

'Sorry,' I mutter, my eyes quickly flitting back to the pair to check whether Jackson's touch stays careless rather than possessive.

'That's a little weird, huh?' Johannes sounds almost as bothered as I am, though I'm probably imagining it because I want everyone to share my frustration with Kian so I don't feel like a twat.

'Didn't know they were so friendly. Looks cosy.'

Johannes looks questioningly at me. I find I can't meet his gaze.

'Very. Any chance there could be something going on there?'

I'm not about to out Kian. I know he said he doesn't care if people know if he's bi, but it's not my place to say anything. If he wants Johannes to know he'll tell him, or tell the world. I also don't think I could say it in a way that wouldn't betray my interest.

I watch them, listening to the sounds of the coffee machine, but when they take their drinks, the cups aren't to-go. And then suddenly they're walking towards our table.

'Oh, shit,' I mumble under my breath. 'Incoming.'

'Hey, Harper,' Jackson says cheerily. Time to fake it till I make it, I really can't afford to be on the bad side of the principal's son.

'Jackson, hey man. How's it going?'

'Not too bad, mate. This guy, though –' he jostles Kian's shoulder for good measure, just in case I don't know who he's talking about '– has me run ragged. A 6am swim and then an afternoon run! Does he ever stop?'

'Well, you know Kian. Dedication is his middle name.' Everyone laughs though it feels a little artificial.

'Sorry, not that he needs introducing considering you wrote so many blog posts about his performance last year, but this is my best friend – Johannes Muller.'

'Sure, sure,' Jackson says, offering Johannes his hand to shake.

I can tell that Johannes isn't thrilled – Jackson might have called Johannes's season last year 'sub-par' in his podcast – but he takes the proffered hand anyway. And being the polite guy he is, Johannes asks how Jackson is enjoying Canada, and this launches into a conversation about Jackson's study abroad year here.

Kian doesn't contribute, just calmly sips his coffee as though there's nowhere he'd rather be. I look up at him and try to catch his eye but he stubbornly refuses to acknowledge my presence.

I watch a bead of sweat run down the side of his face, past his ear and over the edge of his jaw. I observe its progress as it clings to his neck and then disappears beneath the neckline of his running vest. I'm well aware of what his chest looks like and I take a moment to imagine tracing the progress of that droplet all the way down his body.

I have to shift in my seat to hide what this little daydream is doing to me, and when I look up again at Kian's face, I catch the briefest flicker of an expression that tells me he's just as aware of me as I am of him.

Gotcha.

I can't help but smirk.

And then Kian's interrupting to make his excuses. Of

course he is. 'While this has been lovely,' he says, 'I need to get back to FaceTime my sister.'

He takes their empty cups back to the counter and then they're off. Together.

'See you guys later,' Jackson tosses over his shoulder as he exits the café.

'Well that was awkward,' I say once Jackson and Kian are out of earshot.

'All good, mate, all good,' Johannes replies, but his right eye twitches, and if I know anything about him it's a sure sign that he's lying.

'He's just some stupid sportscaster. Don't let him get to you.'

Johannes dismisses me with a wave of his hand, quickly changing the topic to a restaurant he thinks we should visit whilst we are here. He talks a good game about how he's gonna whip my ass next weekend and I join in the mutual ribbing because it takes my mind off what Jackson and Kian might be doing back at the hotel.

He said he was going to FaceTime his sister, but that could have just been a cover. They could be shagging right now, sweaty clothes on the floor, a tangle of limbs on Kian's bed.

Okay, so maybe Johannes isn't doing a good job of taking my mind off the other pair.

'You're so spacey today.' I blink and Johannes is standing up and starting to check his phone, our empty drinks cleared from the table.

'Sorry,' I tell him. 'Think I might need an early night. I'm knackered. Why don't they do Montreal and Miami back-to-back? Why make us go to Europe for Monaco and Spain only to drag us right back over here?'

Obviously I'm not going to say I'm stewing over my teammate shagging someone who's not me.

'Kian's really is rubbing off on you if you're going to bed early. You gonna give up drinking, too?'

I nudge his shoulder as we leave the coffee shop.

'Dickhead. It's you that's turned into a boring old fart. Can't believe you didn't even join me at the casino in Monaco.' Johannes had been somewhat MIA in Monaco; I couldn't even get a hold of him for a couple days.

I want to pry, but I know he'll talk to me if there is something bad going on.

'Been there, done that – last year, while your sorry ass was still down in lower tier.'

We continue in that vein until we get back to the hotel. The fans outside the hotel are noisy and the crowd has almost tripled in size since we left this morning.

I'm glad there's some security and they've lined the path with rope barriers to keep the hoards back, but it doesn't stop them flinging things at us to get our attention. One woman going as far as throwing her bra at me.

I peel it off my shoulder and laugh. 'Sorry, love. This does nothing for me. You're barking up the wrong tree.'

She takes it well, since I make the effort to return her underwear.

'Worth a try,' she replies with a saucy look, and I can respect that.

God loves a trier.

Soon, Johannes and I are laughing along with the fans, and they seem happy that we stop to sign shirts and programmes instead.

Jo and I part ways at the lift, making plans for tomorrow.

Except I don't see him again until qualifying. He looks tired when I catch a glimpse of him and his tech team on the track getting him into the cockpit.

I'd be lying if I said I wasn't concerned. Radio silence from Johannes isn't the norm, at all. He always has his phone in his hand, quick to jump on a plan for the day if he isn't busy.

Seems like he's been incredibly busy.

I don't let it throw me off though – I never let these things get to me on the track – and I manage to smash out some fast times.

This plays to my advantage in the Hendersohm team meeting because Anders is hyped up about today. There are bonus points available in Montreal because there's a sprint race the day before the main event. Hendersohm is currently in a too-close-to-call battle right now to be top of the Constructors' Championship against the Swedes in the McLaren team. We need every possible point to give us the edge. Anders lays on the pressure, and I lap it up like it's gonna turn me into a diamond. Kian looks serious – no change there – and doesn't glance at me once.

I've already qualified in P4, but I love the sprint races – it's where I get to really show off what I can do – and it also gives me a chance to secure a higher position on the grid for tomorrow.

I can see why it's the favourite track for so many drivers. Whilst there's a lot of stop-start in some of the corners, the low downforce of sector three allows for us to be quick and flowing. And then there's the millimetre precision necessary to avoid splatting my brains out on the Wall of Champions. You have to hit the previous apex just right, but when you do, it feels like pure magic.

After the meeting I run through checks with Ash and my tech team, and then I get into the cockpit. A flash of nerves gets my adrenaline pumping. I'm almost more nervous than an actual race day. This is just a snapshot of a race. Twenty-two laps instead of the seventy we'll perform in tomorrow.

Then Ash comes into my ears. 'You've got this one, Harper. We'll monitor the car, just push when I tell you. Eyes on the prize.'

I can see how Kian and Cole have become so symbiotic, as Ash's words perk me up and reassure me that I've got this.

And I do. It's lights out and I'm burning rubber.

I'm out of the gate at full throttle, holding my own in P4, going round the excruciatingly stop-start bends, but the second I hit sector three I'm flying. Feeling weightless, like I'm literally darting through the air.

Everything about the race feels perfect. There's a moment – a very small moment – when I'm completely out in front. It's like I'm the sole car on the track for about five seconds, and then fucking Kian pulls a move and zooms past me.

It's such an incredible manoeuvre and I'm still so high from the feeling that I'm not even mad about it. When I cross the line for the final time, I've been shunted down to P3 but Kian holds P1. I hold on to the memory of being out in front. This is only my first year in Championship racing; my time will come.

Kian looks absolutely overjoyed. He doesn't always win these things, despite being one of the best drivers in the world. He's much happier grinding out laps, reeling people in, biding his time and pouncing when the conditions are just right. He's got stamina and endurance, but today it's like he's told the world *fuck you, I do have speed. There's still so much I have left to offer.*

Maybe the retirement rumours are bullshit, after all.

The pure joy radiating off Kian is infectious, and I find myself gravitating towards him.

I clap his shoulders, so happy for him, and I'm not sure if he even realises it's me, but he's pulling me closer.

We're hugging, his arms around my waist, mine around his shoulders, and dancing up and down like a pair of loons, pure mindless exhilaration. Everyone's celebrating and the noise is deafening. I feel my heart deep inside my chest, booming and thundering – *this* is where I belong!

It's pure excitement to be taking away eight and six extra points from this sprint. Would I have liked to have been taking away seven, instead of six, of course, but Yorris was a sneaky bastard catching my tyre causing me to have to slow for less than half a second.

It didn't matter though, because the whole of the Hendersohm garage is alive and Kian's touching me, hands gripping the back of my shirt, as Cole and Ash join the hug, followed by the techs, until we're trapped in the middle of a massive group hug.

The victory's made sweeter by the fact that the Swedes struggled to get going, the younger brother finishing in P8, whilst the older one ended up in P6. It gives us a twenty-four-point lead over McLaren. Anders is even more excited than we are, if that's possible, as we head towards the main European phase of the Grand Prix.

Kian pulls away to look at me. Excitement creases the outer corners of his eyes and he's properly smiling at me. Like, a true, toothy smile that you can't contain. The moment's brief and his smile slips, almost as if he catches himself and realises who he's stuck with, but it has me fizzing on the inside. I've never seen him like this. It's ... mesmerising.

Something erupts inside of me, something I've only ever felt about a perfect lap or a podium finish. Butterflies. Fluttering in my stomach right now, causing it to churn. Kian Walker's given me bloody butterflies.

The group breaks apart and someone pops champagne. Obviously no one can drink it because we've still got the main race tomorrow and there's work to be done tonight, but it adds to the mood in the garage as it's sprayed all over everyone. It's everything I dreamed it would be when I was down in the lower leagues, trying to get noticed, trying to get my shot at the bigtime.

For once, I'm happy to kick back chatting with Ash about my lap times from yesterday, watching the rest of the team party.

Kian's in his element, soaking up the praise and talking ecstatically with Jackson and Cole about what's turned out to be a record-breaking sprint time today. He looks almost blissed out – all his muscles are relaxed, his eyes a little hazy, and he's not shoving earbuds in his ears and rushing back to the hotel to be alone. It makes me wonder what he's like in the off-season. When he allows himself to just be. Does he smile like that all the time? I'd like to see that.

The news gets even better the next day when we romp home, having maintained our starting positions of P1 and P3, but there's no euphoric hugging today. Kian gets called to do media with the Swedes, Dorris and Johannes, leaving me feeling miffed that I'm not being called up with the big names after how well I've performed so far this season. I know I'm not a contender for the Drivers' Championship, but still.

Next season, I tell myself. Next season they'll be knocking down my door to get to me.

I'm more offended when Kian doesn't come over to congratulate me once all the cameras disappear. He's back to his tactic of complete avoidance. Back at the hotel, I try to talk to him on the walk between the lift and our rooms, but he looks through me like I'm not even there, and then disappears inside, leaving me alone in the corridor.

Well, he can try to ignore me all he wants, but it's not going to work for long.

For the European leg of the tour, Hendersohm have sorted us a state-of-the-art luxury motorhome. That's right. Motorhome, *singular*.

To share.

All around Europe for twelve weeks.

There'll be no escape – for either of us – and I can't wait. Sooner, rather than later, we're going to have to talk about what happened.

Chapter Thirteen

Kian

I'd never considered arson before I found myself living in a motorhome with Harper James. Right now, sending the whole thing up in flames so I can return to my quiet hotel room sounds like a really good idea.

Sharing one of these with Elijah for the last three seasons was nothing short of brilliant. In the first season it helped us bond, in the second season it kept us sane when so many different weather fronts threatened to ruin various Grands Prix during the European leg, and last season it was home to many pizza nights and quiet beers as we celebrated every win.

This year it feels like a prison, the same four walls but somehow smaller, and suffocating.

I'm already at boiling point with the situation and it's only day five.

'You've got to be kidding me!' I shout. Yet again Harper's left half of his outfit from last night all over the living room floor, and he's already coating all of the kitchen surfaces in a loaf's worth of toast crumbs.

Harper's eyes shoot open from where he's leaning, half-asleep, against the counter, feeding himself toast in just his boxers. If I weren't so angry, I'd let myself appreciate the picture in front of me a little more.

'What?' he grumbles, rubbing a buttery hand through his curls to get them off his forehead. It's gross, but the boner trying to make an appearance in my shorts doesn't agree.

'It's disgusting in here, Harper. How can you live like this?'

'Seriously, the sun hasn't even come up. It's like 8am. Why are you screaming?'

The blinds are still down and he's clearly hungover – I can smell stale beer in the air – so he has no idea that the sun came up hours ago and it's definitely not 8am.

I go round opening each blind one by one to prove my point. He covers his eyes, squinting and groaning. The Austrian sun's not warm by any means, but it's undeniably daylight.

'We have to share this space,' I say, gesturing angrily to the mess he's generated in the wake of making a couple pieces of toast.

'Okay, Grandad. I'll clean up after a couple hours' sleep. Give me a break.'

A break? He's treating the whole of his racing adventure like one big break.

'God, you'd think I was asking the world from you, not the bare minimum.'

Maybe this is the world for Harper. Like he's never had to tidy up in his whole life. I don't really know much about his background. Maybe he had a butler following him around with a dustpan and brush, or maybe this is a form of weaponised incompetence.

'I always plan to clean up and then by the time I get to it you've already done it,' he says.

'Because you leave plates and bowls in the sink for days on end. We're going to end up with a fucking fly infestation.'

'They're soaking. You're meant to leave them to soak.'

We aren't getting anywhere with this conversation and I know I'm just wasting my time. Leaving him to it in the kitchen to argue with himself, I grab my sports bag and give myself a once over in the mirror to make sure I'm presentable.

'Where you off to?' he asks, hovering over my shoulder as I try to sort my hair out in the mirror by the door.

I probably shouldn't be worrying about what my hair looks like when I'm about to head to the gym and get sweaty, but there's press and fans lurking everywhere right now. I have to pass through the access-all-areas point for fans in order to get to the gym and, call me vain, but I don't need shit photos of me circulating on social media.

'To the gym, not that it's any of your business.'

'Do you always preen this much to go and work out?'

'I'm meeting Jackson.' I'm not sure why I feel the need to add this. It's not like we're going on a date – it's just the gym.

'You two seemed to be joined at the hip lately. Anything you want to tell me?'

'No.'

'I'm just surprised. Didn't think he was your type.'

'My type to work out with?' I shoot back, even though I know exactly what he means. Apart from the curly hair, there's no other similarities between Harper and Jackson.

'Hmm. Well, have a good day, I guess.'

He drops the subject way faster than I expect, returning to collect his half-eaten toast from the kitchen counter.

Infuriatingly, he leaves the knife – with butter smeared on both the blade and the handle – on the side, not bothering to even put it in the sink, never mind washing it up.

I'm tempted to do it for him, but he's never going to learn if I do. So I leave, not caring if I'm too early to meet Jackson. I just need to be anywhere other than within throwing distance of Harper right now.

Jackson, unlike Harper, is punctual and doesn't flake without letting me know, so he's actually waiting outside the gym when I arrive. We're both early, it seems.

I know I have a face like thunder because the corridor of fans I had to pass through on my way here all told me to cheer up.

I'm grateful Jackson doesn't ask what's up straight away, because I'd probably explode. Instead, we head to the locker room, discard our bags and jackets, and get to work warming up.

He side-eyes me as we use adjacent cross-trainers, like he's trying to figure out how to ask whether anything's wrong. It's making me slightly paranoid, because it feels like he sees everything. I don't know what Anders has told him about the bollocking he gave us earlier on in the season, or whether Anders knows that Harper and I took his suggestion of faking a friendship in public literally. I also don't know what influence Jackson has over decision-making within the team, which makes this situation a bit of a political tightrope.

Maybe I shouldn't have told Jackson about the kiss. I didn't name Harper, but I have a feeling he suspects it was him. It was tearing me apart; really messing with my head in a way that was translating onto my track stats. And I can't afford that. I just couldn't keep it in any longer, the intrusive thoughts and the overthinking, and one day I just blurted it out while we were grabbing a coffee. Plus, I've known Jackson for about a decade, even if this is the first season he's joined us on the tour as part of the Hendersohm management team. He's just a year younger than me, and if the circumstances were different, I think we'd probably have become close friends a long time ago.

His dad is my boss, which didn't help at the beginning, and Jackson was always a little standoffish. It's hard to write objectively and critically about your friends, and since he's built his career and reputation as a Championship race reporter I know that presents a challenge. When he was starting out, there were the usual accusations of nepotism because his dad is the principal of one of the most successful and competitive teams. In some of his early long-form pieces – articles for motor racing magazines, and one TV documentary I remember in particular – he went too far the other way, in my opinion, and made some unfairly scathing pronouncements about Hendersohm drivers, including me, and about his dad and the latest engineering choices. Looking back, I think he was just trying to establish himself, and now, more than a decade on, he deserves his reputation as an insightful critic, a good interviewer, and one of the top motor racing pundits around.

His sabbatical as part of the Hendersohm management team comes at the request of his dad. I know Anders is proud of his son's career, but I think he also wants to encourage Jackson to swap sides and use his knowledge and experience to become a team manager and eventually a principal, like him. I'm not sure it's what Jackson wants, but I suppose that's the point of trying it out.

Sitting opposite each other on the floor while we stretch, we discuss what weights we're going to lift today. I'm still stewing over the Harper situation and obviously not doing a good job of hiding it.

'You doing okay?' he asks as I scrub the rag across my sweaty forehead with a little more vigour than is perhaps necessary.

We're alternating Russian twists and kettle-bell swings and I'm channelling my frustration into faster reps, leaving me panting more than usual. 'Mmm. One more set.'

'How're things going?'

Jackson's skirting around the topic of Harper, like he doesn't want to pry or insinuate what he thinks he knows. Which is probably for the best.

'Urgh,' I groan, falling back completely on the mat so I don't have to look at him whilst I moan. 'I've never lived with anyone like Harper James. It's been five days and I already can't take it. I miss Elijah. *He* never left toast crumbs and butter knives lying around like he expects me to be his personal maid.'

'So he's a bit messy?'

I glare at Jackson. A *bit* messy?

'And the rest. He's an inconsiderate, selfish asshole. He comes in at all hours of the night, crashing around the kitchen and making so much noise. He drowns the bathroom every time he showers because he can't seem to pull the door completely shut. He also wears no clothes, like, all the time.'

'Oh, no. Imagine having to look at a half-naked, sexy athlete all day. It must be so hard for you.'

If only Jackson knew how hard. I saw Harper towel-drying himself the other day. Does he not know how to close a door?

Jackson knows I'm bi, and a careless use of pronouns when I was telling him about the kiss means he knows it's a guy who's currently messing with my head.

'I'd rather he put on a shirt and did the washing-up from time to time.'

'No you wouldn't.'

Savage. I fake a gag, but Jackson doesn't let it go. I guess years of interviewing has given him a pretty good radar for bullshit.

'You're the only person I know who doesn't want a front-row seat to the Harper James show,' he says.

'I came to the gym to get away from him. Can we talk about something else?' I'm sick of hearing his name.

'Okay,' Jackson obliges. 'You looking forward to going home for a couple weeks after this one? Silverstone's always such a good track for you.'

'You can say that again.' I've never scored below P3 on that track, even in my rookie year. Home turf, and all that. But, most of all, I can't wait to see Elise and the kids, and Mum too, of course. That's what is most important this year about going back to the UK. 'Of course, I love Silverstone. A P1 in front of a home crowd would be sweet. Plus, seeing the family is needed right now, feels like I've been away too long.'

'Yeah, family's important,' Jackson continues. 'You'll never hear him say it, but I don't think Dad ever got over losing Mum. He's excited to have me on tour for a few weeks.'

Five years ago, in the middle of the season, Anders's wife, Brita, suddenly passed away and it hit him hard. He'd actually taken a day off during the season because of it, something he'd never done before. For months he walked around like a dark cloud, barking orders and storming out of meetings. It got to the point where people were afraid to approach him, but eventually the senior trainer, a long-time friend and colleague of Anders's, took him aside and had a word. I don't know if he went to therapy or not, but by the time the next season rolled around he was mostly back to his normal self – at least in public.

'That must be tough,' I say. 'And what about you?'

'Oh, you know. I felt really lost for a while, but…' Jackson visibly swallows and he blinks a few times. 'I miss her all the time, obviously, but it's different for Dad. He's not very good on his own.'

'He's definitely happy to have you here,' I say. 'He seems a little more relaxed.'

The look on Jackson's face tells me he wants to say more, but then he changes his mind. My spidey senses tell me there's something brewing amongst the senior leadership team, some big secret I'm not supposed to know. Except Jackson quickly schools his face back into the open, friendly, approachable expression he usually wears and the moment passes.

I'm close to asking what's going on, but if he wanted to tell me he would. We're friends, aren't we? I should just ask.

But there's a part of me that's a little afraid. I'm afraid it's about the future, about next year, and I don't know how I feel about that. I still get asked in every interview about whether I'm going to retire at the end of the season, and although I always brush it off and give an answer full of stock phrases that give absolutely nothing away, the truth is that I don't know. It's been so much harder this year, harder on my body, harder to deal with the chaos that Harper's brought to the team, harder to stay focused.

And for all Harper's chaos, his results have been incredible. Even if Elijah recovers before the end of the season, they might choose to keep Harper anyway. They might even select him over Elijah for next season. It's unthinkable.

The only person I want to talk about this with is Elise, and she's not here. She's also got so much on her plate already that I don't want to add to her burden. It feels like Jackson and I are building a real friendship, but he's still the son of my boss and I clearly have trust issues.

'Ready for bench press?' I ask. I want to get this workout done so I can face whatever shitshow Harper has waiting in the motorhome while I've still got the will to live.

But, when Jackson and I are done and I eventually get back to the motorhome, Johannes is in the living room, and Hendersohm catering containers are scattered across the floor. They've both got their feet on the coffee table and they're playing videogames on full volume.

'Really?' I ask, wiping my feet on the team-branded welcome mat. I know I sound like a nag, but I can't hide the annoyance in my tone. It's one thing being out and about with Johannes, but another bringing the competition into our current home where he could catch a glimpse of sensitive team documents or overhear any kind of calls.

'Nice to see you too, Kian,' Johannes replies, unconcerned.

'Nothing against you, Johannes, but just wondering if you could maybe take him to puppy-training classes, cos I'm sick of living with someone who isn't house-trained.'

'I'm right here, you know,' Harper says, like I could possibly ignore him.

'I'm going to take a nap before the strategy meeting. Is there any chance you could keep it down in here for the next hour?' It's a long shot, but as I'm being nice enough to ask, maybe he'll be polite enough to oblige.

Harper says, 'Yeah, sure,' but neither of them is looking at me as they continue to compete in whatever pointless bullshit shooting game they're playing. The volume stays exactly where it was.

For fuck's sake.

I'm so bloody close to losing it with him.

Chapter Fourteen

Harper

I have entered a whole new level of petty. I set an alarm for ten minutes before Kian's usually goes off – he sticks rigidly to a schedule so it's not difficult to notice. I make a mushroom and ham omelette and a cup of hot blackcurrant, making sure to create as much mess as possible, and then I plonk myself down on the sofa in the lounge and wait. Anticipation tingles in my stomach, spreading to my whole body.

Just like clockwork, at 6.28am, Kian emerges from his bedroom to begin his 6.30am yoga. At first, because it's still dark in here, he doesn't see me. But when he turns the light on, he jumps out of his skin.

It's hilarious.

'You wanker! What the hell?'

He's growly, his morning voice thick and rough. Christ, it's almost enough to have me sporting a semi. If I could get him to say my name right now I'd probably cum in my pyjama bottoms.

I say nothing, just kick my feet up on the coffee table as I take another bite of my toast.

'Do you mind?' he asks irritably, from where he's unrolling his purple yoga mat in our living room. He's wearing an oversized vest and the tightest shorts I've ever seen. They cling to the tree trunks he calls thighs and I'm mesmerised by the way his quads clench when he's annoyed.

'Do I mind what?' I play dumb because it's just so much fun to see him wound up.

'This is not a spectator sport.' It comes out in his best teacher voice, but it doesn't deter me.

'Coulda fooled me,' I say, eyeing his junk in those tight, tight shorts.

This is going to fill my wank bank for years. I'm not giving up the opportunity to see him do downward dog for anything.

'You're not moving.'

'Thank you, Captain Obvious.' I tuck my feet under myself and get cosy, grease dripping out of my folded omelette and onto my fingers. I lick off the drips and hear him take in a sharp breath.

It's too easy!

I stumbled to the bathroom yesterday morning to go for a piss and caught the end of the routine. I might have been bleary-eyed at first, but I was very quickly wide awake. Appreciating how every single one of his muscles was on show, extended and bulging, as he held the position. He was beautiful. His eyes were closed and his breathing was controlled, his face relaxed and blissful. I don't think I've ever felt the way he looked. I didn't know whether I wanted to fuck him or be him.

I'd even made an early morning snack. What did he want me to do, throw it away?

'Whatever,' he grumbles, and proceeds to start his routine by sitting cross-legged and closing his eyes. He then rolls his neck and shoulders and moves fluidly into a full-body ritual that makes him seem like he's on elastic or made of water. I don't know how to describe it except that it's an experience to see him be so completely centred, so relaxed, and so incredibly hot at the same time.

I actually start to feel like a voyeur, watching something deeply personal or private. His ass looks amazing, strong and muscular with hollows in the cheeks as he clenches.

Especially when he bends over into what I believe is called a sun solution.

'That's right, worship me.'

He chuckles, before quickly rearranging his face into a scowl, turning away from me completely.

Not that I'm complaining because it only gives me another perfect view of his perky ass, hugged by the thinnest layer of Lycra. If I didn't know Kian, I'd think he was doing it to tease me.

But I do and I know there's probably a reason he's wearing these shorts. Most likely for breathability or so he can move with more ease.

I don't care what the reason is, I'm just grateful he decided to pull them on this morning.

I want to bend him over the coffee table and then take him from behind. The compulsion becomes so strong that I've forgotten my hot drink and the toast in my hand. Completely lost in the way his body moves. Until it's over and he finishes up with some breathing.

He lies on his front, his palms flat on the mat and then pushes up so his spine is curved and his head is thrown back. I watch his pulse throb in a vein in his neck and think what an absolute killing he could make selling videos of himself doing this on OnlyFans.

I'm also starting to consider giving yoga a go – how hard could it be?

My mouth feels dry.

I'm not even sure why I'm doing this anymore – not *this*; it's obvious why I'm still doing *this*. I mean, winding him up. Pissing him off. Trying to get a reaction out of him. When I set the alarm last night I was chuckling with glee at how mad he was going to be, but, sitting here now, the only one who's being tortured is me.

Kian's gone out of his way to make it clear that the kiss was a mistake. I can take a hint, and since he exits every room I walk into, well I've taken the hint massively. To the point it's starting to make me mad.

Right now, though, I'd do anything to convince him to kiss me again. I want to feel the drag of his lips over mine, his fingers digging into the skin of my hips, my stomach, my thighs. I am dying for any kind of touch from him. Just one touch, one time. I need something to take the edge off.

Except I know it wouldn't be enough. Once will never be enough with him.

I know this as clearly as I know my own name.

And that's the problem in a nutshell.

I'm a lone wolf, not a pack animal. No one has ever believed in me the way I believe in myself. I was always told

I'd never amount to anything. I was always abandoned, left behind, tossed away like rubbish in a skip. The only person I can count on is me. Even Johannes – the one person I trusted with my whole life – is barely around anymore. I know he's found someone else, and at first it felt like the sky was falling down. I couldn't breathe, I couldn't think, I couldn't see. So I drank until I didn't care anymore.

And then I called Kian.

But I don't want a relationship. I don't want to start to depend on someone, to need someone, to love them.

It would be the end of me.

That was what I needed to remember to stop myself doing anything stupid.

Wanting someone more than once would never work. Not for me. Not ever.

I sneak out whilst he's scrunched up in some kind of contortionist shape on the mat. The fun's over.

I'm still straining in my pyjamas, though, so I need to go and take care of that.

I can't have him, but that doesn't mean I can't get off to the image of him being so perfectly elongated in a sun-salutation pose.

It doesn't take much, a couple of tugs and I'm spilling into my fist. It should be enough. I should be spent, but it doesn't work.

I just want more. I want his mouth on my dick. I want his hands digging into my ass while he sucks my balls.

Fuuuuck!

Luckily, my day's packed with interviews, a sports massage and some physio, followed by some social-media commitments to advertise the Austrian event. They've asked for me, along with one of the Swedes, Johannes and Yorris. At least they've picked some of the more entertaining drivers, the ones with personalities, so I'm sure we'll have a laugh.

Even better, afterwards we all head out together for dinner and drinks. Kian might not want to socialise with his competitors but I don't see what the problem is.

Yorris is an interesting one. I don't know him that well, and I'm not sure about him at first. He gives off ultimate asshole vibes in a way that's neither cool nor sexy, but once you get a couple drinks in him he's bloody hilarious.

'That guy's been staring at you all night.' He's pointing the neck of his beer bottle at a gorgeous twink who, as correctly said by Yorris, can't take his eyes off of me.

The twink's not even trying to be discreet and when we make eye contact he beckons me over.

'Right then, lads,' I say, clapping my hands against my thighs, 'enjoy the rest of your evening. Don't do anything I wouldn't do.'

Johannes slides out of the booth so I can get out, shooting me a disapproving glance that almost replicates one of Kian's, but there's no stopping me.

The cute guy's an easy score. My hand on his shoulder and three seconds of unwavering eye contact is all it takes for him to agree to get out of there with me.

It's only when we're outside the bar and getting into the Uber I've summoned that I realise I'm not quite sure where I'm going to take him.

My bed in the motorhome is really comfy, but the walls are paper thin and Kian's definitely going to hear.

Which is perfect.

I'll show him what he's missing out on.

'I've never been fucked by a celebrity,' says the twink the second we're inside the motorhome. It's an instant turn-off. They're all the same, just looking for their five minutes of fame.

It never used to bother me at first – it felt nice to be worshipped – but recently it's started to give me the ick. I almost want to stop and tell him to bugger off home.

But I don't. Instead, I pull him towards my room and we start fumbling in the doorway. He's trying to unbutton my jeans and I'm working my way down his buttoned shirt, trailing little kisses and nips across his collar bone until his skin flares red and he's mewling every time I sink my teeth in a little further than I probably should.

'You're so fucking good at that. My friend was right about you last year.'

Bloody hell! Why couldn't he just keep his mouth shut? I'm regretting not keeping a ball gag in my travel kit.

I don't justify his stupidity with a response, instead I bite into the skin of his shoulder, and this time he winces.

Good.

I quickly kiss it better though. I don't want tomorrow's tabloid headlines to be calling me a biter – or some kind of weird fetishist cannibal.

Anders would *not* like that.

The twink works my jeans and boxers down my thighs, leaving them around my ankles, and then sinks to the floor. He's eye-to-eye with my dick and he starts running his tongue over the tip before tracing the underneath of my shaft, leaving me whimpering out a moan. I reach for something to brace myself against and find the door frame as this man does magic things with his mouth.

He's loving every second of it, hollowing his cheeks and

177

sucking hard, taking as much of me as he can into his mouth. He gags slightly as my dick slams into the back of his throat.

He's talented, I'll give him that, and at least it's stopped him ruining the mood by saying stupid shit. I really need this release after what occurred in this trailer earlier today. Eyes closed, summoning up the memory of this morning's yoga session, I can almost imagine it's Kian on his knees in front of me.

Nothing's going to stop me getting off right now.

'You're taking the actual piss now!' Kian hisses from his doorway. The guy, whose name I can't remember, is startled into choking on my dick. 'Do whoever you want in your room, but this is a joke. We have to share this space. I don't want to be stepping in your fucking cum on the way to the bathroom.'

The twink is terrified and gets up off his knees. I'm lucky he doesn't take my dick off with how quickly he pulls away.

'Fuck! Is that Kian Walker? You share with Kian Walker? Man, you're so lucky. I'd much rather be blowing him than you – no offence.' Why do people bloody say that when they've clearly just said something offensive?

'No, thanks,' Kian says, but it does nothing for my bruised ego. I'd rather be sucking Kian Walker's dick, too.

'You should probably leave,' I suggest, and he's out of here faster than a rat up a drainpipe. 'Thanks for that,' I say, turning my attention back to Kian.

The front porch light illuminates him in his doorway. He does not look happy, the tips of his ears and high points of his cheeks are beetroot red and I'm not sure if it's because he caught me getting my dick sucked or because he's been woken up.

Either way, he looks cute all ruffled up like this.

It's only then I remember that my dick is still hanging out, and it definitely did not get the memo that it's time to stand down. I think I'm even more turned on now than when I was balls-deep in the twink's mouth.

Yet I know that if I don't pull my boxers up Kian's probably going to amputate my dick, so I tug them up quickly, along with my jeans.

'About fucking time,' he says, still lingering in his doorway like the dirty little creep he is.

'Disappointed?'

Even in the dim light it's hard not to see how his eyes darken, almost like he maybe is disappointed. Or maybe it's just wishful thinking.

'Only that I have to share this place with you for eleven more weeks.'

It's a stone-cold lie. He's not even selling it to himself, never mind me.

'Keep telling yourself that,' I say, dropping the bombshell almost as quickly as I dropped my trousers for the guy whose name I still can't recall. I step back into my room and slam the door closed behind me, imagining him rushing over to peep through a crack while I finish myself off.

It's fast, hard, and I don't even try to be quiet when I cum.

My only regret is that this door doesn't have a peephole so I can see just how much I've shocked him.

Chapter Fifteen

Kian

Seeing that guy on his knees in front of Harper affected me in a way I can't even begin to admit.

The original reason for me seeing them – a desperate need to piss – was no longer possible afterwards because my dick was so hard and I'd silently had to relieve myself when I climbed back into bed. It was the way Harper's eyes rolled back as the guy enthusiastically sucked his cock that tipped me over the edge. It felt like the image was burned onto my retinas so that when I climbed back into bed and stared blindly at the ceiling, I could see nothing but the utter bliss on his face. I got harder and harder, maybe even more so when he realised I'd been stood in the door frame watching wordlessly for a couple seconds before I announced my presence.

I'd had to readjust to stop it being obvious that the sight was turning me on, but Harper knew. His shit-eating grin told me so.

Yet the second I snapped out of the trance, there was nothing left but rage. It's one thing being a bit untidy, leaving dirty dishes on the side and clothes all over the floor, but having sex in our shared space? That's inconsiderate, unforgivable and downright gross.

I'm still thinking about it when I wake up. It's taken years of practice to focus during qualifiers, and I need the structure of my routine more than ever in order to centre myself and approach the race in the right frame of mind, but the images of last night are a constant in my brain. I fall into bed that night and have another terrible night's sleep.

As a result, I'm late to my morning yoga practice. It's way after eight when I finally roll out my mat and get going in the lounge, but I have to trust the process and follow the steps that I know work for me.

I'm in the sun salutation pose when Harper appears. I think for a second that he's about to piss me off and watch me from the sofa again, but he's fully dressed in team apparel and sprints out of the door before I can even say good morning.

He doesn't say where he's going, and when I check our shared calendar once I finish my routine there isn't anything in his diary for this early in the morning.

It's strange. I'm almost a little bit worried about what the hell he's up to, but it only takes a flash of his rock-hard dick appearing in my mind to dash away any worry. Harper's a selfish fucker, and I need to focus only on my own performance.

Several hours later, he returns from wherever he's been, a blaze of silent fury trailing behind him. He locks himself in his room, the whole place eerily quiet until it's time to leave for the track.

What's even weirder is that he doesn't say anything the whole way over. Normally he's rattling on about anything and everything, or ribbing me about the yoga and meditation he's *'caught'* me doing more times than I care to admit.

If anyone accused me of having moved to doing it in the living room so he can watch, I would deny it to my dying breath. But you know what they say about love and war.

The second we enter the garage, I'm pulled into a couple of pre-race interviews on the track. There's always so much more of a buzz when you're being interviewed in front of the crowd. People cheer and chant, and I spot at least a dozen people in Hendersohm merch, some of whom are holding up signs with my name on them. The backdrop won't do my reputation any damage, and my ego does a little happy dance. *They're* not asking when I'm going to retire.

'We always see you with headphones on when you're warming up on the side of the track. Who or what are you listening to?' the Sky Sports presenter asks. I haven't heard this one in a while, maybe because when I was asked this a lot at the beginning of my racing career, my answers always used to be the same.

Not anymore. 'Sometimes it's a guided-meditation podcast, sometimes it's Noah Kahan or Hozier.'

She nods along as though I'm going to expand on that but suddenly I'm frozen. Harper, his hood pulled up over his head, is standing in the shadow of a feather flag branded with the logos of the team and our major sponsors, and he's wiping his eyes. It's not something I ever thought I'd see.

The reporter's started speaking again and I thank God this isn't live because I miss every single word she's saying. All my brain power is focused on Harper.

What the hell is going on?

'I'm so sorry, could you repeat the question?' I ask as politely as possible, trying not to come across as an arrogant prick.

'I asked why guided meditation?'

'I find it helps me get my head into the right space. Racing is as much a mental game as it is physical. Being in the right headspace is just as important as putting in the gym work or time on the track. It affects my performance massively. I know most drivers sway towards more upbeat music to get them pumped, but this is what works for me.'

Or at least, it normally does. It's failed me a couple of times recently.

Not today though. I won't let it fail me today.

Today I have to have my wits about me. I can't afford to worry about what's going on with Harper. He certainly won't be worrying about what's going on with me.

We both have good starting positions, but that's the last time the picture looks good.

Lap one, we lose two people straight away. A minor crash that neither of their cars can recover from happens right in front of me. Even with only minimal debris, I have to fight to avoid hitting it and that slows down my lap.

It's their accident, but it's beyond frustrating for me when every single second really counts.

Then, just two laps later, it happens again.

'What's going on out here, Cole?' I ask as another yellow flag appears and I have to slow again.

'It's one of the Ferrari guys – we're just waiting to find out. Could be serious. Crashed into the barrier. May be a safety car incoming. I'll keep you up to date.' This track isn't really known for crashes so I'm shocked there's so many.

'How many people down are we right now?'

'Four.'

'Who's in P1?'

'Yorris. You're close, though. You're still in P2. Keep pushing.'

'And Harper?'

There's silence for a brief moment, almost as if he's letting me finish my lap before he replies. Even though he knows me well and has been my race engineer for, like, five years, he doesn't see how stressed this delay makes me.

Especially after how Harper was this morning.

I zoom across the line again, gearing up for another lap, when he says, 'P16.'

I've got time still to push Yorris and try to get up to P1, but Harper's clearly having a shocker.

'What's his problem?' I ask, but Cole doesn't know. Harper must be absolutely gutted. Dead last, on a day like today, is not where anybody wants to be.

Luckily, I'm able to push the thought of him upset to the back of my mind. I don't manage to overtake Yorris and have to be content with a P2 finish, but I'll take it.

Harper, on the other hand, limps home.

I hope someone's checking in on him and that he's not alone right now. Ash will be on it, I'm sure. It can so easily become a dark time when you have a really bad day after previously doing so well. It's a gut punch that just keeps on punching while your mental game spirals into a hole. And it's not like you can forget about it, because you'll have to answer press questions about your performance and then read about the analysis of your mistakes. Then, ahead of the next race, you'll be asked about how you're going to fix your mistakes, and what you do to pick yourself back up after such a failure. It's like being slapped in the face with your failure right when you need to be talking yourself up.

When I get out of the cockpit, the garage is quieter than normal after a Hendersohm driver finishes second, and I know instantly it's because of Harper.

He's sitting in the corner, a team hoodie pulled on over his suit, the strings tightened around his face so he can't see or be seen. I don't even know what to say. It's a devastating sight, and I suspect he's crying under there. To finish outside the top ten can be soul-destroying, and he doesn't have the resilience of an experienced driver. Sometimes I forget he's a rookie still in his first season.

It must only be making him feel worse that we'll slip into second place in the Constructors' Championship as part of the fallout from his result. He knows it's his fault – there's no two ways about it. This isn't like football where a mistake could be made by three or four or more players, or compounded by different incidents, to cause the loss overall. The way the points get divided up in the sport makes it obvious.

When he's sitting there, completely miserable, especially after how quiet he was this morning, I don't have it in me to be annoyed at him. He has to write off Austria and focus on what comes next – Silverstone. That's our home turf and we have to smash it. It's not like I finished first today, even I could have done more to be first rather than second.

I just hope Harper knows how to deal with setbacks and doesn't end up spiralling, and that Johannes is the kind of friend who doesn't kick a man when he's down.

Normally, by this point of the post-race analysis, Harper's joking about with Ash, finding out specific lap times and going through individual points of the race where the tyres didn't feel great or looking at footage of key moments.

Ash tries, bless him. He brings up highlights of Harper's laps, but it's not working. Harper's heading for a meltdown, and because this is the first time this has happened, nobody knows how to help him. Is he an angry whirlwind, does he smash and break things, or does he sulk? There's a kind of collective breath-holding while we wait to find out.

Instead, it just breaks him.

He shuts down completely. It's like the soul is sucked out of him. It's utter devastation.

Thankfully, Anders releases him from doing any media and Harper leaves so quickly that it's almost like he evaporates. Unfortunately, there're journos already lingering nearby and he has a battle to get to a car while savage questions are being fired at him about his performance. I hope to God that he's 'no commenting' everything, mostly so that he doesn't say something he'll regret.

Anders jogs after him, calling out that 'no media' doesn't mean he can just leave, but Harper's already gone.

I'm left to tackle the media alone and not a single one of them wants to talk about my P2 finish. Everyone wants to know what's up with Harper James.

'Was it a technical or engineering issue?' one of them shouts, microphone stick dangling over a whole other heap of columnist and radio presenters.

'Not that we're aware of. There will of course be in-depth post-race analysis of the car, but it didn't seem to be a mechanical fault.'

'So we're looking at driver error for his poor performance today, then?'

That boils my blood a little. Could he have done better? Of course he could, but he didn't cause any accidents on the track, he didn't screw up the car, he just had a really, really shitty day.

'Everyone has bad days. None of us are perfect – we're not robots. But the season is far from over. That's the beauty of motor racing. We learn from this race and put it into practice for the next one.' I drawl out so many answers like this to anyone trying to goad me into bad-mouthing Harper, especially when they bring up the fact that Harper might have cost us a win in the Constructors' Championship. My tone gets sharper as the questions continue. I don't know when I became so protective of Harper James, but it's got nothing to do with Anders's threats and everything to do with the image of him huddled in the corner looking like his heart was going to break.

I just want to get home now – mainly back to the UK where I will see my family and feel the strength of their love and support, but also back to the motorhome.

Even though I'm not quite sure what I'm heading '*home*' to.

With how distraught he was when he stormed out of the pit, taking his frustration out on all the waiting journalists, and ignoring Anders's calls for him to stop, I have no clue.

Maybe he's trashed it, set it on fire, or maybe he's drowning his sorrows in vodka or blow-jobs with randos. It's hard to predict with Harper.

It's quiet as I step in through the door. All the lights are off and as I turn them on one by one, I take note that nothing's broken, smashed, or on fire.

There's an eeriness to the silence, though. It's almost too much. I didn't hang around that long after the team debrief so I'm surprised he's managed to come home, shower, and head out in this time, but then again nothing should surprise me about Harper James anymore. He does whatever he damn well wants and screw the consequences – or the collateral damage.

I'm about to take a shower myself, my hand hovering over the button, when the softest noise leaks under the door of the Jack and Jill bathroom. It's almost inaudible, as though my mind's playing tricks on me. Until I press my ear up against the door, and there it is again: small sobs. I can almost picture them wracking his body, his chest rising and falling as he struggles to control the sound.

It's downright heartbreaking. Even more so from a guy who has the toughest shell going.

I can't stop listening, and I feel like the world's worst person that I'm just standing here eavesdropping on his pain instead of going in there and checking on him.

But what do I say to the guy who's got a hard layer of arrogance around him that he wears like armour? Who would likely vigorously reject any attempts to comfort or console him?

A guy I've kissed once and not stopped thinking about since?

Chapter Sixteen

Harper

Words like *'final chance'* and *'time to get it together'* and *'you're one more fuck up from having to look for another team'* ring in my ears as I stride back to the motorhome. I'm bypassing the journalists with a face like thunder, yet it doesn't stop them crowing about my fall from grace right now.

Sixteenth. Six-fucking-teenth. I can't even remember the last time I placed so low. I can't remember the last time in either my lower or top-category career to date that I've placed outside the top ten.

Even worse, we've been knocked off the top spot in the Constructors' Championship. It's gutting. The only thing more gutting was the look on everyone's faces as they realised what this would mean – and then Kian's whole face just dropped. Anders did not look happy at all.

And it's completely my fault. I'm to blame.

I always ignore the fun police who try to get in the way of

me living my life. But I'm not a complete idiot – since getting called up to Championship racing, even I've been more careful. At the beginning of the season, Anna laid out a clear set of expectations of the behaviour of a Hendersohm driver. A basic list of do's and don'ts, if you will. And since I signed my contract, I haven't deviated greatly from it. I haven't done anything that could get me fired. Whatever Kian thinks, I *want* to be here. The irony is that what's going to get me fired is something I did before the season even started.

I had a foursome about two years ago, and now it's come back to haunt me, because of course someone made a video. My agent's PR team has apparently been run ragged trying to contain the story. I guess I wasn't high-profile enough before now, and my blackmailer was waiting until I hit the big time so he could get more money for it. He planned to sell it to the media, but instead I am apparently going to be buying it, with a hefty portion of this season's payout.

There's nothing wrong with the foursome in principle, since it was all fully consensual and everyone was of legal age, but Anders lost his mind because of course the owners, the sponsors and the VIPs would be extremely unhappy. I haven't crossed any hard lines this season, but I know I've skirted some grey areas, and after the bollocking Anders gave us back in Bahrain I knew I couldn't take the piss. But even if I had behaved like golden boy, Mr Boring Bastard, himself, this thing would still have come back to bite me in the ass. Apparently they held a senior team meeting and decided I would be on a final warning. One more fuck-up and I'm out. Whatever Kian's been whispering in Jackson's ear has obviously filtered up to Anders. I'm just lucky that Elijah's not fit enough to return yet otherwise I think they'd have fired me already.

People have been telling me my whole life to get my shit together. Not to do anything that would jeopardise my career. I've always told them to fuck off. But they were right. They've always been right. Maybe that's why I push so hard, and drive so fast – because I'm trying to escape the demons I know are chasing me. The demons that are always chasing me. The mistakes I've already made. If I drink enough, fuck enough, win enough, then one day I'll be big enough that the demons can't hurt me anymore. Isn't that the dream of every kid like me? To leave behind the fear that one day you'll be found out and tossed back on the shit-heap you came from? I heard someone call it imposter syndrome once, but that's some serious therapy bullshit right there. It's different for kids like me, the ones with nothing to fall back on, with nowhere to go and no one to run to.

I'm fucking up all over the place – with the team, with Kian, with my life in general. I've probably been fucking up my whole life.

Now I've cost the team points and possibly the Constructors' Championship. And for what? A couple of sub-par orgasms from guys who are clearly absolute dickheads.

I can't even call Johannes. I've barely seen him recently. He's always busy with the secret he's keeping from me, and I don't think he'd even understand anyway. And who else would care? There are so many names and numbers in my phone, but not a single one I can call about this.

So I slump back to the motorhome and lock myself in my room.

For what feels like hours, but in reality is just too many long minutes thinking about what's gone wrong, I lie staring up at the dark ceiling. I'm not used to so much silence.

I'm so quiet that I hear Kian return, the way he potters around the living area. He's probably tidying, but maybe he's looking for me? Or maybe I must be delusional to even think Kian would care what I'm doing. There's something comforting about the sound of him moving about. I imagine him being relieved that he's got the place to himself for a bit. Of course he wants me gone. Who wouldn't?

Well, he'll get his wish soon enough. I knew this couldn't last. I knew I'd mess it up eventually. Just like I mess everything up. I don't belong here, after all.

I turn into the pillow and stuff it into my mouth to hide the sounds I'm making, but I don't seem to be able to stop.

Eventually, I hear the shower turn on and I'm almost relieved that the noise of the water splashing against the tiles will cover my sobs. Maybe it will also drown out the noise in my head.

Except it's short-lived. Kian's either taken the quickest shower in history or he turned it on so I wouldn't hear him shitting. I couldn't decide which was worst, because a long shower was always needed after a race day to get rid of the stench of rubber and petrol. I carry on crying into my pillow until I'm all cried out. I think I heard Kian go out and I hope he's just being kind and giving me some space, although I know I don't deserve it.

The light knock on the door, when it comes, is both expected and unexpected.

Expected in that I thought he'd be straight in here the second he got home, shooting his mouth off about how shit I am, how disappointed he is, how I've fucked it for both of us. And I wouldn't have even blamed him.

Unexpected, because when I mutter for him to come in

there's a bag of takeout in one of his hands and a couple of beers dangling between the fingers of the other.

'Am I okay to come in?' he asks from the doorway, a shaft of light creeping into my room.

I can't remember the last time someone saw me cry. I was maybe ... fourteen? That great foster home, the family I thought would finally adopt me, asked me to come in and sit down one evening. I knew exactly which conversation was coming.

Time to go. Again.

I was long past sobbing like a kid by then, but I hadn't been able to prevent silent tears from running down my face as they let me know that the social worker would be by in the morning and they'd help me pack up my bits into a couple of bin bags. The bits which had made the room upstairs my own.

While it's still relatively dark, I make an effort to wipe my face, just in case there's any chance he doesn't know. He rests the takeout on the end of my bed before whipping out two trays from under his arm. It's a little fumbly until he turns on my bedside lamp which casts a warm glow over us both. It's just enough light to plate up.

He's brought a mixture of everything – noodles, rice, a variety of meats in different fruity sauces. Most importantly, salt-and-pepper chips. I'm not even sure what's happening or why, but I can't tell him how much I need this right now. I don't have words to express how comforting this food is, and how much it reminds me of cheap dinners when I was young. No matter where I was living, salt-and-pepper chips from the Chinese tasted the same – and filled me up.

'It's not that I'm not grateful for this,' I start, snuffling as I try to think of the best way to finish my sentence, 'but ... why?'

It's not graceful, but then neither is the way I wipe my snotty nose on the duvet, but it's who I am.

'Today was shit and it's Chinese takeout. I think we both might need it.'

He's calm and composed as he sits on my bed, resting his back against the wall at three o'clock to my twelve. The Chinese feast sitting in between us at one and two as he starts to eat.

'It was only shit because *I* was. Sorry about that, by the way.'

He looks at me like a white rabbit just hopped out of my mouth and is dancing a jig on the floor.

'Blimey! Never thought I'd hear that word coming out of Harper James's mouth.' He pops off the cap of one beer and hands it to me before doing the same to his.

'You're voluntarily drinking a beer. Never thought I'd see the day, either.' We clink the necks of the bottles and tuck in. I take a sip and then look at the label. Non-alcoholic beer. Some things never change, I guess.

Silence descends again, but with every mouthful I can sense him watching me. There are questions on the tip of his tongue, and queries in the way his eyes have softened at the sight of the tear tracks still there on my face. For once, I kind of want him to ask. I *want* him to ask so I can tell him. I think I want him to know.

But, until our plates are cleared and the leftovers are packaged back up, we don't speak. When he leaves the room to put them in the fridge, our empty beer bottles with him, I'm not convinced he's going to come back. He's done his good deed of the day; he has no responsibility here. He could go to his own room, call his sister and pretend this never happened;

that we didn't have a civil moment when it felt like we could breathe the same air with fighting or fucking.

Yet he comes back, a second beer each in hand and settles himself back on the end of my bed. The way we're both sitting makes our feet meet in the middle, and neither of us make a move to pull them away.

'What happened?' he finally asks. 'You've held it together all season. Even the harshest critics say you've had an amazing first half of the season for a rookie. Tabloid headlines aside, your game on the track has been great.'

'I'm surprised you don't already know. Everyone else seems to. On my last chance now, aren't I?'

'And you thought throwing away your performance, too, was the way to deal with that?'

I almost growl at him. 'Of course I fucking didn't. Couldn't get my head in the game, could I? This is literally all I've ever wanted.'

'I don't get why you act like you don't care, then. All the partying, drinking, and one-night stands … you're your own worst enemy. It's almost like you're self—' He stops suddenly, as if he only figured it out while he was saying it. 'It's self-sabotage, isn't it? Harper?'

He shoves my shoulder.

'Messed up, right?' I shrug because there's no point trying to hide anything now. It's not like we're talking about my future in the sport I love, the only thing I know how to do. 'I don't know how to stop.'

'Why, though? You've got the world at your fingertips right now. What are you so scared of?'

That the thing I want more than anything won't want me back.

Tears sting the backs of my eyes. How is there anything left in my ducts right now?

'I think it's called abandonment issues.'

That's what the therapists said, anyway. I saw several when I was a teenager, but it was always patchy and inconsistent, depending on where I was living at the time. I was never with any one therapist long enough to learn how to open up or be vulnerable, and life taught me not to rely on anyone but myself. 'Probably some trust issues, too.' I've always managed to skate over the top of team psychologists and performance coaching as part of my professional career, and now here we are.

Here we are, I think to myself. He's here, and he's asking, and I want to tell him.

I take a deep breath and launch in.

'I was an accident. Teen parents, still in college, who definitely didn't want me, but found out too late to do anything about it. I think they still tried, though. I don't remember them really, but they kept me till I was almost six and then dumped me on my grandma and disappeared. Or at least, that's what my file says. Gran was great, but when I turned ten she was diagnosed with stage four cancer and was gone within five months.'

Kian reaches for me and I let him pull me into his side. It can't be comfortable for him but it feels nice for me. 'I went into care at that point. No other blood relatives would take me and my parents were long gone. I was just about old enough to understand that nobody cared about me, nobody wanted me, and there wasn't a single person in the world who loved me.'

Kian tenses against my side. I don't know what he was expecting, but I'm sure it wasn't this. He has his arm around me and he's holding me against him like his life depends on it. Or like mine does.

'Over the next eight years I bounced around nine different foster families, and none of them wanted me, either – not enough to keep me. Other kids I knew were fostered and never came back. They were adopted, and I wasn't, and that cemented it for me, I think.'

'I didn't know...' he starts, but I shake my head, cutting him off. Obviously he didn't know. It's not something I've ever talked about publicly.

'Don't get me wrong, most of the families were good to me. The last family really tried – they paid for my karting, tried to get me into therapy, tried to make me feel like I belonged, but I think all my walls were up by that point. The damage was done. It's easier to be constantly on the defensive. No one can hurt you if you don't give them a chance.'

'Christ, Harper! If it didn't make sense before, it does now. I know you want this because I can see it – everyone can – but you fuck about because you want to make sure that you have plenty of reasons tucked up your sleeve to explain why you got kicked out so it can never be because you aren't good enough.'

'Jesus. Maybe you should go into therapy when you retire.'

He groans. 'Not you with that word again.'

'Why does it make you so angry?'

I see the way frustration pulls at his face every time a reporter asks about his plans once this season is over.

'I'm not angry. I just feel like it's a done deal in everyone else's mind but mine. I'm not thinking about it until after this season is over. I'm here and I want to hold on to my title, and that's all that matters. I'm not sure if it'll be my last or if I'll have five more.'

'You're having a great season, but sometimes it seems like you're not having a very good time. Like you don't love it anymore. Like you don't want to be here.'

I've noticed this, I realise now. He still seems excited about every win, but at the same time detached from the magnitude of how great he is and not able to actually enjoy the experience.

'I don't always want to be here, that's why.' His words are so simple, and I know he means it.

'Because of me?' I'm almost afraid to ask, but this might be my only chance.

'You know about my mum, right?'

I nod. Of course I do. The whole of the UK was rocked when the news dropped that Chastity Walker had been diagnosed with early onset Parkinson's.

'She's gone downhill a lot and my sister is now her primary carer. Elise has given up so much to look after her, and then there's me, gallivanting around the world as though it's not my responsibility'

'I can't see your mum disapproving of you living your dream. I mean, isn't that what she did? I think I read an article that said she took you and your sister on tour when you were younger.'

I'm not about to admit that I've read every article there is about Tyler Heath and Chastity Walker.

'The difference being that neither of us was sick. She didn't abandon us for her dreams. She made sure we had the best life, even when we were living out of a tour bus.'

'But you didn't have a normal life. It can't have been an easy childhood, and you paid the price for her achieving her dreams. It proves she was willing to do anything to have her pop career. How is that different to what you're doing?'

It stumps him for a while, almost like he's trying to wrack his brain to prove me wrong. But he can't and that should be a good thing, yet it clearly isn't. He looks as shattered as I feel.

We both still smell like the track, and sadly not like drivers who've been sprayed in victory champagne – something that definitely should've happened in Austria. We were the favourites to win P1 and P2 and we threw it all away. Well, I did at least.

We might be a team, but right now I don't feel like there's anything we can do to make things right for each other. And I find I actually want to make things right for Kian. Not because his father is Tyler Heath or because he used to be my idol. But because tonight he tried to make things better for me.

So I do the only other thing I'm good at outside of racing. I lean into his personal space, eyes searching for any signs that he doesn't want this as well. When the signs don't appear, I capture his lips with my own and silently plead for him to open up for me more in this way instead.

When he does, I sense it immediately and I don't hesitate. It takes only seconds for me to be on top of him, our tongues tied together, hands cupping each other's faces in a moment that feels sweet and sensual. It's not the sexy explosion I've imagined a thousand times with Kian as I've laid in bed alone, wondering whether he's thinking of me, too. Somehow I know he won't pull away this time, so I slow down and take my time, no longer desperate to get in and get out before I'm rejected.

The whole thing is overwhelmingly different as a result. From how leisurely we're moving together to the way we're both sporting rock-hard erections but neither of us is rushing to get naked or move on to the next stage.

Even this kiss doesn't feel like it's just a precursor to sex, even though I'm hoping we'll get there eventually. It's almost as if we're finally getting what we want from each other, what I've needed from him since the second he put me in my place on the jet to Bahrain.

It's like I'm consuming him, sampling everything he has to offer, and properly savouring it like it's enough just to be doing this. But then, hands finally roaming, I find the hem of his T-shirt. I play with it until he gets the message and breaks the kiss to whip it over his head.

Kian's a beautiful specimen. He has a wide, toned chest with a smattering of dark hair poking through and V-cut that I know is the result of some spectacular gym work and yoga. He needs to get a full body wax soon so that the suit doesn't ruberfect the dusky pink nipples that I'm dying to play with. I plan to worship it, to give it the adoration it surely deserves.

Except he takes control. I'm not sure why I'm surprised, since he performs best when he's in charge, and honestly I'm happy to sit back and let it happen. The thing about going slowly is that it feels like there's going to be time for everything. It's a new experience for me.

He nips and sucks at my bare chest, his other hand undoing the drawstrings of my sweat pants so he can force them over the curve of my ass and down my thighs. His joggers quickly follow suit until only boxers stand in the way. Mine are not doing a good job at all of restraining the heavy bulge between my legs, and I hope he knows it's all for him.

He reaches his hand inside and curls his fingers around my cock, rubbing up and down over the head. I let out a hiss – I'm not sure why everything feels so hypersensitive but I love it. He starts to pump up and down and I reach for him too before I lose my mind completely. He's just as hard as I am, and he feels so fucking good in my hand.

Every ounce of patience goes out the window at this point and suddenly we're a sweaty, frantic mess grinding against each other. We discard our boxers so our erections can slide along each other, creating that delicious friction we both seem to be craving. I grab his ass, the ass I've been fantasising about for weeks – no, months – and pull him hard against me. He cups my face again while he kisses me, and I think there is a sweetness to the moment that I've never known before. There is enough space between the action for me to *feel*, too, and I find I am not afraid of it.

It doesn't take much for us both to be panting, moaning messes. And when Kian's hand leaves my face to tug my balls, there's no holding back for me.

'I'm coming,' I pant. He's only seconds behind me, though, and two last pumps has him following suit on mine.

There are no words.

None are needed.

The high I feel isn't wearing off anytime soon, and in the blissful state that follows, there's nothing else I can do other than fall asleep pressed tightly against his side.

Chapter Seventeen

Kian

Never have I longed for a flight to be over so quickly. It's only a two-hour journey, but with how I've been counting down the minutes it's felt about twenty.

The crew even manage a dinner service but it's definitely contributed to making the flight feel ten times longer.

The guys who've flown with us are all napping, preparing for what's going to be an incredibly busy time back in the UK where everyone wants a piece of us, but Anna's wide awake.

Wide awake and striding down the aisle to where Harper and I are sitting, his head resting on my shoulder and his hand on the top of my thigh under the blanket I conveniently have spread over my lap.

I nudge him so he doesn't give anything away, but he only grins when he cracks an eye open to see Anna coming our way. He even brushes my cock as he pulls his hand back, and I know he's teasing me.

Asshole.

'Well this is cosy. Are we finally playing for the same team?'

I almost choke on nothing but the recycled plane air. She has no clue what's going on, but her comment has me almost losing it. Next to me, Harper cracks up, his laughter like a wolf howling as he wakes up half the plane.

'You two are very weird, but we don't have time to unpack that right now.'

She hands us laminated cards, which look suspiciously like tightly-packed schedules, and I groan.

I love the hype I get in the UK, and because Hendersohm has had only British drivers for the last decade and a half, the team is treated like homegrown heroes, but I could do with a break. Especially now.

'Okay, so tonight you'll be recording on the *Need for Speed* podcast and then first thing tomorrow morning there's a four-hour slot for a photoshoot for some of the new team merchandise and then in the evening you'll be on the evening sports slot on the BBC news.'

While Anna's speaking I cast my eye over the details of the rest of the next two weeks and the schedule looks absolutely insane. She continues to run through how every minute of our time is going to be taken up by some photo shoot or soundbite recording and whilst I love this side of being a pro driver, I can't help but wonder when Harper and I are going to get any time together. Or when I'm going to be able to nip back to Norfolk to see Mum, Elise and the kids.

It's a lot, to say the least.

'So what you're saying, Anna, is that I'll be getting around three hours of sleep a night and working out and eating at, like, three in the morning?' I'm teasing, but I also have a system of preparation that I need to follow for each race – important stuff that impacts how well I do.

'Whatever works for you, Kian. Just make sure you're on time and that you drag him along with you.'

'Hey! I'm getting more and more punctual all the time,' Harper interjects, but Anna just laughs in his face. I love that she doesn't take his shit. She's the most perfect fit for a PR manager in Hendersohm.

'Whatever you need to tell yourself, rookie.'

Patting the top of his unruly curls, she takes off back down the plane to her own seat.

The week descends into chaos. Never have I ever been so busy in my life. Even more so when my agent drops into casual conversation that my favourite brand of gym-wear wants me to be one of their new faces, but they need me to do some model test-shots while I'm in the UK in order to be sure. Because of the way Anna's packed the schedule, there's no way I can make it back to Norfolk to see my family.

It's crushing. I'm so close and yet I might as well be on the other side of the world.

And then, two nights before qualifiers, I get the best text ever.

> Managed to sort carers for Mum, so me, Grant and the kids are coming up to Silverstone for the weekend. Will drive up in time for dinner after qualifying and stay till Monday!

Of course, I'm curled up in bed with Harper when I get it. We're both naked, and still breathing heavily after another mind-blowing orgasm, so he catches the way my face lights up at the text.

'Should I be worried that someone else is making you smile like that when I'm lying right next to you?' he asks, lifting himself up on his elbows. His chin rests on my bare chest as he looks up at me with teasing eyes shining in the light of my phone.

Would he actually be worried if there was another guy or girl texting me right now? Would that bother him? Would it make him jealous? I'm not sure, because he's not exactly forthcoming about his feelings. And more importantly, do I want him to be worried?

'Um, Elise is here for the next few days as her husband's got some time off work and she thinks Cassie will enjoy some of the race, even though she won't make it through all of it. I'm gonna go and meet them for dinner, and maybe stay at their hotel the night before qualifiers so I can put the kids to bed.'

I don't know why I feel so nervous telling him this. It's quite normal for family to come and watch your home Grand Prix, but it only highlights the awful truth that Harper doesn't have any family. I can't bear that he's going to be alone. Not *alone* alone, because his best friend is here, too, and so am I, but alone in the sense that there'll be no one on the side supporting him this weekend.

'I'm so excited for you. I bet you're dying to see them?' I can tell by the smile on his face that he means it. His whole stupid, gorgeous face…

'I just wish I could get home to see Mum. It feels weird to know that she's going to be with temporary carers for the next couple of days. Two random strangers she's never met before… But then, it's not like I'm there most of the year so I feel guilty all the time anyway. I don't know. I feel a bit stressed about it and, like, I think Elise is—'

I don't get any more words out as he kisses me to stop me talking. My brain short-circuits, allowing me a few minutes to forget about my worries outside the four walls of this motorhome.

He pushes me back down onto the bed, straddling my hips as he chases my lips as I fall back into the couch. It's delicious in every sense of the word. His lips taste like sweet cherry cola with a side of raw passion. He sighs as I part my lips and let him in, like there's nothing he wants more in this moment.

There's desire spiralling through my body, but he's not hard as I grind up against him. Maybe he needs a bit longer to recover, but I choose to read it as an indication that he doesn't want more than this right now. He's not looking to lose himself in physical release; he's looking for connection. It's caring and, dare I say it, loving. He's kissing me to shut me up, but he also knows this will take my mind off my worries. It feels like he's doing this for *me* rather than for his own pleasure. It might be the most unselfish thing he's done all season.

I push my hands into his hair and grip the back of his head, bringing him closer – if that's even possible. I can feel his heart beating in his chest and the way he kisses me back tells me he would fold himself into me if he could. I don't know what this feeling is, but I know I want more.

I get one of the best nights' sleep I've had on the road so far, and it's even better to wake up knowing that I'm going to get to see my family for the first time in four months.

There's all of Anna's media commitments to get through first. They fly by in a blur of banter with Harper, and then Sky Sports does a piece on my highlights from fifteen years in the sport, and finally I play a reaction-based game on BBC TV against four other drivers.

Then it's qualifiers, and I put on an absolute show for the crowd and most importantly my family. I sweep not only P1, but my personal-best lap time at Silverstone. The next thing I know I'm pulling up at the restaurant, eyes frantically searching every table for my family.

In ultimate twin behaviour, Elise and I spot each other at exactly the same time and I'm sprinting towards her before we hug like it's the last time we'll ever get to do it.

'Oh, God, I don't think I've ever been this happy to see you!'

She all but jumps into my arms and I spin her around like we're little kids again. She snuffles into my shoulder and almost at the exact same time I feel tears pricking my eyes.

It's always been hard being away from my family for nine months of the year, but this season's been the worst. We're both getting older, my niece and nephew are growing up without their uncle, and Mum's not going to get any better. I'm missing out on so many firsts, and so many lasts.

It keeps retirement at the front of my mind all the time, and even more so in this moment.

'No tears, El, please. Let's just enjoy dinner and then tomorrow.'

'We saw you qualified in first place! Smashing it, baby bro.'

She punches my shoulder and then wipes the stray tears from her face.

Grant approaches with Jesse strapped to his front in a baby carrier and Cassie's little hand held firmly in his. I'm glad to be eating at 5pm if it means I get to see this pair. He offers me a half hug and then I quickly kneel down in front of Cassie.

She has her very own toy race car which she holds up to my face for inspection.

My eyes flick up to my sister and she shakes her head.

'Don't start. We were in the giftshop at the Silverstone Museum today whilst you were doing your media thing and free practice and she picked it herself. Don't even think about putting thoughts in her head about getting her into a kart. It's not allowed.'

She sounds serious, but I know she'd never stop her daughter following her dreams, even if it means following in her uncle's footsteps.

'No promises,' I reply. 'Hey, baby girl.' I pat the car. 'Did you enjoy the museum?'

She nods. 'You were on the wall.'

'She told every single person who walked past your mural that you're her uncle. I'm not sure how many people believed her but she was loving life.'

I remember going to see it when they first opened the 'through the decades' portion of the museum. I was shocked and also proud that I was being included in the 2010s section amongst so many of the greats, both past and present. I only wish I'd been able to go with them today.

'I'll take them back when they're a bit older so they can experience the true magic of it.' I know there are a couple of simulators Cassie wouldn't have been allowed on because of her age, and I'm already looking forward to taking both kids back there one day so they can see what their uncle did for a living, once upon a time.

We head to our table in the restaurant. Jesse stays asleep in the carrier, but I plop Cassie in a high chair next to me at the table. She babbles on and on about everything she's seen today and I'm completely at peace as I listen along, asking questions to find out more.

She chows down some pasta and a bowl of ice cream and then promptly falls asleep in the high chair while the rest of us finish eating.

'You look really well, Ki,' Elise says from across the table. Grant has his arm around her and she's leaning her head towards her son, admiring his little sleeping face. 'Better than I've seen you in forever. New skincare routine? Botox?'

'Ha ha,' I say sarcastically. It's not like I can tell her I've met someone, that I'm having the best sex of my life, that Harper James is making me happy and relieving some of my stress. 'Well, my agent did set up this brand partnership with Clinique Men. Anna brought me like two whole bags full of products after I signed on the dotted line.'

'I'm so jealous. Can you try and nab me a lifetime supply of their Dramatically Different moisturiser? It's my fave.'

'I'll see what I can do.'

The second I get home, I'll get Anna onto that. I'm sure there are some strings she could pull to make that happen.

'No, but seriously. Anything we should know?' They're both grinning at me like they already know my secret. 'Have you met someone? Who are they?'

Technically, I've never come out to Elise, but she's always known. She probably knew before I did.

I shrug. I don't want to lie to them. I've never lied to Elise in my whole life. But I'm not quite ready to talk about it. Harper and I haven't talked about what we are to each other, and I have no idea whether he would want me to say anything to my family.

'He's just some guy.' The words feel stale on my tongue as I downplay all the emotions that have been fluttering around inside me about Harper. It's the first time I've said anything out loud about him – about us.

She squeals, not using her inside voice, before squeezing her husband's arm. 'I told you, didn't I? I knew there's been something different about you recently. You've got that relationship glow.'

'It's not a relationship, per se.'

I mean, Harper isn't exactly the relationship type, is he? As far as I know, he's never even been in one. He also deals exclusively in one-night stands and we're definitely not that either. We're teammates. We're … friends, I think. But I don't want to jump the gun and assume we're anything else on top of that. Maybe like teammates ... with benefits.

'Okay, baby bro. You don't want to talk about it. I get that. We don't need the dirty details.' Like I was ever going to give her those! I'm not even planning to tell her his name. 'But he makes you happy, does he?' I nod. 'Well, that's all I need to know.'

And to my absolute surprise, she drops it for the rest of the meal.

Harper's tucked up in bed when I get back. I knew he wouldn't be out tonight considering we're racing tomorrow, but I'm more than glad he's here.

'Hey, handsome.' He's got one eye cracked open, observing

the way I'm lingering in the doorway and taking in every inch of him. His muscles ripple as he stretches out, like he's trying to shake off some of the sleepiness he's feeling. The duvet shifts and it reveals he's wearing a pair of my gym shorts and nothing else.

I almost wish I wasn't too tired to do anything other than sleep.

But we have to race tomorrow and it's more important than ever that we put on a good performance for the home crowd. We also need to get back on top of the league for the Constructors' Championship. In terms of fans and the media, support tomorrow will be immense – but so will the pressure.

'Did you have a good evening?' he asks as I begin to strip off my trousers, folding them neatly back over their hanger, before chucking my shirt into the laundry hamper we're now sharing. If the lovely lady who manages our laundry services has noticed, she hasn't said anything. At least, as far as I know.

'The best, thank you.' I slide into bed beside him and press a kiss to his bare shoulder. He snuggles into me automatically and I sling an arm over his waist, taking my place as the big spoon as per what's become the norm for us. 'The kids were both fast asleep after about half an hour of us being in the restaurant, so Elise and Grant and I got to catch up.'

'Sounds perfect. What did you eat?' I don't know why I love that he wants to know details about the evening, but I really, really do.

'They shared nachos, and then Elise crushed a massive burger and sweet potato fries. It had a hash brown and grilled pineapple on it. I was so jealous. Grant had steak, and Cassie had spag bol and ice cream. I could have hoovered up the lot, but I had grilled fish and an extra side of green veg instead.

Chris would not have approved if I'd had a rib-eye and fries, and I'd be in trouble at the weigh-in tomorrow.'

Our nutritionist would never cuss us out for having a treat, but every gram makes a difference at the elite level, and our kit is specifically designed to meet the specifications for both minimum and optimal weight. The night before such an important race is not the time to be undisciplined. I've made so many sacrifices to get where I am, and this is hardly the worst. The time for a treat meal is right *after* a race so you have time to metabolise and digest it before it will affect your performance on the next circuit.

'Sounds delicious. I Deliveroo'd a Turkish salad and FaceTimed Jo. We didn't talk for long, though. I think his mind was elsewhere and it made it feel … weird. Awkward, somehow. He was obviously distracted and it felt like he couldn't wait to get off the phone. I don't know why he didn't just say he was busy.'

'Have you told him about us?'

After the conversation with Elise this evening, I suddenly really want to know the answer to this. If he were going to tell anyone, it would be Johannes.

'No,' he confirms, and a slither of disappointment drips down my spine. I don't know why that hurts. I don't want this to be on public display when I don't even know what this is, but he tells Johannes everything. I'm not sure I want to be his dirty little secret.

'Oh. Then maybe he's just doing the same.' I don't mean to be cold, but I don't know what else to say. Yet when he tugs my arm to pull me closer and squeezes my hand over his heart, I forget why I'm even annoyed.

I should just enjoy the moment, enjoy having him so close,

enjoy the conversation that flows so easily between us since our truth-telling session back in Austria.

'Maybe.' He pulls my hand up to his lips and kisses each knuckle. 'I know we should probably be asleep, but my brain just feels so awake right now.'

He's started being honest with me too. It's like … since then, since he talked about his shitty childhood, he lets himself be vulnerable with me. He trusts me with his real self and doesn't need to hold anything back anymore.

'You worrying about something in particular, or just pre-race jitters?' I ask.

'Just about Johannes, I think, and why he won't talk to me about what's going on with him and whoever's occupying his attention.'

'Maybe he's not ready. Or maybe he knows you're not exactly the world's best relationship expert. Just keep trying, and be there for him when he's ready.'

'Yes, oh wise one.' There's a pause, and then he asks, 'Did you tell your sister about us?'

'No, well kinda, not about you, but like she knows me so well she could tell there was someone.'

'Oh.'

'Did you want me to?' I ask. 'You and I haven't exactly talked about it, and I didn't know whether you would—'

'No, no, I get it.' It surprises me that he sounds hurt. 'It's not like we're even sleeping together.'

I'm glad his back is to me so I can hide my wince.

'We are *literally* sleeping together right now,' I say.

But I know what he means. I don't want to be just another guy he fucks and forgets, so we've fooled around but that's it so far.

'Speaking of which, can we sleep now?'

He nods, but as I hold him close to my chest, his fingers play with mine like he's still mulling over his thoughts and it takes longer than I'd like for us to finally fall asleep.

Whatever was on his mind doesn't affect his performance the next day, though, because we romp home in P1 and P3. Hendersohm is pleased, the fans are thrilled, and the UK is once again proud of its boys. And Elise and the kids were there to see me do it.

It's a good day, a very good day.

Chapter Eighteen

Harper

I f you'd have told me four weeks ago that this motorhome
would become a blissful bubble of sex and spooning, I'd
have laughed in your face.

One, because I've never been a cuddler, and sex is all about
a quick thrill with no repeats.

And two, because although we've done everything else,
Kian and I have not actually shagged.

I know, I know. This could not be further from my usual
pattern.

I'm sure he wants to. I mean, I'm pretty sure he wants to. I
know I do.

And whilst neither of us seems to have figured out each
other's preference yet around anal, we're still going at it like
rabbits.

It turns out that Kian loves to sixty-nine and he's bloody
good at it. He seems to have this perfect rhythm of sucking me

off, whilst also thrusting down into my mouth. It leaves me with nothing to do other than to choke him down.

It's one of the hottest things I've ever been a part of – and I'm not exactly shy when it comes to sex. I've had my fair share of experiences – partners, groups, you name it – and yet, when it comes to Kian, something feels different.

He's good at taking control, which maybe I've never wanted before. In the past I've always gone for subs and twinks who want to be owned. I've always been a top, and I love to have my dick sucked. But right now there's nothing I want more than for him to tell me what to do. I want *him* to dominate *me* and it's a totally new experience. I usually just take charge, move the guy into position and then fuck him however I want. But I find I don't actually know how to ask for it. I don't know how to tell him what I want.

There was one time when he came back from the gym and pushed me against the wall. He didn't say a word, and when I put my hand down his boxers and started wanking him off he growled into my ear, 'Good boy,' and I thought my head might explode. It was such a turn-on, and when he came it took the barest graze of his hand across the head of my dick and I was right there with him. My obsession with pleasing him has me in a chokehold. Who knew being a good boy would feel like this?

And it's working out perfectly for me. It's taking the stress – which doesn't belong in the bedroom – out of sex. I'm not going out partying. I'm not drinking too much. I'm not picking up randoms and having to worry about what kind of story they'll sell to the press or put on social media.

Most nights I just slip down the narrow corridor, poke my head around Kian's door, and he beckons me in. Others, when the day's been long, we cuddle – *cuddle!* – on the sofa until things start to get handsy and Kian moves us to his bed.

And somehow, I always find myself falling asleep there after we go at it, even though every night I promise to go back to my own bed.

After the first night, I also promised myself that I'd get my fill of Kian, that I'd fuck him and then leave it be, and yet it's been weeks. I don't want anyone else.

Not when he's so mind-blowingly good.

Take right now, for example. We're in our shared motorhome in Stavelot, Belgium. We're moving on to Zandvoort in the Netherlands in a couple of days but we have a small window of free time after a really busy month, and Kian and I are making the most of it.

Kian's lips stretch perfectly around my dick as he hauls my ass forward until I'm hitting the back of his throat. And, like the man of my dreams, he just relaxes and lets me thrust further.

Drool might be gathered at the corners of his lips which are slick with pre-cum, but it only makes him look hotter.

He's looking up at me with lust-filled eyes under a thick fan of dark brown lashes and I feel my balls contract. He's loving every minute as he sets the pace again, slapping my ass when I try to pull back in an attempt to last longer.

The rhythm we then find is delicious. He can tell I'm close, and each thrust is met with a hearty moan, the vibrations in his constricting throat choking my dick and sending fireworks through my brain. He makes a swallowing motion, and I'm not sure if it's the way it clenches the head of my cock, or it's because it feels like a command, but I know I would do anything he asks right now.

Just as I feel myself about to fall off the edge into oblivion, his finger slips between my cheeks and presses on my hole.

Ass play isn't something I normally allow. *I* do the fucking when I'm in my own bed. I'm a top, not a bottom. Yet I can't get enough of his teasing fingertip, and it shocks me back from the precipice of my climax. For a second, I rock back against him, the pad of his finger dangerously close to penetration.

'What are you waiting for?' I groan, my ass so ready to finally feel him inside of me, even if it's just a single finger. And now I'm aching for it, and the gentle fluttering sensation of his touch around the rim isn't enough anymore.

I know he's enjoying the way he's playing my body because he takes me even deeper into his mouth, like the little tease he truly is. Then he pulls his finger away from my ass.

I throw my head back, almost disappointed, and then he drags his teeth a little up my shaft and I'm too overstimulated to care. His hands have already caressed every part of my body prior to him crawling down the bed to worship my dick. Every nerve ending in my body is alive with the touch of Kian. I want him to own me, dominate me, take me. It's a new feeling for me, and I'm not sure what to do with it, but you can't blame a guy for wanting his prostate to be shown a little love too.

We're almost at the finish line as my balls twitch, a tight sensation tugging at them like they're ready to explode. Both Kian's hands are at the base of my dick, working me in time with his mouth, and the orgasm is dangerously close.

He doesn't seem to mind swallowing me down, but I still like to warn him, just in case he changes his mind.

'Kian,' I pant, 'I'm so fucking close.' I test-drive a deeper thrust until his nose is in the soft skin I keep properly manscaped in order to show off my V-cut and my tackle. As

I'm about to pull back for another thrust, a wet finger dives into my ass. Pressing straight on that sweet spot.

My eyes roll back in my head until I'm seeing stars, *stars!* It's amazing.

It's fucking magic. He's … *magic*, with the instincts that mean he's in the driving seat when it comes to how and when to make me cum. Which I do. Repeatedly.

'Fucking hell, Kian.' It's all I can say. I almost want to thank him, but I feel like that would be weird.

His tongue swipes along his bottom lip, lapping up any traces of me he didn't swallow down from my body. I gulp in response – it's like he's got me on a chain and I don't even care.

He stands up and I pull his head towards me for a kiss. A primal urge to taste myself in his mouth.

'You good?' he asks against my lips like an idiot.

Do I look anything other than good? I'm a spent heap of limbs that couldn't move even if I tried right now.

'Mmmm,' I rumble against him before sealing my lips on his. Inside, his mouth tastes warm and salty, and my dick gives a slight twitch of approval even in its exhausted state.

We kiss for what feels like hours, until I don't know anything other than his lips. This is kind of new for me, too. Whilst I never object if a guy wants to kiss me, I don't usually initiate it.

But I'd let Kian kiss me all the time if I get to feel like this.

'Have I ruined you for all the other guys?' he asks when he pulls away.

The room's fading into a hazy darkness, it's only around 9pm, but it could be the middle of the night for how pitch-black it is in here.

But, even in the darkness, the way his eyes search mine

contradicts the teasing tone of his question. He's looking for an actual answer. He wants me to say yes.

In general, Kian's good at being honest, but right now I can tell he's holding back on what he actually wants to say and I don't like that. It sets me on edge.

When he doesn't get an answer, he rolls off me, breathing heavily as his head hits the other pillow.

'What do you mean?' I finally ask, half hoping he doesn't laugh in my face and shrug it off, half hoping he actually was just teasing and not trying to lock down the situation.

A couple of seconds of silence tick by, but then he leans up on his elbows to look me in the eye and asks, 'Are you seeing anyone else right now?'

Is that what we're doing? Seeing each other? Did I not realise that this was more than just sex? Panic rises in one massive ball in my throat and I can't choke it down.

Kian must see it because he quickly corrects his words. 'I mean, you're only with me at the moment, right?' It's a desperate question, and we both know it. The only correct answer in his mind is yes. I nod. 'Okay. So you won't sleep with anyone else, right?'

Does he mean *ever*? Because, like, I can't promise that. Not in a million years. This works right now because we're stuck in here, forced together, but that won't always be the case. Kian will leave me because everyone always leaves me. He'll get ... bored, or I'll piss him off, and he won't want me anymore. Or, I'll feel trapped and I'll need the rush of someone wanting me. I'll need to feel like I have options because I don't want to start relying on him. I'm not stupid – I've had therapy. I know what I'm like.

The panic rises in a heart-fluttering, chest-squeezing

sensation. It's like a cage around my heart, trapping it so that it's struggling to function correctly.

I try to form words, but my mouth is so dry they don't come out.

It's already incredibly awkward that I haven't responded and the more time I take to do so, the worse it gets. I'm desperate to leave and at the same time have no desire to be anywhere other than here, lying next to him. I want to be held, to feel safe and wanted and yet I'm terrified.

It's the most brutally overwhelming feeling, this contradiction that I can't balance in my mind.

Luckily, I'm saved by my phone bleeping loudly and disturbing the awful silence.

'I'm sorry,' I say, pulling my phone out from under the pillow to see a couple of texts from Johannes. The first text says *SOS* and the second is a whole bunch of exclamation marks. 'Oh fuck.'

I swing my legs off the bed, using the torchlight to find my boxers and the rest of my clothes when a third text containing the location of a bar comes through.

'I'm so sorry, but Johannes just SOSed and we have this rule in our friendship that if either of us sends that text we have to go.'

Kian nods understandingly, but says nothing.

I know it probably seems convenient that this has happened at the exact time he's trying to talk about us being exclusive or whatever, but them's the rules of friendship.

It's the first time in ages that Johannes has reached out and I want to know what's been going on with him.

When I get there, I can tell Johannes is looking to pull; he's prowling the bar with a determination I haven't witnessed in a while. It's been months since he's been happy to just let me do my thing and wingman me. I'm not sure what's changed, but tonight he's dragging me into the thick of it.

I try to get him to tell me what's going on and what's happened but he doesn't want to talk about it. He didn't have a great race in Belgium, but I don't think that's what's got to him.

'How do we feel about twins?' he asks, the rim of his glass poised at his lips. I don't know what he's drinking, but he's clearly wanting a sesh.

I follow his line of sight to the bar, where indeed there are two identical men – hot as anything – watching us. One nudges the other and turns his head to say something. It's clear they're talking about us.

If I'm honest, they aren't doing a thing for me, but it's too late. Johannes is sliding sloppily out of his seat, clearly already on his way to being shitfaced. I watch him approach the twins and invite the pair back to our booth.

I'm stuck with Twin 2, who's boring as hell and only interested in talking about his friend from university who he's obviously in love with.

Even after all this, he asks me to go home with him.

'I'm really sorry, but I'm not looking for anything tonight,' I tell him.

Twin 2 looks at me like I've lost my mind and Johannes's expression is comically surprised, too.

'What are you doing?' Johannes almost growls across the booth.

'Going home. This was a stupid idea.'

I feel bad about abandoning him when he's drunk, but then again, that's exactly what he did to me in Miami the night he dropped me for his mystery man.

'You going to be okay?' I ask, because even so, I don't want to be an asshole. He's still my oldest friend.

'Yeah, fine. Maybe I'll get doubly lucky!' I'm not so sure about that, but at least it makes me feel more comfortable leaving. Twin 1 gives me a thumbs-up and it's clear he's going to take care of Johannes from here. I pay the bar bill on the way out and suggest that they stop serving my drunk friend, but whether they will or not I have no idea.

I just want to get back to Kian.

'Hey,' I say, poking my head around his bedroom door the second I get back to the motorhome. His face is illuminated by the light of his phone and I catch the moment he realises I'm home.

Shit, I'm an idiot. It's not like he was trying to tie me down to marriage or lock me in his room forever. He was literally just asking me not to sleep with anyone else while we're hooking up.

He wasn't being unreasonable, *I* was. I knew that even at the time, but I really know it now.

I don't need to sleep with anyone else if I have him. That's more than enough. Not that I'm acquainted with the word. Going from nothing to the high life of motor racing, it doesn't feel like anything could be enough – sex, alcohol, money, success. But the way I've been feeling with Kian, the way I feel when we're … when we're just spooning … it's a kind of emotional comfort I've never had before and I … like it.

Who *am* I? I barely recognise myself these days.

'Hey,' Kian says.

It's not much, but he shuffles over in his bed to make room for me and I feel my heart squeeze. I step out of my shorts and whip my T-shirt over my head, discarding them on his bedroom floor to his utter annoyance.

'Can I get in?' I say as I hover by the edge of his bed. I don't think I've ever felt so unsure about being mostly naked and about to get in bed with one of the hottest men in the world.

Kian flips up the covers and pats the spot next to him. I climb in, instantly feeling refreshed by how cool his sheets are against my limbs. It feels clean and good and almost calming. We lie face to face, not touching, my mind racing a mile a minute because I'm not quite sure what to say to him.

I know I was coward earlier. I know I should apologise. I'm just not sure how. It's not something I've done a lot of before.

'Good night?' Never have I ever heard two words spoken so cautiously. Almost like he's afraid of the answer.

'No.' I shake my head and feel him relax his head into the pillow. 'I'm sorry,' I finally say. Bloody hell! It should have been the first thing I said when I came into the room.

'It's okay—'

'No, it isn't. I completely freaked out. You weren't asking anything unreasonable of me. I just panicked. That's my issue, not yours, and I shouldn't have just run out of here.'

'What did Johannes want?'

'He didn't want to talk so I don't know. He was already drunk when I got there. He had his eye on a pair of twins.'

'Twins?'

'Yeah.'

'Identical?'

'Yeah.'

'Hot?'

'Yeah.'

'But you're here.'

'Yeah.'

It doesn't take a genius to unpack the subtext.

'That's quite the temptation,' Kian says. 'Hot Belgian twins.'

'But I'm here, with you,' I reply. I hope he knows what I'm trying to say without having to actually say it.

Yes, I know, I'm a coward.

He finally pulls me into his arms and I tuck myself into his side, my cheek pressed against his shoulder. He smells of my shower gel, minty toothpaste, and a kind of homeyness that's incredibly soothing.

'Do *you* want to talk about it?' he whispers into the darkness.

Normally I wouldn't, but I find myself speaking anyway. 'There was something weird with Johannes tonight, when we've been out the last couple of months he's taken a backseat, told me he was cleaning his image up and I should, too.' Even in the dark I can see Kian's knowing grin of agreement with Johannes's wise words. 'Okay, maybe *everyone's* been telling me that and I wasn't listening, but that's beside the point for this story. I've barely seen him recently, and I assumed he was blissfully coupled up. He's been having a good season on the track, too, until the other day, and even I thought maybe he was on to something.'

Kian's bark of laughter stops me. I roll my eyes and he gestures for me to continue.

'Yet tonight he was pissed, and constantly scanning the bar. Then he spots these twins—'

'The hot identical gay twins?'

'The holy grail, right?' I say. Kian doesn't respond. 'Before I can say anything, Jo's out of the booth and dragging them over. I said I wasn't up for it –' I'm still hoping Kian will get the message without me having to say it out loud '– but there was no stopping him. I said I was going home and left him to it.'

'Is he okay?' Kian asks. Trust him to worry about whether my best friend is okay, even when that same best friend was directly working against Kian's own interests tonight. He's such a good person – a much better person than I am.

'I don't know. He was shooting tequila, so probably not.'

'And you left him there?'

'Wait a—!' My first instinct is defensive, but I know he's not actually attacking me or accusing me, because he's still holding me in his arms and our legs are entwined. I take a moment to breathe, and then reply petulantly, 'I paid the bill before I left and told the barman to stop serving him.'

Am I a shit friend, though? Kian would have done more, I know. Kian Ubered across Miami in the middle of the night to come and get me when I was a drunken mess. He looked after me when I was sick in Melbourne. He's calmly comforting me now when I know I hurt him earlier on when I didn't answer his question.

'Text him now and make sure he's okay. Get him an Uber home if that's what he wants. You aren't a bad friend –' is Kian a mind-reader now, too? '– but it seems like you both had things going on in your heads tonight and you both need better coping mechanisms.'

I laugh off his comment, but he's not wrong. I do need better coping mechanisms. I need to address all the things that feel messed up inside of me and lead me to make bad decisions.

I sigh and start texting Johannes. Whatever's going on with him, I want to make sure he's being safe. He texts back that he's in an Uber on the way home. He doesn't say whether he's alone or not, but the fact that he's responding to my message suggests his judgement isn't entirely impaired.

Maybe the therapy Anders and my agent suggested isn't such a bad idea, after all.

'You're right,' I admit. I feel like such a grown-up being sensible like this. 'I'm gonna go back to Anders about the therapy. Can't hurt, can it.'

His lips find my forehead and I'd be lying if I said I didn't melt under both his touch and his implicit approval. It's almost disgusting the way I feel so contented right now. It's been a very odd day indeed.

'Good thinking,' he replies and I snuggle up closer to him. 'Sleep now,' he whispers. As I'm falling asleep, it occurs to me that I don't think I've ever been happier than I am right now.

Chapter Nineteen

Kian

Finishing top of the podium in Hungary, Belgium and the Netherlands has lit a rocket up my ass. It's a thrill to be having the best season of my career. It's even possible I could challenge the points record of the championship, but I don't want to get ahead of myself.

I guess it also helps that in my evenings and on down days I'm getting proper quality time with Harper. I'm not willing to credit him for my good fortune, but I'm not denying that I feel great.

But I can't lie and say he doesn't help. I've never cared too much about having someone to 'come home to', but, right now, I can see the appeal. Even when we aren't hooking up, I feel like we hardly leave each other's sides. It's easier in the motorhome than it is in hotels, we cook together and don't rely on the catered meals from Hendersohm. We can curl up on the sofa late into the evening and watch TV like, dare I say it, a normal couple. We aren't one. I don't think? I don't know? I have no clue where we stand.

Since Belgium when I tried to raise the issue of us being exclusive, I haven't mentioned it again. It didn't exactly go well, and although Harper came back and said all the right things, we've still not clearly defined what we are to each other. I'm trying to be cool, calm, and collected so as not to overwhelm him or scare him off.

It's all new to him, this relationship business. He's not said it in so many words, but I think I'm the only person outside of Johannes that he's been with more than once. I'm trying not to pressure him. I figure we just need to take it one day at a time for now, but I can see, in the not-so-distant future, that we'll have to talk about it.

I'm sure it's going to go as well as pulling teeth, but I don't want to be a casual-sex partner forever. If I do decide to retire at the end of the season, I don't just want to be thrown away because it will no longer be convenient and easy. If this is my last season, I won't be his teammate anymore, travelling the world with him and keeping his bed warm.

As I step down from the podium in the Netherlands, I look to my left and see Harper doing the same from where he's been keeping third-place warm. He shoots me the most scandalous look I've ever seen. His eyes are all heat, as if he wants to drop to his knees right now and reward me for yet another first-place finish. I'm glad my racing suit and the layers of fire protection I've got on will disguise my growing erection.

I still look around, scanning the bank of flashing cameras, hoping that none of them caught that look being sent my way or interpreted its meaning.

We've done such a good job of keeping this just between the two of us so far, and I don't want to screw it up now. I don't want to scare him off. I don't want to rock the boat at Hendersohm. And I don't want any distractions from the media that get in the way of our performance on the track.

The comments, I'm sure, would be either incredibly homophobic or would accuse us of cheating by employing team tactics that disadvantaged other drivers. In either case it would be absolute bollocks, but we'd spend hours denying it and the sponsors wouldn't like it. Little do they know, our sexual chemistry thrives on us being competitive. There's no world in which I would give up a podium position to help Harper win, and I know he feels the same.

'Good job, yet again, Walker,' Harper says in a hushed tone. It's a perfectly tame comment that doesn't need to be whispered. To everyone who likes to write about us it'll look like teammates congratulating each other, but I know there's a different kind of praise behind those words. Praise and a promise.

We'll get back to the motorhome and draw the blinds in every room. Before we've even showered, he'll sink to his knees and show me just how proud he is of my win.

Great. Now I'm definitely fighting a boner.

I need to distract myself or there'll be no hiding it and then we really will have a sex scandal on our hands. Journalists aren't stupid and they love to put two and two together and come up with five – except this time it would be four and we'd either have to lie and deny it or go public with our rel—

With whatever we are.

'Not too bad from you either, James. Any chance of you breaking second any time soon, though?'

230

'And take the shine off you, golden boy? Hardly. But don't worry, I'll take you *down*. Can't be *on top* forever.'

If his tone doesn't give him away then his cheeky smirk will.

I start planning exactly what I'm going to do to him when we're back in the confines of the motorhome, with no eyes or microphones on us.

Except first of all, we have to do the press call. Deep breaths. Nails down a chalkboard. Buckets of vomit. Rats in a bag. Car accidents and serial killers. ARGH!

It's not perfect, but it's helping.

'Kian, how does it feel to take home three first-place finishes in a row?' the first journalist asks. She's got a microphone outstretched on a long stick, and there's a camera man moving behind her to get the best shot. I'm not even sure who she works for.

'Incredible, absolutely incredible. Of course, this is every driver's dream to be on top of the podium and defending my title, but I treat every circuit like a completely new start and never take any win for granted.'

'I'm sure, especially in your final season?'

I smile tightly as I reply. 'I'll let you know when I get to my final season.' It's a diplomatic answer and she laughs, and that's enough for me to move down the row to the next.

'You're having an incredible season, Kian,' the next guy comments. He's got a handheld recorder reached out over the barrier to capture my answer to whatever he's about to say next. 'Some would say your best one yet. What would you say is contributing to that?'

Harper.

His name almost rolls off my tongue and I have to work really hard to keep my thoughts in line.

The journalist clears his throat, prompting me, a single brow raised as if trying to figure out what's taking me so long to answer. Apart from the handful of bad interviews at the start of the season, I have a good track record of being pretty slick when it comes to the media. Mostly because I've been used to it my whole life, I reckon.

When Mum was at the height of her fame, we couldn't leave the house on our own. We were escorted to school, to friends' birthday parties, to clubs and activities – anywhere, really. There were reporters at the end of our drive, outside the gates, hounding us from such a young age, desperate for Chastity Walker's kids to say or do something silly.

I'm so zoned out that the journalist has repeated the question and I finally find my voice again. 'Sorry man, apparently the high of the win has gone to my head. Must be some kind of extra altitude on top of that podium, eh?'

I'm sure he'll run with some quote about me being on top of the world or even being cocky about winning again. I don't care.

'I'd just have to say it's experience now. I've been doing this for well over a decade, and at Hendersohm we work like a family. We're a well-oiled machine and we've got some incredible guys in the garage making sure these cars are perfection for us. The team's nailed it this season. Paired with good driving and weather conditions ... I'm hopeful it can continue for the rest of the season.'

'A lot of changes for Hendersohm this season, though. At the start you seemed a bit shaken both on and off the track by Elijah Gutaga's injury and the subsequent arrival of Harper

James.' Here we go again. 'How do you think Harper is getting on? It's his rookie season and he's making quite the splash. Has his presence had any effect on your performance?'

'I think the rankings both today and over the season so far speak for themselves. Harper's having a great first season after dominating lower-category racing last year. He works incredibly hard and deserves all his success.'

'And what about when Elijah's back to full health? Who would you rather have as a teammate?' He's a cheeky fuck. Not in any world would I be able to comment on that and I would be in big trouble if I did. I also don't know what I would say.

'You know I can't comment on that. I'm sure the bosses will make the best decision for the team and they're lucky to have two fantastic drivers to choose from.' I step away quickly to avoid saying anything stupid. I have no clue what the line-up will look like when Elijah's better or even this time next year. I haven't even decided whether I'll be here.

Elijah and I have obviously kept in touch throughout his recovery and I know he had a set-back when one of the incisions became infected. He's still got a way to go before he's back.

The rest of the interviews move along in the same kind of fashion. There are a lot of questions about what's going well, and thankfully not a lot of nit-picky questions about what can be improved. Though I'm doing well enough to start thinking about challenging the record for championship points within a single season, even I'm not immune to the knowledge that there's always more I can be doing.

Anders claps me on the shoulders as I make my way into

the pit. I can't think of many teams where the principal is always there waiting for us when we come off the track.

'Son,' he starts, and I have to work on steadying my breathing in order to keep my emotions in check. My own father may be a piece of shit, but I'm lucky to have been blessed with a father figure in this sport. A proper role model. Someone who isn't only concerned with the money we draw in, but who actually loves the sport and his team. 'Absolute brilliance. I thought I saw some good drives from you in your early career, and last season especially, but this was fantastic. Your poise and focus, and your ability to decide when to take the risk and when to cut it smooth … it astounds me. I'm so proud of you.'

It's high praise from him, and I'd be flushed a deep shade of rouge if I were back in my teens or early twenties. Now, well, now I soak it up. My muscles cry out with a decade's worth of aches and pain from the toll this sport takes on the body, so it's nice to hear that they've been worth it.

'Thanks, sir. Really appreciate it.'

'And the way you've taken Harper under your wing… I know he still needs a few of the sharp edges knocking off, but he's learning some really good habits from you. Becoming a proper asset to Hendersohm.'

It's almost nicer to hear good reports of Harper – why is that? I'm still contemplating my future on the track, but I know that whether I stay or go at the end of the season, it will be my choice. Harper doesn't have leverage yet – one good season doesn't guarantee his seat next year. Especially when Elijah's fit and ready to go again.

I don't envy the tough decision Hendersohm will have to make.

'He's doing great, but I don't think it's anything to do with me. He's got natural talent.'

Fingers drag across my back and I feel my whole body go ram-rod straight. I don't even need to turn around to know he's behind me, and that he heard at least some of what I just said about him.

Thankfully, no one seems to notice his intimate touch. Anders congratulates Harper and they start talking about the specifics of opportunities he had to sneak up into second, before going over to Ash so they can see the details in the data.

I don't know how he still has so much energy. The thrill of winning wears off quickly nowadays, and I'm left with nothing but a heavy weight of exhaustion. I can feel it in my bones. They want nothing more than to collapse into bed and take the weight off for a little while. I don't even have the energy to look at data today.

At just thirty-four, I probably shouldn't feel like this. I'm in my prime, but it feels like the sport has aged me. I'm sure most drivers feel like this – and sports professionals in general. It's a short career to stay on top of elite performance, whether you run, throw, kick or hit. I need a good massage. I'll get one in the diary from the physio before we head off on the road to Italy next, for our final stop of the European tour.

Or maybe I'll get Harper to put his magic hands to good use when we get home. He can iron out some kinks in my more intimate muscles. I'm sure I've probably pushed my glutes *real* hard today.

I have a fair wait, though. Harper's mind does not stop working nor his mouth moving as he sits beside Ash at his makeshift desk in the garage, stats and figures flying across the screen as Harper analyses every number. Not that I'm complaining – I'm happy to sit back and watch his pure enjoyment of this sport. No one seems to enjoy it as much as him. Whatever might be said about his lax attitude towards training and self-discipline, no one can knock his passion.

Or maybe it's just because I see it all going on behind the scenes. I see the way he lies in bed some nights watching hours of footage to learn from other drivers and his past races. He stews over his slower laps, his mistakes and his missed opportunities, and takes even more care analysing the details of his faster laps. Harper James just wants to keep improving and that's damn admirable, whatever way you look at it. Forget the choices he makes in his personal life, I want to tell every journalist, just keep your eyes on his drive.

It's over an hour later when he tugs on his team hoodie and strides over to where I'm scrolling through my phone and texting with Elise.

'You didn't need to wait.'

There's surprise on his face, that I've hung around for him. Little does he know I'd have waited longer. Another hour. Two. Longer, even.

'Thought we could walk back together, that's all.' I'm measured as I speak – a lot of the team staff are still milling around and packing up our team pit to prepare for transport to Italy.

'We'd best get going then, huh?' Surprise morphs into excitement and then quickly into pure lust as he takes me in. I've had some physio and done some stretching in the meantime, but I've still got my kit on. I don't think I've ever been subject to such appreciative eyes.

We don't speak on the walk back to the motorhome, but we don't need to. Even though we're keeping our distance as we move, there's a zing of electricity bouncing between us. It's the promise of what's to come the second the door to the outside world closes behind us.

I haven't even taken off my trainers when he mounts me like a bloody tree. He's lucky I have the upper body strength of a weight-lifting pro, because I'm practically having to hold him up as he mauls my face with his lips.

'Sometimes, I wish I could watch you drive from the sidelines again,' he murmurs between kisses. 'It's so fucking hot. Even when you overtook me I think I was turned on.' His lips are on mine, then on my cheek, my jaw, and my neck until he's meeting the fabric of my T-shirt. 'Need this off.'

'Need you in the bedroom first,' I reply, releasing him from my grip so he can jump down.

His hand finds mine and he leads us to my bedroom like it was his idea. My back can't take another session on the couch.

He's stripped off my clothes before I can even cross the threshold of the room. He yanks his own clothes off, too, and then we're falling back on the bed, hands and lips everywhere they can reach.

It's undoubtable how much we want each other. It's been weeks of messing around, switching between blow jobs and hand jobs, a little rimming and the occasional venture into ass play. Yet we still haven't discussed what comes next and who'll be doing what.

I'm vers, so I'm happy either way, but I'm intrigued to discover how this will change our dynamic.

I don't want to ruin the moment, but it's time. We both want more – the question is am I fucking him or is he fucking me?

'How do you wanna do this?' I ask, injecting my voice with a casualness I don't feel.

'You. Inside me,' he replies. Despite not having been sure of his preference before, somehow this surprises me. His hand snakes around my dick, and he gives it a sharp tug to get this party started.

I decide to take the prep work slow and steady since something tells me it's been a while since he's had someone inside of him and I don't want to ask. Better to be safe than sorry.

I intend to go slowly, but once I start licking and using my spit to get him nice and ready, I'm as keen to get going as he obviously is. I push in first one wet finger and then a second, in and out, while my other hand plays with his dick and his balls. I get a third finger ready and start pressing.

Harper's writhing against my fingers, begging for more. He starts to back himself on to them and I love the sight of his ass working its way onto my hand. It's not something I ever thought I would see, but I know it will live rent-free in my head for the rest of my life.

I can't wait to get inside him, but the second I pull out my fingers, I realise I don't have a condom.

I don't even remember the last time I packed them, never mind kept them to hand. I really don't do this a lot.

A laugh escapes my lips and Harper's eyes fly open, startled by the change in pace. I've been dying to get inside him and now I'm stalling.

'What?' he asks, leaning up on his elbows. 'Why'd you stop?'

'Do you have a condom?'

'Oh, for fuck's sake, Kian. I thought you were Mr Prepared?'

'Just hop off the bed and go and get one. I know you have a stash – at least, I hope you do.'

When Harper comes back with one and gets back on the bed, I thrust my fingers back inside him and find his prostate right away, which has his hips pistoning up off the bed.

'You bastard,' he pants as I set a frantic pace.

Ignoring him, I line up our dicks, both of them slick, and with every thrust of my fingers we slide against each other. It's nearly too much even for me and I don't have someone stimulating my G-spot at the same time. I can't even imagine how good Harper's feeling.

Before we both slip over the edge, I slide on the condom and start to nudge my way inside of him. At first, just the tip, but he's quickly breathing out so push fully inside of him. It feels so damn good, and when I look up from the way his ass is stretching around my cock, he's enjoying it, too. He's looking at me with an intensity that surprises me, and I know for sure then that this isn't something he's done much of before.

His breath hisses between his teeth, and he grunts as I push all the way in.

'Fuck!'

He reaches down and starts pumping his dick and he groans and closes his eyes.

I start thrusting and it doesn't take much to coax him to the edge, our sweat pooling between us. With one more thrust I can feel I'm close, but the sight of his release coating his belly is the final trigger and I cum hard, calling out his name as I do.

I collapse beside him and he rolls into my side, both of us struggling to catch our breath for a second, before the room falls quiet. I take the condom off and dispose of it, and when I return, he whispers something into my chest which I don't quite catch. I go to ask him to repeat himself, but his eyes are closed and he looks peaceful.

Harper's breath evens out, little puffs blowing against my chest hair, and we fall asleep in a tangle of limbs, our bodies slick with cum and sweat, my heart full of the prospect of what this thing between us could be.

Chapter Twenty

Harper

It's 5am when I realise Kian and I have been sharing a room, like a couple, since Hungary. The rooms in the motorhome aren't big enough to hold all the kit and gear for two people, but I've been slowly drifting into his space. Not to the extent that a casual observer would notice, but there are signs.

My clothes on the floor by his bed. My phone charger plugged in behind the bed frame. My Deep Heat on the bedside table.

It's all looking very intimate in here and I can't lie and say I'm not enjoying it. And here's something else I never thought I'd say: though the sex is phenomenal, it doesn't compare to being held by Kian all night.

Kian Walker has turned me into a cuddler. The other guys I've let grace my bed in the past never got the pleasure; they were lucky if I let them catch their breath before they were out the door. Even when Johannes and I were sleeping together it was never like this.

I'm not sure what's different about Kian. There's proximity, obviously, and sexual chemistry, so maybe he's just convenient. I've always liked low-effort convenience.

But there's so much that's just plain wrong about calling Kian purely convenient.

I know that's not why this is good between us.

Maybe that's why I feel so on edge right now, because this is starting to feel very cosy and comfortable and ... like a relationship. I mean, I've never been in one before so I don't really know, but these days, when I feel bad, I'd rather go home to Kian and cuddle him in bed than go out and get shitfaced and shag a random.

This scares me, but I also really, really want it. Hence why I'm so on edge.

I also really care about whatever it is that sometimes gives him nightmares, which is another new experience for me.

He sometimes mutters in his sleep, often just complete nonsense, but whatever he's got to say tonight has his tongue moving a mile a minute.

'It doesn't go there,' he grumbles, arms squeezing around my waist, pulling me closer and out of my messy thoughts.

I'm desperate to ask him what, what doesn't go where? But I don't know if I should disturb him or not. Instead, I hold him closer, so he knows he's not alone.

'No, no, no!' He chants the words over and over again and as I peer over my shoulder his face twists and contorts with pain. 'Not yet, no!'

I'm not sure if sleep screaming is a thing, but his words get louder. He's almost crying out at this point for whatever's going on in his dream to stop, and I slink out of his arms to roll over.

'Hey, Kian. Kian, it's okay.' I gently shake the side of his arm, but his legs start to thrash at the sheet, almost as if he's trying to run. 'Baby, come on, it's okay.' The pet name slips out, but I can't find it in me to care. I just want to stop the pained expression on his face.

I shake him once, twice, three times, and only on the third time do his eyes fly open, his breath coming out in heavy pants. His eyes go wide, startled, before he pushes himself into a sitting position.

'I'm sorry,' he whispers, like I'm looking worried because he's inconvenienced me by being like this. 'Sorry if I woke you.'

'You didn't. Are you okay?'

Instinctively, I reach for him. Normally this is his move, but it looks like he's the one who needs to be held this time.

'I don't know … I don't know what that was, but … but I was dreaming about my mum dying.' His voice cracks as he says the final two words and wet eyes shine in the dark as he finally looks at me.

He finally lets me pull him completely against me, my arms wrapped tightly around him as he bawls into my shoulder. Tears drip down my bare skin, our bodies flush together as I hold him for ten, twenty, who cares how many minutes. I'd stay here with him forever if it meant he'd be okay.

When did I start thinking I'd move heaven and earth to see Kian Walker happy?

Daylight begins to drip in around the edges of the blinds in the motorhome. Kian pulls away from me, snuffling into the back of his hand.

'You're all wet, sorry.'

His face splits into laughter as he realises what he's said and the sound envelops both of us, the tears he shed just moments ago forgotten.

I'm sure the healthy thing to do would be for us to talk about his nightmare, but this is all new territory for me, and I don't know how to navigate it. So I do what I do best and lean into him again, this time capturing his mouth with mine.

There's a saltiness to his lips as I swipe my tongue across the seam of them, pleading with him to let me in. It's a lazy kiss, and we slide back into a horizontal position, sharing one pillow, our bodies hot from the duvet we've slipped back under. Yet I don't care. I can't find it in me to care that this might not lead to sex. I'm content to just lie here with him and explore each other's mouths until I know every inch of his and mine becomes his second home.

It's enough.

And it feels like it's enough for him, too.

Like I'm enough.

I've been working on this in therapy, and I try to slow down and just exist in the feeling of being enough. It's strange and unsettling. And also wonderful.

When my jaw begins to ache and my lips feel beyond chapped, only then do I pull away.

For a couple of beats, Kian just stares at me, his gaze soft as he pushes a couple of floppy curls off my forehead.

In a swift moment, it's as though he shakes himself before springing out of bed. I should probably follow suit – busy day and all – but I'm not excited to leave this room, or this bed. I swing my legs over the side of the bed and try to get my brain in gear.

Kian lifts the blinds and full-on daylight floods the room.

'Argh!' I hiss as I shield my eyes like a vampire.

'I think we may have become actual hermits over the last couple of days and we have a podcast to go record and some short-form videos to capture in the team lounge. And, uh, I was thinking—'

'Wouldn't recommend doing that too hard. Your tiny brain might explode.' I giggle. Fucking giggle! Like a teenage girl trying too hard with her first crush.

He either doesn't notice or doesn't care as he pulls me into his chest, hands finding the sides of my stomach as he tickles me like a wild animal. My laughs turn to screams and I'm scrambling to get out of his grip when there's a knock at our door.

We both shoot apart, even though it's not like whoever it is can let themselves in. They haven't caught us, but we know this can't happen in the open.

'Coming,' I shout and I'm out of Kian's bedroom like a bullet from a gun. I slide across the lock, finding Anna on the other side.

'You're both late! Where's Kian? I'm surprised he's not already in the team room.' Because Kian's always so damn punctual and I'm clearly corrupting him.

'We were just about to leave.' Anna scans my naked chest and boxer-clad ass and gives me her best don't-bullshit-me smile.

'I was just about to leave, I promise,' Kian says, appearing behind me fully dressed, his minty breath floating past me as he barges his way out of the motorhome.

'I never doubted you for a second,' Anna chuckles. 'You have two minutes to be dressed and out, Harper.'

Kian shrugs from behind her, holding back a snigger, and I'm sad that our blissful bubble of sex and pizza has been broken.

I'm sad we have to let the outside world in and for the next few days leading into the Italian Grand Prix we have to be Harper James and Kian Walker, teammates, Hendersohm's top racing drivers. Not *us*.

The days go so fast, though. They whizz by in a blur of soundbites, photoshoots and management finally being happy with what we're putting out for them. There's no more speculation about the rift dividing the Hendersohm team. Anders's face is constantly split in two because of how much good press we've been given. Even Jackson is easier to be around when he sits in on every team meeting and video session, now that I know he isn't a threat with Kian.

It's not just that, though. The pit is more energetic, too, now there isn't as much animosity between the two of us. The technicians aren't walking on eggshells around us when we're practising in the simulator. Everyone's laughing and joking with each other, including me and Kian.

Yet we still keep our distance. Kian doesn't come within a two-foot radius of me, almost as if he can't touch me without giving our secret away. I can't think too deeply about why that might be, because if I do I know my brain will think it's because he's embarrassed or ashamed to be with me.

Nope.

Can't think like that.

I think quickly back to my last therapy session, in which we spoke about the reasons why my parents left, and how it wasn't about *me* or anything *I* might have done. They left because of who *they* are – or were – and their own issues. It's not like I've never heard this before, but it's hard to undo a lifetime of internalised trauma and the behaviour that results from it. I'm trying, though, and working through it with a therapist keeps it top of my mind. I try to apply that rationale to Kian right now.

I stew on it for a few days, and then, in a rare free moment before the qualifiers, we both find each other alone in the motorhome one day. Kian's wearing just the base layer that goes under his suit and I'm in nothing but a Hendersohm team hoodie and my boxers.

'Hey.' I smile as he turns his head to find me pressed up behind him. 'Fancy seeing you here.'

'Blimey, you really are a horn-dog.' My dick is nestled again his ass, pushing against the valley between his cheeks, and I pull him as tightly as possible against me.

'What were you thinking about the other day?' I ask. It's taken me several attempts to voice this, and now that I find myself able to, I have to keep going.

'Huh?'

'When Anna basically shattered our door with persistent knocking.'

'Oh.' The hot and heavy mood I was trying to initiate disappears and he pulls away from my grip.

I brace myself for whatever's coming.

'Ki?' He comes to a stop at his name, though he's managed to put some serious distance between the pair of us.

He remains silent, contemplation scrunching up the little nub of skin between his brows. Uncertainty radiates from him and I begin to wish I'd never brought it up. So much for open and honest dialogue!

'I was, uh, thinking about if you wanted to get dinner.'

Wait, what? I thought he was going to say something about keeping *us* a secret from the team.

'Instead of breakfast?'

'No, like, uh, you know … I was wondering if you wanted to go out. For, you know, dinner.' His jumble of words washes over me like a tsunami and I'm glad I'm white-knuckle gripping the edge of the island to stop me falling to the floor. I don't know what I was expecting, but it's not this.

Why does this feel worse than him telling me he doesn't want anyone to know about us?

'Like a date?' I ask, fearing the worst.

He doesn't speak; just nods shyly.

'Oh.' There's a ringing starting in my ears and I feel the moment the air whooshes out of the hard to open motorhome windows.

It's clearly not the one-word answer Kian was looking for. In some ways it's worse than a straight-up *no* because it seems to express incredulity that he's even asking.

Disappointment etches into his face and I raise my eyes to meet a very sad version of Kian. I've seen him cry over nightmares, fume at a loss, and downright lose his shit in frustration at my antics but this is a new low.

If devastation needed to be captured in a photo, I'd take out my camera right now and provide an endless catalogue of the look.

'Kian…' I start.

'No, it's fine, honestly. A stupid suggestion. Ignore me. Clearly the cabin fever is getting to me.' He busies himself at the sink, rinsing out a glass that was already clean. I'm presented with his back, but I don't need to see his face to read his emotions.

'Motorhome fever,' I correct, forcing out an awkward laugh in the hope of breaking the tension.

He doesn't reply. While I'm still trying to think of something to say to diffuse the situation, he grabs his jacket and trainers, tugging them on as he heads out of the door, kit bag of everything he needs for today thrown over his shoulder.

The door slams behind him and everything falls apart.

It quite literally falls apart when Kian qualifies in Q10 that day, and I know it's one hundred per cent my fault.

And then, just when I thought it couldn't get any worse, I find myself shut out of Kian's bedroom. Relegated to the cold room that used to be mine.

Unable to charge my phone or soothe the aching pain in my chest.

It doesn't make for a good night's sleep and when I wake up the next morning with a plan for how to approach Kian and talk about it, he's already long gone.

We don't speak as we get ready to race. He's locked into whatever's playing in his earbuds – it's probably one of his guided meditations – but his whole body looks tense as he tries to shake himself free of his mood.

During our walk to the garage, he didn't stop to sign stuff or take selfies with every fan like usually does. He's like a ghost as people yell his name. There are people literally holding up cardboard cutouts of him, begging for them to be signed, and his focus is entirely on getting into the garage and shutting out everything and everyone.

As I climb into my cockpit, I have to shut off all thoughts of

Kian. I cannot afford to worry about him. I didn't work my ass off to qualify third only to mess it up on the Sunday because I have *feelings*.

And for the most part, the race is brilliant. It's my favourite kind of battle, with a few of us upfront tussling for pole position, but Kian's nowhere in sight.

I've asked Ash for updates on Kian's position a few times and been told a mixture of P5, 6 and 7. He's struggling to make up the ground after qualifying so far back.

Then, on the lead up to the seventh-from-last lap, a brief glimpse of a yellow flag catches my eye. Since the weather conditions are perfect, it means something's happened. An accident, most likely.

'Ash,' I grunt out, trying my best to give the circuit nothing but my laser focus. 'What's going on?'

The line goes silent for a second and an anxious, gnawing pit opens in my stomach.

'Ash, I swear to God, tell me what's going on. I'm a bit blind here, man. You're meant to be my eyes on the side.'

Nothing.

Radio fucking silence.

'Someone's come off the track. Just slow down a little when you're taking the eighth bend. I'm not sure what the issue is but they skidded off like there was oil or something. Keep an eye out for stripes if this changes next lap, okay?'

'Who?' I can still see the pair of McLaren Swedes in front of me blocking my way into first or second and my brain is stressfully imagining my best friend in a heap of metal on the side of the track. 'Is it Johannes? Ash, please! I need to know.'

I'm not beyond begging, but I really don't want to when I'm trying so hard to remember to steer right now. The bends are vicious on this track and I'm almost glad Ash stays quiet until I finish a tricky set and head back down the narrow straight to finish this lap. The yellow flag is still showing in the distance and I slow down, almost reluctantly.

'It's not Johannes,' Ash finally confirms and I heave out a sigh of relief, my grip on the steering wheel releasing a little.

I slow a little more as I come closer to where Ash indicated the accident happened, driving carefully and conservatively in case there's oil spilled on the track and I end up flying off, too. Except, in slowing down, I catch sight of the car that careered into the barriers ending up on its side.

It's not Johannes, but I'm all too familiar with the colour and design.

'No!' I yell. 'Please don't tell me that's Kian? Please?'

Now I really am begging. If I thought the stress of it being Johannes was bad, it's nothing compared to the spine-crushing dread that washes over me at the thought of it being Kian.

'They're working on it now, Harper. Just focus on the track, buddy. There's nothing you can do right now.'

Like hell there is! I can pull off and get out and help. I'll drag him from the car myself if it means being sure that he's okay.

'Is he okay? Just tell me he's okay, for fuck's sake!' The words come out frantically, desperately. My foot's on the pedal and my eyes are on the track, but my mind is on nothing but Kian.

I see an opening between the pair occupying the top two positions – they must be distracted, too. One swift movement and I could be top of the podium... And suddenly I'm pushing, acting on muscle memory and pure instinct, I feel as though I'm going faster than I ever have before as I focus on the gap that's appeared, and even as I zoom into second I can't feel anything other than a shit-ton of fear.

'They're getting him out now,' Ash confirms.

'Is he okay, though?' I feel like I might spontaneously combust if I don't hear how he is in the next five seconds.

'He's talking, that's all we know right now.' Well, that's something. More than something because it means he's alive. 'Yellow flag's still up, but they've confirmed there's no spill of any kind on the track.'

'So why did he come off, then?'

'That'll be a question for later. Focus now, Harper. You were point eight behind first on that last lap. You could take this all if you really try right now.'

I've never had a problem separating what's happening on and off the track before. I've never had an issue with my focus. But now, when my mind is flooded with images of Kian hanging out of the side of his car, lifeless, covered in blood, gasping his last words, I throw it all away.

My chance to be on top, to bring home those twenty-five points, to be remembered as a legend of the sport … it all goes out the window as I struggle to make the most of the opportunity to overtake just one more car and win. I'm so close, so fucking close, but I can't do it. I see a gap open up but I wait a split second too long to go for it and miss the window. I hear Ash grunt in my ear, and I know I'm messing this up. My big chance, the opportunity of a lifetime, it's draining away… I've worked hard, but it also took Elijah's unlucky leg break to put me in this seat, in this car, on this track and I might not get another chance like it. I might not be good enough…

Then it hits me. Kian wouldn't lose his shit like this. Kian wouldn't want me to fall apart because of his crash. He wouldn't want it to distract me from capitalising on the situation and getting a P1. So I channel the great Kian Walker and take some deep breaths. I wait it out, staying less than half a second behind the leader for a lap until we blast into the straight.

And then it happens. It's one of the Swedes in P1, and he screws himself over by trying a bit too hard to block my path. He overcompensates on the bend and, like a predator in the jungle, I can smell his fear. He's thinking about what's behind him instead of what's in front of him. I know I won't get another chance, so I hit the gas. My chance has come and I'm fucking taking it.

The win is a blur. My first podium top in the Championship and it's nothing but a hazy fog in my mind. I probably won't even remember it – I already have no memory of being sprayed with champagne or of any of the interviews. I have no idea what I said – I hope it wasn't totally stupid.

Because all I can think about is Kian.

'Where is he?' I demand, the minute I find Ash.

'They've taken him to the local hospital for X-rays and to be certain about his concussion status.'

'Is he okay? What the hell, man! I was blind out there.' I know, in the back of my mind, that it's not Ash's fault and he has orders he has to follow in the garage, but I'm desperate.

'We never report accidents unless there's risk to your car. You know this,' he says calmly. It's impressive, actually, how well he's handling my reaction.

'It's Kian! Not some random. I deserved to know.' I'm raising my voice now, and everyone's staring. My paranoia is screaming at me that they're all figuring it out, that they all know what's been going on, that we've been rumbled and it's all my fault – it's always my fault – but I don't care right now.

'Can someone take me to the hospital?'

'You need to finish up here first, son,' says Anders. But he can fuck off with that 'son' business. He's never once said it to me before and he doesn't get to now just because I'm clearly having some kind of freak-out.

'I don't care. I just want to see him.'

'I'll go with him,' Cole says, stepping in. He and Kian have been close for years, so I'm surprised he isn't as ready to go as I am. 'I'll get us a car right now.'

'Okay, okay,' Anders finally relents. 'We'll have Anna give a statement to explain why you disappeared. She can give it a good team spin – how you wanted to be at the hospital to make sure Kian was okay.'

I couldn't give a crap how he spins this or how it makes the team look, I just need to see Kian. I need to see that he's okay with my own eyes.

In the back of the car, with the driver partition locked, Cole spills to me everything he knows. He tells me that Kian was breathing and alert when they got him out. Initial track-side assessments showed no signs of any broken bones or a concussion. That last one is always important, and means the helmet and the halo did their jobs.

My breathing's rapid and I will my heart rate to slow down. He's as okay as he could be after a crash, but I won't believe it until I see him for myself.

'He looked worse than he was – lots of blood, but they said

it looked to be just cuts and bruises. But you know protocol means he needs to be properly assessed and they need to check for any internal bleeding.' I've known this for years – every driver does – but hearing Cole say it out loud is reassuring, and it gives me time to collect my thoughts.

'I have to say, I'm surprised,' he says, when we've been sitting in silence for a minute or two.

'Surprised how?' I ask.

'That you're so concerned. I know you and Kian have put your differences aside during the European leg but I didn't know you were … *close*. I didn't know you were actually friends or whatever.'

Or whatever, indeed.

Chapter Twenty-One

Kian

'Elise, I promise, I'm okay. The doctors have done thorough checks and nothing's broken. It's just a few cuts and bruises,' I reassure my overly worried sister for the fourth time in this phone call.

'God, I'm so glad I didn't let Cassie watch this one. I have no clue how I'd have explained it to her.'

It's a relief to me, too. Even at almost four years old, Cassie's way too young to be worrying about anything in her life.

Plus, I also hope to get her in a kart one day and that can't be done if she's afraid because of something that happened to me.

'They'll let me go after the concussion period has run out, but please, honestly, don't worry about me.' My sister has way too much already on her plate to be worrying about. I've noticed that in our recent calls she's quite short in reporting to me about Mum.

I tell myself it's because the kids are growing up and every time she calls there's more to say about them. Jesse's grasping more words every week and tottering around like the toddler he's becoming and Cassie's a ball of artistic energy who loves painting and making things with clay.

I'm missing so much. It makes retirement seem that little bit more appealing.

'Are you listening to me, Ki?'

I clearly wasn't. 'Sorry, what did you say?'

'I asked what happened. Even I know that was a bend you can do in your sleep.'

She's right. More than. I've never had any issue on this course the last fourteen times I've driven it. But I can't tell her that the guy I'm falling for won't even go on a date with me. I definitely can't tell her it's Harper James. She'd kick his ass.

'I don't know what happened,' I lie. I absolutely hate myself and the guilt that eats me up as the lie continues to spin. 'I don't know if I just misjudged how sharp it was or if there was a problem with the car.' It was neither of those things; my mind just wasn't on the track.

It would be a dangerous admission, and I'm already dreading the possibility that I might have to tell the team when they investigate the car and track to see what caused the crash.

'I still hate this. I know it's been, like, fifteen years but I still hate that you do this every other weekend for nine months of the year.'

Might that be another reason to retire? Does it seem like there are more and more reasons because they're valid reasons, or because the press keeps putting them into my head every time I'm interviewed? Some days, it feels like I've already decided.

'I know, I'm sorry, El. I promise I'll be more careful.' The nurse who's been coming round checking my vitals pops her head around the door and signals to get my attention. 'One sec, El.'

'You have a visitor in the waiting room. He's been here waiting a long time. Do you want him to come in?' I nod and the nurse leaves.

'El, I'm gonna have to go. I think Anders is here, or maybe Cole, I don't know. Someone from Hendersohm.'

'Okay, baby bro. Love you. Let me know when they discharge you.' I return the love and she hangs up.

Before I know it, lurking in my doorway is a very sheepish-looking Harper. The guy who laughed in my face yesterday when I tried to ask him to go for dinner with me.

'How're you feeling?' he asks, letting the doors close softly behind him but not taking any steps towards my bed.

'Fine. Just a bit achy all over but I'll be discharged in the morning as I'm on concussion watch.'

I'd like to be heading home right now, but I know concussion protocol better than I know my own name after more than a decade in the sport.

Before Harper can even take a seat at my bedside, Cole's popping his head around the door too. 'Hey, Cole, thanks for coming,' I say.

'I won't stay long. Track report, you know. And…' He looks at Harper. 'I'll tell everyone you're okay. Good to see you.'

'You, too, Cole. Thanks again.'

And with that he leaves. He's clearly picked up on the

weird energy bouncing off Harper but I can't afford to think about that right now.

'I thought…' Harper steadies himself with a hand resting against the wall. 'I don't know what I thought. Shit! For a moment I thought you were dead. Ash was being so slow with updates and then he said it was you and I thought, fuck, he didn't want to tell me because it was already too late.'

For a second, the terrible conversation from yesterday is completely forgotten. The raw emotion on his face makes it hard for me to breathe. His hair's a floppy, sweaty mess of curls from both his helmet and what looks like hours of running his fingers through it. There are red blotches on his cheeks that can only be from repressed emotions and his eyes are swollen with unshed tears. His gaze is so intense as he scans my body to check I'm okay.

How am I meant to be mad, how can I push this man away when he comes to me like this?

Except, I know I have to. I know I have to because if it's not going anywhere then what's the point? I don't want casual sex, I want a *lover*, in every sense of the word.

'Thanks for coming to check on me, but I'm all good. You should probably head back. The motorhome's a mess and we have to hand the keys back in less than forty-eight hours before we fly to Singapore.' I don't think for a second that he's going to be responsible and do any tidying up but it'll give him a chance to get his stuff from my room. I also need him out of here and it feels like the perfect excuse.

'I, um, ordered pizza to the hospital when they came out and told me you could have visitors. I thought we could eat together. It's probably not the most romantic setting, but you did suggest we go for dinner together.' He laughs, nervously, and there's a pink flush creeping up his neck.

If my head weren't throbbing with a raging headache right now, I would roll my eyes. When I asked him out for dinner, this isn't what I meant, and I think he knows it. But I don't think I've got the strength to have the conversation that's long overdue while I'm recovering from a 300km/h crash.

'Pizza sounds good.'

I really am too tired and bruised to put up more of a fight right now. I feel like I've been tiptoeing around his skittishness for months. We've been acting like a couple in private, and things have felt really good, but the second I push for more he freaks out. I know we never even explicitly agreed to be exclusive, but we were always together so it's not like he was out seeing anyone else. But he won't go out on a date with me yet he shows up at my bedside with big feelings and pizza? It's more exhausting to figure out than two hours on the track. It's gruelling for my brain, having to hold myself in check so I don't scare him off. I don't know if I'm coming or going and I won't sacrifice my performance on the track for the sake of his comfort. Italy has been a total shitshow for me, and I've got no one to blame but myself. We've been operating on his terms so far, but what I want and what I need matter, too.

Except, every time he runs, he comes back quicker. It feels like progress, and the way he's looking at me right now it's clear I must mean something to him. But how long can we keep doing this for? How far would he run if I asked him to be my boyfriend? Would he ever stop running if I got down on one knee?

Woah!

Now is not the time to be thinking about marrying

someone who won't even go on a date with me. I must have hit my head really hard.

'Where did you finish?' I ask.

He meets my eye with a shy pride I didn't know existed in him. I know arrogant Harper, teasing Harper, seductive Harper, sad Harper, but this is new. And it's a good look on him.

'P1,' he says.

'Well done. You should be really proud of yourself.'

'I am, you know. I mean, it's only cos you're in here, but still.'

'No, you deserve it Harper,' I say. He does. He's an incredible driver. I don't know why it's taken so long for him to get called up to the top category. Sponsors and team owners must really dislike his off-track antics to have passed him over for so many years.

'Thanks,' he says quietly.

'What pizza did you get me?' I ask in an attempt to discharge the sudden tension in the room.

'Pepperoni with hot honey.'

He's too good at this. For me this is the perfect mix of meat and spice and sweetness on a pizza and I hate that he knows me so well.

I know he sees my reaction because he looks really proud of himself.

He obviously takes this as an invitation to get closer, because he sits down in the chair next to my bed, scooting it right up next to my pillow.

'I did good, huh?'

'Depends. Did you order just pizza?'

'What do you take me for? Of course I didn't. I got tomato

and mozzarella arancini and then garlic bread with chipotle jam and caramalised onion chutney.'

He's right. He is too good. It's the post-race cheat meal, and because we're in Italy, it's going to be phenomenal and I'll end up falling even harder for him.

Then he'll probably say no to an actual date and we'll never sleep together again. He'll disappear to another team or I'll retire and that'll be it. One hospital pizza date and a whole heap of excellent sex. Then nothing.

It's depressing that my thoughts stray like this around our non-existent relationship.

'Maybe I am good at this dating business.'

I'm not sure if he means to say that out loud. His face says not as it contorts with a mixture of surprise and shock and a healthy dose of fear.

I push myself into a sitting position and the undignified action pulls apart the hospital gown they forced me into.

His sharp intake of breath echoes in the sterile room. 'Fucking hell, Kian! That's not a few cuts and bruises. It's like fifty per cent of your body is black and blue, and that's only what I can see.'

I try to adjust both my gown and the blanket to cover up the marks, but I'm not exactly mobile right now and every joint and muscle is sore. Harper bats away my hands and surveys the damage in full. His fingers dance lightly across the darker bruising on my forearms and biceps and my elbows, which are practically black. There's a painful cut on the top of my shoulder where something dug into me on impact, but it doesn't hurt half as much with Harpers fingers trailing over it.

'It's just what happens, innit?' I try to sound casual, but it's true that getting injured is part of any sport. Ours is just slightly more extreme when it comes to weighing up risks and benefits, because we could end up dying in a pit of fiery hell. I'm glad Elise won't see it.

'You crashed, Kian. I haven't seen one like that before. I kept holding my breath every time I passed the scene. I wanted to see you but I didn't want to at the same time, you know? They had to pull you out. Imagine trying to drive and still rubberneck at the same time?' The words fall out of his mouth fast and breathless. It's almost like he's on the verge of panicking – and it's not at the thought of being in a relationship but at the thought of me being injured.

'Hey, hey…' I reach out to grab his hand and lace our fingers together whilst praying that a nurse doesn't walk in. Harper would run and we'd be tabloid fodder and I don't have the energy to deal with that right now. 'I'm actually fine. They've X-rayed and scanned every inch of me. They've checked for a concussion more times than I can count and mostly I feel fine. A bit sore and tired and a bit of a headache because my body needs to repair itself, but that's it.'

He sinks back into the uncomfortable plastic chair, his other hand on top of mine to hold me in place. Not that I'm going anywhere, seeing as I'm hooked up to a monitor for my heart rate.

It's the most worried I've ever seen him about anything and I know I should be honoured but the doubt is still there, niggling away. I'll want something from him that he isn't ready for, I'll push him too far too fast, and he'll leave again. And one day, he'll stop coming back.

'I just need to rest and take it easy for a couple days. But don't you worry, I'll be kicking your ass again the second we're back in the gym.'

We'll be staying in a hotel in Singapore – no more motorhome! – and apparently we're taking over a whole wing that's newly built, on the same floor as the spa and gym facilities.

My body almost melts at the thought of a good soak in a hot tub.

'Sure, sure, because it's always you kicking my ass, baby.' The gulp that follows the pet name assures me he didn't mean to say it. That's two things he didn't mean to say out loud – his defences are clearly down right now. I don't know how to acknowledge it without scaring him off, so I'm grateful that the nurse decides to interrupt us just then.

Our hands spring apart in what feels like an obvious way, but the nurse must not notice. 'Sorry, visit over. Mr Walker needs rest.'

She doesn't leave the doorway, so Harper has no choice but to say a quick and casual goodbye and follow her out. I guess I'll be eating that pizza on my own after all.

———

The following afternoon, Kev, one of the drivers, delivers me to the door of the motorhome and I'm surprised someone doesn't race over with a wheelchair to transport me the couple of metres up to the door. I've been thoroughly coddled for the last twenty-four hours, and I can't wait to have some privacy again.

I thank Kev for his help getting out of the car – my abs seem to have suffered disproportionately – but the opportunity to finally stretch properly is heavenly. The fresh air is delicious, and even though every part of me hurts, it's nice to extend my limbs and get some motion back into my body.

Harper appears in the doorway, almost as if he's been watching for my arrival. There's a soft smile on his face and I hear him audibly breathe out, relaxing his shoulders and holding open the door for me to pass.

'It's good to be home,' I say stepping over the threshold. I stop short, though, when I see that the place is spotless. 'Who'd you hire?' I joke.

'Asshole.' He goes to thump my arm before he remembers and stops short. 'I'll have you know I did all of this, by myself, with only a little help from Johannes who held the sofas up so I could vacuum under them.'

'You vacuumed? I didn't know you knew how.'

'I wasn't actually sure where any of the cleaning equipment was, but it's all kept in that.' He gestures to the grey storage caddy like it's the first time I've seen it, too, during the twelve weeks we've been living in the motorhome.

'Yes, I'm aware. Who do you think's been cleaning up after you for the last three months?'

'Yeah, yeah.'

It's good to be back with Harper, even if my brain's still mush – I'm telling myself it's from the crash but I know it's mostly a result of uncertainty about our situation.

'Thanks for sorting some clothes out for Kev to bring to the hospital this morning. Leaving in the very short hospital gown would have produced some interesting headlines tomorrow.'

'You're welcome. I didn't want anyone coming in here and realising our shit's all in your room.'

And there he goes again. He could have left it at *you're welcome* but now I feel like his dirty little secret again.

'Right.' It's all I can manage without revealing my disappointment.

'I also cooked dinner. Don't get me wrong, it's only pasta with pesto – nothing fancy – but the cupboards are pretty bare with us flying out tomorrow.'

'I'll take anything over hospital food.' I hate that the conversation now feels awkward again.

He spoons pasta from a pot into two bowls and we settle on the sofa to eat it. We're side by side, but we may as well be thousands of miles apart. Silence settles around us as we eat and then he even volunteers to do the washing-up.

I can't quite believe my ears, but I'm not about to protest. I don't think I could stand up for long enough anyway, and I want nothing more than to sleep for a year. I'll have to pack in the morning because my head's in a spin.

'I'm going to get the shower going. I got you some eucalyptus shower gel – it's supposed to be good for you and it smells amazing. I also got you some magnesium spray for afterwards, and some arnica cream. Is that okay?' I'm not sure why he's asking so hesitantly. Maybe because I'm shocked into silence by what he's clearly been doing for the last twenty-four hours.

'That sounds perfect, thanks.'

His shoulders straighten at my words and he quickly finishes up the dishes before disappearing into the bathroom.

I don't know what to make of his acts of service. I'm in danger of reading way too much into them and thinking it means something it probably doesn't. I can't afford that. I don't need to look very far to be reminded of that.

As I slip into bed, clean and refreshed and looking forward to sleep, Harper appears in the doorway in a pair of what I believe to be my boxers. He presses a kiss to my shoulder and then my forehead and I realise he's not sure whether he's welcome in my bed or not. I lift the covers and he slides in beside me.

'Do you wanna be the little spoon tonight?' he asks.

I don't know why but my throat suddenly feels too thick to swallow and my eyes begin to mist over. Maybe it's the relief that I'm okay after the crash. Maybe it's the painkillers I'm on. Or maybe it's the way *he's* looking after *me* for a change. I don't know.

I nod and he wraps his arms around me gently and scootches close until my ass is flush against his crotch. He's not hard and neither am I, yet this feels like the most intimate thing we've ever done.

We fall asleep, his chest pressed to my back, and the last thing I remember thinking is how much I'd love to spend every night for the rest of my life like this.

But then, in typical Harper James fashion, the next evening he chooses a seat away from me on the plane. He jokes that he wants to be closer to the bar, but that doesn't fly with me. Especially when he spends the whole flight in his seat, minus a bathroom break, and doesn't take a single drop of alcohol.

Just like in the moment of the crash, I still can't get my mind off of him and his feelings towards me. Even when he acts like this.

It's the famous hot-and-cold routine we've settled into and I feel utterly deflated. From the highest high to the lowest low.

I pull out my phone, itching to text Elise for advice, but

what would I even say? How would I put into words the situationship I'm in? How can I explain how I feel about him when I'm on such an emotional roller coaster.

At this point, with how shit I feel right now, we might as well be nothing.

And that's the most heartbreaking thing of all.

Chapter Twenty-Two

Harper

The first week in Singapore feels different. I can't quite explain why, but it's like Kian and I are dancing around each other.

Being back in a hotel, having separate rooms at opposite ends of the corridor, puts space back between us, because now, for us to spend time together, we actually have to make the effort. There's no more motorhome enclosing us in a bubble; it's a choice not the default and that gives everything a complicated layer of significance.

The first day, we spend more time apart than together. He's obviously still resting and recovering so he can be fighting fit for the following weekend, and I'm trying to stop worrying about him. If he wasn't okay the doctors wouldn't have allowed him to fly.

The second day, he texts me in the morning and we head to the gym together. He's quieter than normal, focuses on his workout, and doesn't make any digs at mine. It's eerie when he finishes up on the treadmill and leaves me to it.

Days three and four we don't have a choice but to spend all day together. We're both in the same photo shoot for Hendersohm merch and some of the pictures require us to pose together. I wouldn't say it's strained, but the banter we have feels forced and no real laughter is shared between the two of us.

By the end of day five I've had enough and I take matters into my own hands. I miss him. I hate that I do, but that doesn't stop it. Every night, falling asleep alone in my hotel bed, I think about going over to his hotel room in a nice shirt and asking if he wants to go for dinner. Or if I can spend the night – whatever he wants.

I don't even care if we have sex, I just miss how his body engulfs mine when we're sleeping and how I wake up to a tangle of his limbs and mine.

So I do it. I shower and put on a fresh shirt and I go over to his room.

The second I'm outside his door, I feel so nervous that my throat goes dry and I can't swallow. My lungs don't seem to want to work, either, and apparently I can no longer make a fist to knock on the door. What the hell's going on with me?

Forcing myself to do some of the breathing exercises I've been working on with my therapist, I stand there in the corridor like a lemon, visualising calm seas, warm winds and sandy beaches in the hope it'll stop the light-headedness and the panic attack in their tracks.

It's just Kian. It's just dinner. It doesn't have to mean anything.

Before I can back out, I knock, and for a heart-stopping

moment I'm met with silence. But then, in a quick second – almost like he's been standing on the other side of the door for a while – Kian pulls open the door.

He's fresh from the shower, water droplets cascading down his bare chest and getting tangled in the array of body hair I love to nuzzle. His hair's a wild, wet mess and even though his skin is still mottled with yellowing bruises from the crash I want to abandon the dinner plans I've made and climb him like a tree.

'Um, hi.' The words stumble clumsily out of my mouth and I can't find a way to recall everything I planned to say to him. Dinner. Staying over. Missing him. My brain's screaming at me to say it but I just open and close my mouth like a fish flopping on a river bank.

'You going somewhere?' Kian asks, eying my outfit and the bag I'm clinging to like it's my lifeline here.

Come on, brain.

'Um, yeah. Out. Or not. Or we could just go to bed right now.'

No, no, no! This isn't what I planned. Tell him about the dinner reservation you've made. Tell him you miss him.

'Fuck, you look so hot. Do you answer the door like that to everyone?' This is not going well.

'No, but I could see it was you and—'

'You wanted to tempt me inside? I see your game, Mr Walker.' The words don't come out in the teasing way I intend, making this conversation feel even more awkward.

'No, but I could hear you pacing outside and I watched you stand there being weird, so I thought it would be best to find out what's going on before you bolted.'

Bolted? I'm not bolting. Do I look like I'm bolting in my

favourite jeans and the shirt that makes my eyes pop? I'm not yet sure that I'm not making a total tit of myself.

My hands are trembling by my sides. Do normal people feel this much stress and anxiety when trying to ask a perfectly decent guy out for dinner?

Why does this feel so difficult? It's what I want. I want Kian. And I know he wants me because he asked me first. Yet I can't force the words out. The silence engulfs me and I feel like I'm drowning.

He looks expectantly at me, his eyes pleading with me to ask, and I still can't. I can't give him what he wants.

And when I realise that, my heart shatters.

I'm glad I'm leaning against his door frame when he asks, 'What's the point of this, Harper? Like what? You show up here and we fall into bed together and pretend it doesn't mean anything?'

Would that be so bad? I didn't hear him complaining about our routine in the motorhome. It was nice, weirdly domestic, but I thought he was happy.

I go to reply, but he doesn't give me the chance.

'Where do you see this going? Like, I'm talking long-term. Are we still sneaking around when the season finishes? In a year's time? What about two? Are you still showing up at my door for a quickie whenever the mood takes you? Are you still pretending there isn't something more going on between us? Do you see a future for us or is this all just some game to you?' Kian releases a deep, heavy sigh, like he feels better to have got all of that out in one go. I wonder how long it's been building up for.

Knowing him, a while.

My head is spinning, every question passing through my

brain like a big flashing neon sign making me wince. I don't even know where to start at this point. All I know is that he's asking whether I see a future with him and I just … can't. I'm not sure I see a future with anyone. I don't even know how to start seeing that. My brain doesn't seem to have the right setting. I don't think like that; I never have. I think about today, and I know that tomorrow will take care of itself. I never had any control over what happened to me as a child so I learned that plans and expectations only lead to disappointment and rejection. I started this season in the lower category, wondering if I'd ever get called up, and then on day one of pre-season training I'm catapulted into the top category through someone else's misfortune. And now I'm here, with a win under my belt, rolling with the punches and making the most of what's landed in my lap. It's a dream to be here, and to be getting these results, too. And alongside Kian Walker, the man who's been my idol for years, the man who's making me feel things and want things that are new and exciting and … terrifying.

Kian's still staring at me, knuckles white where he's gripping his towel for it to stay wrapped around his body. With every silent second that goes by, the look on his face changes from hope and expectation to painful, bitter disappointment. I can't give him what he wants, and maybe he already knows that.

Maybe it's why he asked, finally, so he can put an end to this all together.

I wouldn't blame him. He doesn't really need this mess in his life. He's trying to retain a title, maybe even break a record, and he has people in his life who need him. Who love him. He doesn't need someone who can't even think about a future without having a panic attack.

273

I watch anger set into his face and his jaw tense. His eyes harden and I can feel the wall he's building between us, brick by brick.

I can't even blame him. Every time I think about the crash, I can't help but think it might have been my fault. I've been such a distraction to his routine. A dangerous distraction. I could have cost him his life. Am I really thinking it could be a good idea for him to be starting a relationship with someone like me?

'Harper? What's going on?'

The sound of my name snaps me out of my thoughts and the nervous ball of energy morphs into anxiety. The scramble of pain in my chest and the way my hands begin to tingle tell me it's time to get out of here. There's no fight, only flight. I can't do this.

'I'm, um, I'm going out. Johannes—' I quickly fire his name out even though I haven't spoken to him today. 'I'm going out with Johannes. I was gonna see if you wanted to come, but you look ready for bed. So, um, see you tomorrow.'

It's mortifying how quickly I take off along the corridor. I summon a car to take me somewhere dark and dismal. I don't even stop to check reviews of the place online, I just ask the driver to take me anywhere I can drink and dance, and he obliges.

Once I'm inside it's not difficult to find someone to try and lose myself in. He smiles when he realises he doesn't even need to buy me a drink.

He then proceeds to act like I'm easy in every other way too. The first song hasn't even finished when I feel him playing with the button of my jeans, his other hand dangerously close to cupping my dick.

I shake him off from my crotch area and his hands roam across my chest, playing with my nipples through the thin fabric of my shirt. Normally they are so receptive, pebbling at any kind of attention, but I'm just not feeling it.

I give him one more song so he can't accuse me of being a prick-tease, but when the song ends and I try to push him away, he fists my shirt and pulls me closer like it's part of a game we're playing.

'Sorry, I need to go piss,' I say way too quickly, but his grip is tight and I feel my chest struggling to expand against the tight fabric. Any normal person would just knee him in the nuts and run, but I can't. Someone will pull out a phone, get it on camera, and it'll be headline news tomorrow.

So I squirm and wriggle, hoping to slowly slip out of his grasp, and when the music changes, I manage to slip out from under his arms and dart towards the back of the bar. I trap myself in the bathroom, slumping down against the wall to try and centre myself again. I used to do this all the time – go to bars and pick up guys – but it doesn't feel right anymore.

I don't even know why I'm here. Nobody in here is Kian, and apparently he's all I want now. No one compares to him; no one looks at me like he does, like I could hang the moon and stars and still have time to race in every Grand Prix of the year. He thinks too much of me and I know it. He thinks far better of me than I deserve, but it was nice for a while to be with someone who cares so much.

There's such a familiarity to Kian now that I love—

Love?

What does love have to do with being compatible in the bedroom? When did that ever matter?

My brain starts spiralling down a path that I've never wanted it to wander before.

Because I know what's at the end of it: a future with Kian. We could race together as teammates and come home to each other at night. We could spend the downtime between seasons together. We could cook meals together, eat at a proper dining table, go on runs together, wake up together every morning and fall asleep every night ... together.

When I finally allow myself to picture it, it's thrilling. The future looks so bright, so promising, like something that could bring me so much joy.

But that's the problem, because now I want it. And wanting things like this, things that rely on other people, is dangerous.

And I've thrown it all away.

Maybe *I'm* the problem. I didn't need therapy to tell me that.

I know I push people away before they can reject me – I know that's what I did tonight with Kian. Not just *with* Kian, but *to* Kian.

How much have I hurt him by playing down what we have? I saw his face; I know what he wants from me. It hurts me so much to be rejected that I avoid any situation in which it could happen, so why would it not also hurt Kian?

Asking us to be exclusive. Trying to take me on a date. Asking if he sees a future for us. He wants to build us into something more and all I've done is treat him like I don't care, like he doesn't matter.

Dropping to the floor of the dingy toilet, I pull out my phone and select the only contact I have on speed dial. Hoping he picks up.

'Harper?' Johannes says groggily, as if I've woken him.

I check the time and see it's not that late, but we do have a free practice tomorrow so it makes sense that he's already asleep. I shouldn't have come out. Anders is going to be so pissed off at me.

'Hey, Harper, you there? Did you butt-dial me?'

I'm trying to summon the words, but they come out as nothing but a gasp of his name.

'Harp, you okay? What's going on?'

'It's all too much…' I feel breathless as I say the words. It's overwhelming, this feeling… My airways are shutting down…

'Hey, hey, Harp, I think you might be having a panic attack,' Johannes says softly over the phone. 'Take some nice deep breaths and focus only on your breathing. Come on, follow me, breathe in, two, three, and hold it for one, two, three. Breathe out for one, two, three, and hold it there, two, three.'

I try to breathe, I try to follow the rhythm that Johannes is setting, but the air gets trapped in my claggy throat and it goes nowhere when I try to choke it down. It's like I'm only using the top ten per cent of my lungs and I can't get deeper.

'Not. Working,' I pant out as my chest grows tighter. This is so humiliating. I'm in a grotty bar-bathroom, losing it because a guy told me he likes me.

Likes me. Properly likes me. Wants-to-talk-about-a-future-together likes me. And apparently that's too much for me. 'He's a fucking idiot, Johannes!' I growl, my throat dry as my heart rate quickens. 'Imagine liking me. Why? Why would anyone do that?'

'Harper, I don't understand what you're talking about,' Johannes replies, I can hear every bit of how patient he's trying to be right now. It's because I've kept him in the dark. I haven't

277

breathed a single word about Kian to Johannes. I've barely seen Johannes, to be honest.

'He asked me –' I pant between words, taking in any air possible whilst feeling as thought my lungs won't re-inflate '– he asked me … if I see … a future … with him. Jo, I don't … know how … to see … a future with anyone.'

There's a sharp pang in my heart. It might be the realisation that this might not be as true as I've always believed it to be. But in the moment it feels so sharp and heart-wrenching that I gasp.

'Harper, man, you need to get it together. Tell me where you are and I'll come and get you and we can talk about this. It'll be okay.'

'It won't, because, because…' There are a million reasons flying around my head – so many that I can't put them into words for Johannes. How do I tell him that nothing will ever be okay in this situation, because I will always want Kian but he will quickly realise that he can do better, that I'm holding him back, that there are more exciting things in the world than Harper James. And he will leave, in the end. People always leave. It's a given. So I can't tell Kian I want more with him, too, because wanting more will only destroy me.

'Because what? Harper, you're scaring me, bud. I didn't even know you were seeing anyone. Why didn't you say something?'

'Because it was private. It was meant to be just sex.'

'You normally tell me about every sexual conquest.' He's right; he's so right. Maybe I've kept this from him because in my subconscious it's already more. Because it's Kian. It was never *not* going to mean more and I should have been smart enough to spot that.

'He wouldn't want that. It's not the same.'

'What's not the same?'

Shit. Now he's probably going to hate me even more. 'Him. *He's* not the same. Things are different and it's messing up my head. I can't do this, Jo. I need to do something. I need to rid myself of him.'

'Don't do anything—'

I hang up before he can finish that sentence. He can tell me not to do anything stupid all he wants, but we both know I'm going to do it anyway.

I need to do this for Kian. To save him from all the hurt and pain I'll eventually cause him, or that he'll cause me.

Chapter Twenty-Three

Kian

How many times am I going to find myself here? It's almost as if I watch him every time realising he's a little too emotionally invested in what's going on between us and then he shuts himself down completely. Cuts me off.

At what point do I accept that he means it? How many times do I need to be shut out before I'm done? If he can't even acknowledge that this is more than sex, that we are more than two people who just stick their dicks in each other, then what's the point?

There really isn't one.

I should know that by now.

It's time.

Time to move on.

It starts with deleting all of our texts. Every shared memory of the last several months, gone. Every bit of banter, every flirty message, every random meme is banished to somewhere they can never come back from.

A few of his things got mixed up with mine because I had to pack while I was feeling very sub-par and didn't have the energy to separate them out: a hat, his Deep Heat, a couple of T-shirts. I find a bag and chuck the items in, leaving it by the door to drop off at his room tomorrow.

I want to include a hoodie of his that I've basically adopted and to which I feel very attached, but in the end I keep it. Then I change my mind and put it in the bag.

I change my mind again and pull it out, holding it to my nose like a pathetic teenager crying over a first crush.

I'm not sure what I'm expecting it to do – it's not like it's going to magically make Harper appear or change his mind. He won't decide he wants to be with me just because I'm clinging to an inanimate object of his. So, I ball it up and chuck it into the bag again.

Yet it does nothing to loosen the grip he has on my heart.

To the point I find my thumb hovering over his name in my phone contacts. I'm desperate to call him and tell him to come back so we can talk.

But what's the point? That's the thought I keep coming back to. There is no point with Harper. He doesn't want to commit to me and I have to accept that.

Kicking my bags under my bed, I hate that I haven't unpacked properly like I usually do. The energy I normally have to make a place my own little home for the two weeks we're here has been zapped by something painful in my chest.

I won't label it heartbreak. I won't let Harper break me. He can't. He doesn't have that power.

It's a lie I'll keep telling myself until I believe it.

Elijah's been messaging me recently saying he's doing much better and is back in the gym. He needs to get signed-off from his physical therapist and then he can get back in the simulator. Maybe Anders will pull him back in for the rest of the season and Harper will be out. Maybe he'll take London's position as our back-up driver – or maybe he'll be sent back to the lower tier. That would be the ultimate preference.

I wouldn't have to deal with him at all, then; there'd be so much less temptation. No more mistakes, like in Italy.

Trying to settle back into bed is hard.

When I saw him fumbling around outside my door this evening, all dressed up and panting like a dog, I thought the few days of distance we've had in Singapore because of the change in living situation had worked their magic and he'd come to tell me he missed me and wanted to be with me and that he love—

Obviously I got ahead of myself. For a split second he seemed determined and brave, and full of a light and warmth I'm not used to seeing in him, but then that all vanished in the blink of an eye. It was so fast that I doubted whether it had ever been there, at all. I must have imagined it because I wanted it so much.

Of course he's out with Johannes tonight. And I know it's not to talk about whatever was bothering Johannes the last time Harper ran off to be with him. Harper was dressed to go out out. Maybe he's kissing another guy right now. Maybe he's shagging someone else right now.

I really should be trying to sleep. Free practice is early tomorrow and I'm already feeling drained. I'm still recovering from the crash and I need all the help I can get – both physically and mentally. I think of Elise's worry and how I've added to her burden. I can't let Harper mess me up anymore.

Closing my eyes doesn't help, though. Even squeezing them shut doesn't delete the memory of the scene in the hallway. It's on a fixed loop in my head and I can't stop it.

I struggle to get comfy. The bed feels too big and the other side is too cold for me stretch out into. I toss and turn until pure exhaustion finally wins out and the world around me fades.

Until my phone rings out on max volume and I'm scrambling for it from under my pillow. Hope bubbles inside me that I'll see Harper's name on my screen. He's changed his mind and he needs me—

I couldn't be more wrong.

My whole body is frozen. Elise never gets the time change wrong, so if she's calling me in the middle of the night then—

'Elise?' My voice is ragged. I already know what she's going to say. Fear paralyses me, dread dripping down my spine.

'I'm so sorry, Ki,' she chokes out, and I feel my whole body curl inwards, my free hand fisting the twisted-up bedsheet.

She doesn't need to say any more.

Mum's gone.

It's there in the way my sister sobs down the phone and I'm consumed by loss and a need to be with her.

The emptiness in my heart grows more than I thought it possibly could after tonight.

Yet I don't cry. The beginnings of grief numbs my every emotion until I can't feel a thing.

'I'm coming home, Elise. I'll be on the next plane out of here.' It's not very often that I flaunt my wealth or leverage my power within Hendersohm, but I'll do anything to board a private jet on a runway right now if it will get me home faster to my sister.

'But this weekend!' She tries to protest.

'I don't care about this weekend.' I'm shocked by how much I actually mean it. I've never missed a race in my life. I missed the births of both Cassie and Jesse, my sister's engagement party, and Jesse's christening, but nothing will keep me from this. 'I'm coming home. As quickly as possible. I'll figure it out. I'm on my way, Elise, I promise.'

She sobs quietly into the phone and I can't breathe. 'I love you, Ki. I'll see you soon?' she croaks out in between sobs.

'Soon. Love you.'

The line drops and I feel like I might be sick.

I get out of bed and start throwing things in a bag. I call Kelsey, the team organiser, while I'm doing it and when I tell her what's happened she works some magic and gets me a plane that can take me to a private runway in Norfolk. She's arranged a car to meet me, too, and I'm halfway to the airport before I can stop and think.

This is when I contemplate letting Harper know. Whatever's happening, or not happening, between us, he deserves to hear from me that I won't be racing this weekend.

I go to text him when a notification about him posting to his Insta story hits my phone. It's a shaky video taken from Harper's outstretched arm. Neon lights flash rapidly around him and it lights up the way he and another man are grinding to the beat of the music.

It hollows me out completely.

If my heart and soul hadn't already been ripped out and

torn to shreds, this would do it. It's the final nail in the coffin of the saga of me and Harper James.

He was never going to be emotionally ready for a relationship. I should have known that from our first proper conversation in Austria. Hell, I should have known that the second he arrived and caused nothing but chaos for me and for Hendersohm.

I should have walked away completely after the first kiss. I should have locked the memory of it away in the far corner of my mind and left it there. I should have employed even a modicum of my famed self-discipline and maintained a polite and professional distance between us. I should have let him twist himself into self-destructive knots and awaited Elijah's return. Moved on as teammates and teammates only.

Except I couldn't help myself. Harper's an enigma I could not resist and now I've been burnt by him.

Well, he can go fuck himself.

I press the two buttons on the side of my phone, screenshotting the image, and then send it to Harper. I wait to see that it's been delivered and then I block the shit out of him – in my contacts, in WhatsApp, and on every bit of social media I've stupidly followed him on.

And just like that he's gone. I only wish I could start feeling better about it right away, but there's no chance of that with everything else that's going on.

The fucking asshole.

Obviously he's not to know that Mum's just passed, but if he hadn't been out shagging some other guy then he would have been with me and he would have found out when I did. He could have held me like he did when I had that nightmare, and I would have felt better.

I need someone to blame and Harper's a pretty big target.

There are probably so many people I should be contacting right now. The qualifiers are less than thirty-six hours away and I'm one hundred per cent not going to be here. Anders needs to call up our back-up driver to take my place – or Elijah, if he's really ready – and my agent, Will, needs to know I'm about to head back to England. Anna probably needs to know to put out some kind of statement about why I won't be competing. Except I can only bring myself to focus on getting to the airport. I hope Kelsey will handle everything because I just can't right now.

I want and need to be on this flight home.

The plane is waiting on the tarmac as promised, and as I soon as I get on they shut the doors and we start taxiing. Once the plane levels out in the sky, I sink my chair into lie-flat mode and pray for sleep so I don't have to think about how my sister's coping right now. I hope Mum wasn't alone, but I also wouldn't wish it on my twin to have to watch Mum die right before her eyes. I hope Cassie and Jesse are okay – they'll know something's wrong and they're too young to understand. I hope Grant is on a flight home already, too, so Elise has help with the kids. I've forgotten where his conference is, but I know he's not at home right now.

I wasn't there.

I wasn't there when it happened.

I shove my earbuds in and put on some calming music. I need to drown out my own thundering thoughts before I'm no use to anyone.

Eventually, the exhaustion of the day hits and I fall asleep.

When I step off the plane and into the waiting car, I reluctantly turn my phone back on. The BBC news blast about

Mum's death drops into my phone right away and the first articles also speculate that I might not race this weekend.

The driver of the car doesn't say anything, just tips his hat at me out of respect and closes the door behind me. At least he's judged the tone right and leaves me be on the short drive out into the Norfolk countryside.

My phone buzzes non-stop with texts, voicemails, and notifications. I can't bear it – any of it – so I switch it off completely.

Elise must hear the car pulling up the driveway, because she's waiting on the doorstep for me. Her hair's scraped back into a bun on top of her head and she's wearing her comfiest pyjamas.

It takes two steadying breaths for me to finally get out of the car, but the second I reach her I'm pulling her into a hug.

'God, I'm so sorry,' I whisper into her hair as she tucks herself up under my chin. In this moment I'm glad we're the kind of twins who are affectionate, who bicker and fight but who will always love and be there for each other. I couldn't do this without her. I couldn't have done any of it without her.

Her sacrifice has allowed me to have the professional career of my dreams. She gave up her nursing degree and selflessly took care of everything so I didn't have to. The least I can do is take care of her now, so for once she can just look after herself.

I start by running her a bath while Grant puts the kids to bed – he wasn't far away, it turns out, so he beat me here. Then, between us we throw together a somewhat edible dinner and even though we eat in silence at least she's well fed as we send her up to bed early.

'How's she doing?' I ask Grant.

We're sitting in the lounge, the TV playing some rubbish in

the background that neither of us are watching. We've spent hours cleaning the house, running several loads of washing before finally stripping the bedding that Mum passed in. We both allowed silent tears to fall while we did it, but I'm just glad we spared Elise from having to do it. I'm also glad I didn't have to do it alone.

'She can't speak about it yet. She doesn't want to. I think she was waiting for you to get back. I wish I could bear some of the weight of the loss, but I can't even begin to understand it, with two very alive parents.' There's a level of heartbreak to his voice I've never heard before, and I know Elise isn't the only one affected by caring for Mum.

'Well, I'm here now. I want to do everything I can. I don't want her to have to do a thing other than take the time to process what she needs.'

It's the least I can do after being so absent in the final moments.

Eventually, Grant heads up to bed to be with his wife. I know he will comfort and hold her while she cries. I'm glad.

But it's yet another reminder, if I needed one, that I will be going to bed alone. I will cry silently to myself. I will reach out and feel the cold side of the bed and know that no one is there for me.

And I wish, I *wish*, that wasn't the case.

Chapter Twenty-Four

Harper

I've done a series of stupid things tonight, but drinking's not one of them. I would never do that the night before getting in a race car, even if it's just a free practice. Yet, at the same time, I feel drunk. I mean, sober me wouldn't be grinding up against this random guy whose names I don't know. Nor would sober Harper be posting a string of pictures and videos of us together all over my Instagram stories. Anyone with half an ounce of sense wouldn't have come back out here for round two after suffering a panic attack on the floor of the men's bathroom.

Yet here I am again, a different guy dancing behind me like he's won big tonight. Not that he'll be getting anything from me at all.

I'm not even sure what I'm trying to achieve here. To push Kian away? I'm confident I already did that when I freaked out – again – when he asked if we had a future together. He's a saint if he'd even think about giving me a chance after that. And there's whatever I'm doing here.

I suppress my anxiety to the sound of the pulsing beat of the EDM blaring from the speakers in the bar. The bone-shaking volume of the noise helps me to ignore every thought about Kian, but even pressed up against this stranger, there's only one person I actually want.

I don't even want to be here. It won't help. I know it, but I'm too scared to go back and deal with the consequences of my actions. I'm sure my therapist will have something to say about that, but I'm not opening the lid of that box of horror tonight.

Luckily, I don't have to worry about that now because out of the corner of my eye I spot Johannes pushing through the crowd as he makes a beeline for me, a scowl trained on me that would finish off a lesser mortal.

'You're being a fucking idiot,' Johannes growls as he finally reaches me. He's quick to drag me away from the random I'm grinding against. Whoever he is, he's annoyed by the interruption, but one look at Johannes's grizzly face and he scuttles off to find someone else.

'He was hot,' I grumble with a total lack of enthusiasm. I'm not even sure I got a good enough look at him to tell, but he was keen as soon as he realised who I was.

'No, he isn't. He's a two at best and you were humiliating yourself.' He's still dragging me by the hand and before I realise it we're outside the club.

'How did you know where I was?' I ask. I'm completely sober, but the panic attack has screwed with my brain.

'The second you hung up, I saw that you'd posted your gross display of shit dancing on your Insta story. You were stupid enough to catch the name of the bar in the background. Anyone could have seen this. You're lucky you don't have a stampede of fans waiting outside.'

'You're here to save me. My hero,' I grit out sarcastically.

'What the hell is wrong with you? I thought you were on your best behaviour. You're on a final warning, remember? Don't you want this? Don't you want to be in the Championship?'

I shrug, because when did Johannes get so wise or become the boss of me.

He's guiding me into the back of a taxi and giving the location of his hotel over mine. That's probably for the best right now, considering how I left things with Kian.

He doesn't yell again for the rest of the drive home, the taxi not offering a partition between us and the driver to shut him out of our private lives. But the second the door to his hotel room is closed behind us he lets rip.

'I can't believe you. Honestly, Harper! If even *I'm* over this ridiculous behaviour, then surely that must say something.'

I've never been shouted at by Johannes before, but he towers a good four inches over me and his voice booms when he's pissed off. It's kind of scary.

'Says you! Remember Belgium? The hot twins you shagged and the litre of tequila? So don't bring the holier-than-thou act to my door because it won't fly with me. You're forgetting I know you too well, Johannes.'

'What's going on, mate? There's no world in which we should be fighting about this. It's bullshit, Harper. We don't do this. You and I don't do this. We straight talk each other, so tell me, what the hell's going on?'

What do I tell him? I can't believe I live in a world I haven't already told him about Kian, and yet I also enjoyed it being something private that only he and I shared. But now that it's over, what does it matter?

'Me and Kian, we, er, we were sleeping together.'

He laughs. Like, fully laughs. 'Are you drunk? Because if you are, that's a new low, even for you. We've got track time tomorrow.'

I shake my head, and his eyes widen. 'Well, that's a surprise. So, what, you had a fight or something?'

'It's more complicated than that. It's not just tonight... It's ... it's been, like, a couple of months actually.' He can't think I'd be this upset after just one night with Kian. I would never let a one-night-stand make me feel this bloody awful.

'So you're together?'

I shake my head. Whatever we were, we're not that anymore.

'No, it was just sex.'

A snort escapes him and I am glaring, because when did my life become so ludicrous. 'What?'

'So, you've been like a different person for months, you've been sleeping with the same guy for months, and when it's over you have a panic attack in a bar, and it's *just sex*? I don't think so.' He thumps my arm. 'You're a fucking dickhead.'

I hate that he's right. I hate that it's so obvious when he puts it like that.

'You should see your face right now,' he says, and I expect him to laugh, but he looks me over with concerned eyes. 'You look gutted, man. I can't believe Kian Walker has you all twisted up in knots.'

'He's...' I let thoughts of Kian fill my head again and there aren't enough words to describe him or what he's come to mean to me, even if I've been too chickenshit to see it. I can't describe his beauty in words or do his character justice in even a whole book. I'd need an epic series to capture his heart and explain how big it is.

'Kian Walker, racing legend, your hero and the love of your life.'

'Don't.' Not that word. Not right now. Maybe not ever. It holds too much power over me and I'm afraid of what it will do to me this time.

'Harper, man, it's okay. Kian's a good guy and you can't shut him out because you're a bit scared.'

A bit scared? Understatement of the bloody century. The thought of opening my heart to Kian, even a little, makes me shudder.

But, when I look a little deeper, I realise he's already there. He's wormed his way into every tiny space. It's too late and I know it.

'Oh, you big idiot.' I'm grateful when Johannes doesn't say anything else on the subject and pulls me into his broad chest instead. His scent hasn't changed in the many years I've known him. His clothes always smell freshly washed, like a true clean-linen scent that mixes nicely with the soft scents of vanilla and sandalwood in his cologne. It's almost comforting as I take a big sniff, my hands fisting the back of his vest.

I need this. My best friend and his brilliant bear hugs. I'm nestled neatly into this arch of his shoulder when I spot the hickey.

Punching his arm, my voice comes out a little screechy. 'Who's the big idiot now? Is that what I think it is?'

He laughs before going round to the other side of his bed,

sliding back under the covers. If he thinks he's getting away with this, then he's having an absolute laugh.

I shuck off my jeans and climb into bed with him.

'Was he at least hot? Or is this the guy who's been stealing your attention?'

He tries his absolute best not to react, but his whole face cracks into a grin that he can't contain. Blimey, he must have been good.

'No comment.'

That only makes me more suspicious and I'm desperate to push him, but I've kept Kian from him for months. If he needs to hold a little secret in, I'll let him. For now.

We're both tucked under the duvet, looking up into the darkness. I'd say it's quiet, but I can hear both of our minds running wild.

'Kian Walker,' he mutters before we both start to laugh like absolute maniacs.

It is kind of insane, I guess. Kian's always said to me he doesn't care if people know he's bi, but he's never openly said it and he's definitely never had a boyfriend in public before. Not that I'm his boyfriend.

'You remember when we went to Silverstone, what, eight years ago? Or was it nine? And you tried to get his attention from the crowd when he was signing autographs after his race?'

Of course I remember, but there's no way Kian would ever be finding this out. Especially not now.

'Nope, never happened.'

'Oh, but it did, and when the two of you sort this out and we all become friends, I'm looking forward to telling him every single detail of how you screamed his name and cried when he won.' Because of course my best friend is going to absolutely torture me.

'If. *If* we sort this out. I don't even know what there is to sort right now. I've been kind of a prick.'

'Shocker. What's new?' I strike the back of his calf with my cold foot and he winces. 'Yep, definitely a prick.'

'Aren't you meant to be comforting me through this heartbreak or whatever.'

I don't even know if this is heartbreak. All I know is that I've never felt this kind of despair about anyone before, and when I think too hard about Kian being done with me it makes it impossible to breathe.

'I'd rather help you come up with a way to fix it than throw you a pity party.'

It's late and he's probably right, but that doesn't stop us staying up for the next two hours talking about the grand gesture that will fix our relationship. It's almost perfect when we fall asleep and I'm beyond excited to see Kian's face when it all falls into place.

For the first time in ages I feel hopeful, so very hopeful as I drift off into a peaceful slumber.

Only to find myself being shaken awake by Johannes what feels like no less than five minutes later.

I hardly even have time to crack an eye open when he's waving the bright screen of his phone around.

'Shit, shit, shit! You need to see this.'

It's hard not to see it when Johannes thrusts his phone straight in front of my face. The fact that it's morning catches me off guard, but not as much as the newsflash there in black and white on his screen.

Pop legend, Chastity Walker, dies aged 59 after a four-year battle with Parkinson's.

'Fuck, fuck, fuck.' I reach for my own phone, heading straight for his name in my contacts. I hit the call button but it doesn't even ring. I don't even get a dial tone. Which can mean only one thing.

'Maybe his phone's off?' Johannes suggests and I want to believe that, but he didn't see how angry Kian was when I told him he couldn't like me.

'He's blocked me. I need to go back to the hotel and make sure he's okay. Fuck, fuck, FUCK! I can't believe I abandon—'

'You didn't know his mum was going to die, Harper. You couldn't have known. But you *were* a fucking idiot for going out when you should have been talking to him and being honest with yourself.'

I want to glare at him, to tell him he's wrong, but I can't. He's so right it hurts. I screwed up and now Kian's going through this on his own. There's no way I can fix things right now without making his grief worse. He's got to do what's best for him and his family, and that doesn't include me. I can't imagine he'll be competing this weekend, so I'm guessing I'll be racing London. I've barely spoken a single word to him all season. Free practice today is going to be interesting.

'I should, uh, probably – definitely – go back to my hotel. I'll check on him. Do you think that's the right thing to do?'

'Maybe, I don't know. Maybe just go and offer your condolences and leave it at that for now.'

'Yeah, you're right.'

'Always am, man. Things will be okay, Harp. I promise, it'll all be okay.'

I decide to walk back to the hotel instead of taking a car. I need the fresh air to clear my head, and the walk will give me a chance to think about how I'm going to approach him and what I'm going to say. Maybe he'll shut the door in my face, but I have to try.

I barely start thinking when my phone begins ringing. My heart leaps for a moment at the thought it might be Kian, but of course it's Anders. I've already deleted the Insta stories I put up last night, but it's probably too late and I'm probably going to be dropped next season.

'Good morning,' I croak out, my throat suddenly drier than the Sahara Desert.

'Harper, hey, sorry it's early. I know you have a free practice later this afternoon but I wanted to give you a heads-up that London will be racing this weekend. As I'm sure you've heard, Kian has returned to the UK to be with his family and won't be racing this weekend.'

Kian's gone?

'Uh, yes, thank you for letting me know, sir.' The call's short and sweet and I'm just grateful not to be getting the bollocking I deserve right now. Somehow, though, it feels worse.

Kian's gone.

And I'm blocked.

I can't even try to be there for him.

I was a mess last night. How could I do this to him? How could I hurt him like this? How could I hurt someone I love like this?

Why has it only just hit me that *I love him*?

Why has it only just occurred to me that I don't have to repeat the patterns of my past, the patterns that hurt me, by hurting others? I could choose to let him love me without throwing it back in his face. And I could love him, too, couldn't I?

I feel sick to my stomach.

Is it fear? Adrenaline? Hope?

I honestly don't know.

I get up and go to his room. I know it's pointless but I want to be amongst his things. Trying the handle, I almost burst into tears upon finding it open.

Everything's gone, but you can tell he left in a rush because his bed isn't made and the bathroom's a state. Not that I care, because I just want to feel close to him for a moment. I throw myself down on his bed. Oh, God, it still smells like him, and I let myself just inhale him, duvet tucked right up under my chin. I sit up and see the plastic bag by the door with my hoodie spilling out of the top.

Oh, God, it really is over.

I pull out my phone to send him a message. I need to say something to express how sorry I am for everything, to offer my condolences, to tell him I'm here for him if or when he needs me.

I compose something that doesn't go halfway to saying everything I want to say, but then I remember. He really has blocked me.

The worst part is, I deserve it. He has every right to be done with me. I'm done with me too.

Chapter Twenty-Five

Kian

I just about make it down the drive without running over the fucking pariahs of the press who line the gravel path down to the farmhouse. I make a mental note to talk to someone about some security. I'm not sure if it's something my agent can do, or Kelsey, but maybe there's someone they can recommend. It's a relief to get back inside the house.

'It's awful out there.' I shuck off my jacket and throw my shades down onto the counter where Grant's preparing lunch for the kids.

'Worse than yesterday?' he asks, continuing to chop cucumber into sticks, each slice of the knife a little bit more aggressive.

'Much. Not sure who gave them the right to ask such invasive questions, but yeah, definitely worse. Today they were mainly asking if I was worried about missing Singapore?'

'They either don't have family or are complete monsters.

Who wouldn't miss a race to come home and grieve for a much-loved parent?'

It's a good question, but not one I can answer.

'I'm going to talk to the team's head of security and see if there's anyone they can recommend to help give us a bit more privacy until this dies down.'

I actually can't think of anything more awful than Elise having to face these vultures right now. While she and I both grew up in the public eye because of our celebrity parents, she's made every possible life choice to take herself as far from the spotlight as possible.

She's never had media training on how to handle such intrusive questions without snapping, especially when she's under emotional duress, like she is now.

It would be nothing short of a bloodbath if she steps off the property.

'Maybe we could try an electric fence or something, so if they get too close they'll get zapped.' I laugh in response but it's not a bad idea at all.

I'm just opening a couple of beers when I hear movement upstairs. It sounds like Elise is heading to the bathroom, but at least I know she's out of bed.

'How's the to-do list looking?' he asks as I extend a beer bottle to him.

'Awful, Grant. I don't know how to do this.' I'm not even saying it for sympathy or so he'll help me more, I truly mean it. I'm good at being organised about my racing life, but outside of that I don't feel like I can get a grip on anything most of the time.

'I chose the flowers.' I didn't have a clue what I was doing but I have a memory of some flowers that Mum loved to have on the windowsill and I went for a whole lot of those ones. They're pink and white, but I don't remember what the florist called them or what they're supposed to mean.

I've felt like that a lot recently. With Elise not getting out of bed and Grant looking after the kids, all decisions are on me. Which is fine. I'm happy to do it. It's time for me to bear the weight of this responsibility for once in my life. But I do wish I wasn't doing it alone. I want it to be perfect for Mum and I think that can only be delivered by Elise.

'I hope you got Astrantias.' Hearing Elise's voice in the doorway sends goosebumps down my arms and tears pinpricking the backs of my eyes. 'Mum planted them in the garden and picked them all the time. While she still could, she used to leave them in our shared bathroom. They symbolize strength, the strength that she wanted us to have.'

My arms open and Elise attaches herself to me and I finally let myself cry. The kitchen fills with sounds of sobs and apologies on both of our parts which neither of us really need to be saying. All we need is to grieve in our own ways, to process the loss, and to remember Mum together.

The jet lag is brutal, and I've spent the last two sleepless nights running over different memories of Mum from the last three decades. There are so many good ones and that's what's been important to me while trying to come to terms with the loss.

I can't even begin to think how it's been for Elise, because although we've both known that Mum's been sick for years, Elise is the one who's had to live with it every hour of the day since then. I'm just hoping all of her good memories haven't been taped over by the ones of Mum losing her motor functions, and her ability to recognise people.

We hold each other for what feels like hours, while Grant busies himself around us, feeding the kids, tidying up, and starting dinner so Elise and I can just be together. I'm going to have to thank him in a major way when things start to feel more normal. Elise picked herself a good guy. I'm almost jealous. No, that's not right – I'm *envious*.

I'm envious that Elise has someone to look after her while she grieves. I'm envious she has someone to hold her when she cries. I'm envious she has someone to listen to her stories and memories of a person that they've heard a hundred times already.

Could Harper ever have become that for me? I almost snort into my sister's hair. Not likely. He must know by now that Mum's passed away – it's on every news outlet, and of course I wasn't there in qualifying – but he hasn't rung.

Well of course he hasn't, you idiot. You blocked him!

He can't.

I'd almost forgotten about that picture and that I'd blocked him off of everything.

I don't even know the result from qualifying.

Elise pulls away from my hug and tears flood my cheeks as she produces a picture on her phone of the flowers in question.

'Yeah, that's what I picked, amongst many others. I could see them in my mind and when the florist pointed to these ones I just knew.'

'You did good, baby bro. I don't need to know what else you picked to know that. Mum will love it regardless.' The way she speaks in the present tense, as if Mum's still here watching over our good and bad choices, breaks me again and this time it's her holding me up as I cry.

She's so strong, she just soaks it all up, giving me my

moment to grieve. I'm sure, because I know her, that she'll give me all the moments I need. We'll give them to each other.

Grant's off chasing the kids somewhere, giving the two of us a moment of privacy.

'Bloody hell,' I say, reaching for a tissue from the counter to blow my nose. 'I don't think my tear ducts have had a workout like that in a long time.' I can't even think of the last time I cried that much.

'Sometimes we just need it. I'm glad you let it out. I was worried when Grant said you hadn't cried yet. Now, tell me more about the funeral.' A switch has flipped and Elise is back in organised, superwoman mode, ready to take on the world.

'I still have all this to do.' Thank God for my to-do list on my phone because it's easy for her to scan and understand where I'm at with funeral planning.

'We can do this.' She squeezes my hand, and for the first time since I've been home, I can agree with that. Things start to feel easier when you don't feel so alone doing them.

We eat together, my sister, brother-in-law and I, discussing the outstanding decisions and splitting up the tasks between the three of us.

Once everything's been loaded into the dishwasher, I spot a text from Anders asking if I'm free to jump on a video call. So, I head upstairs to the guestroom I'm staying in and prop my phone up on my pillow and make the call.

'Hey, Anders.' As I say his name, Jackson appears in shot, too. 'And Anders Junior.'

They both laugh and it breaks the ice. There's no way in the world they don't notice how bad I look so at least this eases the conversation slightly.

'How're you doing, son?' Anders asks. And just like that,

I'm on the edge of tears again. Growing up without a father and now Mum's gone, I'll probably never hear anyone say that word to me again.

'Dad,' Jackson warns and I'm grateful to him, but he doesn't need to protect me from this. Anders is one of the best men I've ever known and I'm beyond thankful to have had him in my life, guiding me in my career and nurturing my ambitions.

'I'm doing okay. We've decided to have a quick turnaround on the funeral so we have a lot of planning to do, but it's going as well as it could. How's everything out there?'

I want to apologise for not being there, but I'm not sorry to be missing it for something this important. That would be doing a true disservice to my mum.

'Ah, you know, we'll do what we can. London's trying not to be excited about his first Grand Prix as he doesn't want to seem insensitive.' Anders shrugs like he doesn't quite know what else to say to him.

'He should enjoy it. It's a rite of passage.'

I don't ask how he did in qualifying, because then I would also have to ask how Harper did, and I can't bear to say his name out loud.

'Yes, it is. Not that you need to be worrying about us out here right now. We just wanted to check in and make sure you're doing okay. We hear that you're not looking for flowers for the funeral so we're making a team donation to Parkinson's UK. I hope that's okay.'

It's more okay than he'll ever understand. It means everything to me. 'Thank you so much. It's perfect.'

'If you need us, any of us, Kian, just text or call. I know

Cole's already missing you, but he doesn't want to intrude. None of us do, but you are constantly in our thoughts.'

It's beyond noticeable that he doesn't mention Harper and that I don't ask about him.

'Tell Cole to text me, the idiot. And thank you, I really appreciate everything you've done to make sure I could be here with my family.'

'You're family to us, too, Kian. That's what we do for family,' Jackson says.

I nod, knowing that if I say anything else right now I'll break down.

They say their goodbyes and I exit the call. I smash my face into a pillow and scream out my pain, thumping the other pillow beside me.

It's not fair.

It's not fair.

It's so not fair.

Mum was so young, and the way she gradually lost her faculties was just so cruel. And despite knowing it was coming, I wasn't ready. Maybe I'd never have been ready.

All the tears in the world don't help, nor do the muffled screams. I just feel so drained. So wrung-out.

The only saving grace is that exhaustion takes me quickly and sleep puts me out of my misery.

Chapter Twenty-Six

Harper

My first qualifiers without Kian are tough. He's on my mind constantly. I worry that he's grieving and hurting with no way for me to check that he's okay. I'm sure, with the way Anders loves him like a second son, he's been in touch with him, and Cole, too, but I don't know how to ask either of them. If they know I haven't been in touch with him, they'll want to know why and then that would raise more difficult questions, with complicated answers.

I take the Q8 finish badly, but without Kian here to buy me Chinese and then kiss me silly, it's even worse.

Thankfully, I still have Johannes.

Win or lose, we're always there for each other.

Hence us currently sitting together on the floor of my hotel room with the weirdest picnic spread of snacks that we could find in the local store. Neither of us know what half of it is, but most of it tastes okay and that's the main thing.

'You missing him?' he asks, out of nowhere.

'Mmm.' If I start telling him how much, I'll never stop talking. I don't think I've ever felt this lonely, even as a kid who'd been abandoned by his parents.

I miss everything. The cuddles, the sex, the way he'd tell me endless stories about his childhood and his sister and his niblings. I even miss him cussing me out for doing something stupid. I'd take him being mad and here, over him being gone and ignoring me completely.

'Still blocked?'

I don't justify that with a response other than the growl that escapes my throat.

'Christ, loves turned you into an annoying motherfucker. I'm trying to talk to you here. Get you to open up so tomorrow's a better day for you.'

This time I don't stop him. I don't try to deny that it's love, because Kian doesn't deserve that injustice.

'Wow, Harper James, speechless and in love. It's a bad day for all the guys who still think they have a chance of a night with you.'

The thought of someone else almost makes me want to be sick. In a scary turn of events, I don't want to imagine ever sleeping with someone else again.

'I mean, Kian's not exactly here loving me, too, is he? I've blown it there – we both know that.'

I can't even hide the self-pity and bitterness I feel towards myself. It's my own fault completely, yet I still feel stupidly sorry for myself.

'Just give it time, okay? He has to deal with everything else first, especially with the funeral only being a couple of days away. I'm sure he'll be back before you know it and you two can talk.'

I'm lucky, so bloody lucky to have a best friend who didn't break up with me when we became full-on rivals on the track. It's a rarity in the sport for drivers on other teams to be so close, but we really do embrace it.

He's so good he even changes the subject. It can't be a late one as we have the race tomorrow, so we decide to call it a night early. As he goes to leave, he turns back to me and says, 'Look, just do your best tomorrow, for Kian. He'll be so mad if you undo all his hard work in the Constructors' Championship. He wouldn't want you to be anything other than your best out there. You have to do it for the both of you.'

And clearly, I take that on board.

It's not easy, starting eighth on the grid and trying to scramble back from that, but I do it.

I'm nothing but grit and concentration as I climb into the cockpit, Ash in my ear and all the lads around me making sure everything about the car is ready to go. I've never had a problem with overthinking, and today is no exception. It feels like Kian's with me in the cockpit, and I don't try to block him out. I welcome him and hold him close to my heart. I channel him; I use him to inspire me.

The five red lights go out and I'm off.

It's the perfect start, and even when my tyres feel like they're beginning to wear, my determination doesn't dim.

We have our fastest pit stop of the year so far, everything going smoothly and to plan and then I put everything I've learned out there on the track. I remember all the tips and tricks from my early karting days, everything I cherished about racing, and everything I've learned from watching Kian over the last decade and a half.

I embrace his technique and match it with my total fearlessness. I indulge in the mental game he practises so hard to maintain and tack it with my slight recklessness on the track.

In a moment of absolute incredibleness, it pays off.

It takes the first twenty laps for me to find the rhythm I'm looking for and to feel comfortable out there. Then it takes another ten for my speed on the beautiful straight to reach its maximum potential.

On the fortieth lap I truly engage. I'm switched on to the drivers around me and Ash is doing a perfect job of keeping me in the loop.

Especially when I move up to P3. 'Great job, Harper. Yorris and Johannes out in front of you. Show them what you're made of.'

'How close am I?' I ask.

'Johannes is point four ahead, Yorris point nine. After this bend is your best chance.'

Sorry, Jojo. This one's mine. And then I take a risk – some might call it reckless, but I can feel the magic today. I can do no wrong, and I accelerate past Johannes.

If we were still back in our karting days, fourteen and fifteen-year-old boys behaving badly on the track, I'd have stuck my middle finger up at him as I went past.

Kian would be furious that I was even having this thought so I let it go and set my sights on Yorris.

He's been a menace on the track this year. It's his third top-category season and I think he's become tired of finishing around P5 or P4 for the last two years. He wants a win so badly, and without Kian here this is his best chance. Yorris is fast, sharp-witted, and he takes every bend and sharp corner like a pro. He balances his faster laps against his slower laps so he doesn't burn out, a skill which is so hard to learn when all you want to do is hit full-throttle every time you're out on the track.

But wanting it doesn't mean getting it. I want it, too – every guy out here wants it – but I'm channelling Kian today, so I'm not going to make a mistake. And then Yorris is spinning out in front of me. I'm lucky it's in a wide enough part of the track that he doesn't clip me, but even luckier that I can speed past him.

'P1, fucking P1, man!' Ash is going crazy in my ear, but I'm not about to relax. I still have twenty laps to go and I have to stay focused.

Twenty beautiful bloody laps. Johannes gives me some trouble when Ash announces he's caught up to me and is point eight behind me, but I keep pushing, keep channelling Kian, and fight him off until I see that checkered flag.

Fireworks explode around me in the warm night sky and then I'm climbing on top of the car, jumping up and down because I've done it. I've bloody done it. I could remember in this moment that the two wins I've had this season have been Kian's only two DNFs – one because of his crash and one because he's not even racing – but I'm not going to let that take away from what I've achieved.

I look around the cheering crowds and I expect to feel absolutely incredible, beloved and successful. But I realise there's no one there who's mine. Sure, there are fans and it's obvious that plenty of them are cheering for me, but there's no special person I want to celebrate this with. No family, no partner.

For a second, that realisation hits home so hard that the

disappointment drowns out the fans and team screaming around me. It's silent and I'm alone. Even when I'm on top of the world, I'm still alone.

I know this is not what I want. I know it is a hollow victory without anyone to share it with. I know it means nothing without Kian.

The thought isn't fleeting, but I don't get time to engage with it as I'm hauled down from the top of the car and thrown into getting ready to head to the podium.

There's more than a few tears as I stand top of the podium, Hendersohm's name on the screen behind me, the British national anthem ringing out around me.

It's a moment of a lifetime. There's many a petty thought as I step off with my medal and am handed a magnum bottle of Hendersohm branded champagne. I take great pleasure in spraying it absolutely everywhere, washing away all the people who didn't believe in me, the parents and foster families who gave me up, everyone who didn't love me enough.

I'm absolutely hounded by press on the sideline, every radio station, TV crew member and journalist screaming to get my attention.

Is this what it feels like to be wanted? It's emptier than I thought it would be.

'Harper James, what does this win mean to you?' a petite lady with a fluffy microphone extended across the press barrier shouts my way.

There's only one thing I want to say, and only one person I want to say it to.

'First of all,' I say, and I see other recorders jammed into my face to capture my words of wisdom. 'I just want to say that me and all of the rest of the Hendersohm team are thinking about the Walker family right now. Chastity was an incredible woman who paved the way in pop music for so many, plus she was a fantastic mum to her two kids, and Kian always spoke about her with such fondness.' I clear my throat. 'I don't need to tell anyone whose watched a single race in the last decade and a half how good Kian is on the track. But behind the scenes he's an inspiration, he's taught me so much about determination and drive in this sport. How important it is to take care of myself off the track as well as on. He's challenged me to become a better driver. This win today, well, it isn't mine. This is for Kian. He would have taken this track by storm today, I'm sure of it, so my win is his and I can't wait to be back on the track with him soon.'

I'm not sure if it was appropriate to say any of that, but I don't care. I'll never know if I would have won today if Kian had been racing but dedicating this to him is the least I can do.

***

'Good work out there,' Anna says from where she's sitting a little too cosily next to Cole. 'Guess that media training finally paid off, you little shit. Almost had half the pit in tears.'

Well this is new. Making the team proud. Wow.

Anders is shaking my hand like a maniac. I've probably just made him a ridiculous amount of bonus money – and myself, which will help in paying off the blackmailing dickheads who my agent had to bribe – but he does actually look proud of me, too. He seems to be a good guy. There aren't many people I trust. I've never had reason to. But the therapy's starting to help – I can see that; I can feel it. Maybe it's working because

I'm older now, or maybe it's because I have a reason to want to be better. Maybe it's time to take a risk off the track, too, and trust some people.

'Sir, I'd like to ask permission to do something you might not like.'

'Considering you're asking, rather than just doing it and letting me find out about it from the press tomorrow, then I'm almost bound to say yes. Within reason. What is it, son?'

'I'd like to fly back to the UK tonight. I'd like to support Kian at the funeral. He needs someone and—'

'And that person should be you?' He raises a sceptical eyebrow at me.

'It should.'

'Sure thing, kid. We'll get you on the next plane out of here.'

Chapter Twenty-Seven

Kian

'I thought I'd find you in here.' Elise's quiet voice in the doorway scares the crap out of me. She lingers in the darkness, only illuminated by the glow of the TV.

The volume's on low, but the subtitles tell me everything I need to know. The race is coming to its conclusion and I'm trying not to watch it.

Sure enough, I've heard my name way too many times for someone who's not actually competing. They even talked about Mum and I'd cried into one of my sister's decorative couch cushions.

'Apparently, even when I'm not there I still can't keep away.' She joins me on the sofa, tugging a blanket over both of us. It might only be mid-September but we could both use the comforting warmth.

It just reminds me that we probably need to talk about

what we're going to do with this place. The land all belongs to Mum, so soon, once we get probate, it will be ours. I have a cottage on the edge of the estate and Elise and Grant have their house that they've been renting out for the last four years while they were caring for Mum. I don't know if she'll want to stay in this house.

But Elise has raised the kids here since they were born and I know there are just as many happy memories as sad ones, even though they're not top of mind at the moment. I'll support her in doing whatever she wants.

I'm even thinking about moving back into the cottage if I retire at the end of this season. It would be perfect for just me. I could escape everything, but still only be a forty-minute drive from Norwich town centre. It's just a two-bed cottage, but I love the living room and kitchen. I renovated it a while back, but kept all the period features like the sliding barn doors to the pantry and the beams on the ceiling. It has an incredibly cosy, homely feel. Maybe I'll get a cat. Maybe some chickens. Who knows. The world is going to be my oyster supposedly when I retire at the ripe old age of thirty-four.

'Do you wish you were there?' she asks as the race starts.

'It's weird that everything just carries on like it did before Mum died. Like, doesn't the world know that this major thing has happened? But no, I'm not sorry to be here with you.'

I'm not resentful that I've had to come home. There have been so many moments of relief to be here with my twin, if I'm truly honest, but I also have terrible FOMO. I definitely miss being behind the wheel. I miss the way different tyres grip the track. I miss being in control of a powerful engine and constantly smelling like rubber and petrol. I miss the adrenaline high and the importance of every split second during a race. How do you not miss a job that's been your whole life for the last fifteen years and beyond if you count the many years of youth karting I did?

Yet this season *has* been different. In more ways than I care to admit right now.

'I can't tell you how happy the kids are to have their uncle KiKi home.'

'I think, um, I think I might be home more often after this season. I think. Don't say anything to anyone else. I'm not a hundred per cent yet, but I'm getting close.'

Elise dives at me and crushes me into a hug. 'Oh, Kian,' she murmurs into my shoulder like I'm giving her the best news ever.

'I know,' I reply as she pulls back. 'I'm just ... I think I might be ready to say goodbye.' It seems like a common theme right now, saying goodbye – to Mum, to my career, and to the guy who could have been the love of my life.

Mum did always use to say that things happened in threes. Rain, thunder, and lightning. Three's a storm, she'd tell us when we were little. Very apt for this moment.

'You know we'll support you no matter what, right? Whether you come home for good or for a year, or not for another few years, we'll all be here.'

'Don't make me cry, Elise. My eyes have never hurt so much in my whole life.' Ever since the flood barriers opened, I've hardly stopped. It's like Niagara Falls coming out of my tear ducts.

'I just want you to know. I'm sure right now everything seems horrific and maybe you'll change your mind when you go back, but we'll always be here, even when motor racing isn't.'

She's right. She's always bloody right.

'I know. I just think this might be it. I'm tired, and kind of ready to think about what comes next. Might as well have one big fresh start, right?'

'Like with a particular guy maybe?' She nudges me in the side, ribbing me with a cheeky grin and I am rolling my eyes when I catch sight of what's on TV. Harper is being interviewed. I can't believe I missed the end. I don't know what happened or how he did.

'I don't think so,' I say turning back to Elise. 'I think we're done.'

'Who could ever be done with you.'

I can't tell if she's worked out who it is? I haven't said his name since I've been home, but maybe she's guessing.

'He doesn't want what I want, and we're so different,' I say. 'No, we're done. I need to get over it and move on. He already has.'

'Has he? Are you sure?'

She takes the remote control and starts to turn up the volume.

I look at her, and see a familiar smugness in her expression that's always bugged me. She's only older by a few minutes, but she acts like those extra minutes gave her the wisdom of an ancient philosopher.

'Yeah, I'm sure. He really hurt me, El, and I can't have him messing with my head anymore.'

'Just watch it, Ki, and then tell me he's done with you.'

My eyes go to the screen, and we both watch as Harper makes his speech.

Live on international television, Harper James is dedicating his win to me. Not only that, he pays tribute to Mum and what I'm going through. I'm struggling for air. These words aren't possible from the person who went out and banged someone else just a few nights ago.

Elise's hand is clutching mine.

'Now tell me he's done with you.'

I roll my eyes. I guess we're not pretending anymore that she doesn't know the guy I've been sleeping with is Harper James.

'But we've been here before. This is exactly what he does. It's a constant push-pull. He wants me, he doesn't want me. He screws up, he comes back and does something sweet. I can't do it anymore.'

'I agree, that doesn't sound great. It also sounds like he's trying to figure some things out. Have you talked about it?'

'That's the thing, El. He won't – or he can't … I don't know. I've tried, and he just shuts down. It's been really messing with my head.'

'Is that what happened in Italy? With the crash? Because if it's becoming dangerous—'

'Yes and no. That was my own fault,' I reassure her. 'If I make a mistake on the track, that's on me, not him.'

It feels so good to finally be able to talk about this with someone. I wish I'd opened up sooner. Elise squeezes me and sighs. I know she worries about the risks I take, and especially now when we only have each other left.

'What would Mum say?' I ask.

She's quiet for a moment while she thinks.

'Mum would say that life's too short not to have what you really want. If you were … if you were on your deathbed, and you looked back over your life, what would you want to remember? What would bring you comfort and joy? Is it Harper James? Because if so...'

Okay, fine, I admit it. Those extra few minutes did give my sister the wisdom of the ancients.

Damn.

Chapter Twenty-Eight

Harper

Whilst I know both Kian and his sister are grieving right now, it's going to be completely pointless if I've flown all this way in the middle of the night and I can't get Elise on the phone. Luckily, Kian gave me her landline number ages ago when I was sick and I've tried every hour on the flight when finally it rings more than once on my like fifth try. This time, she finally picks up. After a short preamble in which we are finally introduced, I let her know I've been trying to get hold of Kian for days. I don't mention he's blocked me, but it seems like Elise knows more about our situation than I thought.

'Bloody hell, I didn't think I'd ever meet anyone more stubborn than my brother until now. You do know we are burying our mother tomorrow, right?' She's fiery, maybe even more so than Kian, you can definitely tell they are twins.

'I do, hence why I'm currently thirty-six thousand feet in the air and seven hours away from landing.

'Christ, which airline lets you make calls from the sky?'

'A private jet, of course.'

'Of course, silly me. What do you want, Harper?'

'To be there for Kian, I'm coming to him; I just need the address the cars are leaving from in the morning. I'm going to make it no matter what.'

The line goes silent and I have to check she hasn't hung up on me, but the call still shows as active. 'You're a real piece of work, you know that right, Harper?' I nod even though she can't see me. I can only imagine the stories her twin has told her. 'He's so torn up right now, not just about Mum; I don't even think he's begun to process that guilt and grief properly yet. But about you, you really hurt him. I almost want to tell you to keep away from him, but…'

'But…?' I let out a hopeful breath.

'But, I think he will need some support tomorrow. I'm lucky, I have my husband and friends and my kids keeping me strong. Kian, well, he thinks he can do this on his own and well, maybe, it would even be a miniscule bit easier with you here.'

'Elise, thank you. I promise you I won't be in the way, I'll sit at the back if I have to, I just want to be there for him.'

'Cars are leaving at one, are you going to make it?'

I don't know. We land at nine-thirty and Norfolk is a trek. I'm going to be cutting it fine.

'How far are you from Gatwick?'

'Like two-and-a-half hours.'

Roughly calculating that as long as we aren't delayed and I can take the priority line for passport control, I should be fine.

Good thing I only bought a cabin bag. 'I'll be there. Come rain or shine.'

'Hopefully shine, the wake is in the garden.' That doesn't surprise me considering how much land they have.

'See you in the morning.'

'I'm trusting you, Harper. He's been through enough,' she warns one final time.

'You have my word.'

I hear a scoffing sound. Clearly my word isn't worth much to her right now, but I'm determined to prove her wrong.

After taking my mobile number, she hangs up, but then texts me the address of her mum's, where the funeral cars are leaving from, so I'm taking this as a win.

The plane soars on and I sleep until we're about to land.

The airport is in complete chaos; someone's clearly got the word out that I've left Singapore to fly here and they are like piranhas trying to get proof. Even worse I think I've spotted a bigger asshole than me coming through the airport at the same time as me.

He has to be fucking kidding me. I can't think of the last time I saw him in the papers or any good headlines about him, he'd pretty much dropped off the radar. Yet here he is, paparazzi trailing him with flashing cameras as he walked through the airport in his funeral suit and sunglasses. He is an absolute joke of a human; I couldn't believe I'd ever looked up to him.

Eventually, my security begins to push back all the press. It's not like I can declare the real reason why I am here. Plus, Anders had told me to avoid commenting on the matter at all. Which leaves me, my security and Tyler fucking Heath on the same path out of the airport.

It may be the stupidest thing I ever do, but I can't help but call his name. 'Tyler,' I shout. I can't be sure he still even follows the sport until he turns to see who is calling him and stops completely in his tracks.

'Harper James, bloody hell what's the likelihood of this. A racing legend and one in the making both here today? No wonder the press was manic in there. I don't see much of that in Spain.'

So that's where he'd taken himself when he'd walked out on his kids and wife. Two hours away on a plane. My blood only boils more at this.

'Why the fuck are you here?' I ask and the bite to my tone catches him off guard and I watch as the spiteful man he truly is takes over.

'Not sure that's any of your business, kid. But, in case you missed it while you were off winning, my wife died last week.'

'Ex wife. I really don't think it would be a good idea if you attended today.' My tone's icy as I try to keep the volume down; the press don't need to hear this.

'My kids will need their father.'

I scoff at him and he flinches, clearly not expecting a twenty-five-year-old to be calling him out on his bullshit. 'Kian and Elise don't need you,' I say. 'I don't think for a second Kian wants you there today after you abandoned them both before they were even born.'

'Who put you in charge of Kian's life story? You his boyfriend or something?'

I wish. I bloody wish. Yet my silence must speak magnitudes, because Tyler sucks his teeth at me, his stare brutally disappointing. 'You can tell he was raised by his mother, no son of mine would become a pansy.'

He's lucky that I don't want to create anymore bad headlines for Kian. Otherwise I would have decked him. I would have wiped the smug look off his face.

Finally, my security form a wall around me and I'm escorted away from the potential subject of my fist and into a car which I'm praying gets me to the funeral just in time.

Chapter Twenty-Nine

Kian

Nothing can prepare you for a final goodbye.

Not all the grief counselling in the world or knowing in advance that the end is coming for your loved one. They've already left the world, but this is the last time you'll get to be in the same room as them before you subject them to ground.

We decided to have a small, private funeral without celebrities from Mum's career or big crowds. It feels like what she would have wanted. She left that world behind a long time ago, and neither Elise nor I want to be subjected to the glare of the media.

I watch my sister and her little family as they get ready, and I envy what they have on a day like today. I know my twin is there for me, but it's not the same. I see the loving touches and comforting looks that she shares with Grant, and I know that I want that for myself, too.

As they walk ahead of me into the church, a wave of profound sadness washes over me.

If only…

'Hey.'

His voice startles me, but I know immediately who it belongs to.

I turn and there he is. It's like I dreamed him into existence. He looks so good in his black suit and I am too stunned at first to say anything.

'Is it okay that I'm here?' he asks, uncertainly. 'I'm really sorry about…'

I don't know whether he's offering his condolences or apologising for being a prick back in Singapore, but right now I don't care.

I nod, and when he opens his arms to me I walk into his embrace. I can't believe he's really here.

'How…?'

'I asked Anders to arrange it, and I got the details from your sister.'

I pull back from the hug and look at him in shock. Then I turn and see Elise looking back at us with a small smile. Of course my sister was involved in this. She shrugs and tilts her head, as if to say, *what did you expect?* then continues into the church.

'Thank you for being here,' is all I can manage.

He squeezes my fingers, and I look down to where he's still holding my hand in his, and then I meet his gaze again, a silent question floating between us.

'Is it okay…?' he asks again.

Yes, Harper's hand is in mine and I don't want to let go. I'm not going to let go.

'It's okay,' I reply.

Now is not the time to ask him what any of this means. He's here, and I don't feel so alone anymore. We walk together into the church and I don't care who sees us or what they may be thinking. Today is about saying goodbye to Mum. Everything else can wait.

The service is beautiful.

I think it's what Mum would have wanted. Her oldest friend and one of her sisters did readings, and her former agent spoke very movingly about her career in a way I think she would have really liked.

And then Elise gets up and makes her way to the podium.

My sister is so brave to get up there and speak. I'm struggling to keep it together just sitting in the pew, never mind trying to speak publicly about the person who raised us single-handedly, who loved us and encouraged us, who shaped us and—

I swallow the lump in my throat.

But, of course, Elise is prepared. She's has the eulogy printed onto little cue cards and holds back her tears just enough to speak clearly and movingly to the assembled mourners.

She tells tales of Mum's younger days, how she shot to fame and then raised us for the first couple of years on a series of tour buses and private jets. She even extracts some laughs from Mum's closer friends about the wilder times of her teens and twenties. She speaks on behalf of both of us about the kind of mother she was, and the things we will remember most about her.

It's perfect. No one could have done it better.

And I would be a wreck if it weren't for Harper, who never lets go of my hand. He's an absolute rock. He's everything I need him to be on the hardest of days.

And then it's all over. Just like that it's time to say our final goodbyes.

Elise squeezes my other hand and I know we are both silently sending Mum on her way.

We walk out for a final time behind the coffin, hand in hand, only Elise, Grant and the kids in front of us.

The celebrant moves through the formalities and then, finally, Mum is lowered into the ground, and the only thing holding me up is Harper. His touch keeping me grounded, stopping me from losing it completely. Grant leads the kids away after he lets his rose fall on top of the casket. The rest of the mourners following suit until we can hardly see her anymore. Eventually, it's just the three of us at the graveside.

'Do you, uh, want me to give you two a moment?' Harper asks, hand still gripping mine as he offers me and Elise some space.

Yet I'm shaking my head. I can't do this without him.

'Shit, I'm not doing this right, am I?' Elise walks round to link her arm through my free one.

'I don't think Mum would expect any less, she always had such a potty mouth even when we were kids,' she says and it's like at that point we're all holding each other up.

'Love you, Mum. So much.' There's nothing else I can croak out. This is it. The second I throw in my own rose and walk away the ground will be filled and there won't be any other moments.

I know I can come back and visit the grave, but nothing will be the same.

'Me too, Mum. Love you forever.' Stepping forwards arm in arm we both drop in our roses and step away from the grave.

Grant is waiting, arm outstretched to catch Elise as she chokes down sobs and I'm standing strong with Harper's hand in mine.

'Goodbye, Mum,' I whisper finally, leaving her to rest in peace.

The wake we host after the service has a different vibe entirely.

The list of celebrities is like nothing I've ever experienced. The press would have a field day if they got a whiff of the names currently inside a large white tent in our garden. It's overwhelming how many people loved Mum, and both Elise and I enjoy hearing increasingly tall tales from Mum's life and career. It feels like everyone is trying to outdo each other with their stories and I am absolutely here for it. I'm glad this bit feels more like a party.

I spend some time chatting with Mum's sisters. They've both been in and out of my life since I was a kid and are still travelling the world as back-up singers to some of the most famous names in the industry.

They coo over Cassie and Jesse and try to dig around in my life, asking if I'm planning to have any kids in the near future, but I brush that off with excuses that involve my hectic schedule and how much time I spend on the road.

It's all smooth until Harper joins the conversation, putting a comforting hand on the small of my back. Then the pair go wild.

'Introduce us, please,' Aunt Judith says, curious eyes dancing between the two of us.

'Judith, Angie, this is Harper James. Hendersohm's second driver and my, um, my … man friend.' The pair snicker, and Harper joins in with them like he's in on the joke, while I only want the ground to swallow me up.

Man. Friend.

Brilliant. I will never live this down. Ever.

'Well, don't be knocking this one up. He's having a great rookie season, and we need to see more of him next year,' Angie says, smirking at me. Because of course she knows exactly who Harper is. She's always loved motor sport. She's actually the one who introduced my parents way back in the day.

'Don't worry, we're waiting for marriage,' Harper replies.

My knees lock on instinct to stop my jelly legs from plummeting me to the floor. Did he just say marriage? Where did the commitment-phobe go?

He keeps my aunts entertained while I take a second to step outside the marquee to collect myself. I'm having an out-of-body experience that isn't entirely down to the fact that this is my mother's funeral.

Unfortunately, the cold air only wakes my mind up even more to what he said. He might have been joking, but no one, not even Harper, is glib enough to throw around that word when they know the other person cares so much. Too much.

Would he even want that? I just didn't see him being the kind who would want to legally sign up to forever with someone. No matter how much I wanted … want … to hope that could be our future.

Harper finds me not long after, wrapping an arm around me and pulling me in close.

I'm so confused. It's hardly the time, but it feels like there's an elephant in the room.

'That picture…' I say.

'It was nothing. I promise, it was nothing. I was doing what I always do; being an absolute wanker because you bloody scare the life out of me. You've gotta remember, I'm totally new to all this romantic bullshit. I'm a one-night, one-time guy and then you went and took over my whole brain and heart.'

His heart? Are we really about to have our first relationship moment at my mum's wake? It feels weird and highly inappropriate.

'I can't keep doing this, Harper. I was crushed, and it feels like you're playing a game. Every time I'm done and try to move on, you come running back and find a way to hook me again.'

'I know it seems like that, but that's not my intention. I care about you so much, and I'm trying to work through all my issues in therapy, but it's gonna take time. Can you give me time?'

I sigh and take a deep breath. I remember Elise's words about what Mum would say. Maybe this is the perfect setting for this conversation after all.

'If we're going to do this,' I finally say, 'there needs to be some boundaries, and the first big one is that we are exclusive. You're mine if you want to be, but that's it. No one else.'

'Kian,' he says seriously, 'I don't want anyone other than you. I haven't for a while. It's a defence mechanism when I get freaked out, and then I panic and push you away because I'm afraid that you'll get bored and leave me and it will hurt so bloody much, but I promise you, I only want you.'

'Why couldn't you have just said all of this a month ago, I can't even imagine how happy we'd be right now.'

'Because I don't know how to do this!' he says. 'And because I'm an idiot, obviously.' It's the most honest he's ever been with me.

'We've already been doing it. We just need to tidy up the edges a little.'

'Yeah, I guess.'

'Tidying up isn't exactly your strongpoint, I know.'

'Get lost,' he says, laughing, and thumps me on the shoulder. 'Can I kiss you now?'

It feels like heaven to be holding him and kissing him, today of all days. I don't know how I would have got through this without him. I think Mum would approve, and that feels good.

He pulls back and says, 'While this is great and all, I don't think it's appropriate to go back in there with a hard-on, so maybe we can press pause for now?'

'Well that's a first. I could get used to responsible Harper...' I tease.

'Well, responsible Harper is also wondering when you think we should tell Anders, because you know he'll shit bricks if he finds out on social media...'

Wow, that really is a first.

Chapter Thirty

Harper

'Oh shit,' the words slip from my mouth as I scroll through my Instagram. Kian *was* fast asleep behind me, like the big spoon he loves to be, but my words must startle him and he tenses behind me.

'Do I even wanna know?' he grumbles, his voice thick and sleepy.

He doesn't. He really doesn't. I wish I could protect him from what's to come, but there's nothing I can do.

It's the first intimate photo I've ever seen of us. It's not like we've ever taken any selfies together or been papped on a date. Mainly because we've never been on one of those, my fault obviously.

Some absolute asshole must have either flown a drone over the garden during the wake, or taken pictures over the walls, because they have a selection of different photos of me and Kian outside the marquee. Hand in hand, hugging, and to make sure there's no possible misinterpretation, there we are kissing.

It's beyond disrespectful and I can't even begin to think what the newspaper in question paid the soulless monster who took these photos.

It's bittersweet, because we look so good together, but it was such a private moment that this feels like a real violation.

I know, the irony, coming from me.

'What is it?' He sits up, blinking sleep out of his eyes. I'd forgotten how adorable he is when he first wakes up.

I tilt my phone screen away so he doesn't immediately see it, but I've promised no more running and hiding.

So, I turn inwards to look him in the eye and he's picking at the seam of his duvet. 'Yeah, so the cat's out of the bag.'

'Us?'

He's clearly still half asleep as he tries to figure out what I mean.

I tip the screen towards him.

'I'm so sorry, Kian.'

'Why are you apologising? God, Harper, I don't care about that. We both knew this was coming. Are you bothered because they're speculating about what this means?'

He gestures to the one of us kissing.

'Bothered? No. They've published way worse photos of me in the last couple years. But this outs us. You can't unbreak an egg, you know? It's obvious we're…' I don't want to struggle to say the word *together*, but it's not something that just rolls off of my tongue.

'A couple?'

He laughs at me and I pinch the side of his belly.

'I mean, we are a couple, right?' he continues. 'You're my boyfriend, correct?'

'Correct,' I say. There, I've said it. Kind of.

'Perfect, glad that's solved. Makes it easier than one of us having to ask the other. I feel like I'm too old for that game.'

He pulls me back until we're lying down together again, his arm outstretched so I can snuggle into him. Me. Snuggling. But it's incredible. I've never felt so safe in my life. I want to stay here forever.

Except we can't.

The season isn't over yet and sooner rather than later we have to reunite with the team. We have to catch a flight to Japan and get back on the road again.

'Do you want to call Anders or shall I?' he asks.

'You do it. He likes you better.'

'Oh, I see how it is. You're palming off the hard jobs on me already.'

'Couples shoulder each other's burdens right?' That makes him laugh, exactly how I wanted him too.

'Who made you such an expert in couple behaviour?'

I hit him with his pillow and he hits me back as we fall into the most childish pillow fight until it turns into kissing, and then fucking on top of a stack of fluffy pillows on the floor.

In the end, though, we still have to leave behind the cosy cottage to fly to Japan. I know it's a tough goodbye for Kian when he would rather be here with his family.

We're both also all too aware that once we grab our bags and step outside that door, everything changes. The bubble we've lived in for the last couple of days will burst and it'll be back to real life. The promises we've both made mean nothing until they've been stress-tested in the field.

'I love this place,' I comment, taking one final look around. It's so very Kian and I can't believe he doesn't spend more time here. 'I'm not sure what your Norwich house is like, but I doubt it's as lovely as this.'

'Didn't realise I was getting judged on my interior-decorating skills while we were having sex,' he laughs.

'It's nothing to do with that. It just really suits you.'

I can imagine him pottering in the kitchen, making all his favourite meals, lounging in the small sitting area with the log burner roaring and a book in hand considering there's not a TV in there. The bathroom is perfect with its big rainfall shower and wood-panelled walls, and then there's the clawfoot tub in the corner.

Then his bedroom… I've never felt more at peace in a room. There is a zen in here I didn't know you could create in just one room. The neutral colours with the one dark wall behind the bed give the cosiest vibe. It's masculine but not aggressively so. I feel at home here too, which is weird because I've never felt at home anywhere. Maybe I just feel at home wherever Kian is.

Now it's back to hotel rooms for the final cities on the circuit.

'Well, it's not going anywhere.' *And neither am I.* The words are unspoken but they may as well have been because his meaning is loud and clear. He punctuates his statement with a kiss to the lips. It tastes of the promise that this is not the last time we'll be here together.

I think about his words during the flight to Japan, over-analysing their meaning as he sleeps peacefully next to me. Will he want to spend the whole break here? Will he ask me to move in? Is it too early to be thinking about this?

I'm still mulling over every possibility when we land.

We probably should have thought about the chaos of landing in Japan, because we get absolutely hounded at the airport. There are still floaters in my eyes from the avalanche of flash photography and journalists screaming questions at us – some curious and speculative, some gross and inappropriate.

'Christ,' he breathes out as we slide into the backseat of the car.

'Yup. That was…'

I slip my hand across the middle of the seat and take his hand as the car pulls out of the short-stay car park, heading to the hotel.

Whilst Anna couldn't be there to meet us at the airport, she had sent us a bunch of texts reminding us to ignore everything thrown at us and say 'no comment' till we're blue in the face. Those media sessions would probably have come in handy right about now.

I feel like we could both use a nap in our hotel room, maybe a light workout to ease us back into everything, but no. The second we're back at the hotel we're being pulled into a 'Relationship Strategy Meeting'. Because of course there needs to be a strategy meeting about our relationship.

Relationship.

I've barely been in one for forty-eight hours and I'm having a meeting about it with my boss.

Completely normal.

Completely fucking normal.

'For a second, I thought we were going to be steamrolled by the crowds. We should probably talk to our agents about temporarily having some more security until the hype dies down,' Kian says.

I agree with a nod. I don't want us to have to hide, but we still need to focus on the races that are coming up and Kian still needs privacy to grieve and handle everything else that's going on around him.

Him being further protected will give me more peace of mind.

We're shielded under big golf umbrellas as we step out of our car from the airport, and are bundled straight into the conference room of the hotel we're staying in for the next two weeks.

Anders is immediately out of his seat, tugging Kian into a hug. For a moment I just watch from the hallway. This team is Anders's baby. It might not belong to him as such, but he's the one who built it from the ground up. It's a newer team in the sport and Kian's been part of it for most of that time. So the scene playing out in front of me makes sense.

I'm glad Kian has Anders. I noticed there was no mention of his actual father during his mum's funeral. I'm glad he did what I told him and stayed away. Weird how I used to idolise Tyler Heath. Since I've got to know Kian, I know they couldn't be more different. If you'd asked me at the beginning of the season, I'd have said I admired Tyler's fearless style and his desire to squeeze every drop of pleasure out of life. I'd also have said – and I believe I did actually say – that Kian is a boring bastard. But the thing is, I've slowly, gradually, little by little, come to admire what Kian brings to the sport far more. He's dedicated, patient, reliable and I've never met anyone who works harder. He gets results because he's brilliant; he earns his wins. Tyler got results because he was talented and because he was lucky … and then he threw it all away, like I nearly did, because he didn't understand that you need strength of character to race, not just personality.

I give Anders and Kian a minute to hug it out before cockily clearing my throat.

'I'm back too, you know?'

They both laugh, but Anders claps me on the shoulders in a version of the same welcome. 'Back to being a pain in my ass.'

There's a second of awkward silence while Anders undoubtedly wishes he'd chosen a different expression, but then everyone laughs and I can't help myself.

'I mean, actually that's only something I provide to—'

Kian slaps a hand over my mouth before I can say anything that's going to get me in trouble. It doesn't stop me licking the palm of his hand, though, before he guides us to our seats.

'Let's get your agents dialled into this meeting, and in the meantime, I just want to check in with you both. The last week has obviously been a lot to handle and your brains must be scrambled. The schedule here in Japan can be reduced as much as you both need, but I would love to have you both on the track this weekend.'

It's more than I expected and I can't even begin to explain why I want to bawl like a baby right now. It almost makes me uncomfortable and Kian must sense it as I shift in the seat next to him, because he takes my hand and rests it trapped in his on my thigh.

'I'm ready to race. I'd appreciate it if we could limit some of the pre-race press calls, just so we can focus on performance,' Kian says.

'Of course. If you're sure? We can send London out again if we have to.' I don't know why I'm shocked that Anders is trying to give Kian an out. Any other team principal would be pressuring him to get back out there and win. If we're to stay competitive in the Constructors' Championship, Hendersohm needs both of us back out there to make it happen.

'Very. Mum wouldn't want me to throw the season away. She'd want me to finish it in style. There's no chance of the championship-points record now, but I'm still just about top of the Drivers' Championship and I want to stay there, and that doesn't happen if I don't drive.'

'Well, that's very good to hear. Just keep us in the loop if anything changes,' Anders replies. 'Now, the other thing…'

'Us being … together?' I say. I'm trying to show Kian that I meant what I said, and that I won't let him down again.

'Exactly that. It goes without saying that you have mine and Hendersohm's full support, and if anyone in the garage or the wider team has a problem with it, they'll answer to me.'

Anders is firm with his words, and I appreciate his clear, no-nonsense approach. Maybe it's because he has a gay son or maybe because he genuinely cares, who knows. It hardly matters when he's creating a good atmosphere for us in the team.

'We just need to discuss how this is going to play out so Anna can stop freaking out about a PR strategy now that the pictures are all over social media. There's some work we need to do with the sponsors as well, but that's not your responsibility, so don't worry about it.'

'We aren't looking to hide,' I quickly confirm. 'That's not what we want, but we also understand that there are competing pressures. We're going to Qatar next, and then there's Abu Dhabi at the end of the season, and that will present its own challenges.'

'Okay then.' Anders claps his hands. 'Let's properly put Hendersohm on the map. How do we feel about doing the double and bringing home both the Drivers' and Constructors' Championships this season? Anna, do you want to start with a summary of our key points?'

And just like that, Kian and I are a couple. And everyone knows.

Chapter Thirty-One

Kian

T his is it.

No one, except Elise, knows that this will be the last race of my career.

The top of the table is so tight that if I don't come first today, I don't come first overall. Missing the Singapore Grand Prix dramatically reduced my lead, and the top contenders are bunched together now. I want to retain my title. I want to be World Champion one last time. I want that trophy I promised Cassie.

I also want Harper to see me win. I know it's stupid, but I want to be amazing for him. I want him to be proud of me. We've been inseparable since Mum's funeral. The team has continued to book us separate hotel rooms, and we do make some use of them. We stayed apart while in Qatar and Abu Dhabi, for obvious reasons, but everywhere else we've basically been living together.

We keep it professional when we're in the garage, or training, or in meetings.

'Like William and Kate,' Harper joked when I told him that we needed to agree on our PDA boundaries. I don't know that it's quite the same thing, but I have no problem with him comparing our relationship to the romantic royals. We're a couple, but we're also at work a lot of the time – the Hendersohm team is more than just its two drivers, and we have to respect that. We're also still competing against each other, and it's just easier if we keep work and home separate.

I realise that there's a deal of irony that this is how we're finishing up the season – making sure that we remember that we have personal goals outside of how we operate as a team.

I'm just beyond thankful for him right now, because whilst I'm undeniably anxious about where I finish on the podium, he's a calming presence. He never overthinks things, and I could use a bit of that attitude today.

If I hadn't missed Singapore or had that crash in Italy, I'd already be guaranteed the win based on accumulated points. But that's not how things worked out, so here we are. Yorris has a chance, as does the older Swede, and if all hell breaks loose then there are a few others who could challenge for the top spot.

No pressure, huh?

Maybe I'll feel better if I talk to Harper about it, I think, and then he can help me not overthink it. I can't afford a single mistake, after all.

I know I pick a terrible moment to have the conversation – just an hour before we climb into our cockpits – but he seems to be pretty much bombproof when it comes to being able to focus during a race.

'This is it,' I say, the words feeling thick and heavy on my tongue as I truly come to terms with my decision.

'I know, baby. Last race. Can't believe that this is the end of my first season.'

'No, I mean, this is it. This is my last race,' I say, hoping he'll finally get the point.

'What?' His eyes widen.

I didn't think this was going to come as such a shock to him, considering how much speculation there's been, but I've well and truly caught him off-guard.

'My last race ever. I'm ready to retire.'

For a second he's nothing but silent and then he's pulling me into the hardest, tightest hug I've ever had. He practically squeezes all of the air out of me in one big whoosh, but his hands cling to the back of my T-shirt, and in this moment I'm not sure who needs this hug more.

Tears bristle at the backs of my eyes but it's okay because we're together and at this point that's what's important.

'I can't believe it,' he snuffles. 'I don't know why it's hitting me so hard, but you've been my hero on the track for so many years, and then we ended up on the same team, and now you're my boyfriend, and I just wasn't expecting it to be over so quickly.' He chokes down the last few words and he pulls away to look at me properly, almost as if he's making sure I'm serious.

'You do realise I'm not breaking up with you, right?' He chuckles – he's got such a great smile. 'You don't need me here to be great – you know that, don't you?'

'I just thought, I don't know, that we'd get another season together. It would have been nice. I don't know what's happening with Elijah, but I thought…'

'Yeah, it would have been nice, but I'm done. I'm tired and I don't know how much more my body can take. I want to go home. I want to be near my sister and the kids. I want to live in the cottage on Mum's land and maybe get some chickens or a few goats. I'm ready for some peace.'

'I don't think getting farm animals is going to bring you much peace,' he says with a laugh, but a choked sob in the back of his throat comes out, too.

I don't know if the worry lines that crease his forehead are because he's not sure where he fits into this, or because he doesn't understand why I'm doing this, but I want to reassure him anyway.

'I'm not sure what your plans are for the next three months, but do you fancy coming to live in the cottage for a few months? It'll be Christmas soon and we can decorate and have log fires and wrap presents together…'

He tenses and I squeeze his hand.

'You sure?'

'More than anything. So what do you think? Do you want to move in with me?'

'Yes, I'd love to. Move in, that is. I'm not sure about goats and chickens but one step at a time, right?'

'Guess I should probably drop my agent a text and tell Anders I'm leaving, too.' Probably should have done it when I decided, but I really want to get through the race today without anyone knowing so people don't make a big deal out of it. I'm putting enough pressure on myself as it is to make this the big finale.

'They don't know?'

I shake my head. 'I've only told Elise so far and that was a lot to do with me wanting to move back into the cottage. It shares land with Mums house and Elise's, although, Elise hasn't moved back out there yet and I have a feeling she isn't going to.'

I'd thought after Mum had passed she'd want to return back to the home her and Grant had started to build, because Mum's place might hold too many bad memories. But she seems so content there, like it's keeping her close to Mum even though she's gone.

'Bloody hell, motor racing is about to be a whole other world,' he says, before resting his head on my shoulders.

I don't think that'll be the case at all, I'm just one small moving part. But it's nice I'm at least a bit of a legend in my boyfriend's eyes. That's what is important.

He waits outside Anders's office as I go in, my agents on speaker as I let them both know. I've probably chosen the best time to do it because we're so close to race time neither of them have a chance to quiz me about it being the right decision or to convince me to stay.

More than anything, they both seem to have been expecting it anyway so I'll take that as a win as I step out of the office unscathed.

'One step at a time. So, we should, uh, probably go out there and win this then?' I say.

'Absolutely,' Harper replies as we get our gear on and then head towards our separate cars.

For once, Elise, Grant and the kids are here. I wanted them to be here to see me. I had to tell Elise it would be my last race ever in order to persuade her to come, and I know she'll be anxious for me, but it wouldn't be the same without her. Cassie's made a sign and she's waving it furiously, hooting and hollering in the friends-and-family section. I blow my niece a kiss and wave to Elise; it's all I need to feel geared up to go one final time.

For so much of the race it feels like it could go either way. I lead, then Yorris leads, and then I lead again. Yorris has clearly decided he's going for it, too, and as Cole confirms it's ten laps to go, I still can't find a way around Yorris. He's maximising his speed on every bit of straight and the second we get to a bend or corner he's so central in the track I can't get round him. It's aggressive driving and I can feel how much he wants my title.

Until we arrive at the penultimate lap. I'm running out of chances, and we both know it. And then, perhaps it's the magnitude of the occasion, or perhaps he loses focus for a split second, but on a tight bend he's gravitating so close to the edge that a gap appears beside him. It's the moment I've been waiting for.

It's time to be bold. One last time. It's time to risk everything.

'Cole, I'm going for it. If it doesn't pay off, then—'

'Go, Kian. Go! Go now!'

In a snap decision, I swerve out from behind Yorris and blast past him in a slick manoeuvre that forces all other thoughts from my head. It's a massive risk because he could clip me as I pull around but he doesn't.

'Yes, Kian, yes! That's it!' Cole is shrieking in my ear.

And I've done it. I've taken the lead. I only have to hold it for one more lap and then I'll have done it.

Hold your nerve, Walker. Hold your nerve, man.

I think about all the people who are cheering me on and willing me to this victory. Mum, Elise, Cassie. Harper. I'm so lucky. How did I get so lucky?

Time starts to slow down and I picture a crackling fire in the log burner, and Harper beside me on the sofa, the cottage decorated for Christmas. Maybe a cat.

This is so not the time for overthinking. Last push, and then I can fantasise all I like.

Cole is screaming in my ear, 'Go, go, go! Fuck yeah! Go!'

I see it now, the finish line, the sum of all my ambitions.

'Harper's up your ass, man!

What?!

'Harper's got P2. Go, go!'

Cole's going crazy now because Harper's right behind me, and I think it'd be just like the cheeky twat to take me on the line. I won't give him the satisfaction, though. I want a clear win so he can never claim he handed it to me, and as I cross the finish line in P1 I know I've done it.

I've done it.

My final World Championship.

My last race.

I'm screaming into the mic because I know Harper's done his job, too, which means we've got the Constructors' Championship as well. It's the most incredible high I've ever experienced. Sheer and utter joy envelop me as I pull into my spot and let the technicians help me out.

The second we're both out of our cars, Harper and I are running towards each other and he jumps at me so I'm holding him in a bear hug that lifts him off the ground.

'We did it,' he whispers against my ear. Tears in his eyes.

'We did it,' I repeat, before lowering him to the ground so

we can be pulled into congratulatory hugs by every single member of the Hendersohm team.

We've just given them the best result of the team's history, so of course everyone's screaming, crying, embracing and generally going nuts. They're all about to get the biggest bonus ever.

Before we know it, we're on the podium and I know that nothing will ever come close to this feeling. With Harper by my side, I always feel on top of the world, and this podium just proves it.

I can't think of a better way to be going out.

Chapter Thirty-Two

Harper

Standing on top of the podium with the guy I'm falling so hard for was the most unbelievable experience. A once-in-a-lifetime moment, literally, since he's announced his retirement.

I love seeing him celebrating with his family and including the kids in everything. I know the passing of his mum came up in a lot of the interviews and he spoke movingly about the impact this had on him during the season. He spoke too about his sister's sacrifices in caring for their mum so that he could achieve his dreams, and I know this will have meant a lot to Elise.

We're taking a low-profile approach to our relationship with the press. It's not that we're trying to hide anything, and it's not that we're afraid of prejudice within the world of motor racing. It's just that the way I lived before, splashing every hook-up and bar crawl onto my social media, desperately seeking validation and approval from strangers, is not something I want to do with the precious connection that Kian and I share.

It's private, but not secret.

It belongs to us, and only us.

At the Hendersohm party, the celebration has a different vibe. Here, we are not on show. Here we are not 'working royals', so we can be a couple as well as teammates. The whole team and their invited family members, guests and friends get a chance to meet and share stories and to put the proverbial icing on this season's cake.

The first person to approach us is Elijah, who's here with his family.

Elijah hugs Kian like he's a soldier returning from war, but it's a beautiful reunion and I can tell how happy they are to be back together. I feel bad that Elijah missed out on being a part of this incredible season, but I also know I never would have fallen in love with my idol, the great Kian Walker, if not for Elijah's accident.

'The infamous Harper James.'

Elijah sticks his hand out for me to shake and I take it with a firm grip. He's probably not trying to be intimidating, but I want him to like me. He's Kian's best friend, so it matters what he thinks of me.

'Not as infamous as you, Elijah Gutaga. Trust me, at the start of the season this one –' I thumb towards Kian '– sulked so much that he was stuck with me and not you. They were big shoes to fill.'

He grins and I almost breathe out a sigh of relief that he doesn't seem to completely hate me. 'That probably changed, huh, when you started sucking his dick?' I gulp, not sure what

I was expecting from Elijah, but it wasn't this. 'He doesn't get that from me so I think you've probably one-upped me there.'

'Touché,' I reply and Kian tugs me into his side.

'I'm going to regret introducing you two. I know you're going to bring out his immature side.' He nudges me in the ribs.

'I can't believe my best friend's in love,' Elijah says.

'What can I say? How could he resist falling for me?'

We might not have said those magical I love yous to each other yet, but I know how he feels about me and I hope he knows how I feel about him.

'I mean, it was touch and go at first when you couldn't stop being a dick,' he says with nothing but sarcasm to his voice.

'Me? A dick? Never.'

'Did you or did you not once suck a guy off in the hallway of our motorhome?' I wince as he reminds me of one of the low points of the season, but he squeezes me closer and I know he's over it.

'They best be bloody disinfecting it before I move back in next season.' Elijah rolls his eyes.

'Don't worry, I didn't get to finish before Kian strode out of his room and told me off.' I wasn't about to mention that we'd also had sex on the couch, kitchen counter top, in the shower and in both of the bedrooms. What Elijah didn't know wouldn't hurt him next season.

'You ready to come back?' Kian asks Elijah, and it's clear that Elijah's champing at the bit.

'You bet your ass I am. Can't believe it won't be with you, but I don't suppose I'll be grumbling if we get to keep your boyfriend around.'

It's nice to hear, but I'm not about to get my hopes up just yet. I'll let my agent work on the contract negotiations and only once the ink is dry will I be confident about next season.

'I hope so,' I say. 'I really hope so.'

I spot Grant coming over with Jesse on his shoulders, so I'm sure Elise and Cassie aren't far behind. Nudging Kian, he quickly spots them too.

'Would you excuse us?' Elijah peers over his shoulder and steps aside with a nod, returning to his wife and two kids.

Kian's off at a sprint before I can even move a muscle, and then Elise is running and Cassie is falling over and picking herself up without a single tear and then running again to catch up. Kian spins Elise around, hugging her tight. And then Cassie is there and he's spinning her around too, and the little girl is screaming with delight as her hair and her dress stream out behind her. It's downright adorable. There are no other words.

Grant and Kian shake hands, and then Grant hands over a squirming Jesse who has no idea what's going on but is clearly wildly overstimulated. I'll never get enough of watching them like this.

I don't catch much of their conversation, but it's full of love and pride and joy.

'And on Cassie's birthday!' Elise exclaims.

Kian hoists the little girl up again and does a little routine as though *she's* the trophy and he's kissing her and showing her off. 'I won you a cup, baby girl, did you see?'

She nods, talking a mile a minute – largely incomprehensible, as far as I can make out – and giggling as Kian spins her around again. I find it almost painful to watch. Tears threaten, and I don't know if they're tears of second-hand joy, or if they're also a kind of self-pity too, mourning what I never had as a kid.

It's beyond clear that Kian wants this for himself. He dotes on his niece and nephew, always reading them stories on FaceTime and buying them little gifts from every country we visit. He'll be a fantastic dad one day.

In moments like these I can see us doing it. Raising a family. It's bloody scary and overwhelming considering I don't know the first thing about being a father, but for the first time in my life I have some good role models to learn from.

I think we'll have at least a couple of years before that, anyway. If I know Kian, he'll want me to have my moment in the sun like he's had, and if we do decide to have kids then we'll both want to be around all the time to parent properly. After we've both experienced the pain of absent parents, I know we'll agree on the importance of doing it right.

Elise nudges me as we watch her brother and her firstborn share such a beautiful moment. 'I can't believe my baby brother has a boyfriend.'

'You're all of thirteen minutes older,' Kian reminds her with a groan, as he puts Cassie down. She still clings to him, her tiny hand wrapped around two of his fingers.

'You should get yourself one of those, Kian.'

Elise eyes me for a second and I shoot a desperate glance to Kian almost pleading for him to confirm that I'm doing okay. But Elise's expression is speculative, rather than critical, and I wonder if she's read my mind about the possibility of future children.

She gestures to where Kian's looking at me like a prized possession and I have to gulp down the emotion that threatens to spill out of me.

'He's so happy, and I don't think it's just because he's won yet another trophy.'

I hope she's right. I want to make Kian happy – forever, if he'll let me. There's so much I probably need to tell him. I'm not sure I could turn all my feelings into words right now, but that's okay because the great thing about the off season is that we have time. There will be time to tell him in a way that won't be messy and chaotic. We have time.

'I mean, the trophy's great, but look at me...' I gesture to my body and everyone laughs. I'll take it while I'm not quite sure how to have these sappy conversations with his favourite people yet.

Chapter Thirty-Three

Kian

The crowds have cleared and for a few moments it's just me and Harper leaning up against the railing looking over the Yas Marina Circuit. The sun's begun to blend into the horizon in a yellow and purple haze and it illuminates the track in a way I've never witnessed before. It's so beautiful.

'Harp?'

'Hmmm?' I feel the rumble of his response next to me and it makes me nervous about what I'm going to say next.

'I'm in love with you.' I wait for him to squirm, or to run, but he doesn't. There's a second of unbearable silence, before he turns to look me in the eye.

'Me too,' he whispers back.

'You're in love with you, too?' His fingers dig into my ribs and I can't help but laugh. I know exactly what he's saying but I need to hear it from him.

'No, you idiot. I love you. I really bloody do.'

There are no more words after that. There's only the future, and I can't wait.

Epilogue

Harper

Before coming up to Championship racing, I don't think I ever could have imagined a world where after coming first in a Grand Prix, the most exciting thing would be getting a text from Kian which is nothing but a screenshot displaying the top three rankings of the season so far.

1. Harper James.
2. Elijah Gutaga
3. Johannes Muller.

There's no denying the way it fills my heart with a little burst of joy, I almost want to save the picture and put it as my background, but that would mean replacing the one of me and Kian and I would never.

We've become a tight little threesome at the top of the championship rankings, but this is the first time I've been on top. Johannes might not be a Hendersohm, but all three of us; me, Kian, and Elijah, route for him like one in private.

If we could be a team of three we would be, but sadly that's not possible. It also didn't stop me from constantly wanting to come out on top in our little trio. There is nothing I love more than lording it over the other two as the driver who had the least experience in the lower category.

'Oi, James, come on we need to address the media before we can go out and celebrate.' And yep, I've turned Kian's best friend to the dark side. He loves going out for our celebratory drinks and dinners after a win or even to commiserate a loss.

'Remember who you're talking to, Gutaga. The rankings don't lie.' I flash him the screenshot and he shoots me the middle finger.

'It was actually your bestie who sent me that, how sad are you that he loves me more than you?'

'Dream on.' He rolls his eyes at my behaviour, but I know he's nothing but happy for me and Kian.

Last season it'd taken us a moment to get in the swing of things after Hendersohm offered me a three-year contract alongside Elijah. I'd almost slipped back into bad habits of partying and not being a good team player, but Kian had flown out to Canada for the seventh Grand Prix of the season and whipped my ass back into line.

There is no denying I found it harder to get back into my A game at first with him not on the team and tracks, too. But, the second me and Elijah found our groove it was like magic. And has been ever since.

Anders had been so grateful that Kian had come four-thousand miles to make sure I sorted myself out and things with Elijah that he paid for his flights.

Anders is still the absolute best, it almost hurts to hear the rumors that he is thinking about retiring and handing over the reins to his son.

Not that I'd be complaining, I might be tied down now but I could appreciate every bit how gorgeous Jackson is. His tanned skin, chocolate curls and velvety-brown eyes wouldn't hurt to look at for nine months a year.

He's been around more recently again, hanging out in the garage, becoming chummy with Cole and Ash and Anna. Making his mark, it feels like.

He's the same age as Kian, so maybe I just have a thing for older men who enjoy telling me what to do. Who knows. I'm just excited to see how it all plays out.

The press have harped on and on about the dream team Hendersohm has become in their short period of existence and how there are now drivers all over the world wanting to be part of the best team currently in the sport. It's been an absolute core moment that I've been a big part of putting the team on the map. An honour.

Elijah takes the lead with a lot of the team-based questions, but the journos love to try and gain an insight into my personal life.

'Is Kian Walker here today?' One of them asks and I shake my head. 'Trouble in paradise?'

I almost laugh in his face, but I'm not willing to sit through media training again right now.

'Not today, he's building our forever home as we speak.'

I can't believe I ever wanted to hide us behind closed bedroom doors. Now I take great pleasure in talking about him all the time. Especially to journalists who doubted us during the early stages of our relationship.

Our relationship has taken the racing world by storm. I can

only imagine how it would have been if Kian hadn't retired. If we'd been a team again with Hendersohm or, heaven forbid, on rival teams. The rivalry is strong enough between teammates, never mind opposing teams. Everyone would have had a field day with it, I'm sure.

'You must miss him, does that have any effect on your performance on the track?' This time, I do snort at their ridiculous commentary.

'I think my lap times and overall finishing place today speaks for itself .'

Shooting Elijah the glare he's become so used to he hurries us along the press line and we're quickly back in the garage with our second family.

I have a second family. It's bizarre to think about having one, let alone two. Yet the Hendersohm family have looked after me for the last three years and then when I leave them, I head home to the Walkers. I can't wait to become a Walker, even if Kian doesn't know yet that I'm planning to take his name.

'I can't believe how much progress you've made in the last couple of months. The panelling in the guest room looks amazing. Who knew my fiancé was such a dab hand at DIY?'

FaceTiming is something we've got really good at over the last season and a half of being apart. Missing someone the way I miss him when we're on opposite sides of the globe is a new experience for me.

The first month of last season, when Kian was at home and trying to settle back into normal life, was the worst. To the point I actually flew home for two days between the Saudi and the Australian Grand Prix's. Whilst money isn't an object, and I'll charter a private jet every day of my life to see Kian if I have to, it was probably really stupid considering how much the jetlag messed me up when I returned to Australia.

Now we have healthier coping strategies, and Anders loves Kian so much he's happy to let him join us on the road whenever he feels like it.

'I hope you still think so when you see it up close. It looks better on screen, I think.' There's sweat dripping down Kian's forehead as he works on the extension we had built earlier this year.

I was able to be at home with him for the whole of the British Grand Prix, and then I left for three-and-a-half months, and when I came home the cottage had basically doubled in size and we had acquired eight animals.

He obviously didn't actually build the extension himself, but he's decorating and furnishing every inch of it to perfection. I convinced him to start a social media account to chart his progress, and it now has over a million followers on Instagram and TikTok, thank you very much.

'You know what I'd love?' I say. 'A pool.' I've been dropping subtle hints about us having one on the property – there's so much land it would definitely be possible – but Kian's been reluctant to agree.

'An outdoor pool in the UK just seems so pointless. Like, we get two weeks of summer and that's it. Plus, the maintenance is a hassle.'

'We'll get a pool boy,' I suggest.

With a roll of his eyes, Kian replies, 'Yeah, you'd love that, wouldn't you?'

'Not as much as I love you.'

'Wow, being engaged has made you cringeworthy, Harper.'

'You love it.' And I know he does. He embraces every bit of me, from my competitive stubbornness to the cringey way I express my love to how I hog the duvet. I have no doubt about that. Not anymore.

I'm just about to suggest maybe a quick round of phone sex or at least ask if I can watch Kian beat off in our new guest room, but I'm quickly interrupted by loud knocking on my bedroom door.

'What's going on?' Kian asks, the noise loud enough for even him to hear.

I peer through the keyhole to find both Elijah and Johannes lingering in the hallway. 'Just a couple of jokers,' I say. 'One sec.' I lower the phone and unlock the door to let the pair in. 'Say hi to my fiancé.'

I practically shove the phone in both of their faces but they only laugh. 'Kian, please ask your man when he's gonna be tired of that word. He's gonna wear it out!' Elijah's playful tone only makes me laugh.

He and I have become close in the last eighteen months. We work well together as a team, and we've had some great success too. He's also happy to listen to me go on about Kian for hours, which I also like.

So yeah, maybe I've made a big deal of this engagement, but Kian asking me to marry him means more than anything in the world. More than any championship, cup or million-pound brand deal.

Because it means he wants to keep me around forever. That's not something anyone has ever wanted of me before, and I'm finally not afraid to embrace it and show it off to the world. I deserve it, I deserve him, and I deserve to be happy – thank you, therapy! I don't worry anymore that he'll up and leave me.

It's not a development that happened overnight, by any means. It's probably why I flew home for two days and gave myself chronic jet lag – to make sure he was still interested. Yet here I am, ready to commit to forever. I'd do it tomorrow if Kian would let us, but he wants to have everything just right – the cottage, the extension, the barn, the off-season timing.

That's his gift to me – the perfect wedding. And mine to him – is that I'm going to become a Walker. I want to take his name, because the Walker family have embraced me and welcomed me in a way that has changed my life.

Another thing that's very different about our lives now is the way we're all starting to lean in to farm life. I was very sceptical at first, but both Kian and Grant were obsessed and I saw how happy it made them both. Grant has cut down on his work trips significantly, and he and Kian have been developing Chastity's land together. It has become a beautiful bromance and it makes no one happier than me and Elise.

With Cassie in school and Jesse approaching nursery age, Elise is finally back finishing her nursing degree, and because Grant is home more, her dream job is something she can pursue again. I couldn't be prouder of both the Walker twins.

At this point, I've zoned out of the conversation so much that Johannes is holding my phone as he, Elijah and Kian chatter away.

Johannes. Well, Johannes remains a mystery. It's crazy that he's become my biggest worry in life over the last year. Something has changed in him, he's become reserved in himself, quiet, only wanting to hear about my life and never talk about his. It's made being friends difficult at times, but we push through.

It's something I've spoken about in depth to both my therapist and Kian, he'd been so full of life and then all of a sudden so full of secrets. He still enjoys going out to eat with us and for a couple drinks here and there, but he never looks at any of the many men who throw themselves at him. He's not looked at another man for the last eighteen months and none of us know why. At first, I used to push him about it, but it only made him clam up more. Now, we're all resigned to the fact that he'll tell us when he's ready. Just like I did with Kian.

The worry niggles away at me as I watch him talking to Kian, he's animated in his teasing but I can tell he doesn't mean it. Insight that comes from knowing each other for almost a decade now.

'Can I say goodbye to my fiancé, please?' I ask holding out my hand to retrieve the phone.

'And there he goes again,' Johannes jokes, but he hands over the phone anyway.

'I'm going to take these two jokers out to dinner. You know, because I'm earning the big bucks now after winning the world championship last year.'

Yep, that's right, I won the Drivers' Championship the year after Kian. If my place hadn't been secure on the Hendersohm team before, then it was after that win. The whole team has begun to feel like family, too – a 'found family' – so now I have two. I feel rich beyond my deepest desires. Family, a man I love, and the career I always dreamed of.

'Okay, baby.' Johannes and Elijah gag behind us at Kian. 'Speak to you later. Call me when you're back and in bed.' He throws me a wink that thankfully neither of them see. 'Love you.'

It doesn't matter that it's the millionth time I've heard him say it, it still warms my heart. 'Love you, too. Enjoy the clean-up from that panelling.'

I hang up and head out for dinner with the boys.

It's not long until the season's over, and then I'll be back home with my fiancé, my Kian, my love. I can't believe how much time I spend thinking about the future now. I barely used to think beyond the day, the hour, the second – and I admit it led me to make plenty of bad decisions – and now I'm just thinking about walking through the door of our home. I think about the kids we might have one day. I think about the fact that when I get home I'll discover that Kian's acquired a flock of sheep or a pack of llamas – or something equally as daft. And I won't care.

I won't care at all.

Acknowledgments

Always beyond thankful for my mom, my best friend in life and my biggest supporter in anything and everything I do. To my dad and brother who will buy this book and never read it, I'm still grateful.

To my best friends in the whole world – Ella and Paige, thank you for being the loves of my life, cheerleaders and emotional support. I adore you more with every day of friendship.

To my writing friends who get it – Alicja, Hannah and Louise – thank you for being part of this journey every single time!

To being one of those girls whose made some of the most amazing friends in her 20's – Taylor/Charlie, I treasure you with my whole heart and can't imagine you not being part of my life anymore. Thank you for making sure I take writing breaks and always wanting to know how the book journey is going.

ONE MORE CHAPTER

The author and One More Chapter would like to thank everyone
who contributed to the publication of this story...

Analytics
Abigail Fryer
Maria Osa

Audio
Fionnuala Barrett
Ciara Briggs

Contracts
Sasha Duszynska
Lewis

Design
Lucy Bennett
Fiona Greenway
Liane Payne
Dean Russell

Digital Sales
Hannah Lismore
Emily Scorer

Editorial
Kate Elton
Arsalan Isa
Charlotte Ledger
Bonnie Macleod
Lydia Mason
Jennie Rothwell
Caroline Scott-
Bowden
Emily Thomas

Harper360
Emily Gerbner
Jean Marie Kelly
emma sullivan
Sophia Walker

International Sales
Bethan Moore

Marketing & Publicity
Chloe Cummings
Emma Petfield

Operations
Melissa Okusanya
Hannah Stamp

Production
Emily Chan
Denis Manson
Simon Moore
Francesca Tuzzeo

Rights
Rachel McCarron
Hany Sheikh
Mohamed
Zoe Shine

**The HarperCollins
Distribution Team**

**The HarperCollins
Finance & Royalties
Team**

**The HarperCollins
Legal Team**

**The HarperCollins
Technology Team**

Trade Marketing
Ben Hurd

UK Sales
Laura Carpenter
Isabel Coburn
Jay Cochrane
Sabina Lewis
Holly Martin
Erin White
Harriet Williams
Leah Woods

**And every other
essential link in the
chain from delivery
drivers to booksellers
to librarians and
beyond!**

ONE MORE CHAPTER

One More Chapter is an
award-winning global
division of HarperCollins.

Sign up to our newsletter to get our
latest eBook deals and stay up to date
with our weekly Book Club!
<u>Subscribe here.</u>

Meet the team at
<u>www.onemorechapter.com</u>

Follow us!
@<u>OneMoreChapter_</u>
@<u>OneMoreChapter</u>
@<u>onemorechapterhc</u>

Do you write unputdownable fiction?
We love to hear from new voices.
Find out how to submit your novel at
<u>www.onemorechapter.com/submissions</u>